GREY LADY

BY PAUL KEMPRECOS

SUSPENSE PUBLISHING

ALSO BY PAUL KEMPRECOS

Aristotle "Soc" Socarides Series
Bluefin Blues
The Mayflower Murder
Feeding Frenzy
Death in Deep Water
Neptune's Eye
Cool Blue Tomb

Matinicus "Matt" Hawkins Series
The Emerald Scepter

GREY LADY

by
Paul Kemprecos

PAPERBACK EDITION
* * * * *
PUBLISHED BY:
Suspense Publishing

Paul Kemprecos
Copyright 2013 Paul Kemprecos

PUBLISHING HISTORY:
Suspense Publishing, Paperback and Digital Copy, November 2013

Cover Design: Shannon Raab
Cover Photographer: iStockphoto.com/glaflamme
Cover Photographer: iStockphoto.com/bpalmer

ISBN-13: 978-0615918228 (Suspense Publishing)
ISBN-10: 0615918220

To Terri Ann Armstrong, who urged me to write another Socarides book. I wish she were here to know that I followed her advice.

PRAISE FOR PAUL KEMPRECOS

"What a character. Aristotle Socarides is a diver, a fisherman, and a PI who just can't seem to stay out of trouble. He's the brainchild of a genius—Paul Kemprecos—who knows a thing or two about writing action and adventure. I bow to the master and urge all of you to read this latest installment in a first rate series."
—Steve Berry, *New York Times* and #1
Internationally Bestselling Author

"#1 *New York Times* bestselling author Paul Kemprecos shows once again he is the undisputed master of high-action adventure, better on his own and better than his former co-author Clive Cussler period. Returning to his roots in *Grey Lady*, he brings back old friend Aristotle "Soc" Socarides in a rapid-fire tale chock full of historical mystery, cutting edge technology, and sea-going daring-do with so many twists and turns you'll need to take a Dramamine before you plunge in. Masterfully paced and brilliantly constructed, this is reading entertainment of the highest order."
—Jon Land, bestselling author of *The Tenth Circle*

"Paul Kemprecos has crafted another winner! The *Grey Lady*'s dogged and irreverent private investigator Aristotle "Soc" Socarides is a blast to spend time with, and the story's clever twists and turns will have you rocketing through the pages until the very end. Don't miss it!"
—Boyd Morrison, author of *The Loch Ness Legacy*

"The gods visit the sins of the fathers upon the children."
—AESCHYLUS

GREY LADY

ARISTOTLE "SOC" SOCARIDES SERIES: BOOK 7

BY PAUL KEMPRECOS

PROLOGUE

The Pacific Ocean, 1822

Obediah Coffin crouched in the bow of the open whaleboat under the hungry gaze of the two men who yearned to gnaw the flesh from his bones.

The skeletal fingers of his right hand clutched a pair of dice carved from the tooth of a sperm whale, but he could not bring himself to make the throw.

"*Do* it!" one of the men growled. His name was William Swain and like Coffin, he was a whaler from Nantucket.

"Aye, Obed," said the third Nantucket man, Henry Daggett, his voice a bare whisper. "No use putting it off. God's will be done. What will be, will be."

Coffin wanted to shout at Daggett that God's will would be to condemn him and the other men in the boat to eternal damnation for the abominations they had committed, but his lips were as cracked and dry as parchment. He gazed with red-rimmed eyes at the lonely sea stretching to the horizon in every direction.

"God's will be done," he mumbled. He took a rattling breath, pried his fingers from the ivory cubes, and tossed the dice without shaking them. They rolled a few inches and came to a halt in a puddle of water that had leaked through the seams of the boat.

A five and a three. *Eight.*

William Swain cursed, then scooped up the dice, shook them in his cupped hands, blew on his boney knuckles, and gave the whalebone cubes a loose toss, careful to aim for the driest part of the deck where they would have a full roll. They bounced off the base of the harpoon resting post and came to a stop showing two fives.

"Hah!" Swain said. "A *ten.* Your turn, carpenter." He picked up the dice with his left hand, placed them in his right palm and offered them to Daggett.

Daggett stared vacantly at the dice lying on the calloused palm.

"Can't move?" Swain said. The fierce, deep-set eyes under the sloping brow bored into Daggett's ravaged face. "Your hands were fast enough back at the island when they grabbed for my woman."

There had been no love lost between the two men since their ship, the *Moshup,* had set sail from Nantucket Harbor on a sultry August day nearly two years before. The animosity between them was inevitable. Daggett was young and handsome, and his position as ship's carpenter gave him privileges such as superior sleeping quarters and food and a bigger *lay,* as shares in the whale oil profits were called. Swain was a harpooner, a misshapen troll of a man whose muscular body and scarred face had been marked by the dangers of his profession.

The crewmates had nearly come to blows on a Pacific island where the ship customarily stopped for supplies. Despite lectures from the captain against the dangers of venereal disease, the men unleashed their libidos on the willing young female natives. A beautiful bronze-skinned woman who had been Swain's on a previous voyage had been attracted to Daggett. Swain had pulled a knife on the carpenter, only to be stopped by order of the first mate.

A few weeks after the island stop, the ship had chased down a sixty-foot-long sperm whale. Swain tossed a harpoon into the great creature, but it was a bad throw and the barb came free. The enraged whale had upended two boats, then rammed and sank the ship. The surviving crew had gathered provisions before the ship went under and set off in four whaleboats led by the captain, who was navigating for the fleet.

The twenty-eight-foot-long, double-ended whaleboat was a synthesis of function and beauty. The demands of the whaling trade for a speedy and maneuverable lightweight craft imbued the whaleboat with a sleek elegance. The whaleboat was built to chase and dodge giant sea mammals and carry the implements of the trade used by the six-man crew. With good men pulling at the oars, and if the boats stayed together in a flotilla, the thousand-mile journey to land would have been hard but possible.

But a storm swept in one night, and a boat had been separated from the flotilla, which included the only whaleboat carrying navigational gear. The boat had lost its oars in the storm and began to drift aimlessly. The survivors were reduced to skeletons; their bodies were covered with scabs from constant exposure to salt water and sun. Their joints swelled and the men became lethargic and weak. They suffered from blackouts; the lucky ones never regained consciousness.

As their shipmates began to die off, the desperate survivors did the unthinkable. They cut open the dead bodies of their fellow crewmen and devoured the hearts. Then they sliced what flesh remained, dried it in the sun and ate it like jerky.

Finally, only three men were left alive. They managed to collect drinking water from the frequent rains, but they had nothing to eat. Driven half-mad by starvation, they had agreed that one man must sacrifice his life to feed the others.

Swain produced the dice. Low man would slash his wrists and bleed out. Now it was Daggett's turn to make the throw.

"*Do* it, man," Coffin urged. "For godsakes, don't drag this out any longer."

Daggett slowly took the dice from Swain, cupped them in his hand for a second as he murmured a prayer, then let them roll.

CHAPTER 1

It was one of those seamless Cape Cod days in late spring, perfect in every detail, as if the gods were atoning for the nasty, raw winter they had visited on the narrow peninsula. There wasn't a cloud in the sky, and the flat-calm surface of Nantucket Sound looked as if it had been steam-ironed. The twin 250-horsepower four-stroke Yamaha outboard motors sent the thirty-six-foot Grady-White powerboat skimming over the teal-green water like a skipping stone thrown by a kid. I felt like a prisoner who'd escaped from a dungeon. Each breath of the sweet sea air filling my lungs was laden with the expectation of good things to come.

The dumb smile on my face would have vanished in a second if I'd known about the trouble brewing thirty miles to the south, and the fact that soon I'd again be reminded that no abyss in the sea is deeper than the depths of the human soul. But there was not a whisper of danger in the breeze blowing off the bay when I had levered my body out of bed that morning. The rosy fingers of a Homeric dawn streamed through the windows of my converted beach house. I had showered, then pulled on a new pair of cotton chino slacks and a Mediterranean blue polo shirt.

While the coffee brewed, I spooned out a glob of food for

mature cats into a plastic dish. Kojak, my old Maine coon cat, has a hard time chewing dry food, but he sucked down his breakfast like a runaway vacuum cleaner. He was too full to object when I stuffed him into a wicker pet carrier. I hauled the carrier and a thermos of coffee to my 1987 GMC pickup truck, and took it as a good sign when the engine started on only the third try. The truck had replaced a 1977 pickup, but it seems to have inherited the old junk's balky genes. I jounced out the long, cratered driveway to the road that ran along the bayside, and ten minutes later parked at the harbor where I keep my boat. I rowed a skiff out to the mooring and climbed aboard the Grady-White. Kojak stuck his nose out when I opened the carrier in the cabin, then emerged to settle in the nest of cushions I'd arranged for him in an empty fishing gear box.

Unlike my temperamental truck, the boat started with the first turn of the ignition key. I listened to the pleasant purr of the outboards for a moment, then cast off the mooring line and cranked up the throttle. A southwest breeze brushed my cheeks with the gentle softness of a bride's veil as the boat slowly moved into the harbor. The sun rising above the low dunes of the barrier beach was burning off the morning mists.

The Cape is a narrow, seventy-mile-long arm of sand dunes and beaches curled into the Atlantic like the clenched fist of a muscle man showing off his biceps. I live and work about where the elbow would be. I navigated the channel markers of the no-wake zone and notched up the throttle when I hit open water. The boat left a creamy wake as it raced west across Nantucket Sound parallel to the low-lying southerly shore of Cape Cod.

Forty-five minutes after leaving my home port, I steered the boat around the rocks of Point Gammon, headed into Lewis Bay and followed the channel markers to a large marina. I tucked the boat into my rented slip and tied up to the dock. After I checked in with the dock master, I went back to the boat. All was ready for my first charter. The shiny new fishing rods and reels were in their racks. Fishing lures were within reach. I plunked into a swivel chair, waiting for my charter to arrive, and smiled as I examined one of my newly-printed business cards. On the front of the card was the name and silhouette of the boat against a blue background. Under the boat was a line, with my home phone, saying the boat was available for charter. On the backside is the name of the captain: Aristotle P. Socarides. The P stands for Plato. People sometimes trip over their tongues trying to navigate the string of syllables. I usually tell them to call me by the shortened version. *Soc.*

For years, I had worked with a Yankee gentleman named Sam, on his commercial trawler the *Millie D.* Sam taught me how to smell out fish. We made a good team until age and a temperamental heart caught up with him. Our high-line days of big catches came to an end after his cardiologist gave him a warning he couldn't ignore. Sam quit fishing for good and headed south with the migrating snowbirds.

I scraped some savings together, took out an equity loan on the waterfront property that surrounds my boathouse and used the money to buy Sam out. He and Mildred retired to a gated community in Florida and an easy life of early bird specials and bingo. He picked a good time to abandon the fishing business. The codfish were becoming harder to find than a bar tip at a miser's convention. The scientists got alarmed at the declining stocks and the feds reacted by tightening the catch regulations.

Squeezed between my loan payments and the shortage of fish, I decided to go to Florida to consult with Sam. I almost didn't recognize him. Sam had traded in his work outfit—faded blue chambray shirt, khaki slacks and tan long-billed cap—for Madras shorts, espadrille sandals, and a pink flamingo Hawaiian shirt. He and Millie looked like a couple of kids. The southern sun that had tanned Sam the color of a walnut shell must have melted his Yankee reserve because he gave me a bear hug. We sat around the pool and I explained what I had in mind. I wanted to quit commercial fishing and go into the charter business. Years of backbreaking work in all kinds of weather had washed away the last trace of sentimentality about the boat. No amount of painkillers can cope with the aching joints that come from a lifetime at sea. He said to sell the *Millie D.* if I wanted to.

"Maybe you should think about movin' south, Soc. You're not getting any younger."

I didn't need to be reminded that my dark brown hair and mustache were streaked with gray, and the laugh lines around my eyes are sprouting branches. I glanced at the old folks sunning themselves around the pool. They looked like leather back turtles. Sam would have liked to have me around to talk about old times, but we both knew that routine would get stale.

"Maybe in a few years, Sam," I said with a wag of my head.

He nodded and pronounced the fisherman's phrase for all things good: "Finestkind, Cap."

Sam suggested that I swing by Sea World to see Sally Carlin, an old girlfriend who was working at the marine theme park as a biologist. Sally is a terrific woman, but I said I'd have to make it another time. Sam knew my checkered history with Sally and didn't pursue it. I dined with Sam and Mildred that night at an all-you-can eat restaurant that wasn't half-bad and stayed in their spare bedroom. The next day we said our goodbyes and I took a plane back north.

I was disappointed but not surprised at the low-ball appraisal figure for the *Millie D.* The old gal had taken a lot of hard knocks from the Atlantic Ocean. I sold the boat to a young fisherman who'd been helping me, but the money fell short of the amount I needed for a new business. I bit the bullet and went to my family for a loan. My dad is pretty frail and spends most of his time at home, but my aging mother still rules the family frozen pizza empire with an iron hand. The family has more money than Fort Knox and it's just as impregnable. The request for a loan went to the Parthenon Pizza family tribunal, consisting of my mother, my younger brother George, and my kid sister Chloe. George, who runs the operational side of the business, was against the loan; his argument went something like this:

"I work my butt off for this business while my big brother, who *should* be working for the family, wants us to buy him a boat so he can screw off even more than he does. No offense, Soc."

"None taken, George," I said.

It was a refrain I'd heard before. George lives in a five-bedroom house in a North Shore suburb, drives expensive cars, indulges a wife who likes to shop, and sends his kids to private school, but in my opinion, working with my mother entitles him to his comfortable martyrdom.

Chloe is head of marketing. We've always been close, so she was in favor of the loan.

"This isn't a gift, George, it's a *business* proposition. Don't pay any attention to George, Ma. I think we should give the money to Aristotle."

As company president, my mother was the tiebreaker. "Chloe's right, George. The family must do what is right for the family."

My mother's version of doing the right thing wasn't based entirely on family loyalty. She said she would approve the loan in return for a stake in my new business and a promissory note to pay the money back at slightly less interest than a loan shark. Oh yes, she said. One more thing. With my mother, there is *always* one more thing, but what she wanted in return brought a smile to my face.

With cash in hand, I bought a Canyon 366 center console boat with a sleek white fiberglass hull. My mother's "one more thing" was a request to name the boat *Thalassa*—a poetic Greek word for the sea—that sounds like the whisper of waves on the shore. Coming from Crete, Ma swore by the healing powers of the sea. I ordered business cards and bought some blue polo shirts monogrammed with the name of the boat, matching baseball caps to sell to customers, and I was ready for my first season as a charter boat captain.

My faithful old companion Kojak is twenty years old, and it won't be long before the Maine coon cat who shares rooms with me, as Watson would say of Sherlock Holmes, is chasing blind mice through a celestial field of catnip. He can barely walk, but he still likes to eat. Putting him in a cat kennel would hasten his demise. The old guy and I had been through a lot together. I had a heart-to-heart and asked him if he wanted to go fishing. He had yawned, which I took as a *yes*.

My charter party arrived a half-hour late. The big black Toyota Sequoia pulled into the marina parking lot and four men got out. Three of them ambled down the dock carrying coolers like porters in a safari. The short, hairless man in the lead climbed onto the deck of my boat.

"I'm Glick," he said.

Glick was around five-foot-five and maybe half that wide. His stout body was supported by two short legs as thick as tree trunks that extended from plaid shorts containing a melange of every color in the rainbow and then some.

"Welcome aboard the *Thalassa,* Mr. Glick."

Glick had called the day before. He said that he ran a string of nursing homes. He wanted to take three associates for a fishing trip, and we negotiated a price.

I stowed the coolers in the storage compartments and asked Glick if he and his friends were ready to go fishing.

"Not quite yet," he said. "I'd like to renegotiate the price."

I stood firm, legs wide apart, my arms crossed across my chest. "Sorry, Mr. Glick. A boat can't run on air. Price we agreed on yesterday stands."

Apparently, he didn't understand my body language. He moved

so close that our bellies almost touched, although mine was a lot flatter. My guess was that he used his intimidating frontal bulk to bully residents in his over-priced old folks' warehouses when they asked for an extra helping of Jell-O.

When physical intimidation didn't work, he jutted his fleshy jaw out. "What guarantee do I have that we'll catch fish?"

"*No* guarantee. I'll put you and your friends on top of the fish. The rest is up to you."

He placed his forefinger on the second of his three chins. "How about prorating the fee based on the number of fish caught?"

"Sorry. That won't work. I'll show your friends how to catch fish. If they don't land the fish they hook, I'm out a day's charter."

Glick gave me a sly smile. "You could be out a day's charter if I canceled the trip."

"And you'd be out a deposit. Don't forget, you gave me your credit card number."

The smile vanished and the eyes in his pale face narrowed to a squint.

"We'd better catch fish," he growled.

I gave him a lop-sided grin and poked him in the tummy like the Pillsbury doughboy. He stepped back and glared at his friends, who'd been listening and watching. I started the outboards, untied the dock lines and eased the boat out of its slip. We followed the channel markers to the mouth of the harbor and I pointed the *Thalassa*'s bow southeast. The seas were barely a foot high. We made good time to Monomoy Island, a long slender finger of dunes that hangs off the Cape's "elbow," then ran south to Nantucket shoals.

Although it was morning, Glick's friends dug beers out of their coolers and got into the sandwiches I provide as part of the deal. They finished their breakfast and beer about the same time we arrived on the shoals. The fish-finder screen displayed dozens of finny silhouettes. Sea birds dove into the water to catch bait being chased to the surface by bigger fish. A strong briny smell filled the air. I handed out rods and reels and gave a quick lesson in how to use them. A couple of passengers had fished before, and within minutes, they began to pull in striped bass.

The waters were thick with stripers. It was almost impossible not to hook a fish. When the schooling fish moved on, I followed.

I measured each fish, and tossed back those that weren't keepers. The fish box rapidly filled. In between sizing fish and tending the wheel, I tossed a line over the side and hooked a few big lunkers for myself. It had the makings of a great first trip, but as the boat rocked in the waves, I began to notice that the smiles were vanishing. The combined effects of the beer and food, the smell of fish and engine exhaust, and the rolling of the boat, were taking their toll.

The faces around me were tinged with green. One guest made a gurgling sound, set his fishing rod down and leaned over the side to disgorge the contents of his stomach. Another followed his example. I held the two men by the back of their shirts so they wouldn't go overboard. Within minutes, every passenger was sick except for Mr. Glick, who had not had any beer. This was probably a blessing given the potential volume of his digestive system. He protested heavily when his friends said they wanted to head back to shore.

"You *morons!* I'm paying for a *whole* day of fishing," he said.

A chorus of pitiful moans greeted his announcement. I took pity on the seasick guys.

"Your friends here look like a bunch of avocados, Mr. Glick. Why don't you put it up for a vote?" Before he could answer, I added, "Who wants to call it a day?"

Two hands went in the air. The third man bent over and emptied his breakfast at Glick's feet.

"I'll take that as a vote," I said. "Looks like we're out of here."

Glick glowered, but he didn't argue when I rinsed his splattered boat shoes with the deck hose. I gathered up all the fishing rods and headed the boat back to the mainland. The passengers looked better by the time we coasted into the slip and tied up, but they couldn't wait to get off the boat. I pulled the fish from the cooler and laid them out side-by-side on the dock so the guys could take photos of their catch.

Glick took a wad of cash from a wallet and made a big show of peeling off the bills with his stubby fingers.

I counted the money and said, "This is only pays for a half day, Mr. Glick."

"We only went *out* for half a day."

"Not my fault. There was a vote."

"*Screw* the vote."

"Suit yourself. I've got your credit card number, remember?"

His jowls quivered and he snarled an order at his friends, who started to pile the fish into a plastic wheelbarrow.

"Each man gets two fish," I reminded them. "You can choose the biggest. Rest goes back to the boat. You caught three fish, Mr. Glick. You can take two home."

"What are you going to do with my *third* one?"

"I'll sell it. Policy is plainly printed on the contract you signed. Folks tend to waste fish if they take too many."

That's when things began to get ugly.

Glick yelled that he paid for *all* his fish. He snatched up the monster striper I had caught, holding it in both hands at the narrow part where the tail meets the body. As he started to walk away, I reached out and grabbed the fish by one of its gills. Glick pulled. I stuck my fingers in the other gill and pulled back.

I was wearing gloves, and the gills offered better hand holds. But Glick outweighed me by fifty pounds. He put his flab to good use, leaning back at an angle. I used my arm strength to compensate. We stood on the dock playing tug-of-war with the fish. His weight began to tell. His lips widened in a smile of triumph. That's when I jerked the fish, hard. The tail parted company with the body. Glick toppled backwards. His short legs tried to catch up with his body and did a funny little dance walk, then he went off the dock and landed in the water with a mighty splash.

He went under and bobbed to the surface with a wet curse on his lips. He shouted at his friends, who pulled him back onto the dock. Water dripped off his nose. His clothes were glued to his body. He was still holding the fish tail.

"Okay, Mr. Glick," I said with a shrug. "You can *keep* your half of the fish."

I imagined that I saw steam coming from his ears. He tossed the tail in the water, whirled around, and sloshed back to his car, followed by his entourage. He got behind the wheel of the Sequoia and slammed the door. His hand shot out the window and he flipped me what in polite circles is referred to as a single finger salute. I held up the mutilated fish and pointed at it. I guess that irritated him. When he pulled out of the parking lot, he left half his tire rubber stuck to the tarmac.

I threw the shortened striper into an ice chest, rinsed my hands off and walked up the dock to Trader Ed's. I slid onto a bar stool and ordered a glass of Cape Cod Red beer. I was on my second glass when I felt a tap on my shoulder. I turned and looked into the smiling face of Sheila Crumley.

She slid onto the stool next to me. "Hi, Soc. I had the feeling I'd find you here."

Sheila was a reporter with the daily newspaper. I had met her at the bar while I was organizing my charter venture. She was middle-aged plump but still sexy. She'd been intrigued when I quoted a couple of the philosophers I was named after. She had the curiosity and disarming manner of a good reporter, and my brain was slightly lubricated with alcohol.

I had given her the Cliff's Notes version of my life story. How I had been a Marine in Vietnam and later a Boston cop, couldn't handle the politics and the ghosts of war that haunted my memory. And how, when my fiancé died in a car crash and I drowned myself in an alcoholic sea of self-pity, I gave up my cop career and moved to Cape Cod hoping the demons who had taken up residence in my head would choke on the salty air. I told her about fishing with Sam, and pushed my charter boat plans, hoping for some ink. She really got excited when I said that I sometimes hired out as a private detective and a diver.

"Buy you a beer?" I offered. I was feeling flush with the cash from Glick in my wallet.

"No thanks, but I'll take a margarita. Easy on the sour mix."

I ordered a drink for Crumley and we clinked glasses. "What's new with the Fourth Estate?" I said.

She pulled a copy of the newspaper from her oversized purse and spread it out on the bar. The long red nail on her plump finger tapped a front-page banner headline:

POLICE IDENTIFY BURN MURDER VICTIM AS RUSSIAN

"Cape Cod ain't what it used to be," I said. "I remember when a stolen bucket of clams was considered a crime wave."

She took a sip of her drink. "Professional opinion?"

"Speaking as a fisherman?"

"Don't play coy with me, Soc. Speaking as an ex-homicide cop and a private eye. Whaddya think?"

I slid the paper over and read the article. The guy had died a hard death in the woods near the county airport. Someone had tied him to a tree with baling wire, emptied a can of gasoline over his head, ran a trail of gas, lit it from a safe distance and turned the victim into a human torch. He must have seen all this happening and would have known it was going to end badly for him. Duct tape sealed his lips. Poor guy couldn't even scream.

In an irony that must have escaped the victim, the flames spread into the woods, attracting trainees from a nearby firefighting training school.

"Tough way to go," I said. "Someone didn't like him."

"I talked to some of the firefighter trainees. They've decided on career changes. I saw the photos of the victim. I don't blame them."

She told me that the cops had traced the dead man to his motel room. They found no luggage, but his car was still parked at the motel. The registration identified him as Viktor Krasnov from Brighton Beach, New York. He had earned a police record as a supplier of Oxycontin and had spent a few years in jail. No one knew what he was doing away from his home turf. She asked my opinion.

"It's obvious," I said. "*Ivan* did it."

"Ivan? Ivan who?"

"Ivan nobody."

"Sometimes I find it hard to follow you, Soc."

"Ivan is a generic term for a Russian. Not exactly politically correct, but it was very big during the Cold War."

"Okay. And—"

"The guy came from Brighton Beach. Russian Mafia. Drug trade. He drove up here to make a deal, or he was on the run. Maybe the deal went bad, and someone caught up with him. Maybe he held back some money from his bosses." I went on in some detail, making up a fictional scenario that might have fit the facts.

"Why not just shoot him? Why play Joan of Arc with the poor bastard?"

"It was a warning to others. Don't cross Ivan the Terrible or you're *toast. Literally.*"

She pondered my words for a moment, then slid off her stool. "Thanks, Soc. You've been a big help." She gave me a peck on the cheek. "Got to go. Deadline."

"Always a pleasure, Sheila."

I had another beer and decided I had better feed Kojak. I strolled back to the dock, passing a police cruiser, and saw a female uniformed officer standing near my slip, talking to another boat owner who pointed to me.

The cop came over, asked if I were Mr. Socarides, and identified herself as Officer Tucker. She was young, mid-twenties maybe. I asked what I could do for her.

"I'm following up on a complaint of assault and battery from a Mr. Glick. Says you pushed him in the water."

"That's not exactly what happened," I said. I told her about the fishy tug-of-war and pulled the mutilated fish from the cooler as evidence.

"Exhibit A," I said.

Her mouth did a little on-and-off smirk. She was having a hard time maintaining a cop face.

"Any witnesses to this, ah, incident?" she said.

"Three guys who work for him. Not sure if they'll be impartial, though. Mr. Glick strikes me as a rich guy who doesn't like being embarrassed. I embarrassed him in front of his employees."

"I looked up your background," she said. "Saw the stuff about Vietnam and your cop work in Boston and the PI stuff, which makes me believe your version of events."

"Don't forget Exhibit A."

"Oh, I haven't."

"Then that's that." I tossed the fish back into the cooler.

"Don't be too sure, Mr. Socarides. Even if the criminal complaint doesn't stick, he'll probably sue you. That's a pretty boat you've got there. Hate to see you lose it."

I glanced at *Thalassa*, thinking about all the trouble I'd gone through to acquire her. "Yeah, me, too, Officer."

"So I'd advise you to get in touch with a lawyer. In the meantime I'll file a report and see where it goes from there."

I thanked her and we shook hands. I stood on the dock and gazed at the *Thalassa*. Nice going, Socarides. First day of operation and you're up to your eyeballs in a sea of trouble. I could lose my boat and my business. I tried to put a bright side on things. The police officer seemed sympathetic, and I had right on my side.

And I still had the fish with no tail.

CHAPTER 2

Daybreak in a busy harbor creates a concert all its own. The high-pitched cry of gulls is the flute section. The low rumblings of boat engines are the bassoons. The ting of halyards against aluminum masts is like the E string being plucked on a violin. The horn blast of the Steamship Authority ferry is like a tuba on steroids, and it's a potent alarm clock as well.

I rolled out of my bunk, set a pot of coffee to brew while I took a quick shower and got dressed in shorts and blue polo shirt. I whipped up a feta cheese scrambled egg bagel. Then I carried Kojak and his dish out onto the deck where we dined *al fresco*. He happily munched the mature cat salmon treats, which are about all his old teeth can deal with.

After breakfast with a water view, I put my pal back in his bed below. He promptly fell asleep. I cleaned up the galley. At eight o'clock on the nose, my charter party arrived. The two middle-aged couples from Ohio were giddy with excitement at the prospect of their first fishing trip. The women were sisters, and as it turned out, they had a fisherman's instinct. They pulled in more striped bass than their husbands, who cheered them on.

It was a great charter. The Ohio folks didn't get sick from too much beer. They didn't demand to keep the fish, preferring to take photos of their catch. The weather was beautiful. The people were fun and they displayed their appreciation with a fat tip. The trip wiped out the nastiness of the previous day's charter. I hosed down the deck and flushed out the fish box, using routine tasks to put off pressing business. But eventually, I went below and was looking through the scribbles in my address book for the name of the lawyer who'd handled the sale of the *Millie D.*, when the boat settled slightly. Someone had climbed aboard.

The waterfront crowd is a pretty informal bunch, but it's still considered a breach of etiquette to board a boat without an invitation. If you see someone on a boat, you say hello and wait for the wave that passes for the informal invite. If no one is visible on deck, you call out an *ahoy* or ask if anybody is home. If there is no answer, you come back later.

Having to think about legal matters hadn't put me in the best of moods. I slapped the address book shut and emerged from the cabin. Two men were standing on the stern deck. One man was almost my height, and his companion was several inches shorter. Both had on tight-fitting, shiny black leather jackets, even though the temperature was in the seventies. They wore snug black jeans and black running shoes. Mirrored aviator-style sunglasses with blue lenses hid their eyes.

"Can I help you gentlemen?" I said in a tone that could have been friendlier.

The shorter man glanced around. "Naz bot," he said.

I didn't have a clue what he meant, but said, "Nazbot to you, too."

They exchanged glances and the tall man said, "His English not so good like mine. He is saying you have *nice boat*."

"Thanks. It's available for charter this afternoon. Are you gentlemen interested in going on a fishing trip?"

The tall man unfolded a newspaper he'd been carrying.

"No fishing. Interested in *this*."

In his hand was the front page of *The Cape Cod Times*. My eyes went to the banner headline above the fold: PRIVATE EYE SAYS IVAN THE TERRIBLE KILLED THE BURNING MAN.

The story had Sheila Crumley's byline on it. Set into the story was a photo of me, a publicity head shot that I'd sent into the paper's business page. I saw my name repeated a number of times in the article, and each mention was circled with heavy black ink.

I took the paper from the stranger and read the lead sentence.

"Ivan the Terrible was the killer of the Russian man found burned to death in the woods near Barnstable Municipal Airport. So says Aristotle P. Socarides, a retired homicide detective formerly with the Boston Police Department who is now a part-time private investigator living on Cape Cod."

I scanned the next few paragraphs. Sheila had done a pretty good job cobbling my alcohol-fueled bar ramblings into a story. Enshrined in print was my off-hand theorizing about the Russian mafia, the drug trade and the possibility of a deal gone bad. There was my comment, loosely quoted, which said, "Don't cross Ivan the Terrible or you're toast."

Crumley had recapped the details of the murder from her original reporting and mentioned that as a private investigator, I only took cases that were highly unusual. She finished up with the plug she had promised, saying that I ran the charter fishing boat *Thalassa* out of the Hyannis Marina. It was clear *how* my visitors had found me, but not *why*. I handed the paper back to the tall man who tapped my photo with his finger.

"This is you?"

I nodded. "Yeah, that's me. Not my best side."

"How are you knowing Ivan is killer from Russian mafia?"

"I *don't* know that," I said with a shake of my head.

He waved the folded page at me. "Is in paper."

I had a bad feeling about this. *Damn* that Sheila! Double-damn my beer mouth. Speaking slowly and deliberately so my new pal wouldn't miss anything in the translation, I said, "The man who was killed was Russian. He's from Brighton Beach and he's been arrested before. The dead man was in the drug business. Someone killed him. It was probably Russian bad guys. Ivan is a common Russian name. Like *John* in this country."

"Russian bad guys?" He chuckled and spoke a few words to his friend.

The short man laughed. "Roosian bed gize."

"Why the questions about someone named Ivan?" I said.

Tall Guy frowned. "Our boss named Ivan. He reads this. He don't like it. He thinks it makes big trouble. He says it stinks."

"It *steenks*," said his shorter friend.

"Your boss isn't the only guy in the world named Ivan."

"He's only Ivan who is my boss," Tall Guy said.

I couldn't argue with his logic, even if I disagreed with the conclusion.

"Please explain to your boss that he was not the person in the story. Offer him my apologies."

"Not enough," Tall Guy said.

He said something to Short Guy, who reached under his leather jacket. His hand came out holding a knife. I heard a snick and a sharply-pointed four-inch blade flicked out of the black handle. I tensed, thinking he was coming for me, but he turned and stabbed the leatherette cushion in the stern seat. He yanked the knife back, leaving a cut about two feet long. Then he pulled the knife out and jabbed the cushion in another place.

My first instinct was to go for him. But the voice of experience was telling me if I moved in, he'd start working on my gut instead of the cushions. The Tall Guy watched me in case I did something rash. The corners of his mouth were tweaked up in a smile.

I backed away as if I were scared to death. He grinned and turned to watch his friend. Using the center console to shield my move, I leaned over, grabbed a boat hook from its holder and snapped the telescoping tube to full length. I stepped back around the console and took a baseball swing at the taller man. He was surprised, but he jumped away from the chest-high blur of metal. I brought the aluminum shaft back again and swung it like a Jedi knight across the posterior of his friend, was who bent over, busily slicing the seat cushions to ribbons.

He let out a scream of pain and whirled around, his face contorted in anger. He pulled the knife out of the cushion and brought it around. I chopped at his forearm. The switchblade flew from his hand and splashed into the water. Pivoting, I faced off against his pal, who had dropped the newspaper and had his hand under his jacket.

My boat is docked between two bigger boats that blocked the view of the *Thalassa's* deck where I could easily be dispatched with no one to witness it. I needed a miracle, which came to me at that moment, courtesy of an angel in a blue police uniform who appeared on the dock.

"Hello, Officer Tucker," I said in a loud voice.

Tall Guy turned and his hand came out from the jacket. He growled in Russian to his friend, who was holding his right arm with his hand.

Tucker glanced at the two men, then at the boat hook in my hand. "Everything okay?" she said.

I didn't know what the tall guy had under his jacket, but if he had a gun and was spooked into using it, Tucker would have been the first target.

I grinned and said, "Everything's fine, Officer. These gentlemen were just leaving."

Tall Guy stared at me as if he were trying to make up his mind, then he growled something to his friend. They climbed out of the boat and walked briskly along the dock. I motioned for Tucker to come on board.

"Who were *those* guys?" she said.

"They work for someone named Ivan." I picked the newspaper up from the deck. "They think I was talking about their boss in this dumb story. I wasn't. I was just using the name Ivan as an example."

She glanced at the headline. "Weird. What did they want?"

I pointed to the mutilated cushion. "I think they wanted to make me sorry I opened my big mouth."

"Holy crap!" She grabbed her hand radio, stepped off the boat and sprinted down the dock. "Gone," she said when she came back a moment later. "Okay, tell me what happened."

I was still pumped up with adrenaline as I told her about the encounter. She shook her head in disbelief. "You seem to *attract* trouble, Mr. Socarides."

"Just call me ol' lightning rod. Glad you showed up. What brings you to my neighborhood?"

"I came by to tell you that I talked to Mr. Glick's three friends. They hate their boss. Said he's nothing but a slumlord for old people. They backed up your account."

"Then it's over?"

"The criminal complaint part is. You may have to deal with a civil suit. Talked to your lawyer?"

"Still looking up his number."

She ran her hand over the shredded seat cushion. "Better do it fast, because at the rate you're going, this boat won't be worth suing you for. Think those guys will be back?"

"I hope not."

"I'll ask around the marina. Maybe someone noticed them or their car. Call 911 if they show up again. In the meantime, be careful."

I thanked her and we walked up to the parking lot. She got into the cruiser and I decided I needed something to steady my nerves and strolled over to Trader Ed's. On the way, I encountered the dock master. He handed me a pink telephone call back slip.

"Got a call for you. Lady said she left a message on your home phone, but called the marina on the chance she'd find you."

I used to get phone messages at a bar called the 'Hole, but I figured that if I was serious about my new business I'd better have a better system. I considered getting a cell phone, but my mother would be calling constantly to ask how her boat was doing. Instead, I hooked up an answering machine at the boat house so I could call in and retrieve messages. The pretty blonde barkeep on duty poured me a beer without being asked, then slid the mug across the bar-top. I took a sip of the cold brew and read the name on the pink slip. Lisa Hendricks. She had called about a half hour earlier.

I asked the bartender if I could borrow a phone and punched out the number. A woman answered. "Hendricks law firm."

I asked for Lisa Hendricks and gave my name.

"I'm Lisa Hendricks. Thank you for returning my call so quickly, Mr. Socarides." She had a nice voice.

"No problem. My fishing schedule is filling up quickly, so I thought I should get back to you right away."

"You misunderstood, Mr. Socarides. I didn't call about fishing. I'd like you to take a case in your capacity as a private investigator."

I hadn't done any PI work in months and the last job wasn't exactly the *Purloined Letter*. A wealthy couple from New Jersey hired me to do security checks on their summer home. I should have done security checks on *them* because they still owed me money.

"How did you find me?" I said.

"I saw your name in the newspaper. I'm an attorney on Nantucket. I need the help of a private investigator. The article said you take unusual cases. This situation certainly fits that description."

"You'll have to tell me more about this case, Ms. Hendricks."

"You'd be working for the defense team of someone who's a suspect in a murder."

"That's pretty routine stuff. Checking alibis and witnesses. What makes this so unusual?"

"It's too complicated to explain over the phone. You'd have to come to Nantucket so I can show you."

I contemplated the wisdom of further complicating my messy life. When I didn't answer right away, she must have taken my silence for a bargaining ploy.

"I know it's a little inconvenient coming over to the island, but this could be quite lucrative." She quoted an hourly rate that raised my eyebrows. I had a damaged boat that would put me out of business until it was repaired, a high deductible on my insurance, and a potential lawsuit.

"When do you want to get together?"

"The Hy-Line's high speed ferry will be leaving in half an hour. I've made a reservation for you. I'll meet you at the dock when you arrive in Nantucket."

"Okay, Ms. Hendricks. How will I know you?"

"That won't be a problem. I'll know *you*. Didn't you know your picture was in the paper?"

I thought about the slashed cushions, and the smiling gent in the picture that went with Crumley's story in the local daily. "Yeah," I said. "So I've heard."

CHAPTER 3

The high-speed ferry was on the other side of the harbor. I tucked my truck into a parking slot, trotted over to the ticket booth, then sprinted aboard the boat moments before the dock crew removed the gangway. Within minutes, the ferry was entering Lewis Bay, moving past the long breakwater that juts out from Camelot, the Kennedy compound at Hyannisport. The ferry swung a few points to port around the Number 4 red harbor buoy, then headed southeast. Once it hit open water, the ferry flexed its mechanical muscles, ramped up to its cruising speed of thirty knots and began its dash across Nantucket Sound, leaving twin rooster tails in its wake.

With their squashed down, streamlined looks, the high-speed catamarans that make the daily run between the mainland and Nantucket resemble waterborne UFOs. Their twin aluminum hulls slice through the water like hot knives through butter. The fast ferries don't have the character of the grungy, slow-moving car ferries that are the lifelines to Nantucket, but they're heavily used by workers who can't afford to live on the island and by travelers who'd rather go by boat than plane.

I bought a cup of coffee at the food counter and plucked a tourist brochure from a rack. Settling into one of the seats arranged in rows like those on an airplane, I opened the chamber of commerce brochure and read, "Because of the grey shingled buildings and frequent fog, Nantucket is affectionately referred to as '*the Little Grey Lady of the Sea*.'

I glanced at a brief history of the island's whaling heritage, then studied the map in the pamphlet. From the air, the island looks like a croissant, with the concave side of the crescent facing the mainland. Nantucket is only fourteen miles long and three miles wide and was shaped by the same ice age glaciers that sculpted Cape Cod. The island encompasses around forty-eight square miles, most of it not much higher than the waves that wash its sandy shores, except for Folger Hill, which soars one-hundred-nine-feet above sea level.

It was too nice a day to stay in the cabin. I set the brochure aside and went out onto the deck for some fresh air. It was hard to believe there was land under the low bank of marshmallow clouds off to the south. At the midpoint in Nantucket Sound, neither shore is visible. The boat is at the center of what Joseph Conrad described in his writing as the wide disk of the sea.

The island first appeared as an unevenness of the horizon. The line separating land and sea darkened in hue. A water tower appeared, then church spires spiked the blue sky. As the ferry neared the buoy marking the harbor entrance, tawny strands of beach and dark green vegetation were visible. Mansions lined the cliffs on the harbor approach. The ferry slowed as it passed between the Brant Point lighthouse and the tip of a thin, sandy island that shelters the harbor, with the Coast Station on our right, then it cruised past Straight Wharf, which encloses one side of a rectangular basin for smaller boats. The ferry stopped and pivoted to back up to the wharf.

I walked down the gangway onto the ferry dock, the busy nexus where the eager newcomers exchanged places with the tanned but sad-eyed vacationers who look like refugees being driven from the only home they have ever known. The foot traffic flowed past gift shops, galleries and restaurants, around the tour vans and hotel shuttles. Handsome young men and pretty young women from the local hotels held squares of cardboard printed with names of incoming guests.

As the crowd thinned, I felt like a pebble left in the ebb of a receding wave. I waited five minutes. Still no one who looked lawyerly. After ten minutes had passed, I went over to an ice cream stand. I was checking out the list of flavors when someone tapped me lightly on the shoulder. I turned and looked into the anxious face of an attractive young woman. She brushed a strand of curly black hair away from her forehead. She had a flawless cinnamon and cream complexion.

She was holding a copy of *The Cape Cod Times*, folded to display the front page. "Mr. Socarides?" she said, glancing at my photo.

"That's right. And you must be Ms. Hendricks?"

She extended her hand. Her grip was warm and firm.

"I'm so sorry I'm late. There was a moped accident on the Siasconset road." She pronounced it properly as S'conset.

"I'm in no hurry, Ms. Hendricks. Can I buy you an ice cream cone?"

Her lush lips widened in a smile. "Thank you. I had a late lunch. Maybe later after we talk business. My office is a short walk from here."

She guided me toward the center of town along a narrow uneven brick sidewalk, moving with the relaxed litheness of a yoga instructor. She was wearing an almond-colored silk pant suit that flowed with her body. Main Street begins its slow rise a short stroll from the ferry dock. The wide street is paved in cobblestones and lined on both sides with shade trees and ritzy shops. Near the top of the hill, at the venerable Pacific Bank, we made a right onto a quiet street away from the hubbub. The law office was in a neat two-story brick building. A brass plaque to the right of the entryway said: Lisa D. Hendricks, Attorney at Law.

Her office was on the second floor at the top of a narrow stairway. Taped to the dark-wood walls were several color-coded maps. Light streamed in through tall windows that looked out on the Methodist church across the street. Ms. Hendricks motioned to a comfortable leather chair and slipped behind a mahogany desk. She removed her designer sunglasses to reveal eyes of startling blue framed by long dark lashes.

"Thank you for coming to the island on such short, may I say *impossibly* demanding, notice."

"It's always a pleasure to come to Nantucket even when I don't know why I'm here."

"Then let me get right down to business. As I mentioned on the phone, I'd like you to investigate the circumstances surrounding a murder. I'm representing the suspect. His name is Henry Daggett."

"When did the murder occur?"

"About five weeks ago. I'm surprised you don't know about it. The story was all over the news because of the unusual circumstances and the prominence of Mr. Daggett and the victim, Absalom Coffin."

"I was busy getting my charter business off the ground about then. You'll have to fill me in. You said both men were prominent."

"Henry Daggett and Ab Coffin come from old Nantucket families that go back to the Quakers who settled the island. Both families originally made their money in the whaling business which they used as springboards to other ventures. The Daggetts owned huge holdings of property which became quite valuable as real estate. In developing that land, they moved into construction and did quite well at it. When whaling faded, many of the Coffin family became successful in other businesses. Ab's branch of the Coffins wasn't one of them, although he was quite respected as an antiques dealer."

"Nantucket's a small island. They would have known each other."

"Yes, but it was more than a casual acquaintance. They were friends, drawn together by their island heritage and common interests. They were accomplished Nantucket historians with an extensive knowledge of the island's whaling past. They were on the board of the historical association which operates the whaling museum."

"Where did the murder occur?"

"In the museum."

"So there were witnesses?"

"No. It was after hours and the museum was closed. As trustees, both men had keys to the building."

"What was the murder weapon?"

She pursed her lips is if she was having a struggle finding the right words, then said, "Coffin was killed with a boarding knife taken from the museum's collection of whaling implements. After a whale was caught, boarding knives were used to cut strips of blubber from the carcass. It's similar in shape to a bayonet."

"Was Mr. Coffin stabbed from the front or the back?"

"From the front."

"Indicating that Mr. Coffin was aware he was being attacked. He may even have known the killer."

"That's what the police believe."

I sat back and tented my fingers. "You've mentioned two of the three elements a D.A. needs to convince a jury that Henry Daggett is guilty. The knife is the means and the museum key presents the opportunity. The only thing that bothers me is the lack of motive. You said they were friends."

"I should have said that they *had* been friends. Both men were strong-minded Yankees. They'd had a serious disagreement recently. An argument over museum policy."

"That seems like a lame reason to make *shish-ka-bob* out of an old friend. Are you sure there wasn't any underlying source of antagonism between them? Business deal gone bad. A grudge over a woman?"

"You're very perceptive, Mr. Socarides. There had been bad blood between the families going back nearly two-hundred years. You've heard of the *Essex* tragedy?"

"I'm not an expert on Nantucket, but I read the *Heart of the Sea*, Nathaniel Philbrick's book. The *Essex* was the Nantucket whaling ship sunk by a sperm whale. The story gave Herman Melville the idea for *Moby Dick*."

"Then you know that the *real* tragedy transpired after the ship sank in 1819. The crew struck out in whaleboats, thousands of miles from land. They avoided some islands out of fear of cannibals, which is ironic, because they resorted to cannibalism to survive."

"That was a long time ago. How is the *Essex* connected with this present-day murder case?"

"Indirectly. Let me keep going. Another Nantucket ship was sunk by a whale a few years after the *Essex* incident. The *Moshup* went down in the same part of the Pacific, possibly attacked by the same whale that sent the *Essex* to the bottom."

"I've read a lot of marine history. I never heard of the *Moshup*."

"That's because the whole thing was hushed up. There were rumors, but they were quickly quashed. The Quakers who ran the whaling trade were hard-nosed businessmen. One act of desperate cannibalism could be forgiven. A second might seem like habit. If outsiders thought Nantucket was home to hungry cannibals it would have been bad for the whale oil business."

"Not hard to see why," I said. "Every time someone saw a candle made with Nantucket whale oil they'd think of someone boiling in a pot."

She suppressed a smile. "Technically inaccurate, but to the point."

"All very interesting, but what does the *Moshup* have to do with your client's case?"

"It goes to the missing motivation you mentioned. Mr. Daggett's ancestor, also named Henry, was carpenter on the *Moshup*. Coffin's was first mate. The police think that a recent museum disagreement turned up the heat and old resentments finally bubbled over into violence."

"That's quite a leap. My ancestors came from Crete where revenge was a way of life, but after a few generations, people tend to forget and forgive."

"Unless the reason for that bad blood was so heinous it could only be washed away with more blood."

"And the heinous reason in this case?"

"Simple, really. Mr. Coffin's great-great-grandfather Obediah *ate* Mr. Daggett's great-great-grandfather."

Lisa must have known that she was delivering a potent punch line because there was a mischievous sparkle in the lovely blue eyes.

"That *could* take a while to get over," I said. "What were the circumstances?"

"It's a complicated story. I'd be glad to tell you more after you talk to my client. He's been allowed to stay home, monitored with an electronic ankle bracelet."

I tried to come up with a way to let Lisa down for a soft landing. I was thinking I should be back on the mainland dealing with the lawsuit that threatened my charter business. "From what I've heard, you might be better off spending the money on a good criminal defense attorney."

"I deal in conservation land acquisition and I'll admit that criminal law is not my specialty. I know my limits. I've brought in a Boston law firm to join the defense. We'll still need a thorough investigation to see if there is enough evidence to convict my client."

"And if there is, and it leads to a conviction?"

"I'll let justice take its course. But it will make me sad."

"You seem to have an emotional attachment to this case."

"You're correct. It's very personal to me."

"Why is that if I may ask?"

She cocked her head and looked at me like a portrait artist searching a subject's face for the inner person.

"It's really not complicated, Mr. Socarides. Henry Daggett is my grandfather."

CHAPTER 4

Lisa Hendricks was a skilled angler. She had lured me to Nantucket using money as bait, set the hook with the cannibal story and reeled me in with the revelation that murder suspect Henry Daggett was her grandfather. Before I had a chance to wiggle off the hook, she gaffed me aboard with the offer to let me drive her classic MG red convertible. Which explains how I found myself behind the wheel of an antique sports car, with the top down and the salty air tossing the raven hair of the lovely woman at my side.

Lisa showed me an escape route that circumvented the traffic gridlock in town. We rode through quiet old neighborhoods where the narrow streets were lined with antique houses. Lisa gave a running commentary on her family history. Near a windmill on the edge of town, she said we were not far from a neighborhood called New Guinea, once home to whalers of African ancestry. There was a cemetery nearby for black and Cape Verdean residents, where her ancestors were buried.

The traffic soon thinned out. I kicked the MG up to an enjoyable, and slightly illegal cruising speed on Milestone Road, which ran in a straight line between thick stands of scrub pine and oak, the tough, shrunken trees that pass for forests on Cape Cod and the

Islands. At one point, the woods opened up into a prairie spotted with trees shaped like umbrellas. Lisa said that the land had been cleared for the benefit of wildlife. The locals called it the *Serengeti*. Someone had put up big cutouts of African animals for those who had no imagination.

I slowed when we got to Siasconset, a picturesque former fishing settlement on the easterly end of the island around eight miles from the main town. The road into the village is a pretty lane shaded by maple trees and lined with white picket fences. Tall privacy hedges cut off the view of many houses, but there were glimpses of rose-covered trellises on the shingled roofs. There's an old casino theater built back when the fair-weather fishing village drew artists, writers and actors from the big city.

Siasconset is a far cry from Times Square. Clustered in the village center are an insurance agency, a book store, post office, package store and a couple of seasonal restaurants. With its silver-shingled, rose-covered cottages and sea-breezes, *S'conset* encapsulates the kind of Nantucket charm that the chamber of commerce talks about in its guidebook.

It took about a millisecond to get through the roaring metropolis. Lisa directed me onto a gravel road lined with tall privacy hedges. At the end of the road was a circular driveway covered in crushed clamshells bleached bone white by the sun. The driveway served as access to a big summer house. With its gabled roof and wide, wrap-around veranda, the house had an understated elegance that bragged about the owners' wealth without boasting. I smelled Old Money. The house was sheathed in white cedar shingles that had weathered to silver-gray. The lawn was so green and perfectly manicured that it could have been made out of AstroTurf. Set back from the house behind a privet hedge was a small cottage, and next to it was a three-car garage. A white Miata sports car was parked near the cottage.

I pulled up to the veranda and we got out of the MG. We

climbed to the expansive porch, which was furnished with rocking chairs and a sofa of white wicker. Lisa opened the front door and we stepped into a large lobby.

A man was descending the wide staircase that went up to the second floor. He was dressed casually in tan shorts and a white polo shirt, and was probably in his thirties. He had a buff physique and a lifeguard's tan. I had him tagged as a personal trainer or masseur. I learned that I was wrong a second later when Lisa introduced him as Dr. Tyler Rosen.

"How's Gramps doing?" Lisa asked.

"Pretty much the same. No better, but no worse."

"I'm going to introduce Mr. Socarides to Gramps, if it's okay. He's on our defense team."

Rosen eyed me with less-than-friendly curiosity. "It would be fine, Lisa," he said with a coolness in his voice. "Not too long a visit, though."

She thanked him and led the way up the staircase. As we stepped onto the landing, she paused and said, "Dr. Rosen has been treating my grandfather."

"Is your grandfather ill?"

"In a way." She shrugged. "Having a resident psychologist on call was part of the deal to get him released to the house." I opened my mouth to ask for specifics, but Lisa said, "You'll understand better after you meet him. *C'mon.*"

We walked down a carpeted hall and stopped in front of a paneled oak wood door.

Lisa turned to face me. "A word of warning. Gramps can be overwhelming and a bit demonstrative, but he's really harmless."

"No sharp objects within reach?"

"Nothing like that. Just play along. Remember that he sees things through a different lens. Literally and figuratively. Relax. Ready?"

I shrugged. "*Ready.*"

She knocked lightly. A man's voice roared out.

"*Avast!* Who goes there?"

"It's me. Lisa. There's someone out here who wants to see you. Can he come in?"

"Is he a whaler ye speak of?"

"I've heard there's none finer."

"Wait not, girl!" The gruff tone had vanished. "Send him aft."

Lisa opened the unlocked door. Seeing my hesitation, she placed her palm on the small of my back. With more strength than I would have imagined in her slender arm, she pushed me through the doorway. The door clicked shut behind me.

I stepped into a room that looked like the Library of Congress. The shelves that lined the two facing walls held hundreds of volumes. There was a wooden trestle table and a captain's chair in the middle of the room. Books and maps covered the top of the table.

At the far end of the room, a section of floor was raised several inches into a platform in front of an arched window that rose almost to the ceiling. Someone wearing a long frock coat and a slouch hat was silhouetted darkly against the afternoon sunlight filtering through the glass panes. The man stood with his legs spread wide apart, as still as if he were carved from basalt.

The face was obscured by the wide hat brim and details were lost against the back lighting. But even if I couldn't see the eyes, I could feel the twin orbs burning through me with a laser-like intensity.

He spoke. "Art thou a man or a spirit?" The deep voice had a hollow ring that echoed off the ceiling and hardwood floors.

Lisa had advised me to simply play along. "I'm a *man*."

He paused as if he were testing the truth of my reply. "*Aye*," he said with a chuckle in his voice. "I can see that well enough. Come aft."

I walked forward under his shadowed gaze and stopped at the base of the platform. He advanced several paces in my direction with a strange lurching walk, and then stopped. In his hand was an antique, telescoping brass spyglass.

The face that peered down from under the brim must have been a handsome at one time. The jaw was firm and the features chiseled. The long nose could have denoted character, or simply a long nose. The face was creased with wrinkles and deep lines, like wrinkled parchment. The eyes were set so deeply in their sockets that it was impossible to tell what color they were.

Without warning, the lips turned up at each corner, transforming his grim expression to one of joy.

"Thou hast come at last!"

"You were *expecting* me?"

"Art thou not *Starbuck*?"

Lisa's voice whispered in my head.

Play along.

"Aye, Captain. That's me all right."

"Aye indeed. Starbuck, the best lance in all Nantucket. The *Pequod*'s chief mate. The most royal prince in Ahab's sea-washed kingdom. Where hast thou been, lad?"

"I sailed across from the mainland."

"*Ah.* Thou hast been to visit your wife and brood on Cape Cod. Too long away, Starbuck. Too long. *Here* lies your true family. Stubbs and Flask. Queequeg and Tashto. Brothers born in the billowing sea and baptized by the blood spray of the whales we have killed."

Sometimes I can be a slow study, and it had been years since I'd read Herman Melville's saga about the white whale named Moby Dick. But I didn't have to be a professor of American literature to figure out Daggett's peculiar pathology. Lisa's dotty old grandfather thought he was Captain Ahab, skipper of the doomed ship *Pequod* and nemesis of Moby Dick. This was *weird.* I backed away toward the door.

The smile vanished. "Whither goest thou?"

I stopped in my tracks. "I goest to see a man about a whale."

"Then thou hast heard the good news?"

"I've been pretty busy, Captain."

"No matter. Come closer. It hast been much too long since the planks of the quarterdeck hast felt aught but my ivory thumper. Lend me your hand."

I walked back to the stage and raised my arm, thinking he wanted to shake hands. His right hand shot out and the fingers clamped on my wrist, then he pulled me up onto the platform with surprising strength. He bore into me with his burning eyes, a manic grin on his lips. He pulled me toward the window, where he released my arm and pointed. I was looking toward Nantucket Sound, but his imagination had apparently burned a different kind of image on his retina. His mad eyes saw the vast expanses of the Pacific Ocean.

He turned, and speaking softly, said, "Thou doubted your captain like the disciple Thomas. Thou said the white whale wast a dumb brute, that smote me from blindest instinct. That which struck my leg off, and made a poor pegging lubber of me forever and a day. Do you *remember*, Starbuck?"

A thunderstorm was brewing on his broad brow as he pulled back the lower part of his frock coat and yanked up his pant leg. There was no peg-leg carved from whalebone as in the story. The skinny white leg was in once piece. Around the ankle was a metal strap holding the transmitter that would let the police track him if he wandered off from the house.

"Yes, Captain. I remember. As if it were yesterday."

His voice rose. "Now burn this into thy memory. That cursed thing which demasted me is soon to learn the meaning of revenge!"

"That *is* good news, Captain Ahab."

He dropped the pant leg and raised his right hand in the air.

"God will guide the lance in my hand. Its point will go to the heart of the great brute. I will kill that which had taken my leg, and consigned me to life as a freak, part human flesh, part spermaceti bone."

He grasped the spyglass as if it were a spear and brought his hand down in a sweeping motion, halting a few inches from the wooden floor. The energy seemed to go out of him and he stared at the parquet for a moment. Then he turned and lurched back to the window.

I stepped down from the platform and walked with a soft step to the door. Lisa was waiting for me in the hallway with her arms crossed.

"Welcome back to the 21st century," she said. "How did it go?"

"I saw the Gregory Peck version of *Moby Dick*. This performance was much more convincing. Your grandfather thought I was Starbuck."

She raised her eyebrows. "Ahab's chief mate? Ranking you second in command was a compliment. Did he let you up on the quarter deck?"

I nodded. "He even showed me his ivory peg leg with the battery pack."

"*Impressive*. Only the ship's officers are allowed on the captain's deck."

Daggett was insane. Bonkers. Crazy-go-nuts. I didn't take the invitation into his fantasyland as the compliment she might have intended. "How long has your grandfather been like this?"

"Since the night of the murder."

"What happened to him?"

She took in a deep breath and let it out. "It's a complicated story. I can tell you all about it over a cocktail. You look like you could use one."

"I always look as if I could use one because I usually do," I said.

She passed me the keys to her MG.

"You can drive," she said.

CHAPTER 5

Ten minutes later, I pulled up in front of the Wauwinet Hotel, tossed the MG's keys to the car valet and escorted Lisa into Topper's restaurant. The hostess smilingly obliged our request for a table off by itself, and found us a two-seater in a corner of the deck. The lights of Nantucket town sparkled like gemstones across the harbor. A sweet salt-spray rose perfume floated on the warm summer breeze.

The waiter came over for our drink orders. Lisa asked for a Kir cocktail. I went for a shot of Macallan malt whiskey. When the drinks came, I raised my glass. "A toast to Ahab and Moby."

Her glass stayed on the table. "I'm curious. Why would you raise your glass to Moby Dick, who sank the *Pequod*, and caused the death of nearly all of its crew, including yourself, Mr. Starbuck."

"Precisely because that's who I am, according to your grandfather. *Starbuck*."

Lisa furrowed her brow. "Maybe I'm just being dense. I'm afraid you've lost me."

"Understandable. Let me lay it out for you. Ahab snapped after Moby bit off his leg. Racked by pain and humiliated at having to hop around on a peg-leg, Ahab let his desire for revenge become a destructive obsession. My namesake, Starbuck, tried to discourage

51

him from his insane quest."

"You have a good grasp of Melville, I see. I'm still not clear why I should join a cheering section for the whale."

"The whale was not evil, Starbuck argued; Moby was a force of nature and had attacked Ahab in self-defense after he harpooned it. Unlike the whale, Ahab had human intellect, but he denied the fact that Moby's reaction was animal instinct and attributed it to human-like malevolence. Blinded by his anger, Ahab ignored Starbuck's warning. Thought of him as a traitor. When Ahab enlisted his crew in his unholy cause, he doomed them. And himself. And *me*."

"You're looking quite healthy for a dead man. Are you saying Moby was the victim?"

"*Think* of it. Guys like Ahab were using him for a pincushion. He had suffered as much physical pain as Ahab. Maybe mental as well. Moby could have been vindictive as Ahab said. Who knows what goes on in a whale's mind? But in any case, *both* Ahab and Moby were victims of their own fate."

"Ah. *Now* I understand. I think."

"Good, because my harpoon-throwing arm is getting tired holding this glass. I suggest that we make the first toast to Ahab."

We clinked glasses. She took a sip of her cocktail, keeping her eyes on me over the rim of her glass.

"Maybe Gramps wasn't being crazy when he made you his first mate, Mr. Socarides. I think he saw the philosophical qualifications that could help him out of his predicament."

"Not sure I agree, but I'll admit that you were right about this being a fascinating case."

The warm evening was too pleasant to fill our conversation with autopsies and murder weapons. We made small talk, exchanging personal information in the cautious way new acquaintances do when they're not sure of each other.

She asked about my background and I gave her an edited version of the Socarides biography. She picked up on my sudden shift from the job of catching criminals to catching codfish.

"That was a drastic change, cutting short what must have been a promising career in law enforcement."

"I had professional and personal reasons. I'll tell you about them when we get to know each other better. Your turn now. My incredible powers of deduction suggest that the *D* in your middle name stands for Daggett."

"I'll give you five Sherlocks on a scale of ten, because it *is* family related. Only not the Daggett family. The D stands for Daphne, my Cape Verdean great-grandmother."

"What's the family tie-in to the Daggetts?"

"It all goes back to the *Moshup*. Remember how I told you that the original Henry Daggett never returned from the voyage."

"How could I forget? He survived the whale attack and ship sinking, but not the hunger of his shipmates."

"Correct. He left a widow with two sons back on Nantucket. They grew up and married. Each had large families, as was the custom at the time. One of their male offspring married my great-grandmother Daphne. Among their descendants was my father, who was a foreman with the Daggett construction firm. He and my mother were killed in a car accident when I was quite young."

"I'm very sorry to hear that. I lost a good friend the same way and know from experience what a hole it leaves in your life."

"My grandparents did their best to fill it. Gramps was my mother's dad. He was devastated, but his biggest concern was me. After the accident, he and my grandmother took me into their house and into their lives. When my grandmother died of cancer, he became my caregiver."

"He did a good job from what I can see."

"Thanks, I appreciate that. A lot of the credit goes to a local widow who pretty much became my surrogate mother. She and Gramps encouraged me to study law. Said I had a natural sense of fairness. I graduated from Harvard law and took a job with a big firm in New York. Married. Divorced. No children. Returned to Nantucket to seek solace."

"And did you find what you were looking for?"

"Yes, I did. There's a lot of development pressure on the island, so as a conservation lawyer, I keep pretty busy. The work doesn't pay much, but I live in Gramps' house and my office building is owned by a family trust."

"His instincts were on the mark when he advised you to become a lawyer."

"Guess I should have studied criminal law instead." A sad smile came to her lips. "I never dreamed Gramps would be involved in something like this."

"You told me that Henry's personality change went back to the night of the murder?"

"That's right. You remember the open land we passed on the way to Siasconset."

"The Serengeti."

She nodded. "A bird-watcher found him there roaming around in a daze. He had a head injury and he was babbling this craziness about Moby Dick."

"The Serengeti is several miles from the museum. Any idea how he got there?"

"The police found his car pulled off the main road, so he must have driven."

"Do they know how he got the injury?"

"They think he fell maybe."

"Could the injury have had something to do with his personality change?"

"I've been told that it's possible. He's been a collector of Melville for as long as I can remember. That library you saw in his apartment contains several first editions of *Moby Dick*. The doctors said the trauma may have caused a shift from his real world to the fictional one. Unfortunately, he couldn't say where he had been that night.

Without a record of his movements we couldn't establish an alibi."

"Any chance he'll come out of it?"

"He might snap back any minute. There's no guarantee that he would remember anything of what happened."

I signaled the waiter for another Macallan and stared off at the glittering lights across the harbor.

"Let's talk about Coffin. Tell me what you know about the murder victim and your grandfather."

She shook her head. "Nothing is simple about this case."

"I'm beginning to see that."

"You have to go back to the cannibalism on the *Moshup* whaleboat."

The waiter arrived and recommended the prime rib or the turbot. Lisa and I exchanged glances, and in anticipation of the cannibalistic topic of our conversation, we both ordered fish. We broke out in laughter for no apparent reason. The waiter simply shrugged, and went off to the kitchen, probably muttering to himself about daffy tourists.

"I'll try to get through this part of the story before dinner arrives," Lisa said. "Picture this scenario. You had three men in the whaleboat. Coffin, Daggett and Swain. They had avoided starvation by eating the bodies of their comrades and were on the brink of madness. When Daggett died, they ate him. A passing ship picked the survivors up a couple of days later. They returned to Nantucket. They hardly talked about their ordeal. Nobody pressed them. As I said, wounds were still raw from the *Essex* loss."

"What happened to the two survivors?"

"Swain opened a guest house. He was quite successful. People liked to stay at a place whose owner was a celebrity of sorts."

"The conversation around the dinner table must have been fascinating."

"He didn't talk much about his last voyage, from what I understand. He eventually made enough money to acquire a hotel in Boston. He expanded this investment into a small empire of hotels and bars."

"Did Coffin parley his reputation into similar success?"

"Not at all. Just the opposite. Coffin never got over the *Moshup* experience. He was broken further when his young wife left him. She couldn't abide living with a cannibal. Ab Coffin was descended from Obed's brother. While Swain flourished, Coffin eked out a living making scrimshaw, which he sold to tourists. As I said earlier, Ab ran a respectable but not very profitable antiques business on the island."

"You said Coffin's descendent and your grandfather were on the museum board and that they argued about policy. Could you be more specific?"

"It was *little* things, mostly. Where to place a display. Acquisitions. It was good-natured discussion for the most part. But that changed when they argued over whether to spend money on a scrimshaw collection. Coffin was pushing for the museum to buy it, supposedly through a third party. My grandfather was against the acquisition. The dispute brought the old cannibalism case to the fore one night. Coffin told my grandfather at a board meeting not to oppose him. 'Remember what happened with our ancestors,' he said. He apologized later that he meant it as a joke."

"Funny sense of humor you Nantucket folks have."

"Henry took it as a threat and that only made things worse. When Coffin was killed, the police theorized that the needling got to be too much. That it pushed Gramps over the edge so that he snapped and killed Coffin. He became the only suspect. I told the district attorney at the preliminary hearing that Gramps is not a violent person. The D.A. said that may be, but he theorizes that the Ahab personality emerged because Henry's inner self could not comprehend the enormity of his actions."

"Which brings us back to Ahab."

"*Yes.* Now that you've met Gramps what do *you* think?"

I know from Vietnam how a shock to the senses can warp your sense of time and space. Something happens, and in an instant you switch from one universe to another.

Henry Daggett could have been the thoughtful old Melville scholar going about his business when his reality shifted. I remember the force the gentle old man used when he swept his telescope down as if plunging a lance into an invisible whale.

I was about to say all this, but Lisa, who'd been patiently waiting for my brain to hook up with my mouth, lifted her gaze and smiled.

"*Michael*. How nice to see you."

She was talking to a man who had come out onto the deck from the main restaurant. He strolled over to the table and said, "I saw your car in the parking lot and the hostess told me you were out here. How are you?"

"I'm fine, Michael. Would you care to join us?"

"Thanks, Lisa. I'd love to, but I've got to hook up with a potential investor."

I thought I saw a flash of relief in Lisa's eyes, but she said, "That's too bad, Michael. Mr. Socarides, this is Michael Ramsey. He's an old friend of the family."

I stood up and we shook hands. He wore olive slacks and a dark green linen blazer over an open linen shirt. He was about my height, with narrower shoulders. He had an athletic physique but his movements were surprisingly wooden and robotic. His face had the same type of dichotomy. It was handsome, with a broad forehead, square chin and even features, but there was little animation except for a shifting of the eyes and a quick jerk of the head as he flashed me a blinding white smile.

"Nice to meet you, Mr. Socarides. On-Island for business or pleasure?"

I glanced at Lisa. "A little of both."

The eyes narrowed and the frozen smile stayed in place. He turned to Lisa.

"How is your grandfather doing?"

"As well as can be expected. I've brought in a Boston lawyer who is working on a delay while Gramps undergoes further psychiatric evaluation. Thanks again for lending us Dr. Rosen."

"It's the *least* I can do, Lisa. Well, let me know if I can be of additional help. In the meantime, I'd like to invite you over for cocktails tomorrow evening. Perhaps you would like to come, too, Mr. Socarides."

"Thank you for the invitation," I said. I sensed the invite had more to do with his curiosity than any desire to see me again. "I'm heading back to the mainland tonight."

"Another time, then."

We shook hands, going through a repeat of our earlier hand-grip contest, then he bent over and gave Lisa a kiss. It was aimed for her lips, but she turned her face slightly at the last second so that he brushed her cheek. I watched him disappear into the lounge and then sat down again.

Lisa gave me a bemused smile. "Care to try your powers of deduction on Michael, Mr. Socarides?'

"That's easy. Nice clothes. Nice dental work. Nice haircut. Strong handshake and a few callouses, suggesting a tennis player. Oh yeah. He's *rich*."

"Is that all you can come up with?"

"No. He has a casual arrogance that some people develop when they think the successful acquisition of money entitles them to respect from peons like me. He tried to crush my hand, which shows he's an alpha male. He didn't like it when I gave him the lobster claw treatment."

She clapped her hands lightly.

"That's Michael. Anything else?"

"Did I say he's rich?"

"He's *very* rich. He scoops up marginal companies and drains them for every dollar. Closes them down or moves operations out of the country. Your deductive powers are going to be a big help to my grandfather."

It was a soft pitch, low and outside. I could have hit it out of the ballpark had I chosen to take a swing. Lisa was one of the prettiest women I'd ever met. She was smart and funny, too. She reminded me of Sally Carlin, who left Cape Cod a couple of years ago when she discovered that slightly alcoholic beachcombers like me are a dime a dozen. But this was no ordinary case, and I had a potential legal problem I had to deal with back home.

"I'm no Sigmund Freud, but it's pretty clear that your grandfather is mentally ill," I said. "From what I've seen and what you've told me, there's a real possibility that he's guilty."

Anger flashed in her eyes. "I'll *never* believe that."

"But a jury might, which is why I'll repeat my earlier suggestion that the money would be better spent having an extra criminal defense lawyer on your team."

"You won't take the case?"

"It doesn't seem necessary. Your grandfather says he wants to kill the great white whale. The prosecutor would have no trouble associating that statement as a veiled confession of a past misdeed."

She gave a sigh of defeat. "I'll give you a ride to the dock. I'm afraid you missed the high-speed boat, but you can catch the car ferry back to the mainland."

She paid the tab. I protested, but she said, "I invited you. Business."

We didn't talk much on the ten-mile drive to the Steamship Authority terminal. We got out of the car and she walked me to the gangway of the car ferry *Iyanough*, where she handed me her business card. She wasn't about to give up, which made me like her even more.

"Obviously, I'm disappointed," she said. She stood so close I could smell the shampoo in her hair. "Would you promise me to do one thing? Sleep on it for twenty-four hours. If you still think it's not for you, give me a call."

I said that I would think it over. We shook hands and she held onto mine.

"Mr. Socarides, my grandfather is my only family. If he died of a heart attack, I could live with that. Having him in limbo is simply awful. You connected with him somehow. So please...." She paused to clear away a catch in her throat. "*Please.*"

She let go of my hand finally and headed back to her car. I watched her walk away, and then climbed the gangway, feeling as if my shoes were full of lead. Moments later, I stood on the high deck as the ferry cast off and slowly headed out of the harbor. On the way past the lighthouse, I had a close view of a big yacht, tied up at the end of the pier that had not been there on my trip in. I saw that it had a helicopter pad and I got a glimpse of the name on the fan-tail.

VOLGA

I wondered what a yacht named for a river in Russia was doing in Nantucket. But I was too tired to think about it. As soon as the ferry cleared the Brant Point lighthouse, I went back inside and found a seat near the cafeteria bar. The ferry was practically deserted. I ordered a beer and chatted about the fortunes of the Red Sox with the night shift cafeteria manager.

The trip on the slower ferry was almost twice the time the high-speed boat took to get to Nantucket, and it was late in the evening when we rounded the harbor buoy and entered Lewis Bay. I walked out onto the deck, and that's when I saw that the entire harbor lit up with a flickering red and yellow light. The cool night air was heavy with the acrid smell of smoke.

The source of the light and the smoke was a fire burning furiously at the Hyannis marina. It was hard to pinpoint the exact location, but as the ferry grew nearer, and details became visible, I grew more worried. And with good reason.

The *Thalassa's* dock was enveloped in flames.

CHAPTER 6

The island ferry makes a 360-degree pivot in the tightest part of the harbor so it can dock stern first in position for the next trip. I've always liked watching the maneuver, but as the ferry went through its agonizingly slow spin, I circled the deck like an ant on a floating leaf. The blaze was definitely at my dock. And my boat was in the middle of the writhing pillar of flames.

The ferry eased up to the bulkhead and the deck hands dropped the gangway in place as soon as the land crew secured the dock lines. I dashed down the gangway like a thief on the run, got behind the wheel of my pick-up, murmured a prayer and turned the ignition key. The engine miraculously kicked into life on the first try.

I broke the speed limit driving to the other side of the harbor, only to jam the brakes on at the entrance to the marina parking lot. A cop was turning people away. I yelled out the window that I had a boat at the dock and he waved me through. The parking lot was pure chaos. Four fire trucks and a couple of fire department SUVs were clustered near the dock. Behind the trucks were more cruisers than you'd see at the policeman's ball. An ambulance with EMTs stood by. Hoses snaked everywhere. The stroboscopic color display looked like the special effects at a Rolling Stones concert.

The *Thalassa* was hidden behind a wall of flames and black, foul-smelling smoke. The firefighters had dampened down the fire on the dock and were advancing cautiously to the source of the flames under a shower of sparks. An acrid, choking cloud hung over the marina. A line of yellow tape had been set up a safe distance from the blaze. The cop standing behind the yellow tape saw me duck under the plastic barricade and came running over to kick me out.

"Hey—oh, it's *you*," Officer Tucker said. "Am I glad to see that you're okay, Mr. Socarides! I thought you might be on your boat."

"I've got to get to the dock."

"Are you *crazy?*"

"I left my *cat* on the boat!"

"Sorry to hear that, sir. *Look* at it. There's nothing you can do until they get things under control."

She was right, of course. Even from where I stood, the heat toasted my face like a bagel in an oven. I placed my cap over my nose and mouth as an impromptu gas mask, but it didn't help much when the wind shifted in our direction. We both broke into coughing fits and the smoke produced by burning fiberglass stung our eyes. Officer Tucker and I retreated another hundred feet from the docks. I raged at my helplessness and stared at the fire with glazed and watery eyes.

Poor old Kojak wouldn't have stood a chance.

Someone called my name. I turned and saw the dock master hustling toward me. As he came closer, I wiped my eyes and saw that he was cradling in his arms what looked like an overgrown fur muff. The dancing light of the fire illuminated the grin on his face.

I yelled, "*Kojak!*"

The old boy heard his name, lifted his head and blinked his yellow eyes. Then he yawned.

I took him from the dock master's arms. Kojak smelled as if he had come from a smoked sausage factory. I thanked the dock master.

"I thought he was a goner."

"Came damned close," the dock master said. "I was on my way to check on the car fire and saw a weird yellow light coming from your boat. Went out on the dock. The door to the cabin was wide open. I could see flames inside. Your cat was on the deck, hiding in a corner. I grabbed him and ran over to tell the firemen working on the car. Good thing the *Hatteras* wasn't in its slip and lucky there was no wind. Woulda been a real mess."

I nodded in agreement. If the bigger boat next to mine had caught fire, its gas tanks would have gone off like a bomb. Every boat in the marina could have caught fire.

"You said there was a *car* fire, too?"

"Near the big boat storage shed," he said with a wave of his hand. "Two fires about the same time in almost the same place. Hell of a coincidence."

Fires rarely start themselves. Spontaneous combustion can happen in haystacks and manure piles. My boat was plastic and metal, and I kept it cleaner than a surgical unit. Even if the boat fire was accidental, the timing of the car fire was suspicious. If someone wanted to walk out to my boat without being seen, a car fire would have drawn attention from the boat dock. People would have rushed over to see what the excitement was about. Someone could come aboard the *Thalassa*, break the lock to the cabin, get the fire going and escape.

"*Yeah*. Hell of a coincidence," I said.

The smoke was getting worse and drifting our way as the firemen tamped down the fire. The dock master started to cough.

He said, "C'mon to my office. It's going to be a while before we can see what the damage is."

I followed him to the small building overlooking the marina. He poured a couple of mugs full from a coffee machine. I put some half-and-half into a dish for Kojak who licked it dry. He seemed unfazed by the fire that had just destroyed my boat and my dreams.

I stared out the window at the drifting haze enveloping the entire marina. The dock master was busy answering the phone, which rang off the hook as boat owners heard about the fire. I thought about another fire, one that had been fueled by the body of a living man. About two Russian thugs who said their boss didn't like what I said in the newspaper. And about the smaller thug who said the *Thalassa* was a "naz bot."

After about an hour, the smoke started to thin. I asked the dock master to keep an eye on Kojak, who had curled up under a chair. I found the fire department officer in charge and told him I had a boat in one of the burned-out slips.

He shook his head, then led the way along the dock until the wooden planking became black charcoal. He played the flashlight beam on the charred dock. I could have cried. My slip was no more. The Grady-White had burned to the waterline. The hull was mostly submerged and the console had melted to the deck. The twin outboards at five thousand bucks a whack were ruined.

I slogged back to the parking lot, head down in the classic pose of dejection. I could argue with myself that my old cat and I were lucky to be alive, but the boat was brand new and when it burned, my plans for a new career sank with it. I wondered how I would tell my family that their investment in the charter fishing business had gone up in smoke.

Officer Tucker intercepted me on the way to fetch Kojak. "How's it look?"

"Like an overdone marshmallow."

She tilted her cap back on her head. "That's a bummer. Sorry, Mr. Socarides."

"Me, too. It's not all bad news. Dock master rescued my cat. Boat's insured. I wasn't sleeping in my cabin when the fire broke out. I won't have to worry about Mr. Glick taking my boat away. All is well." The skeptical look on her young face showed that she knew I was faking it.

"I'm glad you and the cat are okay, but this sort of ruins it for your summer business."

"I can always take parties out in a rowboat. It would certainly cut down on the overhead."

She squinted off at the fire scene. "Those two guys who visited you today have anything to do with this?"

"That's not out of the realm of possibility. I can't prove it. Anything turn up in your records?"

"We have mostly native-borns in our bad guy file." She glanced at the dock. "We'll have to start at the scene of the crime. The fire inspectors have arrived and will check for arson as soon as it's safe."

I thanked her for her help and shuffled back to the dock master's office. The dock master was gone and Kojak was snoozing through the irritating jangle of the phone. I sat in a chair for a few minutes, staring out the window until the ringing stopped. Before the phone could ring again, I grabbed it and stuck it in my ear. I punched out a number from memory, not sure I had it right. After the first ring, a sleepy voice answered.

"Flagg here," it rumbled. "Go ahead."

"I see you're still a man of few words, John."

The deep voice went up a couple of octaves to a throaty growl. "That you, Soc? Christ, it's the middle of the night where I am."

"Sorry, pal. You told me once that Indians sleep with their eyes closed but their minds awake."

There was a chuckle on the end of the line. "Thought you were too smart to believe that crap. Bet you still think Santy Claus is going to bring you a Daisy BB gun."

"This year I'm going to write and ask him to leave a new boat under the tree."

"Didn't you just get a new sport fisherman?"

"Yup, but while I was out of town, someone tossed a Molotov cocktail onto my new sport fisherman. The *Thalassa* melted down to the waterline."

It had been nearly a year since I had seen Flagg in person. You never know when he's going to show up. He simply appears, like a Genie materializing from a magic lamp, and says he wants to go fishing.

"No shit. Any idea who did it, Soc?"

I could picture Flagg suddenly coming alert, the black eyes darting in his broad face as if someone had flicked on an electric switch. His wavy black hair has gone to salt and pepper like mine, and he's thickened around the waist, a development he describes as a southern migration of his barrel chest. But he's still got the powerful shoulders and towering height that make him a formidable figure.

"*Maybe.* I think there's a Russian guy named Ivan involved. A couple of Russian hoods dropped by to see me yesterday." I filled Flagg in on the murdered man and story in the newspaper and quoted Ivan's representatives as best I could remember. "Any idea who this Ivan guy is?"

I could hear a sharp intake of breath.

"*Jeez,* Soc. Of all the guys in the world to get pissed off at you. His name is Ivan Chernko. They call him Ivan the Terrible."

"I've heard about the original Ivan, but not Chernko."

"Not surprised. Anyone who gets too nosy about Ivan usually winds up with a few broken bones. Or even worse. A couple of reporters who wrote about him have been shot by unknown assailants. He's what passes for a businessman in Russia. Ex-KGB. Closely tied to the top government echelon. He's a multi-millionaire. Got a lot of his money through sweetheart deals with the army. Arms acquisition mostly."

"Russia is a long way from where I'm sitting, Flagg."

"It's closer than you think. Chernko jets over to check out the real estate he owns. He's made a few friends with mega-tycoons there who wish they could use his methods to deal with critics. He's got connections in our government, too. Our guys cut him slack because they think he can go around the usual diplomatic channels when they want to talk hush-hush with the top guys at the Kremlin. Let me make a few calls and find out where he is these days."

Flagg asked for my telephone number and hung up. I sat there pondering his words. If Flagg was right, Ivan made Mr. Glick look like a choir boy. I got up and paced the floor, wondering how a quiet, unassuming chap like me turned out to be a magnet for bad feelings. After about ten minutes, the phone rang. It was Flagg again.

"It's Ivan Chernko all right. He's in your back yard. Cruising around in his yacht."

"The *Volga*?"

There was a pause on the line, followed by a chuckle. "Sometimes you scare the hell out of me, Soc. How did you know?"

"I saw a big yacht by that name in Nantucket Harbor a little while ago. Lucky guess."

"Not sure I'd call it *lucky*. What are you going to do now?"

"Talk to the fire inspectors. Talk to the insurance guys. Get Kojak home."

"*Hell,* Soc, that mangy old eating machine still alive?"

"Just barely. He was on the boat when someone torched it. Dock master rescued him. Another black mark against Mr. Chernko."

"I hope that's not a quiet threat I hear. My advice, stay away from Ivan. You've seen what he can do. Get outta his hair, take a trip somewhere, and maybe he'll forget about you."

"Flagg, you're like an old mother hen. I know better than to go up against someone named Ivan the Terrible. You think I'm *insane?*"

"Huh. I'm going to let that question sit there. I know how your brain works. *Most* of the time, anyway."

"I'll take your advice. I've been asked to do an investigation. Working for a pretty lady who allows me to drive her red MG convertible. I'll be busy with that case for a while."

"Call if you need me. Can't stress this enough. Stay away from that Russian bastard."

I was getting tired of Flagg's scolding. I told him I saw the fire inspectors and had to hang up. I turned to the old eating machine.

"What do you think I should do, Kojak?"

He half opened his eyes at the sound of his name and yawned.

"Think you'd be okay on your own for a couple of days?"

He yawned again.

"Yeah, I thought so."

I dug Lisa Hendricks's business card out of my wallet and dialed the home number she had printed on the back. She answered in a low sleepy voice after a couple of rings. I apologized for waking her.

"That's okay, Mr. Socarides. Is everything all right?"

"Everything is fine," I said. "I've had second thoughts about your offer to join your grandfather's defense team."

"And—?"

Flagg's warning popped into my head. I drew a mental picture of a broom sweeping Flagg's words up and dumping them into a trash can.

"I'll see you at the ferry landing tomorrow morning."

CHAPTER 7

The next morning I stood on the open deck as the high-speed ferry cruised past the Hyannis marina. A crane barge was positioning itself to haul the burned wreckage of the *Thalassa* out of the water. Several fire department SUVs were parked in the lot.

After talking to Flagg the night before, I drove back to the boathouse, fed Kojak a night treat, then we both rolled into bed for a few hours of sleep. When I woke up, I showered, downed a gallon of coffee, then called a neighbor.

I apologized for calling at the last minute, told her that my boat had burned, and asked if she would take care of Kojak for a few days while I straightened things out. She said she'd be glad to help. I packed my duffel and his favorite dish, the one with the kitty face on it, gave him a pat on the head and dropped the old guy off at the neighbor's house with a supply of food. Then I headed back to the Hyannis marina where I met the fire inspectors.

I told the inspectors that the boat caught fire while I was on my way back from Nantucket, and that I didn't have a clue how it started. They had said it was a good thing I wasn't on board. Which was when it dawned on me. I had been so intent on taking care of my elderly cat that I hadn't seen what was right in front of me.

This wasn't a simple act of vandalism or arson. Whoever torched my boat was trying to kill me!

A stinking miasma hung over the harbor. I was glad when the ferry entered Lewis Bay and the breeze freshened. I bought coffee and a bagel with cream cheese and carried them out to the sun-drenched bow deck. I stared at the wheeling gulls keeping pace with the ferry, and pondered what I had learned from my talks with Lisa and Grandpa Ahab. I'd let my jumbled thoughts simmer in my subconscious stew. As the ferry slowed on its approach to the island forty-five minutes later, I leaned on the rail, peering at the docked yacht through binoculars. I checked out the blue and white helicopter sitting on its elevated pad. I also caught a glimpse of a sunbather with auburn hair, but she was sitting on the deck with her back to me.

Lisa was waiting for me on the ferry landing. She was wearing a white sleeveless top and her turquoise shorts looked as if the color had been invented to go with her golden skin. She greeted me with a warm smile and a quick hug. We joined the crowds heading into town, but instead of going to her office, she guided me to a small private lot near her office where a sky-blue Jeep Wrangler was parked.

"You can store your bag in the Jeep for now," Lisa said.

I made a sad face. "No MG?"

"I thought you might need more space for your baggage," she said.

I tossed my duffel behind the passenger seat.

"I travel light while I'm on the job. All I need is a toothbrush and my trusty .45."

Lisa looked as if I had told her that my real name was John Dillinger, the notorious bank robber.

"I never *thought* that you might carry a gun. I guess it makes sense for a private investigator." She didn't sound happy.

"Just kidding about the .45," I said. "I haven't packed a gun since

I left the Boston PD." I narrowed my eyes to slits. "I simply demolish a potential assailant with my acerbic wit."

The shocked expression left her face. "I'm sure they must die laughing, Mr. Socarides." Lisa was quick as well as pretty. "Where would you like to begin your investigation?"

"We could start by dispensing with the formalities. Things might move along a lot faster if you didn't have to contend with a mouth full of syllables every time you used my name. My friends use the shortened version, *Soc.*"

"Then I will, too, Soc. And you will call me Lisa."

"Deal, Lisa." We shook hands on it. "Now that the formalities are over, let's start the official investigation with a visit to the crime scene."

"This way," she said, taking the lead. "I don't have the words to tell you how happy I am that you've agreed to work with us. I'm curious about why you changed your mind. You seemed pretty sure last night that you weren't interest in the case."

"My boat developed serious mechanical problems, so I've got time to work on the case. Besides, how many chances will I have to play Starbuck? I've been drinking his coffee for years."

"Maybe fate had a hand in your boat problems, freeing you to work with me."

I thought about the Russian goons who had visited me.

"That could be, Lisa. Fate takes on some unusual colorings. How is your grandfather doing today?"

"Physically, he's fine, but he's still delusional. When I said goodbye a little while ago, he was charting the currents and whale migrations so he could ambush Moby."

"Where does he fit you into his delusional Ahab world?"

"He knows I'm his granddaughter, but my guess is that he thinks of me as a specter, a figment of his imagination that comes and goes. Maybe something a home-sick sailor would see emerging from the mists after a long time at sea. Sometimes he stares at me as if he is on the verge of reality, then he slips back into that crazy Ahab world of his. So I limit my time with him. It breaks my heart."

"Maybe his mind thinks of you as a lifeline that he can hold onto to keep from slipping into deeper insanity."

"Good point. If you're correct, he could climb back from his delusional pit."

"Or he could let go and fall so far into it that he'll never be able to get out."

"That's a chilling thought." We walked a few minutes without talking, then she stopped and said, "Well, here we are at the crime scene."

We were standing in front of the entrance to a three-story brick building. Lisa said the Peter Foulger Museum was a former candle works and pointed to a weathervane in the form of a sperm whale atop the cupola on the roof. A sign informed visitors that the Nantucket Historical Association had its administrative headquarters joined to the museum building.

We stepped out of the warm summer day and passed between a pair of Doric style columns into the cool air-conditioned interior. Lisa bought our tickets and led the way past a series of whaling exhibitions to the main first floor gallery. The massive skeleton of a sperm whale hung from the ceiling. As dead and as dry as it was, the creature's tooth-studded jaw still looked fearsome. It was hard to imagine what it would be like to be that close to an angry whale in the flesh.

Under the assemblage of bones, where it was dwarfed by the skeleton, was a whaleboat, tipped at an angle to display the interior. Folding chairs for those attending lectures were lined up in rows to the right of the whaleboat. A handful of visitors perused the exhibits.

"The room was closed for a time while police did their investigation," she said.

"Where did they find the body?"

Lisa went over to a big cast iron barrel set close to the wall.

"The body was found hanging over the rim of a try pot like this one. The whalers used the pots to boil down blubber. The police moved the actual container out as evidence. I'll show you the type of whaling tool that was used in the murder."

We went over to the curved wall to the left of the boat. Attached vertically to the wall were tools that Nantucket men used to make many a whale unhappy and dead. There were different types of harpoons and lances, and metal heads from both types of implements.

She pointed to a section behind the boat where there were several tools that a plaque described as Boarding Knives. The knives had long double-edged blades, set into short wooden handles. Some had a crosspiece at the tip of the handle as an extra hand grip. Rope was knotted around the handle to prevent the hand from slipping down on to the blade. The sign on the wall said the knives were used to slice the huge strips of whale blubber down to smaller pieces.

One knife was missing. There was a hole in the plaster a couple of feet below it where fastening clips had been pulled out of the wall.

I stared at the blade of one of the remaining knives. "The victim didn't stand much of a chance."

Lisa crossed her arms instinctively in front of her, as if she were trying to protect her mid-section. "What kind of a person could kill someone with a horrible thing like that?"

I knew what she meant. This would have been up close and personal.

"Let me ask you a few questions," I said. "You told me that the two men were here after hours. What brought them to the museum?"

"My grandfather told me he was going to see Mr. Coffin to talk about the scrimshaw collection Ab wanted the museum to acquire."

"The collection your grandfather didn't want the museum to buy."

She nodded. "He said the museum already had one of the finest scrimshaw collections in the world."

We climbed the stairs to the second level and went into a dimly-lit room filled with glass display cases. Spotlights in each case highlighted specimens of the whaler's art known as scrimshaw. Whaling voyages went on for years. To help pass the time, the crewmen scratched images on sperm whale teeth and rubbed India ink or soot into the scratches to bring out the image.

A lot of scrimshaw is pretty crude, but the whale teeth in the cases had amazingly well-defined images of ships, whales, the respectable women they left back home and the loose women they met on their travels. The collection included pie crust crimpers, corset stays and yarn swifts carved as gifts.

One case contained a whale bone around three feet long and ten inches wide. The artist had etched out three action scenes that showed the phases of a whale chase, from the first harpoon tossed, to the kill and the butchering.

"I've never seen a piece of scrimshaw this big," I said.

"It's a *panorama* piece, one of the more unusual works in the collection. It was made from a rear section of the whale's jawbone. This is only a small portion of the museum's holdings."

"Which brings us back to the question of why Coffin wanted to expand the collection."

"That was my grandfather's question, too. He posed it during several meetings of the trustees. Coffin never answered it to his satisfaction."

"How did the other museum trustees feel about the scrimshaw debate?"

"We're talking about a pretty discreet group. They don't like conflict; although some quietly backed Coffin, others supported my grandfather. What they all agreed on was that they would not make any decisions until they actually saw this fabulous collection Coffin described."

"Which is what the two men had come here to discuss."

"Presumably. Is there anything else you'd like to see?"

"Later, maybe. Can I get the files on the police investigation and findings?"

"I have all that material waiting for you at the house."

Before we left the museum, Lisa showed me some first-edition copies of *Moby Dick* and an exhibition on the *Essex*, the ship whose sinking inspired Melville to write about the big white whale. A thought occurred to me.

"Is there anything in the museum about the *Moshup*?" I asked.

"Mostly newspaper accounts of the sinking. There is very little detail about the aftermath except for a self-serving account Swain wrote, and local gossip." She looked at her watch. "Let's get you settled. Michael Ramsey's cocktail party is at six. Some of the museum trustees will be there. You can talk to them. Maybe you'll pick up something that will be helpful in the case. Michael tends to invite the island's movers and shakers so you'll make a quick acquaintance with Nantucket high society."

We walked back to the Jeep and drove out of town. Lisa had a natural skill for taking advantage of openings in the traffic, stomping the gas pedal and brakes until we extricated ourselves from the car-clogged narrow streets. Traffic thinned out when we got on Milestone Road. Not long after that, we were pulling into the driveway of the Daggett homestead. Lisa showed me to my living quarters, a one-bedroom apartment over the garage. "Well, this is it," she said. "I hope it's all right."

I told her it would be fine. She said she'd be back to pick me up in forty-five minutes. I tossed my duffel bag onto the bed and walked out onto a small deck. From the top of the garage, I could see the dunes and the blue of water beyond.

I explored the rest of the apartment. There was a kitchenette with a small wooden table. The space opened up into a living area furnished with a chair, a sofa, and television set. There were some fishing rods and a bird-spotting scope in a closet. The refrigerator was stocked with Grey Lady ale.

When I'm on an investigation, I try to dress like the locals. I figured standard dress code at a Nantucket shindig was green slacks decorated with whales. Coincidentally, I had picked up an outfit just like that, including a pink shirt, and a lightweight navy blazer. I bought the whole outfit at a church thrift store for five bucks. I had a well-worn pair of boat shoes which I wore without socks. Even with a pirate's face like mine, and the gold ring in my left earlobe, I thought the outfit would help me blend in.

I slipped out of my jeans and *Thalassa* polo shirt, which was all I had left of my pretty boat, and got into my party clothes. I popped a bottle of Grey Lady ale and went out on the deck. I was taking a last slug from the bottle when I heard a car horn. I grabbed my blazer and went down the outside stairs to the driveway. Lisa was waiting on the passenger side of the MG. The lawyer in business casual had vanished and it its place was a woman of stunning beauty. She was wearing an ankle-length lilac print summer dress cut low at the top to show off her shapely shoulders. I felt like a hobo in comparison.

"Thou shall takest the helm, Mr. Starbuck."

"Don't mind if I doest," I said. I got behind the wheel and put the car into gear.

A beautiful night. A beautiful woman. A beautiful car.

I've seen far too much of life to be naïve, but I felt like Nick Carraway, the narrator of *The Great Gatsby*. Lisa was a more exotic Daisy Buchanan. And we were off to a party at Jay Gatsby's house. What possibly could go wrong? As I was about to learn, I could have answered that question with a single word:

*Every*thing.

CHAPTER 8

As I drove out onto the road, I told Lisa that she looked great.

"Thank you. You look very handsome," she said. "Pink is a good color for you."

I was glad that she didn't mention the whale slacks. I asked if I was dressed right for the cocktail party.

"This outfit is pretty standard for Cape Cod. Add a sailboat tie and you're a real estate broker. Put on a nautical cap and you're a yachtsman. I wasn't sure what was appropriate for Nantucket, so I improvised."

"You'll fit in fine," she said. "Although it can be tricky to know what *is* appropriate at a Nantucket cocktail party," she said.

"Should I have worn a tux?"

"It's not about what you wear. It's all about *show*. You could be wearing jeans as long as they are $500 fashion jeans. Or you can gain an edge simply wearing thirty-dollar Levi's. If you wear the cheap jeans you have to have the money, but not the desire, to buy the expensive ones."

"Nantucket cultural mores are more complicated than I thought."

"That's only *part* of it. With the Nantucket moneyed elite, it's all about one-*upsmanship*. On Nantucket Island, the rich are divided into two classes. There are the *haves* and the have-*mores*. You can't brag about the size of your house or how fast your private jet goes, because on Nantucket there is always someone who has a bigger house and a faster plane."

"So by being déclassé I could be classy."

"You're getting it." She raised a finger of caution. "Depends who you are, though. If you've got fifty billion in the bank, you can dress in rags. If you have fifty cents, you can't."

"I'm closer to the fifty cents."

She did the finger raise again. "Doesn't matter. Wealth isn't all that's important when it comes to Old Money. If you're an *old* Nantucket family that goes back generations, you believe that ancestry trumps money."

"My family is more Ellis Island than Nantucket Island," I said, heaving a big sigh.

"You'll be fine. You're in the *company* of someone from an old Nantucket family."

At Lisa's direction, I drove to the easterly end of the island and the MG joined a slow-moving line of cars creeping along a winding two-lane road. We were behind a Bentley, a Land Rover, a Beemer SUV and another Land Rover. We breathed in high-end exhaust fumes for a few minutes, then turned off onto a driveway paved in cobblestones. Each vehicle stopped briefly at an open gate. A stylized R had been worked into the metalwork. Standing at the entryway was a young woman wearing a white polo shirt and beige shorts. She was blond and tanned, and had a pearly smile she displayed to its brightest.

"Nice to see you and your guest, Ms. Hendricks." The young woman checked off Lisa's name on her clipboard. "Enjoy the party."

I put the MG in gear and continued onto a white gravel driveway, following the procession for about a half mile. The line slowed to a stop in front of a mansion that was slightly smaller than the medium-size hotel it resembled. A wide stairway led up to a massive portcullis, resting on multiple Doric columns, which connected two wings set at a slight angle.

"I must have taken a wrong turn back there," I said. "We seem to have arrived at *Versailles*."

"Michael's house is a bit on the palatial side," Lisa said with a sad shake of her head. "Ten thousand square feet is lot of space for one person."

"Ten thousand square feet is a lot of space for a *hundred* people."

"Meet the new Nantucket aristocracy. They make the rich whaling captains look like paupers."

A squad of car valets dressed in the white and tan uniform of the gate-greeter was waiting in the front of the house. As soon as I braked to a stop, two car valets stepped forward. One opened the passenger door; the other came around to the driver side.

Lisa and I stepped out, and a valet got in and whisked the MG off to an area of lawn, near a five-car garage, that was being used as a parking lot. The other valet guided us to a line of golf carts. Most of the arriving guests were middle-aged couples. They had the deep tans and well-tuned physiques that come from time on the golf course and hours spent at the health club. Their burnished skin looked good against the colorful off-the-shoulder dresses on the women and the silvered hair on the gents. I didn't see anyone else wearing green whale design slacks.

The cart took us along the front of a two-story wing that looked bigger than the Newport mansions that the robber barons built in the last Gilded Age. We rounded the corner of the house and I saw that the front of the place had been only a preview for the main feature. The two wings were joined at a three-level rotunda.

The big windows in the curved exterior overlooked a wide patio surrounding an Olympic-size swimming pool. The patio was made of pink marble, semi-circular in shape, and it rippled down to the lawn in a series of steps from the massive rotunda. Gas lanterns set around the patio glowed warmly in the gathering dusk. A string quartet sat at the edge of the pool playing something by Mozart. There were two bars, one on each side of the pool, and business was brisk at both. Tables surrounded the pool and there was a food tent on the lawn at the edge of the patio.

The swimming pool patio was joined to a sweeping lawn that looked as if every blade had been clipped with manicure scissors. The lawn gradually angled down to a wooded area. Water shimmered in the distance over the tops of the trees. The grass was so green that even in the low light, it hurt the eyes to look at it. There were probably two hundred guests strolling or seated under the tent. Waiters and waitresses in white shirts, black slacks and matching black bow-ties moved through the partygoers offering drinks and food from the trays balanced on their fingertips.

The golf cart pulled up to the patio where Ramsey waited to greet his guests. Moving with mechanical precision, Ramsey offered a two-handed handshake to the men, a quick hug for the women, and waved them off toward the bars and food. When we climbed out of our cart, his movements became less robotic and he hugged Lisa longer than is usually considered polite. When he finally unglued his body from hers, he held her bare shoulders and let his gaze rove over her body from head to toe.

"I didn't think it was possible, Lisa, but you look lovelier every time I see you."

Lisa must have felt the heat from Ramsey's eyes. "Thank you, Michael, that's very sweet." She smiled gallantly, and turned her body sideways to escape his clutches. She took my hand and pulled me over to her side.

"You remember Mr. Socarides, last night from the Wauwinet?"

Ramsey tore his gaze away from Lisa. His light-switch smile clicked off and on again. He pumped my hand, but I could tell from this narrowed eyes that I was about as welcome as a root canal.

"Yes, of course. I'm *so* glad you could make it, Mr. Socarides. I thought you were going back to the mainland."

"I managed to do a quick turn-around. This is a terrific party. Thanks for the invitation."

Ramsey saw that the line of golf carts was building up. "Please excuse me. I have to prevent a traffic jam. Save some time for me later this evening, Lisa, and in the meantime enjoy yourselves."

"Of course, Michael. I'm looking forward to it."

He smiled effusively and greeted the next set of guests to arrive.

Lisa guided me by the arm away from the host. As we strolled around the patio, she scanned the self-absorbed knots of people.

"*Aha.* I see a gathering of some of the museum trustees. Come on, I'll introduce you."

We neared the group of five people huddled off by themselves away from the main crowd. There were four men and one woman. They smiled warmly when they saw Lisa coming toward them. She shook hands with the men and gave the woman a quick embrace.

There were polite introductions and handshakes all around. The name of the woman with the carefully quaffed snowdrift hair was Lillian Mayhew. After a chatty moment or two, the male trustees said they were glad to meet me, then they headed for the bar.

Which is when Ms. Mayhew looked me directly in the eye and said, "How do you know Lisa, Mr. Socarides?"

"I'm a private investigator. I've joined the defense team for her grandfather."

Her knowing gaze dropped to take in the way Lisa's arm was hooked around mine. She pursed her lips for a second before she turned back to Lisa.

"How *is* your grandfather doing, dear?"

"Thank you for asking, Lillian. Gramps is fine physically. But he's still delusional."

"That's too bad, dear. Is he still chasing the great white whale?"

Lisa nodded. "There's been no change in his Ahab personality. In fact, he thinks Mr. Socarides is his first mate, *Starbuck.*"

Mrs. Mayhew swiveled her level gaze back to me. "Oh. Really."

I struggled to think of a gentle way to say ol' gramps was as crazy as a bedbug. "Mr. Daggett has a vivid imagination," I said. It was the best I could muster.

Her icy blue eyes bore into my face. "Melville describes his first mate as a long, earnest man with flesh hard as a twice-baked biscuit. When you looked into his eyes, you saw images of the many perils he had calmly confronted in his life. Have you confronted perils, Mr. Socarides?"

"A few times, but more with panic than calm."

She regarded me for a second, her lips cracked in a thin smile, then she turned back to Lisa. "If Mr. Socarides can spare you, dear, I'd like to chat for a moment."

She took Lisa's other arm and guided her off to a table. I noticed a trustee who'd been introduced as Sutcliffe standing nearby with a drink in his hand.

"*Wow!*" he said with wonder in his voice. "You really hit it off with Madame Mayhew. She rarely warms up to *any*one that fast."

Sutcliffe was wearing a blue blazer over a button-down blue shirt and rumpled chino slacks. In fact, everything about him was rumpled, including his face. There were deep laugh lines at the corners of his gray eyes.

"I've had warmer receptions from a slab of ice," I said.

"It's all a matter of degree," he said. "Pardon the pun. I've only been on-island fifteen years, but she still considers me a *washashore*. She's never given me a smile in all that time."

Sutcliffe was probably in his sixties. He was slightly shorter than normal, but his height may have been diminished by the slight stoop to his shoulders.

"I thought it was more of a lip curl than a smile, but you know the lady better than I do. Where did you wash ashore from?"

"Practically everywhere you can think of. I was a newspaperman in Washington. I bought a vacation house here before you had to rob the Franklin Mint to pay for it. My wife died a couple of years after we retired. I did some stringer work for the weekly newspaper, the *Inquirer*, and that got me interested in island history."

"Sorry about your wife."

"Thank you. That's nice of you to say." He brushed his thinning sandy hair back in a gesture that seemed to say he still couldn't believe she was gone.

I turned toward the house. "What does Lillian think of washashores who build monuments to their ego like this?"

"She considers them as distasteful *arrivistes*. Maybe *slightly* more advanced on the evolutionary ladder than the jellyfish that float up on the beaches. Lillian comes from a long line of Quaker whaling tycoons who regarded it a sin to show off your wealth. She'll be the first one to admit she's living in the past."

"If she finds new money so distasteful, what's she doing here with a major show-off like Ramsey?"

"Granny believes in the old adage: keep your friends close and your enemies closer."

"That's not bad advice." I glanced over to where Lillian and Lisa were deep in conversation, their heads close together. "A formidable lady in other words. Did you say your name was Matt Sutcliffe. The author?"

"Guilty as charged."

"I enjoyed reading your book on famous mutinies a couple of years ago."

"*Death on the Quarterdeck*? Glad you liked it." He shook his head. "Those amazing whaling skippers would put down a mutiny single-handed, kill a crewman or two in the process, then jot it down as a brief mention in the logbook, in between whale sightings. They could eat nails for breakfast."

"Nails weren't *all* they chewed on. Lisa told me about the *Moshup* incident."

"Did she tell you I was writing a book with Coffin on the tragedy?"

"She never mentioned it. We talked mostly about her grandfather. Quite the tale from what I've heard."

"No one knows the true story. The cover-up was pretty effective. Which is why I hooked onto Ab when he mentioned that he had evidence he hoped would exonerate his family."

"What sort of evidence?"

"He was going to tell me later." Sutcliffe looked as sad as a basset hound. "Talk about a dead-end source."

"Do you have enough to write the book without him?"

"It's going to be much more difficult. He wasn't only a source, though. We became friends. I might mention that I was also friendly with Daggett."

"Do you think Daggett did it?"

"Anything's possible. But *no*."

"What about Coffin's comments about his ancestors eating Daggett's?"

"That was kind of a joke. They'd laugh about it."

"Maybe Daggett was faking hilarity."

"Well, that's always possible. I don't think he could have killed Coffin with that boarding knife. Daggett is the definition of a somewhat daffy but kindly soul."

"What about his Ahab persona? Lisa said the D.A. thinks he might have thought Coffin was Moby Dick and that he didn't know he was killing a human being."

He gave a disgusted shake of his head.

"His lawyer may use that as a defense strategy," I added.

"Yeah. *Brilliant!* That is the craziest thing I've ever heard. Make sense to you?"

I had seen Daggett in his altered state and wasn't sure he was the kindly soul Sutcliffe knew, but I didn't want to argue with someone who might be of help. "No, it doesn't make sense. You said Coffin had some new evidence about his family?"

"That's right. He said he would be able to offer proof that Swain had falsely accused his ancestor of murder."

"Pretty sensational if that's true."

"It would be to me. I think there's a book in it."

I gazed out across the gas-lit patio thinking that when I worked as a cop in Boston I used to read the 87th Precinct novels by Ed McBain, who said he started with the corpse. Then he asked himself how the corpse got that way. I turned back to Sutcliffe.

"Tell me about Mr. Coffin."

"He ran a small antique shop in town, specializing in scrimshaw. Especially pieces made by his great-great-grandfather. His goal was to gather up every piece that had ever been crafted by his ancestor. He told me that when he ran his fingers over a whale bone that his great-great-grandfather had decorated, an electric charge would go through him, as if they were connecting somehow, and that the dead man was telling him something."

"Spectral voices don't usually hold up to scrutiny."

"Don't know if I believe the voices story, but we both agreed that Swain's journal was fishy. Too many discrepancies."

"I'd like to hear more about them."

He dug a business card out of his wallet. "I live on Petticoat Row in town. Give me a call and we can get together over coffee or beer. Your choice."

"That's not even a contest."

We shook hands and he wandered off to the bar to refill his drink glass.

Lisa had broken away from her conversation with Lillian and was walking toward me only to stop and lift her eyes to the darkening sky. The buzz of conversation and the music were drowned out by the thrashing sound of helicopter rotors. Then a noisy moving constellation of blinking lights appeared and circled once over the party before dropping out of sight beyond one of the wings of the mansion.

Years after I left the Marines, I could hear the *whup-whup* of

Hueys in my dreams and to this day, the sound of a chopper can still give me a bad feeling. I remembered the helicopter gunships that came in to give you air cover and how in the heat of battle sometimes they lobbed a few missiles into the troops they were supposed to be supporting.

The appearance of the chopper out of the night sky gave me a bad feeling. Part of it came from the persistence of memory. Part of it was the sudden, uncaring intrusion into the frivolity. But most of it was the quick glimpse of the blue and white fuselage. It might have been coincidence, of course, but those were the same colors of the chopper I had seen on the helipad of *Volga*, the yacht owned by Ivan the Terrible.

CHAPTER 9

Rich people must be used to helicopters buzzing their backyards. The party settled back to its sultry summer night rhythm soon after the aerial inspection. The golf carts continued to drop off well-dressed guests. The lighthearted chatter and laughter played against the backdrop of classical music.

Minutes earlier, Ramsey had shifted from his greeter duties and he'd been moving from guest to guest like a honeybee gathering pollen in a field of wildflowers. He greeted some guests with a quick handshake, a word of welcome, and a gesture toward the bar and food. With others it was a double handshake, a shoulder squeeze, a cheek peck for the women. The smile switched on and off like a strobe light.

When the helicopter flew over, he had broken off his glad-handing and headed toward the rotunda with a stride full of purpose. I stationed myself off to the side of the patio, close to the rotunda doors. I could see through the wrap-around windows into the first level, a circular room furnished with comfortable looking sofas and chairs. Ramsey crossed the room and disappeared through a doorway that must have led to the interior of the house. Minutes later, the door opened and Ramsey reappeared with a man and a woman. Oddly, it was the two men and not the couple who walked arm-in-arm. Their heads were bent low in conversation.

A slender woman in her twenties walked a few paces behind the men. She wore a black low-cut dress that ended just above the knees of her long legs. Oversized red-framed sunglasses covered her eyes and her chin had the upward tilt of an aristocrat. Her auburn hair was the same color as that of the sunbather I had glimpsed on the deck of the yacht on my second trip to Nantucket.

Ramsey and his friends were heading in my direction. The first rule of recon is to see without being seen. I put my glass up to my mouth in a lame attempt to hide my face. I needn't have worried. They strolled past so deep in conversation that I would have had to shout to get their attention. Then Lisa blew my cover. She gave a big wave, and came over to fetch me. Ramsey saw her and called out:

"*Lisa.* Good timing. Come over and meet my friend, Mr. Chernko."

If life imitated art, the string quartet playing background music would have struck a gut-wrenching bass chord at the mention of Chernko's name. Ivan the Terrible. *Da*-dum. My self-preservation instincts were telling me to head for the hills, but by then Lisa linked her arm in mine and there was no escape.

My close-up impression of Ivan was that he didn't look so terrible. He was of medium height and average physique, probably in his fifties. He had on a black suit and white shirt open at the collar. His straw colored hair was thinning and cut close. He had a round, slightly pudgy face that gave him a jolly look enhanced by a calm, avuncular smile. Good old Uncle Ivan. Can't get enough of him. Always in a good mood. Never a bad word for anyone.

Lisa extended her hand. "Nice to meet you, Mr. Chernko. This is my friend, Mr. Socarides."

I might have been taken in by the engaging manner if I didn't know that the man beaming like a lighthouse wasn't what he seemed. I suspected that Ivan had something to do with the human torch found tied to a tree. I knew that he had ordered two thugs to intimidate me, and when that didn't pan out, they destroyed my boat and almost killed me and my cat. My first choice would have been to study him safely from a distance. Outer space maybe.

But here I was, grinning and shaking hands with Ramsey's friend and watching for a reaction at the mention of my name. Chernko was a cool one. The smile didn't vary one millimeter. If eyes are the window to the soul, he was keeping the blinds down. In fact, his laugh crinkles only got deeper.

Speaking with a trace of an accent, he said to Ramsey, "How do you and Ms. Hendricks know each other, Michael?"

Ramsey took the question as an opportunity to wrap his octopus arm around Lisa's shoulders. "Lisa is an attorney who specializes in conservation. I've been active in efforts to preserve the character of the island."

The statement seemed at odds with the mega-mansion Ramsey had built. The house looked like a giant space ship that had landed with conquering aliens. Chernko almost caught me off guard when he turned back. "And *you*, Mr. Socarides? How do know Michael?"

"We only recently met through Ms. Hendricks. I'm on Nantucket doing some legal work for her family."

"You're a lawyer as well?"

"No. I'm a private investigator."

Ivan knew damned well who I was and what I did, but he reacted with surprise, giving me a head-to-toe once over. "I've never met an American private detective, but I've read about them." There was a playful mischievousness in his voice when he said, "Is Sam Spade an accurate rendering of your work?"

"Only the drinking part, Mr. Chernko."

He parted his lips to reply, but instead he glanced over my shoulder and stared at something. There was a slight narrowing of the hooded hazel eyes and a wag to his head that was almost imperceptible.

"A pleasure to meet you both," he said with a smile. "I'm sure we'll meet again." Turning to Ramsey he said, "Thank you for introducing me to your friends. I can only hope your other guests are as charming."

"I'll introduce you and you can judge for yourself, Ivan."

He guided Chernko toward a group of guests. The Russian's female companion glanced at us without interest, and sauntered after them. I turned around and saw what had caught Ivan's eye. The two thugs who had visited my boat at the marina were hanging around near the drop-off point. Unlike their boss, they had been delivered on a golf cart like the rest of the guests. Chernko must have seen them coming up behind us and warned them away with a chin wag.

The thugs looked like professional mourners with their black shirts, blazers, slacks and down-turned lips. The taller one placed his right hand on the left side of his suit where I could see the slight bulge that I guessed to be a holster. He knew that it would not have been the smartest thing to plug me in front of hundreds of witnesses. I wasn't so sure about his mushroom-shaped friend, who looked as if he would like to pay me back for the spanking I'd delivered when he misbehaved on my boat.

They gave me the fish eye and set off to follow their boss. As they caught up with Chernko's girlfriend, the taller one said something to her. She frowned and gave him a foul look. Then she stopped to light up a cigarette. She stood there, weight on her left hip, puffing on the cigarette as if she wanted to demolish it, an expression of sheer boredom on her lovely face. One hand supported the arm of her cigarette-holding hand.

Lisa noticed me staring. "*Pretty*, isn't she? You'd think her friend would be more attentive with someone that lovely."

"From the look of her body language I'd bet she's not happy about being ignored."

She studied the woman's angular pose. "You may be right. Well, that helicopter fly-over made for quite the show."

"Andrew Lloyd Webber couldn't have done better. Chernko and Ramsey seemed to be old pals. Do you know what his background is?"

"I've never seen him before. Rest assured though, if he's close to Michael, there's money involved. *Lots* of money."

"How do you think Mr. Chernko will score on the Nantucket snob scale?"

"The old-timers would be appalled at the obnoxious way he swooped over the party. Lillian has left, which tells you *exactly* how she feels. The newcomers admire brashness, so they wouldn't have cared if the helicopter had landed right in their *fois gras*. They're attracted to money like sharks are to blood."

Lisa was right on the mark. Guests were swarming around Chernko with the ardor of rock star groupies.

"Speaking of Ms. Mayhew, you two seemed deep in conversation," I said. "Did it have something to do with Gramps?"

"Lilly's been a great support throughout this ordeal with my grandfather. He and Lilly used to be a hot item in their younger days. She was the one who mothered me after my parents died. She likes you, by the way."

"Evidently impressed with my boyish charm."

Lisa rolled her eyes. "Sorry. What impressed her was the fact that you are not Michael."

"The Old Money thing again?"

"It goes beyond that. She thinks he is trying to acquire me like one of those companies he buys up, then dumps at great profit. She likes seeing me with another man."

"Then I'm at your service. Shall we walk around and be seen?"

"I'd love to." She scanned the crowd. "Oh darn! Would you excuse me for a moment? I see a high mucky-muck on the conservation trust I should talk to. Sorry for being rude."

"Not rude at all. I'll wander around and see if I can pick up any tips on the stock market."

I strolled closer to where Ramsey and Ivan were still pressing flesh, artfully shielding myself behind the milling guests. Ivan's thugs kept several paces behind. Ivan shook one last hand, then said something to Ramsey, who pointed to the rotunda. The bodyguards slid in close behind Ivan, cutting off a couple of glad-handing guests, and followed the other two men across the terrace and into the house. I plucked a couple of champagne flutes from a tray carried by a passing waiter, went over to the auburn-haired woman and offered her a glass of champagne.

"Compliments of Mr. Ramsey," I said.

She took a last puff from her cigarette, dropped it onto the patio and reached out for the flute without looking at me. She slugged down the champagne like a thirsty longshoreman, handed me the empty glass and took the other one from my hand. She downed the second glass and handed it back to me. When I didn't leave, she removed her sunglasses and appraised me with almond-shaped green eyes.

"You werk hir?" Her husky voice had a heavy accent. I figured out that she was asking if I worked for Ramsey.

"No. I'm a fisherman."

She brushed a strand of hair back from her forehead. "What you doink in this place, Meester Feeshermenz? Only reech people come to these stupid parties." She gave me a look. "You don't look reech."

"I'm not rich. I'm a friend of a guest, just like you and Chernko's associates."

She raised a finely arched eyebrow. "Associates?"

"The two men who went into the house. One is tall and the other was short." I held my hand high, then dropped it to knee-level.

"*Associates?*" She laughed and repeated the word, turning it over in her mouth. "They are eediots."

"I agree. But *dangerous* idiots."

A shadow of fear crossed her face. She slipped the sunglasses back on and tossed her head like a high-spirited filly. "What is your name, Mr. Feeshermenz?"

I told her. "And yours?"

She hesitated, then said, "I am Tanya."

"Russian."

She frowned. "*Bulgarian.* I don't like Russians."

I would have liked to ply Tanya the Bulgarian with more of Ramsey's expensive champagne to find out why, if she despised Russians, she hung out with them, but I could see into the house. The shorter of the two thugs was coming toward the door. I guessed he must have been sent to check on Chernko's arm candy.

I said, "Nice talking to you, Tanya. Maybe we'll meet again."

I stepped away from her, and melted into the crowd of guests gathering around a long buffet table under the tent. I grabbed a plate, but instead of getting in line, I stood where I could see the short thug come up to Tanya. After what looked like a quick but heated exchange, he took her by the arm and practically dragged her back to the house. About five minutes later, the helicopter rose above the roof of the house and darted off in a thrash of rotors.

I wondered what Chernko's connection was with Ramsey. Was it the money thing, as Lisa had suggested? My gut told me that they were more than simply fellow members of Nantucket's Big Bucks club. I was painfully aware, too, that I was over-matched. And that Chernko wasn't about to lift his death edict. There was only one way to protect myself, and that was to eliminate him as a threat before he turned me into a Roman candle like poor Viktor Karpov.

I hadn't gotten off to a very good start. Chernko had met me face-to-face. He knew I was on Nantucket and what I was doing. He'd be able to track me down. I would have preferred to scout him out from a distance. But the meeting gave me a chance to probe him for weaknesses. Chernko was cagey and smart, but I may have found a weak point in his smooth facade. And she had auburn hair.

CHAPTER 10

On the drive back from Ramsey's cocktail party, I was lost in thought. I was wondering if I had screwed up royally. I had taken the Nantucket job so I could scout out Ivan from the shadows. Instead, I'd stepped out into bright glare of daylight in plain view of the Russian and his henchmen.

Lisa noticed that I was uncharacteristically tight-lipped. "Penny for your thoughts, Starbuck."

"Not worth the price. I was thinking what a lovely party that was."

Lisa was no dummy. She burst into laughter and punched me lightly on the shoulder.

"I can't believe you can *say* that with a straight face. You saw all those people who think Nantucket is their own little castle, and that it's surrounded by a moat."

"I was trying to be positive."

"Well, you were being absurd."

"That, too. You know what F. Scott Fitzgerald told Hemingway about the rich being different from everyone else? I'd go one further. Ramsey and his friends are an entirely different species of *homo sapiens*."

"That's more like it. That is *exactly* what they are. And they look at us the same way, only as a lower rung on the evolutionary ladder."

"Isn't that a little harsh?"

"Well it's true. They are clueless when it comes to what my family learned a long time ago. Reputation is more important than money."

Lisa crossed her arms and seemed to go into her own cocoon. It wasn't hard to figure out the source of her simmering rant about the tasteless habits of the newly rich. As crass as they were, at least they didn't have a family member charged with murder.

The village of Siasconset was as still as an abandoned tomb. We drove through the deserted center, then along the shore road and turned off onto the shell driveway between the high privet hedges. By the time I pulled up front of the big house, Lisa's short-lived blue funk was over. She pecked me on the cheek and got out of the car.

Before she whirled up the front steps, she turned and said, "Thank you for a lovely evening. Breakfast is at eight. Dr. Rosen will be there so you can talk to him about Gramps. I'll have the case files for you as well."

I gave her a thumbs-up and headed for my apartment. I snatched a cold Grey Lady ale from the fridge and went out onto the deck. The light from the windows reflected off the droplets of a dank fog moving inland. I thought of Plato's allegory, where people in a cave try to determine the reality of shadows moving on a wall. No shadows danced on the wall of fog. But I didn't have to see the ocean to know that it was real. I knew from the smell of fish and sea that the mists hid trillions of gallons of water filled with millions of living creatures and plants.

I had less success when I tried to penetrate the fog of mad thoughts that had enveloped Lisa's grandfather. Or the mists that surrounded the odd couple relationship of Ramsey and Chernko. After my encounter with Ivan, though, I was sure of one thing. That if I planned to go wandering around in the Nantucket murk in search of answers I needed someone to watch my back.

I slugged down my ale and went back inside to call Flagg. I got his recorded message. At the beep I said, "Hi, Flagg. Did you know that your tribe has voted to build a gambling casino overlooking the cliffs in *Aquinnah*?"

Flagg has the Wampanoag Indian's mystical reverence for the multi-colored Gay Head cliffs and rolling hills of his home village. The tribe had been trying to open a mainland casino for years. If anything got Flagg's attention, it would be the threat of destructive development coming to *Aquinnah*.

I got undressed, crawled into the bed and slipped off into a fog of my own. I woke up to the "*chip-chip*" of a male cardinal serenading his mate outside my bedroom window. I showered, shaved and pulled on a pair of tan shorts and a *Thalassa* polo shirt.

The front door of the big house was unlocked. I followed the fragrance of frying bacon to the large, sunny kitchen. Lisa was helping a pleasantly portly middle-aged woman cook breakfast. She introduced the woman as Mrs. Gomes. She and her husband had been hired to take care of her grandfather. They had been given a room near Daggett's quarters.

I nodded at Dr. Rosen, who was sitting at the table, sipping from a coffee mug, then I sat down and ordered two eggs over easy with my bacon. They were done to perfection and I complimented Mrs. Gomes on her cooking. She thanked me with a smile on her face, and excused herself to tend to some household tasks.

"Does Mr. Daggett ever join you for meals?" I asked Lisa.

She made a sour face. "Only once. It was an experiment. Gramps flew off in a rage when he saw Dr. Rosen at the table. He thinks he's a lowly crewman on the *Pequod* and had no right to be dining with him. He almost had him clapped in the brig."

"What about you?"

"He was confused when he saw me, but not angry. It fits in with his unformed perception of me. Mrs. Gomes cooks his meals. Her husband and Dr. Rosen take turns bringing meals to him. Gramps accepts Mr. Gomes as ship's cook. Gramps thinks Dr. Rosen is the cook's assistant."

"It allows me to observe him and medicate him," Rosen said.

"He allows you to deliver food, but won't dine with you?"

Rosen nodded. "He tolerates me, because he thinks of his study as the main deck of his ship where ordinary crewmen are allowed and the raised floor as his quarterdeck and cabin. Only officers and privileged crewmembers were allowed in the cabin to dine with the captain in the old whaling days. Mr. Daggett fits that protocol into his personality disorder."

"Which is?"

"The broad term is grandiose delusion. It's a subtype peculiar to those in a manic state of bipolar disorder or schizophrenia. Dementia can play a role as well in the aging. The patient thinks he or she is a famous, wealthy or powerful person."

"The captain of a whaling ship could be all three."

"No doubt about it. Successful whaling captains were wealthy and powerful. They were the princes of their society. That role would fit in very nicely with a diagnosis of schizophrenia, which involves hallucinations and delusions. The patient is totally out of touch with reality."

"Lisa said that her grandfather was behaving in a normal manner up to the time of the murder. Is that consistent with schizophrenia?"

He shook his head. "Usually the onset is gradual, starting in a person's twenties. I see where you are going with this and I have no explanation for the swift personality change."

"What about the blow to the head?"

"The blow was to the *side* of the cranium. He received a slight concussion, but it was not hard enough to damage his mental function."

"Could the blow have disturbed his mental equilibrium?"

"*Anything* is possible, but major personality changes would have had their genesis in trauma to the frontal lobe of the brain, which governs behavior, among other functions."

"So how do you explain his change of personality?"

"Mr. Daggett was deeply involved in the study of Melville and *Moby Dick*. It's possible that he retreated to the sanctuary of this nether world as the result of a shock to his *mental* rather than his physical state."

I finished munching on a piece of buttered oatmeal bread toast and wiped my fingers on a napkin before I tossed out my next question.

"Like the shock that would have come from killing an old friend in cold blood?"

Rosen sat back in his chair. "*Whoa!* Sandbagged me with that one. That's a big leap that I'm not willing to take."

"Sorry to ambush you, Dr. Rosen, but these questions are marshmallows compared to the fastballs the prosecution is going to throw at you." I pondered my next question, then said, "Based on your evaluation of Mr. Daggett's present condition and his past behavior, do you think he could have killed Coffin?"

The answer was quick in coming. "He would not do anything immoral that he wouldn't do in his normal state. Mr. Daggett is not a killer."

"Mr. Daggett thinks he's a fictional character. Is that his normal state?"

"No, of course not."

"So what if in his delusion he imagined someone was a thing that Ahab detested. The white whale, Moby Dick. Could he kill him?"

"Yes. It's possible, but farfetched."

"But it is possible."

"Yes. It is possible."

I looked across the table at Lisa, who had been listening to the exchange. She must have known that my line of questioning would be repeated in court and that it would lead to the institutionalization of her grandfather. There was anguish in her eyes.

I said, "Maybe we should do this another time, Dr. Rosen."

"Yes. I'd like that." He cleared his plate and left the kitchen. "I think I'll go for a run."

I stared at his back, thinking that Rosen was going to be a fine tool in the hands of the prosecution.

"How did you find Dr. Rosen?" I said to Lisa.

"Michael recommended him. He had worked in the human resources department of one of Michael's acquisitions." She took a deep breath and let it out. "He's not going to do well by Grandpa on the witness stand, is he?"

"Depends on what outcome you're looking for. If your grandfather is guilty, treatment in an institution could be the kindest thing you could do for him. When he snaps out of the 19th century, you could say he committed the crime while in an altered state."

"But we're not going to let it get that far, are we, Soc?"

The cool determined tone of her voice, the gaze and the use of my real rather than fictional name told me that I had better get working on the case I was hired for.

"No, we're not, Lisa. You said you had some files for me to go through."

She slid a string-wrapped packet across the table. "These are the case files. Some of the pictures are quite graphic, so I waited until after breakfast to show them to you. I've seen all this material. I'll talk to you later after you have read the files. I've got to go off-island for business today."

"I was hoping you could give me a tour of the Serengeti."

"I'll be back late in the afternoon. I could meet you there around five."

"It's a date. Should I bring an elephant gun?"

"That won't be necessary," Lisa said, rising from the table. "The biggest type of wildlife we're bound to encounter is a fox. Before you dig into the police files, I'd like to show you something here on the property."

A minute later, I was following Lisa along a winding sandy path that led from behind the Daggett house for a couple of hundred yards down to the beach. At the end of the path, set into the dunes, was a beach cottage around ten-by-twenty feet in size. The silver-gray shingles had been bleached almost white by the sun and salty air.

A more or less level porch was attached to the front of the building, shading two windows that were framed by faded green shutters. A stovepipe protruded from the asphalt-shingled roof. Behind the building, leaning at a slight angle, was an outhouse, complete with the half-moon opening on the door.

"This is my grandfather's hideaway," Lisa said as she stepped onto the porch. "It was here before the house went up. It was originally built by a couple of local fishermen who liked to surf cast at night." She reached under a shingle and pulled out a key, which she used to open a padlock.

"The lock looks new," I said.

"It *is*. We never locked it before, because there was nothing to steal, but a few weeks ago someone walked in and trashed the place. Luckily there was no serious damage." She replaced the key, opened the door and stepped inside with me behind her.

There was a cot on the right, and a sink with a hand pump under some cupboards against the left wall. In the middle of the room was a small wooden table with two chairs. There were a couple of kerosene lanterns on the table. Next to the table was an old Boston rocker. At the back of the room was the small wood stove whose chimney pipe I'd seen on the roof. There was a harpoon hanging from one wall.

"The rocker belongs out on the front porch," Lisa said. "Gramps would spend hours out there, reading, or simply looking at the ocean, deep in thought."

The cool breeze coming through the open door brought with it the low rumble of waves rolling against the beach.

I guessed that Lisa was giving me a conversational opening, so I took it. "Thinking about *what*, Lisa?"

"His very favorite subject in the world," she went over to the bookshelf and picked up a paperback book from the stack of yellow-paged paperbacks. She handed the book to me and I saw that it was a well-worn copy of Melville's *Moby Dick*. "The first editions and research volumes he collected are back in the house. He'd done a number of articles for the local paper and history publications. He'd sketch out his ideas on a pad, and work on the finished product in his study."

"Can I keep this?" I said. "It might come in handy in talking to Gramps."

"Please do." She glanced around the cabin. "I thought if you saw this place it might give you a sense of Henry Daggett. His greatest interest was simply in reading and writing about a bygone day. He'd lose himself completely in Melville's writing. He even named his powerboat after Ahab's ship. The *Pequod II* is at the marina, if you'd like to take it out. Keys are in the kitchen."

"Thanks," I said. "Do you think any of this explains why he's up at the house sailing the imaginary *Pequod?*"

"I don't know. What I do know is that he is a gentle, introspective man, who would be the last person in the world to hurt another human being."

I looked around. "You said the place was trashed."

She nodded. "The books were thrown everywhere. The old mattress was ripped open. Stove tipped over. It took a little to clean it up. Nothing was taken as far as I could see."

"They left the harpoon?" I said.

"Probably figured it was a replica and not worth stealing."

We walked back to the house and parted ways. I went to my apartment where I sat down at the kitchen table and fanned out the folders. I opened the folder neatly labeled Nantucket Police and read through the report. It was written in Baroque type of cop talk that must go back to Cro-Magnon times when Sergeant Ogg reported how the victim met a sudden death at the hands of Gronk the Neanderthal.

I cut through the clouds of vague phrases like, "Ascertaining that the individual was deceased," and learned that a worried telephone call from Lisa had led to the discovery of Mr. Coffin.

Lisa had come home late from a conservation meeting to find that her grandfather was not home. Since he was an early-to-bed person, she became worried. His night vision had been going and the winding island roads can be treacherous. She knew he had a meeting scheduled with Coffin at the museum. She called Coffin's house. When there was no answer, she called the police and asked them to check on the museum, which was near the station.

Lights were on in the museum and Coffin's car was parked outside. Her grandfather's car was nowhere to be seen. The police called in a trustee who had a key to the museum. They found Coffin's body in the main room. The cops searched for Daggett, but they didn't find him until an early morning bird watcher encountered the old man wandering around the Serengeti. There was a diagram in the file showing where he had been found in relation to Milestone Road.

Daggett was dazed, and bleeding from a head wound. He was taken to Nantucket Cottage Hospital for treatment. The police tried to interview him, but he had slipped into his Ahab nether world. That was the end of the Nantucket police's involvement. In Massachusetts, homicide cases are handled by a State Police team working with local investigators. I read through some newspaper clips which told me nothing that wasn't in the police files.

I went out onto the deck. The sunlight sparkled on the surface of the ocean that the fog had obscured the night before. The Big Blue had been there all the time. Right in front of me. Maybe there were other things that were right in front of me. I left the apartment and went to the main house. Rosen must have taken a long run because the place was empty. I walked down to Daggett's quarters and knocked on the door.

"*Avast!* Who goest there?"

"Tis Starbuck," I said, trying to insert some pirate gravel in my voice. "Request to see the captain, sir."

"Aye, tis my first mate. Enter."

I opened the door and stepped into Daggett's living quarters. Daggett was sitting hatless at his desk, his back to the window. He looked up, cracked his mouth in a crooked smile and beckoned me over. Spread out on the desktop were yellowed sea charts and old logbooks. A set of parallel bars lay at his elbow.

"Good morning, Captain," I said.

He nodded, and then motioned for me to come and stand behind the desk, next to his chair. The charts were covered in pencil markings. Some lines had been erased and the charts were covered with scraps of eraser rubber.

"Doest thou see it?" he said. His voice was calm with none of the animation I had seen on my first visit.

"See *what*, Captain?"

He placed his finger on a chart and followed a line. "Here be the currents whereby the whale's food drifts over thousands of miles." He took the parallel bars and drew a line that intersected with the ocean current. "And here be the vein the cursed white whale follows to the spermaceti's feeding ground." He drew a circle where the lines crossed. "This is where we meet again, thou with harpoon in thy hand, and I with vengeance in my heart."

"Moby Dick?"

He turned and looked at me with furrowed brow. "Aye," he said in almost a whisper. "The white whale."

"How long will it take to find him?"

The manic grin. "Three days hence. Make sure thy harpoon and thy lance are sharp enough to cut a slice from the breeze."

"Aye, Captain. I'll do that. Off to gather my tools."

He bent his head over the charts. I moved quietly toward the door and stepped out into the hallway. I leaned against the wall and chewed over our brief but telling exchange. The police said Daggett had killed Coffin in an insane rage, thinking that he was Moby Dick. Rosen more or less backed this up. But from what I had heard, Daggett was still searching for the white whale, so he could not have killed the imaginary Moby because he hadn't caught up with it.

And if my theory was right, it raised another question. If Gramps didn't do Coffin in, who did?

CHAPTER 11

After leaving Daggett, I went back to my apartment. I went through the police reports again, but nothing caught my eye. I shoved the folders aside, got up and stuck my Red Sox ball cap on my head. I was thinking about my encounter with Chernko. Time to do a recon. I went to the Daggett house. There was no one in the kitchen to see me take the keys to Daggett's boat from its wall hook. I drove into Nantucket town, parked the MG near Lisa's law office and headed toward the marina. I was walking past an outdoor restaurant when I heard a voice call out.

"Hey, feeshermenz."

Chernko's lady companion of the night before was sitting alone at a table on the patio. I stopped and said, "Good morning."

"Where you goink?"

"I was on my way to the *Volga* to see if I could find you."

"You're crazy," she said.

"Never denied it. Are you expecting anyone?"

She managed a lazy half-smile. "Heva seet."

"Thanks for the invite," I said, settling into a chair.

Tanya was wearing her oversized sunglasses and a green shift that set off her hair color. Moving with a feline languor, she lifted a glass of what looked like *prosecco* to her lips and took a sip. She stared off into space like someone in the throes of terminal ennui. Finally, she acknowledged my presence.

"Why do you look for Tanya?"

"I liked talking to you at the party last night. Too bad you had to go off with one of Ivan's associates."

She pursed her lips, puzzled. I held one hand high, one low. She frowned and pointed to the higher hand. "That one is Sergei. The other is Piter. Yes. They go *every*where with him. What was feeshermenz doing at the reechie-reech party?"

"Ramsey invited me. I came with a friend of his."

"The pretty lady with the hair like this?" She crossed her arms and patted her shoulders to simulate Lisa's shoulder-length hair.

"That's right. The pretty lady."

"She *likes* you?"

"I think so. But it's not like that. She's a lawyer. I'm helping her find out things. And you and Ivan? He likes you?"

"He likes pretty things. I meet him in New York. He asked me to go on boat cruise." She shrugged. "He'll get tired of Tanya some day and find other pretty theeng."

"Then he's a fool."

She threw her head back and laughed. Then she removed her sunglasses and gazed at me with her jade eyes. "No, he's not a fool. He has big money. Do you have money, Mr. Feeshermenz?"

"Not much."

"Too bed. You are very nice."

"You're nice too, Tanya. Do you get off the boat very much?"

She slipped the sunglasses back on. "Sometimes he goes off on *Volga*. All night. I stay at Jared Coffin house and he tells me to go shopping."

"Where does he go in the boat?"

She shrugged, then rose from her seat and said, "I hev to go, for manicure, Sookareedees."

"I hope our paths will cross again."

A thoughtful expression crossed her face. "Ivan is going out in his boat tomorrow. I am on island for the night."

"When does he leave?"

"Always the same time, near sunset. Then Tanya is free. Maybe feeshermenz is free, too."

She sauntered off with a relaxed, loose-limbed walk. I watched her until she mingled with the tourists starting to crowd the streets. I pondered her words. *Sometimes he goes off on* Volga.

I could feel the weight of the boat keys in my pocket. A vague plan began to form in my mind. The downside was that I would miss an encounter with a beautiful young Bulgarian woman. The upside was that I might learn where Ivan went on his sojourns. The more I knew about Ivan's business, the better for me.

Leaving the restaurant, I walked over to the marina. Daggett's boat, the *Pequod II*, was a Pursuit model around twenty-five-feet long. I climbed aboard the boat and checked to see that the gas tank was full. I started the twin Evinrude 250 horsepower engines. The four-stroke motors purred like tigers. Everything was shipshape and ready to go. I cast off the dock lines, eased the boat out of its slip, steered past the *Volga* and toward the harbor. When I was out of the no-wake zone, I gunned the throttle. The hull rose at a sharp angle and planed smoothly over one-foot waves.

Just outside the harbor, I encountered gray tendrils of fog snaking in from Nantucket Sound. The sun was trying to burn off the fog, but its futile attempts only served to give the wooly mists an unhealthy yellowish pallor.

I rounded the boat in a banking turn and headed back into the harbor, where I reduced the boat's speed and wove my way through the pack of power and sailboats anchored in the basin to the east of the yacht dock. I cut the engines to an idle. The boat rocked in the gentle swells. From my vantage point, I would be able to see any boat leaving the harbor.

I headed back to the boat slip, tied up and did a survey to make sure the *Pequod II* was ready for a quick departure. Leaving the marina, I walked along Water Street to the whaling museum and bought an admission ticket. I went directly to the room with the whaleboat and the whale skeleton and stopped in front of the portrait wall opposite the whaling tool display.

The oil painting of Prudence Whetherell was one of a dozen or so portraits of whaling captains and their wives that hung in the big room. Using my best Bogart impression, I growled, "Okay, Prudence. You saw the whole thing, don't deny it. *Confess*."

Prudence stared back at me with a blank expression. I stepped in front of another portrait. If the eyes of the resolute man in the painting had been human, they would have seen Coffin's murder. I tried again, appealing to Captain Sperling's civic side, but he kept his lips sealed.

A couple of visitors overheard me talking to the portrait and hurriedly dragged their kids out of the room. I turned away from the silent witnesses and leaned against the whaleboat. I tried to imagine the night of the murder. Daggett calls a meeting with Coffin to talk about buying the scrimshaw collection. In one scenario, Daggett gets there ahead of his victim, pulls the boarding knife off the wall and ambushes Coffin from the front.

Try again. Both men get there at the same time; their chat turns into an argument, Daggett yanks the knife down and stabs Coffin, who presumably resists his instincts to run and stands there to be killed. Unable to face the enormity of his crime, Daggett drives to the Serengeti where a blow on the head from an unknown source transforms him into a fictional character from Melville.

Why couldn't I be working on a good old-fashioned straightforward murder? One guy kills another. Gun. Knife. Beer bottle. *Bam*. That's it. I juggled the different scenarios until my head was spinning. I wandered around the museum and went up to the scrimshaw room. I stared at the whalebone carvings. A question nagged at me again. If the museum collection was so extensive that only a few pieces could be displayed, why did Coffin want to add to it?

I went back to the front desk on the ground level and borrowed a telephone book. Coffin and Company was listed under the antiques section. I asked the receptionist for directions. A few minutes later, I turned onto an alley and walked until I came to a buff-colored, two-story clapboard house that had a small porch with a double stairway. Hanging over the porch was a small black wooden sign carved in the shape of a sperm whale. Painted on the sign in gilt letters were the words: **Coffin and Company Antiques**.

I climbed a stairway, opened the door and stepped into a dimly-lit space. Glass counters ran down both sides. Ship paintings decorated the walls. The musty-smelling shop was twice as long as it was wide and jammed with enough merchandise to fill a WalMart. I imagined a giant foot shoving all the stuff into the small space.

At the far end of the shop, a middle-aged woman sat at a wooden desk, watching a miniature TV screen. When you're about to ask a stranger a question, it never hurts to have an ice-breaker. On the wall behind her was a painting of a whaling ship sailing in a puddle of moonlight, and above the oil was a Red Sox pennant. She had on a Red Sox cap pulled over her short sandy hair. I tapped the visor of my blue-and-red cap.

"What's the score?" I said.

She turned and put a finger to her lips. "Shhhhhh."

Red Sox fans consider their baseball team as a metaphor for life, with all its ups and downs. Ever since Babe Ruth was traded off, triggering the decades-old curse, the erratic and sometimes incomprehensible behavior of the Olde Town Team has made its followers more superstitious than most. The Sox were winning, but to acknowledge such would be bad luck. It was best to ignore them or they would take a dive.

I nodded knowingly. Close call. If she had answered my

question, the shortstop would have flubbed the catch. She turned down the volume on the TV.

"Sorry," she said. "My name is Pat Greely. How can I help you?"

I told her my name and said that I was a private investigator hired by the Daggett family to look into his case.

With her round face, eyes and wire-rimmed glasses, Pat resembled a friendly owl. She enhanced that resemblance when she blinked a number of times and said, "*Good*. Henry Daggett could *never* have done what they're saying he did. Not in a thousand years."

"You seem pretty sure about that."

"I am absolutely sure. He and Ab were *friends*, for godsakes."

"I've heard that they argued a lot."

"*Pshaw!* Sure, they were two cranky old guys who were too strong-minded for their own good. That was all for show."

"You seem to know them pretty well."

"Ab gave me a job here after my husband died. Not big pay, but steady. Henry came by a lot. The two men would talk for hours about island history. Just like any old friends. Sometimes they agreed, and sometimes they didn't. Ab griped about Mr. Daggett, but it was always with a twinkle in his eye."

"Did they talk about the scrimshaw collection for the museum?"

"I'll have to admit that was a doozy. They came as close to breaking up as I've ever seen them."

"I've seen some pretty good scrimshaw," I said, "But it's hard to understand why old friends would go head to head over a collection of carved ivory."

She grinned. "There's scrimshaw and then there is *Coffin* scrimshaw."

Pat got up and unlocked a glass cabinet. She removed three sperm whale teeth and lined them up on a square of green felt under a magnifying glass on a stand. "Scrimshaw varies in quality, from primitive craft work, to downright masterpieces in ivory.

Obed Coffin was a genius. See if you can pick out his piece from the others."

The scene etched into the whale teeth was basically the same on all three, showing a whaleboat closing in on a sperm whale. The harpooner stood in the bow with a harpoon raised above his head. But one tooth stood out. The image was flawless. The shading of the sea and foam were done in a fine detail. Where the other images were stiff, this image had life and flow to it. I moved the tooth aside.

"This one, far and above."

"Congratulations. You picked the Coffin piece."

"It wasn't difficult. Coffin was a true artist."

"He had the luxury of working in this shop rather than on the deck of a whaling ship. But I don't think it would have made any great difference. The art that flowed from his fingers stemmed from his own painful past."

"The *Moshup* incident?"

"That's right. It scarred Ab's ancestor and ruined him personally and financially. He poured himself into his art to ease the pain of his awful experience, and sold scrimshaw to put food on the table."

"I heard that Mr. Coffin was collaborating on a book about his great-grandfather. He apparently had new evidence that would shed light on the *Moshup* case."

"Yeah," she said with a sigh. "He told me that, too, but he didn't go into detail. When I asked him about it, he said he had put the book project off. That his first priority was persuading the museum to buy his ancestor's scrimshaw."

"I can see where that might be a hard sell. The museum already has an extensive collection."

"That wasn't the problem. Daggett was open to buying the collection, and even money wasn't an issue. It was the *source* of the collection that bothered him."

"Why was that?"

"Mr. Daggett was worried about the dealer. He was afraid that it might be stolen property and wanted it authenticated so that there would be no question whatsoever. He was adamant about that."

"Was there any chance Coffin could have changed Mr. Daggett's mind?"

"All I can say is that Henry would have had to hit a grand slam to change Ab's mind. Which reminds me." She had been keeping an eye on the silent television screen, but now she turned up the volume. The batter had just clocked a triple off the Green Monster and the man on second had scored a run, leading the Yankees. It was the eighth inning. I knew I had lost her. Before she was swept up in the game, I got in another question.

"Do you have the name of the scrimshaw dealer Mr. Coffin was talking to?"

She opened a drawer in the desk, pulled out a business card and handed it to me. I thanked her and headed for the door.

I was halfway there when I heard her say, "How about those Red Sox?"

CHAPTER 12

The smoky tendrils of fog that had cut short my jaunt around the harbor merged into a thicket of gray. Nudged by a steady offshore breeze, the fog bank rolled in from the sea, dimming the sun to a pale disk, muffling sound and sending the temperature down to goose-bump levels. The animal cut-outs of elephants, giraffes and rhinos looked less playful in the fog, looming out of the murk like creatures from a Jurassic age.

Lisa's Jeep was parked off the road next to a split rail fence, not far from the plywood animals. I pulled the MG up beside the Wrangler. Lisa stepped out to greet me and swept her arm around like a real estate agent trying to move a dog off a property.

"How do you like a Nantucket fog blow?" she said.

I squinted, but it didn't help me see through the murk. "Maybe we should come back when we can see better."

The Sankety lighthouse tower high on a bluff a few miles distant was completely hidden from sight. The umbrella-shaped trees were obscured behind a misty shroud. Visibility had been cut to less than a hundred yards.

"Don't worry. We won't be operating blind." She reached into the Jeep and pulled out a map, which she spread out on the hood.

"The official name for this area is the Middle Moors. There are extensive cranberry bogs to the northeast and a pond due north. There's even a hill called *Kilimanjaro*. The moors encompass nearly four thousand acres."

I let out a low whistle. "That would be a lot to cover even on a clear day."

"I agree, but we're only interested in a small section." She tapped the map with her long fingernail. "The bird-watcher encountered Gramps here, a few hundred yards off the main trail. Is there anything special we should be looking for?"

"Not that I can think of. We'll know if we find it. Can you think of any reason he'd come to the Serengeti?"

"It was one of his favorite island spots. He liked to walk here and spot birds. He may have sought refuge in a place he loved."

"Let's go with that for now. The medical report in the case file says the blunt force trauma to your grandfather's head was hard enough to knock him out. So why wasn't he out cold at the museum when the cops showed up?"

"Maybe he eventually woke up and drove here."

"I don't buy it. I've been clouted a couple of times and the first thing you want to do when you regain consciousness is to throw up. The last thing you want to do is to get behind the wheel of a car. He would have been dazed and disoriented. His vision would have been blurred. He would have had to navigate the maze of roads around town in that condition, and then find his way here in the dark."

"Are you saying he was *brought* here?"

"Someone could have killed Coffin, snuck up behind Henry, clubbed him and dumped him out here."

"But his car was here. How would you explain that?"

"You be the detective. How would *you* explain it?"

It only took her a second. "Someone followed the driver and picked him up."

"*Elementary*, my dear Lisa."

114

She pinched her chin between her thumb and forefinger. "That would suggest that more than one person is involved."

"It would certainly suggest malice aforethought."

"You mean the whole thing, the murder and framing my grandfather, could have been planned?"

"I can't prove it. *Yet.* So let's go for a walk. Maybe something will jump out at us."

There are times when I wish I'd keep my big mouth shut, and this was one of them.

We climbed over the fence, followed a trail of hard-packed dirt a short distance and stopped near a scrub oak tree. We were only a few hundred feet from the road, but our cars were invisible in the fog. The temperature had dropped at least ten degrees.

Lisa referred to her map. "Here's where Gramps veered off the trail. And here's where he was found."

I pointed to some oaks and pitch pines that were ghostly silhouettes in the rolling mists.

"Since we don't have a compass, we'll have to navigate by dead reckoning," I said. "Those trees will be one point of a triangle. The pines that way, off to the right, are another. And where we are standing is the apex. As long as we can see the trees, we won't get lost. We can always head toward the noise of the road traffic if the fog gets worse."

Using a ballpoint pen, Lisa marked the points of the triangle on the map. We pushed through the knee-high tangle of ground cover to the first stand of trees. The hum of traffic gradually faded until there was only the rustle of our footsteps through the grass.

We reached the trees and stopped. We were surrounded by a deep silence. It was as if the fog were trying to deprive us of our senses. First sight, then sound.

"This place has always reminded me of the English moors Thomas Hardy used to write about," Lisa said.

"I was thinking more about the curse of the Baskervilles. If you hear a dog howling, run for the manor house." The second clump of trees was a hundred feet away. Fog was nibbling away at the thinner limbs so only the main trunks were visible. I warned Lisa that if we didn't move quickly, we'd lose the next way-point.

She started walking, and that's when an odd thing happened. An oak branch was hanging down in front of me, about a foot above my head. As I followed Lisa, a section of the branch separated from the main limb and fell to the ground. The effect was quite magical, and I wouldn't have recognized what had caused such a strange phenomenon if I hadn't heard the *zip* sound that a bullet makes as it shreds the air.

I called out for Lisa to stop. She half turned, and a terrified look came to her eyes as she saw me bearing down on her like an enraged bull. I grabbed her by the shoulders and pulled her down in a way that would allow my body to cushion the fall. The map flew from her hands.

When we hit the ground, I put my mouth to her ear. "Keep your head down! Someone just took a shot at us."

"I didn't hear any gunfire!"

"The shooter is using a sound suppressor."

Lisa looked unconvinced at first, but she quickly became a believer. A patch of bark flew off the trunk of the same oak tree that had lost its branch, exposing the white wood. Two more swatches of bark peeled away. Each piece was lower than the other. The shooter was lowering his aim.

"*Move!*" I said. "*That* way. Stay down. I'll be right behind you."

Another bullet dug into the tree inches above our heads. Lisa didn't have to be told twice. She got onto her knees and elbows and crawled like a Marine recruit on his first day at Parris Island. None too soon. A bullet dug a divot from the earth at the base of the tree where we had been lying. If not for the fog hiding our movements, we would have been dead meat. On the way in, we had walked by a wooden tree perch, probably there for bird-watchers. It would have been a perfect place for a sniper's nest.

We crawled until we got into higher grass. I whispered at Lisa to stop. The sniper would have figured out he had missed his target and climbed down from the perch. I could picture him standing in the fog, ears cocked for the snap of a twig or some other sound that would give our position away. I moved up beside Lisa and placed my hand gently over her lips.

We waited like a couple of rabbits spooked by a hunter.

The waiting game was about to end. We could hear the swish-swish of someone moving through the grass. I pushed myself up on an elbow and saw a shadowy figure coming our way. I coiled my legs under me. If the shooter found our hiding place, I'd spring out of the grass. Maybe Lisa could get away. It was a frail reed to cling to, but it was all I had. But the shadow moved past us, passing within twenty feet, and headed toward the tree where we had been standing when the first shots were fired.

As the footfalls receded, we started crawling again. At one point, I rolled over on my side and looked behind me. I was startled to see that blades of grass had been broken by our passage, leaving a trail that an experienced tracker could follow. I tapped her on the leg and signaled a stop.

For a minute or two there was only silence, then I heard footsteps again. I held my breath and let it out only when the footsteps moved away from us. They seemed purposeful, hurried, as if the shooter had something in mind. I urged Lisa forward. We'd crawl a minute, then stop to listen. Then we'd crawl again. Our elbows and knees were being scraped raw.

The land dipped suddenly and we dropped into an old irrigation ditch about four feet deep.

"We can get up, but we'll have to stay low," I said.

I did a Quasimodo stoop to demonstrate. Then I helped her to her feet and led the way, following the ditch until it came to an intersection. Then another. I tripped over a weathered two-by-four-section of lumber around three feet long that must have floated in when the ditch held water. I picked it up, thinking it might come in handy if the shooter was stupid enough to get within range.

Darkness was falling and we soon became lost. I called a rest stop.

Which was when I heard the sound.

I cursed in the language of my Cretan ancestors.

"What's wrong?"

"Listen."

She cupped her ear, but it wasn't necessary. The buzz of traffic was clearly audible. I had led us in a big circle, back to the road. Assuming we had moved deeper into the Serengeti, we had made little attempt to cloak our footsteps and our voices. If the shooter were still around, we would have put ourselves in jeopardy once more.

I motioned for us to go back the way we had come. Too late! Footsteps were crunching our way. They were no longer stealthy, as if their source didn't care about being heard or not. And they were *near*. I moved Lisa aside and stood in front of her, clutching the board as if I were holding a Louisville slugger:

I was standing in that position when the footsteps stopped, the blinding beam of a light hit me in the face, and a deep, familiar voice snickered.

"Funny place for batting practice, Soc."

CHAPTER 13

Flagg had literally dropped down from the clouds. His executive jet had landed at Tom Nevers airfield only a few miles from where Lisa and I dodged bullets in the Serengeti. He told us this as we walked back to Milestone Road. His rental car was parked next to the MG. He said he had been on his way to the Daggett house to track me down.

"Saw that dinky little red convertible you told me you were driving. Crazy place for anyone to leave a car like that so I figured it was you."

"See anyone else?" I said.

"*Nope*. But I heard someone crashing through the bushes over there. Then a car took off. Must have laid down an inch of tire rubber."

"Someone was shooting at us," Lisa said in a flat voice.

"Huh," Flagg said, in an approximation of a laugh. "How long have you known Soc, Ms. Hendricks?"

"Only a few days."

"Do tell. You really know how to show a gal a good time, Soc. What's going on?"

"I'd be happy to tell you what's going on after you're through making lame wise-cracks, Flagg."

"How about starting now? I'm on a limited schedule. I told the pilot to keep the engines running."

I suggested we go back to the Daggett house. Lisa left the Jeep and rode with me in the MG. Flagg followed in the rental car.

"Are you okay?" I said as we headed toward Siasconset.

"I'll be fine after I clean up. How about you?"

"A little sore in the knees and elbows. But it could have been worse."

She shuddered. "Yes, it could have been. Thanks for getting us out of that mess."

"Wish I could claim total credit. We might still be running around in the fog if Flagg hadn't shown up."

"Who *is* that man?"

"Flagg is a Wampanoag Indian from Martha's Vineyard. We know each other from way back. He works for the government now."

"He's a strange man," she said. "Almost *scary*."

"Flagg is a tough guy in a tough business, but under that imposing exterior beats the heart of a human being."

She paused. "He's a bit like you in that respect, isn't he?"

"In some ways, I guess. Flagg likes to go by the book. I threw the book out the window a long time ago."

"How did you meet him?"

My mind flashed back to the seedy bar in Quang Tri where I first encountered Flagg. I had saved him from being stabbed by a drunken soldier and we became good friends. Flagg was part of Operation Phoenix, a rough-playing counter-insurgency group. Our friendship went down the drain after I thought, erroneously, that he had tossed a prisoner out of a helicopter. I didn't learn the truth, that he had nothing to with it, until years later when we found ourselves working together on a case. We've been friends ever since. Flagg has repaid me tenfold for that night in the bar. He went on to work for a shadowy division of the CIA. I became a cop, then a fisherman.

I could have told Lisa all this, but I simply said, "We met in Vietnam. He works in security for the government. Top-secret stuff. I called him the other day and told him I was working a case on Nantucket."

Lisa slipped into that silent, thoughtful mode I had noticed before. I dropped her off at the house so she could change and Flagg came up to my apartment where he settled into a kitchen chair. Flagg seemed to fill the room with a forceful presence that went way beyond his physical size. I offered him a beer, but he asked for instant coffee.

I grabbed a Grey Lady ale and sat across from him. "It's great to see you, Flagg."

"You, too, Soc. Your friend Lisa is a nice lady."

"She's smart, too."

"All the more reason not to bring her into your little quarrel with Chernko. She could have been hurt tonight."

I felt heat flushing my cheeks. His comment hit home.

"No argument there, Flagg. I got careless. I should have seen this one coming."

"Fill me in. I've got thirty minutes before I have to leave. I was on my way across the Atlantic and persuaded the pilot to make a quick stop to see my old friend Soc. Good thing I did, seeing you ignored my warning about Chernko."

"It's more complicated than that. I'm working for Lisa. Her grandfather is being charged with murder and I'm the investigator hired for the defense team."

"Did he do it?"

"I don't think so, but he's gone off the deep end. He thinks he's Ahab chasing a white whale."

"Serious?"

"Very."

After I gave him a summary of the Daggett case, Flagg said,

"You sure know how to pick them. This sounds like a loser in my opinion. My guess is that you took the case because you wanted to be close to Chernko."

"Can't deny it. I wanted to watch him. Now he's watching me."

I told him about the encounter at Ramsey's party.

"You think there's any connection to the shooting?"

"Seems like an easy call, but there was only one shooter. From what I know, Chernko's hit men work as a pair."

He let out a heavy sigh. "You like Lisa?" he said.

"Very much. That's why I'm helping her."

"Best way you can help her is to get off the island. Go far away for a while."

"Thanks, Flagg. I'll think about it."

"But you won't do it."

"That's not bad advice, but Chernko and I are joined at the hip. I've pissed him off. He'll use every resource he has to swat me down like an annoying fly. You know that."

"I know that it's only luck that he missed you this time. He'll try again."

"I'd be surprised if he didn't."

"Guess that's something." Flagg glanced at his watch. "Sorry, but you're on your own. Got to go save the world again." He reached inside his windbreaker and pulled out a blue folder. "This report will tell you what you're up against. You might want to change your mind after you read it. I wish I could lend a hand, but I'm gonna be out of the country, up to my eyeballs with government work for the next few days. Give me a call and I'll help you find a place to hide. Say goodbye to the nice lady for me."

We walked down the stairs to the car and shook hands.

"By the way," I said. "I was jerking your chain about the casino in *Aquinnah* as a way to get your attention."

"Oh yeah, really had me fooled, Soc. *Really* fooled." He burst into a deep laugh and was still chuckling when he got into the car.

I watched until the red taillights disappeared down the driveway. And suddenly I felt very much alone.

After a warm shower, I changed into running pants and sweatshirt, then I sat down with the report Flagg had given me and read the words on the cover: **Forensic. Ivan Chernko**. I had just turned to the first page when there was a soft knock. Lisa waved at me through the glass panes in the door. I tucked the report on top of the refrigerator and beckoned at her to come in. She was wearing a pink terry cloth bathrobe over red silk pajamas. Her long hair had been tied back in a French twist. She smelled like soap and water. She was carrying a bottle of red wine. She looked around the kitchen.

"Where's your friend? I wanted to thank him again."

"John said something about saving the world and vanished into the night. He does that a lot. You'll get used to him when you know him better."

She sat down at the table. "I hope he comes back soon. After what we went through tonight, I think his help would come in handy."

I shook my head. "We can't count on it. In fact, Flagg advised me to get off Nantucket and go into hiding."

Her eyes grew wider. "What did you tell him?"

"That I've been hired to help your grandfather, and I'll stay until the job is finished."

She let out the breath she'd been holding. "I think I'm hungry."

"That's a good sign. Let me see what I can rustle up."

I found a box of pasta and a can of spaghetti sauce in the cupboard. There was a bag of frozen meatballs, a box of peas, and a container of Ben and Jerry's Cherry Garcia in the freezer. While the pasta boiled and the sauce and peas heated up, I opened the bottle of wine and Lisa set the table on the deck. Running around the Nantucket moors had drummed up our appetites and unlike the food, the wine was top-shelf. Lisa practically squealed with joy when I produced the ice cream for dessert.

The wind had shifted and the fog blow had retreated as quickly as it advanced. The stars sparkled like sequins on blue-black velvet. I waited for Lisa to speak and when she did, she said, "Soc, do you know who wanted to kill us back there in the Serengeti?"

"I think I was the target. You had the bad luck to be with me."

"Then maybe it's time you told me what's going on."

"Maybe it is, Lisa."

I started with the newspaper article that sparked Ivan's ire, the visit from the hired guns, and the destruction of my boat. I leveled with her and said the main reason I took her grandfather's case was so I could keep an eye on Ivan.

"That's an unbelievable and thoroughly frightening story," she said.

"No argument there."

"Thank you for being honest, Soc. I suppose I should thank Chernko. You might not have taken the case otherwise." A serious look came to her face. "Maybe your friend Flagg is right, and you should get off the island."

"I kinda like it here," I said. "And right now I have no other place I'd rather be. But here's my dilemma. I don't want to place you in danger, so the decision is up to you."

Lisa went into her silent mode again, then opened her mouth wide in a yawn and said, "I'm tired."

"I'm not surprised. You've had a long day. I'll walk you back to the house."

"Thanks, but I was wondering if I could sleep with you."

I have spent more time that I should trying to convince pretty women to share my bed, but when the request came from the other side, I didn't know what to say.

Lisa laughed at my slack-jawed silence. "For godsakes, don't look so shocked. I'm not really as forward as I sound. Maybe I should try again. I'd rather not be alone tonight. I'd like to share your bed with you. Sleep with you in the *literal* sense. As a friend. Like bundling in the old colonial days, when unmarried couples got to know each other with a board in between them."

"Oh *sure*," I said. "I don't have a board." Brilliant retort, Socarides.

"Then just use your imagination."

"I'll give it a try. Crawl under the covers whenever you like. I'm going to stay up and do some reading."

She yawned again, thanked me for dinner, kissed me on the cheek, and went into the bedroom. I read a few pages of the report while I waited until she had time to doze off, then went in and stretched out, fully clothed, on the bed beside her. I could feel the heat from her body. I thought she was asleep, but when I pulled the covers up, she reached down and clutched my hand. So much for the imaginary bundling board. We were still holding hands as we slipped off into a deep sleep.

CHAPTER 14

"Sleep well, Lisa?" Dr. Rosen said at the breakfast table as soon as Mrs. Gomes had left the kitchen.

Rosen had a smirky little grin on his orange tanned face. I guessed what lay behind the smirk. He was an early riser, and it was likely that on his morning run around the property, he had seen Lisa walking back to the house from my apartment wearing her bathrobe and pajamas.

"Actually, no," she said. Realizing, when Rosen's grin grew wider, that she had implied a night of unbridled passion, she blushed and said, "I've been worrying about Gramps."

"No need to worry, Lisa," Rosen said in a smarmy know-it-all tone. "I'm keeping a close eye on your grandfather."

It was time for me to jump in. "What *else* are you doing for Mr. Daggett, Dr. Rosen?"

"I'm not sure—" He knitted his brow as the prelude to a glower.

I gave him an *awshucks* smile. "Didn't mean to sound pushy. I'm just curious about the sort of treatment methods you are using to help Mr. Daggett."

"Oh. I see. Well, Mr. Socarides, it's a complex pathology that's hard to explain to a layman."

"Understandable. I'll narrow it down to a couple of questions. Are you popping pills into the captain's food or does he stretch out on your couch and spill his guts?"

Rosen made a game try at plastering an Eddy Haskell smile on his face. "I'm using proven drugs for Mr. Daggett, and I'm still attempting to establish a rapport with the patient."

I glanced over at Lisa and snorted like a winded horse. "Good luck with *that*, Doc."

"What do you mean?"

"Lisa told me that you used to work for a big corporation. Human resources. What they used to call personnel, I guess."

"That's right. I was in charge of psychologically evaluating top-ranked applicants for high-level jobs."

"Pretty impressive, but—"

"What are you getting at?"

"I can't help wondering how sizing up Harvard MBAs qualifies you to deal with, what did you call it, a complex pathology?"

A hard look came to his eyes and his face got even more orange. "If you'll excuse me," he said, rising from the table.

"*Wow!*" Lisa whispered, when Rosen was out of earshot. "You demolished him. You should be a trial lawyer."

"Chalk it up to a misspent youth watching Perry Mason. Rosen was an easy mark, and I didn't like the way he leered when he asked if you had a good night's sleep."

"Thank you for coming to my rescue, Soc. And thank you for last night. I hope I wasn't a pest."

I wanted to tell Lisa that I hadn't slept either. I lay in bed and listened to her soft breathing, inhaled the scent of her and felt the heat of her body, thinking before I slid off to dreamland that the bachelor life is overrated.

The Victorian gentleman in me answered. "No, Lisa. You weren't a pest at all. I was glad I could help."

"Thank you. Now I'd like to help by firing you."

"Was it my cooking?"

"No, it was not your cooking, which was quite, ah, creative. But I think John Flagg was right. You should get off the island. It's too dangerous for you to be here. Go into hiding until Chernko leaves. That was much too close a call yesterday."

"Chernko has connections. He would find me no matter where I went. You know the old saying. Keep your friends close and your enemies closer. My best hope is to bring him down before he does the same to me."

"You can't do that alone. Do you think your friend Flagg will help?"

"If he can. Flagg tends to be busy dealing with international hot-spots. If he's here, he'll help. If not, I'm on my own."

"Then how do you intend to bring Chernko down?" she said, clearly exasperated with me. "He's rich and powerful."

"Still working on it." I glanced at my watch. "I've got a ferry to catch. I'm meeting with the lead assistant district attorney on the case. Maybe he'll toss me something we can use. At the very least, we'll know what we'll be up against in the courtroom. I'll drop by your office on the way back to fill you in."

We both got up from our chairs at the same time. Lisa came around the table and stood in front of me. She took my hand, raised it to her face and brushed it with her lips. It was a touching, affecting gesture. The wise guy who lives in my brain and controls my mouth was struck mute. I mumbled something about seeing her later, and headed for the door.

Despite my reassuring platitudes, I knew that I was over my head when it came to a *mano a mano* with a ruthless killer like Chernko. I would have to be more than careful. I tensed when I saw a car pulled over to the side of the road, but it was only a couple of tourists taking photos.

On the ferry ride to the mainland, I sat out on the deck and let the sun cook my face. My tension melted a little with each passing mile. By the time the boat pulled up to the dock in Hyannis, the whole thing back at the Serengeti seemed like a misty dream. As I walked off the boat, I could feel the soreness in my knees from crawling around, and I knew that the adventure in the fog had been very real.

I crossed the street to a restaurant with a patio that overlooked the ferry dock. Assistant District Attorney Francis Xavier Martin sat at a table holding a cell phone stuck to his ear. He gave me a wave and pointed to the chair opposite his.

"I don't care *what* his lawyer says," Martin was saying. "We gave his client the plea bargain on the first four charges. The last two stick. We're giving him a gift. Tell the defendant that if he doesn't go along, we will pound him into dust."

The fact that Martin was smiling pleasantly as he talked didn't dull the steely edge to his voice. He hung up, put his phone on the table, and extended his hand.

"Hi, Soc. Great to see you. Read in the paper about your boat. What the hell happened?"

"Not much to tell. I was on Nantucket and came home to see my dreams of a charter fishing business go up in very smelly smoke. The inspectors are still trying to figure it out."

"Electrical?"

"Yeah, maybe."

"Sorry, Soc, that's a tough one," he said with a shake of his head.

"Yeah, *real* tough. Looking on the bright side, now I've got plenty of time to take on detecting work. Thanks for meeting me on such short notice."

He made a show of looking around. "The D.A. would kick my ass if he knew I was meeting with you."

I had known Martin ever since he joined the D.A.'s office fresh out of law school. He was a tall, lanky guy in his late thirties. With his Mediterranean features and black hair, it was safe to bet that one of his ancestors was a shipwrecked sailor from the Spanish armada who'd found true love among the Celts of Ireland. I had helped him a couple of times with information that made him look good. A few years ago, I yanked an accused murder suspect out from under the nose of Martin's boss, proving the defendant was innocent.

"Your boss still mad at me?"

"Your evidence made him look like a chump in court and he almost lost the election. What do *you* think?"

"I think he *is* a chump and that I'd better make sure I never get a speeding ticket in this county." I pointed to the cell phone on the table. "How long have you been pounding defendants into dust?"

"Ever since the D.A. filed his papers for re-election," Martin said. "Cases we would have pled out in a heartbeat are getting a hard look."

"Tough time to be a criminal in an election year," I said.

"It will only last until voting day. Then we get the bad boys back on a plea bargain assembly line."

"It doesn't hurt his political prospects to show that his office is being tough in a high-profile murder case."

Martin clutched at his heart. "Do you really think I'm so shallow that I'd turn the heat up on my prosecutorial zeal for political purposes?"

"Wouldn't be the first time an aspiring politician used the courts of justice as a stepping stone to the good life, Frank."

He uttered an evil chuckle. "And it won't be the *last*. Off the record, I'm resigning and will file soon for the state rep job. The basis of my platform will be strict law enforcement. No punks get a break."

"As I said on the phone, I'm working for the family of Henry Daggett. Does he come under the punk category?"

"Henry is in his *own* category. How'd you get roped into his defense team?"

"He has a pretty granddaughter. After my charter business burned up, I needed the money. Did I mention he has a pretty granddaughter?"

"I've met Lisa Hendricks. You're right about the pretty. Smart, too. She got me to agree to house arrest for her grandfather. Caught hell from the boss."

"I don't deny the lady has high intelligence, in spite of the fact that she hired me. What's the status of the Daggett case?"

"It's been fast-tracked. My boss isn't going to waste an opportunity like this, especially one with a predictable conviction."

"Is the conviction a certainty?"

"What do *you* think, Soc?" He ticked off his points on his fingers. "The defendant and the deceased argued over a museum acquisition. The defendant's fingerprints were found on the murder weapon. The defendant and the victim were at an after-hours meeting. Maybe Daggett didn't have murder in mind, but tempers got out of hand; the result was the same. Daggett grabs the knife off the wall. Coffin ends up in a coffin."

"I hope you're not going to use that clever play on words in court."

"Depends on my mood. I'll decide after jury selection. So what does the ex-homicide cop think about this?"

"I can guess what a sharp defense attorney might say. The defendant and the victim were good friends who had a few disagreements. The defendant comes upon the deceased and unthinkingly picks up the murder weapon, thus leaving his prints. I've seen the boarding knife fasteners; it wouldn't have been easy for an old guy to pull that thing down from the wall. In the meantime, Coffin could have run for the hills."

"Okay, say Daggett waited in ambush with weapon in hand."

"Coffin was stabbed from the front. Be a lot easier if murder was the goal, to sneak up from behind. The museum is filled with nooks and crannies where Daggett could have waited."

"Maybe Coffin heard Daggett and turned to face his killer."

"Still lots of maybes."

"None of it matters," he said with a shrug. "Daggett will convict himself."

"Defense will never allow him to take the stand."

"He doesn't have to. There will be testimony to the effect that he thinks he is a fictional whaling captain in search of a white whale with the goal of killing same. We will charge negligent homicide, and get the old guy into a treatment center for the rest of his life. Which everyone will agree is the best possible outcome."

"His granddaughter won't agree. She thinks he's innocent."

"Like I said. Doesn't matter."

I raised an eyebrow.

He spread his hands. "Think of the publicity this will produce. It's totally bizarre. Moby Dick! Crazy Ahab. The D.A. will look competent and compassionate at the same time."

"Which doesn't hurt in an election year."

"Don't deny it, but I still maintain that this crazy old man is dangerous, and putting him away is the best solution."

"Here's my problem with that, Frank. The D.A.'s case against Daggett says he killed Coffin in a crazed rage, and that the trauma launched him into the world of *Moby Dick*. But there's also a case to be made that he slipped into a crazy world when he got a blow to the head, *after* he left the museum. Does that discrepancy matter?"

He slowly wagged his head. "In a perfect world it would."

"But this is an election year."

He gave me a quick tight grin. "Taking the fifth on that, pal."

"How about the Russian guy cremated in the woods near the airport? Will that help the vote?"

"I saw the story in the *Times*. Looks like you sewed that case up, Soc."

"The reporter took a few liberties with our bar talk."

He laughed and said, "Low priority. The guy wasn't a local.

Hell, he wasn't even a *citizen*. Chances are, we'll never find his murderer, not that anyone really cares. Karpov was up to his neck in drug stuff."

"Still, that was a nasty way to die," I said.

"No disagreement there, Soc." He picked up my baseball cap, which I had hung from an empty chair, and plunked it onto my head. "How about those Red Sox?"

The lesson in contemporary jurisprudence had ended. We ordered coffee and bagels and talked about the changes we would make if we were managing the Boston Red Sox. Martin fielded a few more calls in between, and said he had to get to court. I thanked him, we parted company and I headed for my truck, which must have missed me, because it started on the first try.

I drove around the harbor to the marina and talked to the dock master. My burned-out boat had been taken off on a flatbed. We walked down to my old dock where a clean-up crew was hard at work. He said the fire inspectors had determined that the fire was arson, started with an accelerant. I thanked him for the update and walked over to Trader Ed's and borrowed the phone to call my answering machine.

There were a couple of calls from the insurance adjustor saying things were in the works, and from people looking to charter my boat. There was a message from my neighbor saying Kojak was fine, but running low on food. And lastly, there was a message from my mother, who wanted me to call her on a family matter. *That* message filled me with dread. With all the craziness on Nantucket, I had forgotten, maybe on purpose, to tell my family that their investment in the *Thalassa* had burned to the waterline. I called my neighbor, told here where I kept an extra food stash in the boathouse and gave her my Nantucket number.

During the commute back to the island, I pondered how to tell Lisa the bad news about her grandfather's impending court date. As I entered her office, I still hadn't figured out how to break it to her. She looked up from her desk, which was cluttered with land plans, and gave me a smile, which faded when she took in my somber expression.

I flopped into a chair and told her about my conversation with Martin.

"There's no way to postpone it?"

"The D.A. wants to fast-track this case to re-election."

"Have you gotten anywhere in your investigation?"

"Bits and pieces. I'm still trying to put the puzzle together. Do you know where Sutcliffe, the writer lives?"

I hadn't anticipated the depth of her anger, so I was surprised when she pushed the maps aside and said, "Why waste time talking with him when we've got to do something to exonerate my grandfather?"

I blinked, then said, "Your grandfather is living in the past, so maybe that's not a bad place to start."

Her shoulders sagged. "Sorry, Soc. I know you'll do your best. It's not that you don't have other things to think about, like getting shot at. I just—" Her eyes brimmed with tears. She rose from her chair, came around and gave me a shoulder hug. "Sorry for the waterworks," she said. "I've got a conservation trust meeting tonight. Will I see you at the house?"

I nodded. "Maybe Dr. Rosen and I can continue our discussion."

She frowned in disapproval at the mention of Rosen and gave me directions to Sutcliffe's place.

I had tried to mollify her by suggesting that I might find the solution to her grandfather's problem in the historical record, but I wasn't entirely honest. I was going to see Sutcliffe mainly because I didn't have a clue where to go next on Daggett's case.

CHAPTER 15

Petticoat Row is a narrow, tree-lined street a short walk from the center of town. The front lawn of Sutcliffe's two-story shingled house looked as if it had been cut with manicure scissors. Neat ranks of flowers had been planted around the lawn. The gleaming paint on the white picket fence could have been applied the day before.

Sutcliffe opened the door on my first knock. The annoyed expression on his face melted when he saw me standing on the steps. "Oh, hi," he said. "I thought you were the police again."

"Why would you be expecting the police?"

"C'mon in and I'll show you."

He ushered me into the house. We passed through a hallway into the living room. In contrast to the well-tended exterior of the house and lawn, the room was a shambles. Chairs and tables had been upended, and the braided rug was covered with broken ceramics and smashed picture frames.

I looked around at the destruction. "I wasn't aware Nantucket had cyclones."

"Hell, this isn't the worst of it," Sutcliffe said. "Take a look."

He led the way through the living room into his small office at the back of the house. The floor was littered with paper, books and newspaper clippings. File cabinet drawers had been emptied onto the pile. The screen of the computer monitor on a desk was smashed.

"You're right. That *wasn't* the worst of it. What happened?"

"Some bastard broke in and trashed the house while I was in town this morning. That vase in the other room was a favorite of my wife's." He pointed to the scattered papers. "It's going to take days to sort this research material."

"Any idea who did this?"

"The police think it was vandals. Kids maybe."

"Did anyone else get hit in the neighborhood?"

"Nope." He screwed up his mouth. "Maybe all this extra damage was done to make it look like vandals did it. I think they were looking for something."

I flashed back on the story Lisa had told me about the vandalism at her grandfather's beach shack. "That's not a bad guess. Anything special come to mind?"

"I don't have any money or valuables. All I have is stuff to do with my writing." He went over to a wall painting of Nantucket Harbor and slid it aside to reveal a wall safe. He twiddled the dial and opened the door. Reaching inside, he pulled out a flat aluminum box. "I'm an old-fashioned hard copy guy. I back up everything I write on paper and keep it in the fireproof vault. These are articles I've been working on and notes for the book I was going to write with Coffin."

"I can come by another time, after you've straightened things out."

"Naw. I need a drink to set my mind straight. Thank God they didn't steal the beer."

With the Serengeti shooter on the loose, dulling my senses with alcohol could prove fatal. I refused the offer of a drink and settled for coffee. We went out onto a deck that overlooked a backyard tended with the same loving care as the front lawn and settled into a couple of wicker chairs. Sutcliffe explained that the plantings had all been put in by his late wife. She'd come back to haunt him if he ever let the landscaping get out of hand.

"I wouldn't blame her for that."

He laughed and asked me how I happened to be in the neighborhood.

"You told me at Ramsey's soiree that to understand what happened between Coffin and Daggett, I'd have to know more about the *Moshup* incident. So here I am."

A thoughtful expression came to his face. "I'll take it another step. To understand the *Moshup*, you should examine the *Essex* tragedy."

"Examine away," I said.

"First of all, a sperm whale attacked and sank both ships. It could have been the same whale in both cases. It was white around the head, which is common with mature bulls. Both ships were in the same area of the Pacific, just north of the equator near Fanning Island, and the attacks happened a few years apart. In each case, the whale smashed the whaleboats that were giving chase, and then rammed the ship's bow section with its head. It's almost as if he picked out the ship's weak spot."

"Smart whale."

"*Stubborn*, too. It hit the ship repeatedly, hammering away until the *Essex* went down. The crew retrieved navigational instruments, food and water. They were two thousand miles from land. They decided out of fear of cannibals to steer clear of Tahiti and head for South America. The boat with the navigational gear got separated from the others. Two boats managed to stick together. A crewman died just before their food was about to run out. That's when talk of cannibalism first surfaced."

"I'm sure I'm not the first to point out the irony of their Tahiti decision."

"No, you're not. They cast lots and cannibalism won. They

started by eating the man's heart. More guys died and ended up as the dinner special. The two boats drifted apart. The real horror was about to begin with the three men on Pollard's boat."

"Who was Pollard?"

"He was the captain of the *Essex*. They'd been adrift for more than ninety days when a crewman named Ramsdell suggested that one of them would have to sacrifice himself so the others may live. Pollard says *no*. The third crewman, a guy named Coffin, who was Pollards' nephew, supports Ramsdell."

"Any relation to our present day Coffin?"

"Maybe. It was a common name on the island. So they draw lots, slips of paper in a hat, and Coffin loses. Pollard wrote later that he was soon dispatched, but doesn't say by whom. The executioner was never named. Some say it was Pollard, the other Ramsdell. Coffin's body kept them alive until a ship found them, half-mad, trying to suck the marrow out of the young man's bones."

"Coffin's family couldn't have been too happy with them."

"*That's* an understatement. This is a small island. The Coffins crossed paths every day with the local cannibals. Coffin's mother in particular couldn't abide the sight of the guys who ate her son."

"What was the reaction of the rest of the community?"

"The Nantucketers were horrified by the episode, but they knew of the dangers of whaling and were understanding. Sorta."

"*Sorta?*"

"The early death of the black whalers was a scandal that wouldn't go away. The idea that the Nantucket men might have survived by withholding food hit hard on an Abolitionist island. No one talked about the *Essex* except in whispers. There was the practical aspect, too. Cannibalism hurt business. Fast-forward three years. When the *Moshup* crew went through almost the identical experience, there was a massive cover-up. My book would have exposed that cover-up."

"The book you hoped to write with Coffin?"

The sad nod of his head said it all. "I had planned to dedicate the book to my wife."

"You'll get another chance. Tell me more about the cover-up."

"The locals tried to bury the whole *Moshup* thing, but there was an unintended consequence. By keeping it under wraps, they may unwittingly have hidden evidence of a crime."

"What *kind* of crime?"

He dropped his voice to a growl. "Murder most foul."

"I was a homicide cop before I became a private investigator. Run the case history by me. I'll treat it like a contemporary crime."

His face lit up. "*Hey.* That may be a great new book angle. A detective tries to solve homicide on the high seas after nearly two centuries."

"I like it. You can do that dedication to your wife."

He smiled and said, "Okay, here's what is known. The *Moshup* spots a pod of sperm whales and launches the boats. They go after a big white-headed whale. Bad decision. The whale fights back, busts up some whaleboats and rams the ship, sinking it. The crew retrieves supplies from the ship before it goes under, then sets off in a flotilla of whaleboats. They become separated in bad weather. The crew on one boat is alone without navigational equipment. They drift for days, food runs out, and there is a vote to eat their dead comrades instead of tossing the bodies into the sea."

"Sounds like a replay to the *Essex.*"

"So *far.* Eventually, three men are left in the boat. Swain is a harpooner whom contemporaries describe as aggressive and conniving, qualities that are only heightened by the dehumanizing effects of starvation. Swain's quarters had been in the dirty and cramped forecastle. Daggett is the ship's carpenter, a privileged position that allows for a more comfortable shipboard life. Same with Coffin. As the first mate, he should be in command, but Swain is definitely running things on the boat. He proposes that one of them die to feed the others. Coffin refuses, but Daggett supports

Swain. They draw straws, Daggett loses, and is killed to feed the others."

"Who did the killing?"

He raised a forefinger in the air. "That's where *you* come in, Mr. Homicide Cop."

"It's obviously either Swain or Coffin. Start feeding me some facts."

"Not long after Daggett dies, a passing ship picks up the two survivors, each guarding his stash of bones. The ship is on its way to the whaling grounds, so the two men are placed on another vessel headed for New Bedford. That ship runs into some bad weather and has to put into port for repairs. In the meantime, the cannibalism account starts making the rounds of the whaling fleet and becomes common knowledge. When the survivors return home to Nantucket, hundreds of people are waiting on the dock to hear the full story."

"The devil is in the details," I said. "Swain and Coffin could shape the narrative any way they'd like to."

"*Correct.* There is no denying that they ate their crew mates, but they say Daggett died of *natural* causes."

"That was convenient."

"The survivors stick to their story when they testify before the ship's owners. The owners have their suspicions, but they had seen the PR damage that the *Essex* incident caused, and they decide to accept the testimony at face value."

"The bad for business thing again."

"That's right. It wouldn't do for the sordid details of another cannibalism episode to come out. It would unsettle people, cast Nantucket in a bad light. Unfortunately, the cover story starts to unravel."

"It must have been hard to keep a secret on a small place like Nantucket."

"The story would have come out in time, but Swain broke it

open. He wrote an account of the cannibalism incident. Said he wanted to clear the air. He said that Coffin had pushed the other men to cast lots to choose the executioner. That he was supposed to do the job and when he refused, Coffin grabbed the knife and killed Daggett."

"What did Coffin have to say about Swain's account?"

"Nothing. He had died the year before. Swain's story was the only detailed account by a survivor so folks took it as the gospel truth. It offered closure as well. People just wanted to forget the whole thing."

"I'd like to read the Swain account."

He opened the aluminum box and pulled out a slim paperback book.

"This is a reprint of Swain's journal produced years later for the tourist trade. It's got details of the hearing before the ship's owners, contemporary news accounts and so on. Maybe it will be safer with you than with me. I'd better get to cleaning up the mess in my office."

As I walked back into town along the cobblestone streets, I thought about the desperation of starving men, the unimaginable horror that transpired on the whaleboat and how the present is intertwined with the past. A little voice was warning me that the drama hadn't ended a hundred-fifty-years ago. The break-in at Daggett's beach shack and Sutcliffe's house were too close to be a coincidence. Somehow, in a way I had yet to fathom, the tragic story of cannibalism, murder, and cover-up was still unfolding, and like it or not, I had been drawn into the on-going saga of the good ship *Moshup*.

Tanya had said that she was leaving the yacht around five, so I was surprised to see her sashay along the dock around a half hour earlier than expected. I had been finishing up a burger and fries at the restaurant patio where we sat the last time. Tanya was wearing a very short dress of jade green and was carrying an overnight bag in her hand. She saw my wave, walked over and flopped loosely into a chair.

"Hello, feeshermenz. Don't you ever leave this place?"

"I haven't moved from this spot. I was hoping that you would come by and we could have a drink. You're early."

"Ivan kicked me off the boat. He says the *woodzool* man is coming again."

I'd been developing an ear for Tanya's English locutions, but this had me stumped. "What's a woodzool, Tanya?"

She shrugged.

"Could he have been talking about Woods Hole?"

"Maybe."

"This Woods Hole man that Ivan mentioned. Does he have a name?"

"Max, I think. Maybe."

"Max who?"

She frowned, obviously annoyed at my questions and gave me a dismissive wave of her hand. "I hev to go spend Ivan's money. Hair first. Then shopping. Come by hotel later and we'll talk some more."

"I'll try, but I'm busy tonight."

She smiled. "Another woman?"

"I haven't looked at another woman since I met you, Tanya. I'm going fishing."

"Feeshing! Men are crazy," Tanya said with a roll of her eyes.

She stood up and continued on her way into town. I watched her swaying hips until they almost made me seasick and glanced at my watch. I had to get moving. I paid the bill and a few minutes later, I was driving the MG out of town. I stopped at the Serengeti and spent a few minutes looking for clues that might shed light on the night before, but the shooter left no sign of his passing. There were no cartridge shells, no cigarette butts, or footprints. I got back in the car and continued on to Siasconset.

I traded my shorts for jeans and packed a sweatshirt and a windbreaker. It's always cooler on the water, especially after the sun goes down. I borrowed one of the fishing rods from the rack over the fireplace and was on my way out the door when the phone rang. It was my mother. She had called my house again. My neighbor happened to be there to pick up more food for the feline eating machine known as Kojak. She answered the phone, chatted with my mother and gave her my Nantucket number.

"Hi, Ma," I said. "I got your message. I've been meaning to call. How are you?"

"Fine, Aristotle. How is the *Thalassa*?"

"I've taken out a few parties. They caught lots of fish."

At another time, my mother would not have been satisfied with such a brief answer. I would have been subjected to a withering third degree that would have pried the truth from me. Apparently, she had other things on her mind.

"That's good, Aristotle. You remember your cousin Alex?"

"Of *course*. How's Alex doing?"

"Good. And not so good."

It must be a Cretan thing. Life on that rugged island historically had been a combination of disaster amid incredible beauty. Only my mother could put two opposing statements together and have them sound perfectly rational. I cut to the chase.

"He's not ill, is he?"

"No, Aristotle, but he's got trouble from the old days."

Alex was the son of my Uncle Alexander and Aunt Demeter. Both were Type A personalities who had important jobs. When Alex's sister died at a young age, they threw all their energy into spoiling their only child. He ran away from home and moved in with some drug dealers on Cape Cod. I pulled him out of trouble by the scruff of the neck. He went on to law school, set up a practice

143

and had two kids, a girl named Demeter and a boy named Aristotle. The old days my mother was referring to could only have something to do with his flirtation with cocaine.

"What's going on, Ma?"

"Alex wants to tell you himself."

"I'm kinda busy, Ma." I knew that the second the excuse left my mouth it would be shot down like a blind duck.

"I know that." Sigh. "You are too busy with the nice boat that your family bought for you to do something for the family."

I knew when I was outgunned. I caved in without a fight under the guilt onslaught.

"Tell Alex I'll be glad to see him. Tell him to take the first Hy-Line ferry tomorrow morning and I'll meet him at the dock."

"*Efharisto*, Aristotle. Thank you. I'll call him now."

She hung up before I could change my mind, even though there was little chance of that with a maternal decree hanging over my head. A family obligation was the *last* thing I needed. But I tried to be philosophical about it. Compared to my mother, Ivan the Terrible was a pussy cat.

CHAPTER 16

The late afternoon sun was sinking toward the horizon when I dropped anchor off the Brant Point Light near the Coast Guard Station. The *Pequod II* blended into the dozens of power and sailboats swinging at their moorings. I stood in the boat, holding a fishing rod. I heard the yacht's engines rumble into life. Minutes later, the *Volga* slowly moved away from the dock.

I waited until the yacht had cruised past the lighthouse, then I reeled in the line and set the fishing gear aside. I started the twin outboards and pointed the boat out into the channel. I let a couple of boats follow in the yacht's wake ahead of me. The *Volga* emerged from the harbor, made a slow turn to the right and picked up speed, following a course along the *Coatue* barrier beach toward Great Point. The long sliver of land extends northwest from the island like a finger making a rude gesture.

The waters between the point and Monomoy Island are fishing grounds for striped bass and bluefish, so there were other boats in the general vicinity. Rather than risk arousing suspicions aboard the yacht, I kept well back. The yacht's size made it easy to keep in sight as it made the turn around the point to the eastern shore of the island.

Once the sun gets an inch above the ocean horizon it is only a matter of seconds before it disappears completely. The light faded from the western sky and the sea shimmered with the molten afterglow. The ocean was relatively calm with seas no more than a foot high. I kept the running lights off in violation of Coast Guard regulations. After steaming a while, the yacht came to a halt around a mile from shore and I killed the throttle. I peered through my binoculars, and saw people moving around the stern deck in the glow of powerful floodlights.

I could see a crane lift a large object from the deck and dangle the load off the stern. I cut the distance to a quarter of a mile and stopped again in time to see the object lowered into the sea.

I had pulled on my windbreaker, but the air temperature was not uncomfortably cool. The relative tranquility lulled me into an impulsive move. I moved to the edge of the zone of light around the *Volga* and killed the motors.

Twenty minutes passed with nothing much happening. I reasoned that the most I'd see would be the crane hauling the object back on board. I decided to head back to the harbor before the yacht got underway. I turned the ignition key, pushed on the throttle, and began to follow a course closer in to shore.

It looked like a clean getaway. But less than five minutes after I started off there was a sharp rap against the hull, like the noise you hear when a truck kicks up a pebble that smacks your car windshield. I throttled down and stuck my head over one side, then the other. All I could hear was the thrum of the motors. I started off again.

Seconds later, the rap repeated. Then another quickly followed. This was getting annoying. I stopped the boat. There was no repeat of the odd sound. I got moving, and doubled the boat's speed. The hull got hit again. Multiple raps, like someone throwing gravel at the boat. I slowed and grabbed a flashlight. Keeping one hand on the wheel, I leaned over the side and pointed the flashlight beam into the darkness.

I saw nothing close to the boat, but around twenty feet away the water was roiling with a pale blue luminescence.

As I watched, the patch of frothy water began to move in my direction.

I clicked off the flashlight and goosed the throttle. The boat surged forward. There was a scatter shot noise under my feet like hail hitting the roof. I gave the motors more power. The propellers bit into the water and the boat angled up on plane. The roar of the motors failed to drown out the rapping, which had grown in volume and seemed to be coming from the bow. Then off to the starboard. Then port. Then from under the deck.

The starboard motor skipped and coughed. The boat was losing its plane angle when the motor stopped. Then the other motor died. The bow lowered and the boat made headway for a short while on its momentum. Then it came to a wallowing stop. There was brief silence and the hull noises began once more. The rapping grew louder. There was a new sound as the fiberglass hull splintered. I peeled off my windbreaker, grabbed a life jacket and snapped the buckles across my chest.

The boat settled rapidly. Waves splashed over the gunwales and flooded the deck. The stern tilted down under the weight of the water. The prow stuck up in the air like a big shark's fin. I rolled into the cold sea, kicked off my boat shoes and swam around under the angled bow. I reached out to fend off the underside of the hull and my hand plunged through a ragged gash in the fiberglass.

I heard a racket directly overhead and looked up to see the hovering helicopter. Its rotors kicked up the water to a froth and the chopper's floodlights lit up the boat. I took a deep breath and stuck my head into the hole, hiding from the searching eyes.

The helicopter moved away. I slid out, gulped a lungful of air, and ducked back into the hole before the chopper made another pass. At the same time, I was worried that the sinking boat would take me to the bottom with it.

I was about to take my chances in the open when the helicopter moved off again. I came out from under the boat, gasping for breath, and saw the chopper heading back to the yacht. Seconds later, the boat slipped completely below the surface. I swam away from the whirling vortex, pivoted in the waves and saw house lights on land. I had only one choice.

I kicked off my jeans and started swimming.

It was difficult to swim wearing a flotation jacket. The added padding prevents you from slipping through the water. Movement is inefficient. Your flailing arms get tired after a few strokes. I came up with a routine. I'd swim for a while, ten strokes for each arm. Then stop for thirty seconds. After three such stops, I'd stop again, float on my back and look at the star-lit sky. Once I caught my breath, I'd begin the routine again.

Even with the rest stops, my arms were tiring. The chill of the water had penetrated through my soggy sweatshirt to my skin and weakened me further. I tried stroking in rhythm to sea chanteys. I sang them in my head, which limited their effectiveness, but it worked for a while. Then the stops became more frequent and longer. I had headed instinctively toward shore when the boat was first attacked, but it was hard from sea level to judge how far I was from land.

I was almost at the end of my rope. I didn't know if I could swim another stroke. I stopped and sucked in gulps that were half seawater, which is when I felt the change in the motion of the seas. The water was lifting and taking me with it. I was in the grip of rollers, which meant I was close to the beach. I didn't know whether it was a false hope, but it gave me new energy. I struck out again. A wave lifted me. I swam harder. I could see lines of foam where the rollers were breaking toward shore.

I unsnapped the life jacket and slipped it off along with my sweatshirt. I held onto the flotation vest until a wave lifted me, then threw out one arm after another and rode the foaming crest of the breaking wave. I repeated the exercise again and again until I was only yards from the shore where the waves were breaking. I flailed with my last ounce of strength and my bare feet felt the gravelly bottom. The wave receded, leaving me on the wet sand. I crawled slowly up the slope until I had escaped the grip of the sea completely.

I lay on my belly, panting for breath like a beached flounder. Cold had seeped to every part of my body. I was shivering uncontrollably and my teeth clacked. Stripped to only my shorts and T-shirt, I could die of hypothermia if I didn't keep moving. I got up on my hands and knees, then pushed myself to a standing position. The time in the water had affected my equilibrium. I swayed dizzily for a minute or two before my head cleared. I struck inland, staggering drunkenly in the soft sand, which eventually gave way to beach grass. I discovered a path cutting through the dunes.

The path led through a strip of woods, then around a low, brush-covered hill, that rose from the scrub oak and pitch pine. I kept moving until I came to the edge of a lawn. I was happy to be walking on the clipped carpet of grass. Eventually, I came to the edge of a patio and saw the dark mass of a house. I could make out the outline of a tall rotunda against the starry sky. *Small world.* I was at Ramsey's McMansion.

I moved along the sea-facing side of the house, then around the end of one wing, toward the garage. I found a locked door that had glass panels. I picked up a flagstone from a walkway and broke a pane, then reached through to open the door. I thought I heard a footfall on the gravel drive, but when I listened, all was silent.

Three vehicles were parked inside. There was a Mercedes SUV, a Mercedes sedan and a Bentley. In all three cars, the keys were in the ignition. I picked the Bentley.

I got behind the wheel, started the engine and punched the *open* button on the car's remote. As the door lifted above the hood,

I hit the gas. Out of the corner of my eye, I saw two shadows swiftly moving in my direction. I nailed the accelerator and the car took off with spinning tires. I covered the ground to the entrance in seconds, clicked the remote control again and the gate swung open.

I turned the heater on full blast. My shivering subsided to a tremble, but reality set in.

I was driving a hot Bentley, I was barefoot and down to my underwear. I drove into town and parked the car on a quiet side street. I left the keys under the seat and made my way back to the MG using a roundabout route. I encountered a group of college kids, but they were so drunk they hardly noticed the half-naked guy trotting past them. I had learned the hard way never to take car keys out on a boat. The MG's keys were where I left them on top of the front right tire. The MG felt tiny after the Bentley, and the heater was puny, but I would have driven a roller skate at that point.

I climbed the stairs to my apartment fifteen minutes later. I peeled off my underwear and got under the hottest shower I could stand without blistering my skin. Then I changed into shorts and T-shirt and went out on the deck with an ale. As I reviewed my nautical adventures, I knew three things I didn't know before. That I was lucky to be alive. That whatever it was that sank my boat had something to do with Ramsey and Ivan. And that in my clumsy dumb way, I had stumbled into something very, very big.

CHAPTER 17

My chirpy new friends Mr. and Mrs. Cardinal woke me from a dead sleep around six o'clock the next morning. I had dined on warmed-up pasta from the night before, crawled under the sheets and fallen instantly into an exhausted sleep. After eight hours in the sack, I awoke rested and slightly less water-logged. My arms and legs ached, but my thoughts were more ordered. I brewed a pot of coffee and tried to figure out what I had accomplished besides sinking a nice boat and taking an unauthorized spin in a nice car.

Chernko and Ramsey were up to something nasty. That *something* had chased the boat down and attacked it, probing for soft spots until it found one. I remembered Sutcliffe's description about the whale attack against the *Moshup*. How the whale kept banging away until it broke the bow. This *thing*, whatever it was, had the same destructive mindset.

With the *Pequod II* on the bottom, at least there was no connection to me. Then the mental clouds parted and I let out a groan. The registration number on the upturned bow would have been clearly visible to eyes in the hovering chopper. With that number, the boat could be traced to Daggett. I was worried about Lisa if Chernko thought she was in the loop.

I told myself to settle down and get to work. I poured myself another cup of coffee and retrieved Flagg's folder from the top of the refrigerator. Inside was a packet of stapled pages. The cover page was labeled: *"Forensic Report on Volgatechnologi."* Volgatech for short. The next page described Volgatech as a state-owned holding company tied to military contracting and manufacturing. It owned dozens of groups formed to conduct applied research in science and technology. The holdings were worth billions.

The general director of Volgatech was Ivan Chernko. The report said that five years before he slipped into the director's chair, he allegedly was connected to the KGB, Russia's notorious intelligence service. It said, without explanation, that during this time he got his nickname, Ivan the Terrible. I tried not to think of the type of work he would have had to do to earn that honor in a hard-assed outfit like the KGB.

Earlier in his career, he had been the director of a number of arcane organizations that the report described as classic KGB covers. Volgatech sounded like a Russian version of venture capitalism. Like Ramsey, Chernko's outfit took over companies that were on the ropes and used them to expand his corporate reach.

Volgatech had been at the center of dozens of legal challenges, accusations of corruption and misappropriation of funds, patent infringement, and illegal transfer of state property. The report also said that Chernko had built a financial house of cards. Many of his investors were KGB fronts. But even with all the investments, a good percentage of the companies he supervised were on the verge of bankruptcy.

I finished the report and checked the time. Cousin Alex would arrive soon on the ferry. Before leaving for town, I gathered the notes from the conversation at Coffin's shop and tracked down the name of the scrimshaw dealer he had been talking to. I found his number through directory assistance and gave him a call. I told him I was a private investigator working on the Coffin case and said I'd like to talk to him about the scrimshaw collection Ab Coffin wanted to acquire for the museum. Mr. Mandel said he would be glad to meet with me. He gave me his New Bedford address and we agreed on a time later that day.

I thought about my conversation with Tanya. Using directory assistance again, I dialed the public affairs office of the Woods Hole Oceanographic Institution. Tanya thought she overheard Chernko mention the name Max. The nice young lady on the other end of the line looked through her directory, but couldn't find any scientist with that name. I got one of those rare brainstorms that somehow find their way between my ears.

"Do you have a corporate directory?" I said.

"Yes. Would that help?

"Maybe. Could you look under *M* and see if anything sounds like Max?"

"Be glad to. Just a sec. Hmm. I think I found it! Marine Autonomous Corporation."

MAC.

"Anything remotely similar in the listings?"

She went through the rest of the Ms. "*No.* Could the one I found be what you're looking for?"

Tanya's accent had thrown me off. "I'll give it a try. Do you have an address and phone number?"

I jotted the information down in my note pad and left the apartment. Lisa must have gotten a ride to the Serengeti to fetch her Jeep because it was in the driveway. It would be hard to look her in the eye at breakfast, knowing that I had scuttled her grandfather's boat. I left a note on the Jeep's steering wheel saying I had to tend to family business and would be off-island most of the day. As I was walking to the MG, Dr. Rosen came jogging down the driveway.

"Nice run?" I said, friendly-like.

He stopped and jogged in place. "Yeah." Puff. "Thanks." Puff.

"How's the captain doing? Find that white whale yet?"

"*Soon.*" Puff. He put his legs into gear and jogged off around the house.

I decided to check on Ahab when I got back.

On the drive into town, I wondered what kind of trouble Cousin Alex had gotten into. As a kid, Alex had chosen me as a surrogate for the big brother he never had. At weddings and funerals or other family gatherings, he followed me around like a puppy dog. Unlike his parents, I gave the obnoxious little brat a hard time when he screwed up. He admired my unconventional lifestyle, especially the private eye part, and the fact that I had broken away from our tight family circle. My mother had asked me to talk to him after he had run away from home when he was in his teens. She hoped I could make him what the Greeks call *ezginis*, which means civilized and well-mannered.

It would take some doing. Alex was living on Cape Cod with a bunch of druggies. He would have been scooped up in a police bust if I hadn't saved him. I gave him a verbal spanking and sent him home. The close call scared him into civility.

I stopped at a coffee shop in town and ordered fried eggs and ham that at Nantucket prices cost what I would have paid for dinner at a five-star restaurant on the mainland. The eggs were overdone, but what the heck, I was fortified when I strolled over to the ferry dock. The *Volga* had returned and was tied up in its usual place at the end of the dock. I was tempted to hook up with Tanya and ask her how Ivan was this morning, but decided that I had already pushed my luck the night before.

I hadn't seen Alex in a couple of years and was unprepared when the handsome young man in the tan cotton sports jacket stepped off the high-speed ferry and walked in my direction. I say handsome with a hint of self-interest because the cute, raisin-eyed little charmer I used to knock around as a kid looked a lot like a younger me. Same dark eyes and smart-ass grin. Same thick dark brown hair, only his didn't have the gray specks in it.

He gave me a big hug. "Cousin Soc. Wonderful to see you. You're looking great!"

"You learned the art of flattery well in law school, I see."

He threw his head back and laughed. "Still cutting me down to size, Soc. I'm telling the truth. You look terrific."

I ruffled his hair for old times and suggested that we grab a cup of coffee at the restaurant on the dock. I asked him about his wife and kids. They were doing great, he said, and pulled some pictures out of his wallet. Little Aristotle was a handsome kid and his sister was beautiful. He beamed when I told him.

We made small talk, and then I said, "My mother said you need help. She was doing the mysterious Cretan thing and was short on details."

"How'd she know I needed help?"

"Cretan radar. Nothing in the family escapes her attention. What's going on, cousin?"

He took a deep breath and slowly let it out. "You remember a guy named Chili?"

I dug into the mists of my memory. "Yeah. Stocky guy with lots of X-rated tattoos. Twitchy cokehead you ran with before I dragged you away by the scruff of the neck."

He grimaced as if he had a stomach pain. "*That's* him. Well, Chili is back. He's been in jail since you met him. He's out now. He contacted me a few weeks ago."

I raised an eyebrow. "What's the little sleazebag want from *you*?"

"He's picked up where he left off before he went to jail. He wants me to set up a laundering operation so he won't get caught again."

"And you told him go to pound tar?"

Alex leaned forward. He had that stomachache face again. "I told him I'd think about it. He wants an answer by the end of the week." He saw me open my mouth and raised his hand in a stop gesture. "Before you jump down my throat, listen to what he said. He'll spread the word about me being involved with drugs."

"That was a long time ago."

"I *know* that. But he says he'll splice the old story onto more recent deals he knows about. Soc, if he does that I could lose my license to practice law. Doesn't matter if it's true or not. I could be disbarred. It'll kill my family."

"Calm down, Alex. Let's hash this thing out. Does anyone else know about this?"

"No. He contacted me at my office. Used a phony name."

"Where is the little darling now?"

He shook his head. "You won't believe it. *Nantucket.* That's why I jumped at the chance to see you when I learned you were here."

"Chili doesn't strike me as the kind of guy you'd see at an island garden party."

"The island has a big drug problem. Just ask the cops. Oxycontin mostly. Hundreds of workers wait on tables, wash dishes or mow lawns. Think of all the nationalities. They come from all over the world. It's the perfect set-up to move stuff in and out."

"Trouble in paradise," I mused. "Okay. How can I help? Want me to talk to Chili again?"

"I don't know. He's not just a punk like before. Prison has made him a hardened criminal. He's a lot more dangerous. Don't take this as an insult, but you're, uh—"

"Spit it out, Alex. Long in the tooth. Over the hill. One foot on a banana peel."

"Sorry, Soc. Didn't mean it to come out like that, but you'll have to admit that you're a little older than last time."

"Only thing I'll admit to is not running the hundred yard dash in less than ten seconds. Look, Alex, if it were all brawn, I'd have been dead a long time ago. Tell me what you know about Chili's island operation."

Alex said Chili had bragged about his cover. He was working

a kitchen job at a big hotel. It gave him cover and he could hire accomplices he'd met in prison. No one paid any attention to dishwashers and prep cooks or thought anything about people coming and going at all hours. Chili had smartened up since the old days. Spending time in a cell does wonders to focus the mind. I said I would scout out the situation and see what I could learn. I suggested that he stall Chili for a few days.

"You're a lawyer. You must be good at delay."

"I'll do what I can, Soc. Thanks for everything. I knew I could count on you. How's the fishing business going with your new boat?"

"A little slow right now. I thought I'd use the time to work on a murder case." I glanced at my watch. "I've got to catch a ferry to the mainland. Want to go back together?"

He looked around. "I dunno. I haven't been on Nantucket for years. Maybe I'll walk around town and catch the next boat out."

I cuffed him lightly on the head the way I used to when he was a kid.

"Okay. Just behave yourself."

He grinned like a kid I remembered. "Not a problem, Soc."

I hurried toward the ferry dock, intent on catching the boat before it left. Otherwise, I might have remembered something important. Alex and I looked like younger and older versions of ourselves, but we had more in common than physical resemblance. We were both human lightning rods for trouble.

CHAPTER 18

The city of New Bedford is about a one hour drive from the ferry terminal in Hyannis. The National Park Service has carved a historic district out of several square blocks of the old neighborhood that used to be the nerve center for the most efficient whale-killing machine on the planet. I parked the pick-up near a granite Greek revival building that houses the city's whaling museum.

The museum is on Johnnycake Hill, where Herman Melville once trod, absorbing atmosphere for *Moby Dick*. I walked past the Seaman's Bethel and imagined Ishmael and Queequeg sitting in a pew, listening to Father Mappel sermonizing about Jonah and the whale, surrounded by marble wall tablets memorializing whalers killed by whales or lost at sea.

Mandel's antique shop was a couple of blocks beyond the Bethel in a refurbished mercantile building. A pleasant young woman who said she was Mandel's assistant ushered me past showcases filled with relics of the city's maritime trade and to an upstairs office. Mandel was sitting in front of a computer. He got up from behind his desk and came over to shake hands.

The antiques dealer was a trim man who might have been in his seventies. He wore a dark brown suit and a yellow power tie. With his thick mane of white hair, prominent nose and narrow face, he reminded me of a bald eagle. He led the way to a sofa and chairs and told me to have a seat. His assistant brought us an antique porcelain teapot and cups.

As he poured the tea, Mandel said, "You mentioned on the phone that you were a private investigator."

"That's right. I formerly worked for the Boston police department."

"I hire investigators from time-to-time to do background checks on buyers and sellers. In this business it's a good thing to know with whom you're dealing."

He mentioned the names of a couple of Boston cops who had acquired their PI license after retirement. I said that I knew them both from my Boston days and that he had chosen well.

Mandel's watchful black eyes studied me through round metal-rimmed glasses, studying me as if he were peering through a magnifying glass at an antique artifact.

"Well, Mr. Socarides, how may I be of help?"

"I'd like to hear what you know about the scrimshaw collection that Ab Coffin wanted the Nantucket museum to buy."

"Ah, a fascinating story." He leaned back in his chair and tented his fingers. "I've known Ab for a long time. We attended the whaling museum's annual scrimshaw weekends together. He was incredibly knowledgeable in what was comparatively a new field of academic inquiry."

"*New?* I thought scrimshaw went back a hundred or so years."

"That's correct. But the *study* of scrimshaw only dates back to the 1960s. Our knowledge of the art form has advanced quickly, however. Unlike many antiques, scrimshaw has wonderful provenance. Most museum collections were donated by families that had whaler-scrimshaw artists in their family tree. Often you know not only who *carved* the scrimshaw but what ship and voyage the artist was on when he did it. Ab became excited whenever he encountered Coffin work. He was very proud of his ancestor."

"He had reason to be proud. I saw examples of Obed Coffin's carvings in his Nantucket shop. He was a genius at what he did."

Mandel nodded in agreement. "I'd say that Coffin ranked with perhaps the greatest scrimshander of all time, a Plymouth man named N.S. Finney. Like Coffin, he'd served on whaling ships, but once he went ashore, he stayed there. Both men carved ivory commercially. Up to that point, scrimshaw was the product of bored whale men who had time on their hands. Whaling ships tended to be over-manned. You only needed a dozen or so crew to sail a ship, but more than twenty to thirty men to hunt whales and process the oil. The voyages were two to three years long. Contrary to what people think, many whalers were educated, so their art was sometimes quite sophisticated. Coffin took his art a step further than Finney."

"In what way?"

"Both were copyists and didn't do much in the way of original images. They carved a lot of commission work. But Coffin was more of a transitional artist than Finney. I'll show you."

He got up and walked over to a bookshelf. He pulled down three loose-leaf notebooks which he opened and spread out on the table. The clear plastic pages held color photographs of scrimshaw specimens. "These are Finney pieces. As you can see, they had a precise photographic style." He picked up another notebook. "These pieces were done by a much later artist in the more modern style. Around 1950. The lines are more fluid, and the images are three-dimensional. They are done from different angles rather than straight on. You can see that they are full of action and verve."

I picked up the notebook labeled: **Coffin** and leafed through the pages. "These look like a combination of both styles."

"Good eye, Mr. Socarides. Coffin bridged the art form between the traditional and the modern."

The carvings in the photos were romanticized images of men

and women in fancy dress, portraits of male and female subjects, children and symbolic figures representing liberty and freedom. Mandel pointed to the little coffin carved in the base of each piece and said it was the artist's signature.

"*Interesting*," I said. "There isn't one piece here that has anything to do with whaling or the sea."

"You *do* have a good eye. That's correct. Coffin made a few pieces with whaling scenes when he was on shipboard, but after his horrible ordeal he wanted nothing to do with the sea. Which was why I was skeptical about the pieces Ab wanted to acquire for the museum."

"What can you tell me about the collection?"

"It's quite the story. Last February a man named Gerhard Warner came into my office. Warner has a shop on the other side of Johnnycake Hill." Mandel paused for emphasis. "He doesn't have the best reputation."

"Why is that, Mr. Mandel?"

"He's been caught with specimens that have proved later to be stolen property. He's a slippery individual and has always had a paper trail that exonerates him. Anyhow, he said he had a number of rare pieces of Coffin's work having to do with his whaling days."

"Did he say where he got them?"

"He said they were part of a collection of some sixty pieces of Coffin scrimshaw. Coffin was down on his luck and when he died, his estate was not probated. The pieces went off at auction to pay the bills and were scooped up by a collector, now deceased, whose family was trying to sell them.

"As you correctly observed, Coffin stayed away from whaling themes. I told Warner it sounded like a cock-and-bull story and threw him out of my office without even looking at his catalog. The matter should have ended there."

"But it didn't?"

"Unfortunately, no. Ab and I were at a conference and I

mentioned Warner's visit to him in passing. He became extremely excited and wanted to follow up. I cautioned him about Warner's reputation, but he didn't care. He said that it wouldn't hurt to check out the collection."

"And did he?"

"He contacted Warner and actually saw the collection. He came to my shop raving about it. Particularly one piece."

"Did he describe the piece?"

"No. Only that a lot of heads would explode if he could acquire it and that his namesake would jump out of his grave."

"That's a strong reaction from a piece of carved whalebone. Did he give any details?"

"He was very tight-lipped. He said only that he had offered to buy the piece, but Warner refused, saying his source wanted to sell the collection as a whole."

"Is that when Ab approached the trustees at the Nantucket whaling museum?"

"*Correct.* He tried to persuade the board to approve the sale, but to no avail. The museum already has one of the biggest scrimshaw collections in the world and the board didn't like the clouded background of the collection. One board member did some research that suggested the collection may have been stolen from its owner many years ago."

"From what I understand, Coffin thought he could change Daggett's mind. How did he intend to do that?"

"Simple. He was going to show him a special piece from the collection."

"I thought Warner wanted to sell the whole thing."

"He *did*, but Ab managed to borrow a piece. He had to pay Warner a substantial "viewing" fee. Supposedly as insurance. He took out an equity loan on his house and shop to do it. He had persuaded Warner that the deal would go through if he could use this one specimen as leverage."

GREY LADY

"That fits with what I know. Coffin told Daggett he would show him something he that would change his mind. I read the police report. There was no mention of scrimshaw being found. It seems to have mysteriously disappeared."

"Too bad," Mandel said. "It could prove important."

"That's what I think. How would I get in touch with Warner?"

"You could try his shop, but he's rarely there."

He gave me directions and I thanked him for his time. I walked a block or so through the historical district and found Warner's shop. The door was locked. I peeked through the windows, but the place was dark. Tucked in a corner of the window was an index card with the words By Appointment Only printed in ballpoint on it. There was also a telephone number.

I jotted the number down in my notepad and went back to Mandel's shop. He didn't seem surprised to hear that the shop was closed. I asked if I could use a telephone to call the number. I got a recorded message and left my name and Nantucket number. I told Mandel that I would let him know if anything turned up and he said he'd do the same with me.

Before I left he said, "*You're* the detective, Mr. Socarides. What do you think happened to this missing scrimshaw piece?"

"I don't know, Mr. Mandel, but there is one thing I'm absolutely sure of."

"What's that?"

"The scrimshaw didn't walk out of the museum on its own."

CHAPTER 19

You can practically spit from one end of Woods Hole's main drag to the other, but appearances can be deceiving. The quaint little village on Vineyard Sound is known around the world as a center for ocean science. The dock off Water Street is home to the ship that carried the submersible *Alvin* to its *Titanic* discovery. From the same dock, research vessels sail far and wide to probe the oceans around the globe. The dynamo driving this research is the Woods Hole Oceanographic Institution, or *WHOI* for short. The locals simply call it "Whooey." The institution is a magnet for government and research money and dozens of underwater tech labs have sprung up close to Woods Hole like pilot fish around a shark.

I tracked down the Marine Autonomous Corporation on a back road a few miles from Woods Hole harbor. The black sign marking the lab was about a foot square and the white letters spelling out MAC were so small that I almost went past the entrance. I jammed on the brakes, backed up and drove down a hard clay driveway until I came to a No Trespassing sign. I wheeled the truck around in position for a quick getaway and pulled off to the side. I grabbed a pair of binoculars from the glove box, got out and crunched through the forest of scrub oak and stunted pitch pine. After walking a couple of hundred feet, I saw the glint of metal through the trees.

The reflection was sunlight bouncing off coils of razor wire topping a chain link fence. A surveillance camera angled down from a post on one side of a closed gate. A red light glowed on the camera, indicating that it was on. There were other working cameras on the fence itself, all probably motion-activated, as would be the floodlights spaced along the perimeter.

I made my way back to the pick-up. Stored in the fiberglass storage box behind the cab was a duffel bag. Possessing the contents of the bag would merit an arrest in most jurisdictions. The bag's former owner was sent away to a bad boy home and didn't need his burglar tools any more. A green plastic trash bag had been sitting in the back of the truck, destined for the dump. I emptied out the empty beer cans, cut eye and arm holes with my Swiss army knife, and pulled the bag over my head, down to my hips.

It wasn't a cloak of invisibility. And it smelled of yeast from the beer cans. But it would do the job. The cameras would record my trespass, but they wouldn't show my handsome mug. I slung the duffel over my shoulder and followed the driveway to the gate. I waved my arms at the camera's glass eye and waited for a reaction. Then I listened, ready to bolt back to my truck and make a run for it.

Five minutes passed. The woods were still except for the twitter of the birds. I decided to chance an entry. With the metal cutters from the duffel, I snipped the mesh and cut a hole just big enough for me to crawl through. Once on the other side of the fence, I slipped the trash bag off and put it in the duffel. I started walking. The driveway led to an aluminum-sided building. No cars or trucks were parked in the paved lot near the building. I walked directly to the entrance and saw that it was padlocked.

I circled the building and found two more locked doors. Back at the main entrance, I got out a set of picks from the bag. The padlock didn't stand a chance. I turned the knob and pushed the door open. A damp musty odor of mold welled out and smacked me in the face.

I tried a wall switch. Rows of fluorescent ceiling lights blinked on.

The interior was basically a big windowless room. The side opposite the entrance was lined with cubicles. A rectangular pool around twenty-feet-deep took up much of the floor in between. A motor hoist with a hook attached ran along the ceiling above the empty pool.

I walked around the pool to the cubicles. One space was at least three times the size of the others. Folding metal chairs faced a white display board on an easel. The board was covered with squiggles and equations. Taped to the wall behind the easel were photographs of bees swarming around a hive, ants clustered on an anthill, flocking birds and a school of tropical fish.

The cubicles had all been cleaned out. But in one, I found a sheet of paper on the floor. The electric bill was dated more than a month earlier and marked *paid* over the signature of Sean Malloy. I folded the bill and tucked it in my pocket, then went over to a bin that looked like a lumber stall in Home Depot. A sheet of plywood stood upright in the bin alongside rectangles of different material, all around five-by-five feet in size. I tugged at the plywood. The sheet was a lacework of layered wood and a piece came loose in my hand.

Leaning against the plywood was a fiberglass sheet around a half-inch thick. The sheet was peppered with holes as if it had been used for machine gun practice. There was also a plate of half-inch steel covered with dozens of dents on one side and goose bumps on the other. Above the bin was a motor and cable arrangement that would have allowed the sheets of material to be moved to the pool.

I glanced at the nature photos on the wall, wondering if there was something I had missed, then I took a last look around and headed for the door. The fresh air felt good after the musty interior. I refastened the padlock and trotted back to the hole in the fence. Before I crawled through, I shimmied into the plastic bag. Moments later, I was back at the truck where I removed the bag. I drove onto the road and headed to the Hyannis ferry terminal. The big car ferry *Iyanough*, run by the steamship authority, was the next boat to Nantucket. I got on board after a short wait and climbed to the cafeteria deck where I bought a cup of coffee and took it to a window seat.

The view of the blue-green sea had a calming effect and after a while, the thoughts stopped bouncing around in my skull. I spread a paper napkin out on the table and with a ballpoint pen drew a triangle. At the points, I printed the words **Ramsey, Ivan** and **MAC**. In the center of the diagram I drew a picture of a sinking boat. Nothing jumped out at me. I turned the napkin over and drew another triangle. This time I labeled the angles **Coffin, Daggett** and **Swain**. In the center of the triangle I wrote the word **Scrimshaw** with a big question mark over it. I stared at the diagram. Nothing again. I folded the napkin and tucked it into my shirt pocket with MAC's power bill.

After the ferry landed in Nantucket, I walked over to Lisa's office. She was on the phone. She waved and pointed to a chair. As she talked, I studied her face, marveling at the smoothness of her unblemished mocha skin and the animation of her mouth and eyebrows. I decided that I liked Lisa very, very much. It went beyond physical attraction. She was a class act.

She hung up a minute later and gave me a warm smile.

"Sorry to keep you waiting, Soc. That was someone from the land trust."

"No apology necessary. Thought you'd like to hear about my trip to New Bedford."

I told her what Mandel had said about Warner and the collection he was peddling.

"What you seem to be saying is that this missing piece of scrimshaw could be the key piece to the whole puzzle," she said.

"It does seem to be a common denominator." I ticked off the points on my fingertips. "Coffin and your grandfather argued over the collection. Coffin felt something in the collection could exonerate his ancestor. And the scrimshaw was the reason for the meeting at the museum that ended so badly."

"Then we have to talk to Warner."

"I tried. He didn't answer. From what Mandel told me, Mr. Warner is a slippery fish, but there may be a way to lure him in."

I outlined what I had in mind. Lisa didn't hesitate when I gave her Warner's telephone number. She snapped up the phone and called him. She got his recorded message.

"Hello, Mr. Warner," she said. "My name is Lisa Hendricks. I'm an attorney and I'm acting as agent for Mr. Socarides, who tried to contact you earlier. He asked me to stress that he is *very* interested in the Coffin scrimshaw collection and that money is no object. Please call me at your earliest convenience."

After she hung up I said, "Not bad."

The satisfied smile faded from her lips. "On that other matter. The incident out at the Serengeti. Have you made any progress?"

"I'm still assembling the dots. Once I do that, I have to find a way to connect them. In the meantime, it might be wise for you to keep your distance from me."

"That would be very difficult," she said. She must have noticed my raised eyebrow, because she quickly added, "Especially where we're living side-by-side." She didn't like the sound of that either. "Oh, you know what I mean."

"The offer to move out still stands."

She pursed her lips and gave her head a slow shake. "I need you where I can reach you. Dear God. I can't seem to get it right."

Seeing her embarrassment, I glanced off at one of the conservation maps taped to the walls. She had explained at our first meeting that the maps were color-coded to designate land tracts as private, public conservation and property under discussion.

"Isn't that Ramsey's property in the conservation trust holdings?"

"That's an old map. The trust had hoped to acquire the property, but the deal fell apart."

"Too bad. How did Ramsey acquire it?"

She made a sour face. "It's a long story." Before she could tell me, the phone rang. She answered it, then covered the mouthpiece. "I'm going to be tied up for a while. Dinner later?"

"It would be a pleasure. Want me to cook again?"

A pained look came to her face. "Not really. Let's meet in about an hour." She jotted down an address on a pad and ripped off a page for me. "This is where Lillian lives. She can tell you the whole story."

"Ms. Mayhew is familiar with the property?"

"*More* than familiar. The Mayhew family *owned* the land for more than two hundred years. It's still called Mayhew Point."

From Lisa's office it was a short walk to India Street where Lillian lived in a two-and-a-half-story white captain's house topped with a cupola. I climbed to the veranda and rang the doorbell. No one answered. A blue antique Ford beach wagon was parked in the driveway. I left the porch and walked around back. Lillian was bending over in a vegetable garden with her rear end facing me.

I walked up behind her and said, "Nice tomatoes."

She stood and turned, trowel in hand. She looked startled, and then the glimmer of recognition came to her eyes. I gave her a little help.

"My name is Socarides. We met at the cocktail party."

"Oh, *yes*. You were with Lisa." Slowly, the ghost of a smile came to her lips. "I assume you were talking about my plants just now. In any event, thank you. But if you really want to flatter a woman, don't approach when she has her hind-most parts in the air."

"I'll remember that, Ms. Mayhew."

"Call me Lillian if you will, Mr. Socarides."

"And please call me by my nickname. *Soc.*"

She tucked her trowel into a belt holster and stepped out of the garden onto the lawn. She was dressed in a loose, long-sleeved peasant's blouse and baggy, knee-length slacks. On her head was a wide-brimmed Shaker style straw hat. She settled into an Adirondack chair and invited me to sit in the one beside her.

"Well, Soc. How may I help you?"

"I was at Lisa's office a while ago. We got to talking about Ramsey's property."

Her blue eyes blazed like cold light lasers. "In my family, we still call it Mayhew Point."

I had touched a sore spot. "How did Ramsey acquire your family's property?"

"*Indirectly*," she said with unveiled contempt in her voice. "It was taken by the Navy years ago. They used it for some sort of hush-hush work during the Cold War. Something to do with spying on the Soviets, I believe. When the Cold War ended, the Navy abandoned the property, but retained ownership."

"Did your family ever offer to buy it back?"

"The Mayhew family long ago lost the fortune it had made in whale oil. Bad investments and bad luck. We suggested that the Navy turn it over to the conservation trust. They refused, saying the government planned to hold on to it. The next thing anyone knew, Ramsey was building that monstrous monument to his ego. That's the first we knew the navy had sold it."

"The ownership passed from the Navy to Ramsey?"

"*Evidently*," she said. "Don't ask me how or why. It just did."

"Did the Navy say why it changed its mind?"

"I must have talked to a dozen people. The closest I could get to an answer was that the decision was made 'higher up.' "

I ran through the scenarios in my head. Bribery. Political favor. Old school tie. There were probably a dozen ways Ramsey could have weaseled choice waterfront property from Uncle Sam and they all smelled to high heaven. I could see too why Lillian was afraid Ramsey would acquire Lisa in the same inexplicable way.

"I'm very sorry at the way things turned out."

"Thank you. May I ask why you are so interested in Mayhew Point?"

Lillian was no dummy. She'd never believe me if I told her it was idle curiosity.

Deflecting the question, I said, "I'm more interested in Ramsey's business associate. The man who came in by helicopter."

She wrinkled her nose as if her nostrils had picked up a foul odor. "I left directly after that. I'm confused. I thought you were hired to help Lisa defend her grandfather."

"That's right. This is unrelated to Mr. Daggett."

I don't know if she believed me, but she gave me a quick, knowing smile. "How is Henry doing?"

"Still thinks he's Ahab."

She stared off into the distance.

I pushed myself up from the chair and said, "Thank you, Ms—I mean, Lillian."

The frown on her lips changed to a smile. She stood and unsheathed her trowel. "And thank you for helping Lisa and Henry, Mr. Starbuck. I can see that they are in good hands."

I wanted to tell her that those hands were a little shaky after their owner had been shot at and almost drowned. I promised I would do what I could, said my goodbyes and headed back to town. I put aside my self-pledge to stay sober, rationalizing that alcohol would help me think. I headed to a local hang-out called the Rose and Crown.

The place was busy with the after-beach crowd. I squeezed up to the bar and ordered a beer. The college kid tending bar looked at me as if I were the good gunslinger about to ask for a sarsaparilla in an Old West saloon.

"Is there a problem?" I said.

"This is *incredible!*" he said. "Guy just left here could have been your son or brother. He looked just like you. Except a lot younger."

"Did you happen to catch his name?"

"Oh yeah. Said his name was Alex and that he was a lawyer."

"Cancel my order," I told the bartender. Then I headed for the door.

The hotel Chili was using for his drug operation was a couple of blocks from Water Street. It was an old ark of a place that had been renovated at great cost to accommodate guests who wanted to do more than sit fully-dressed in a rocking chair and take in the sea air. There were a couple of benches set on the sidewalk facing the hotel, and sitting in one of them was Cousin Alex. He was reading a newspaper, occasionally glancing over or around it.

I snuck up behind him and yanked the paper from his hands. Then I ripped out a hole in one of the pages, sat down and shoved the paper back to him. "Now you won't have to keep looking over and around the paper," I said.

"Hey, Soc—"

"You told me you were going to leave the island."

"I had every intention, but I as I walked around I thought that I shouldn't hang this all on you. I could help. Maybe I'd see something that you can use."

"Your intentions are noble, Alex, but this is way out of your league. You're—"

"Wait, Soc. It's *Chili!*"

I grabbed the paper page and raised it to my face. Through the ragged hole I saw three men emerge from the service entrance. One man had the husky physique I remembered from Alex's old drug supplier. He said something to the other men, then they left and walked toward the harbor. One man was tall. The other was short. Sergei and Pitir. Maybe I shouldn't have been so harsh with Alex. Thanks to my nephew, I had had just learned that Chili the drug dealer was pals with Ivan's goons.

CHAPTER 20

Alex and I sat without speaking at a table amid the noisy crowd at the Rose and Crown. We were like a couple in need of marriage counseling. Ten minutes earlier, he tried to thank me for buying the round of beers. I told him to shut up. I wanted to think. I sipped my mug, letting the cold liquid trickle down my throat, while I laid out a mental checklist of what I knew. Chili was in the drug business. Human torch impersonator Viktor Karpov *had* been in the drug business. The goons who may have killed Karpov worked for Ivan, and they knew Chili.

Ivan was a KGB guy by trade. He would know that his muscle guys were dabbling in pharmaceuticals. But that didn't make sense. Why would a wealthy businessman risk his fortunes by pushing drugs? I thought back to the Volgatech report that Flagg loaned me. Ivan controlled a pile of companies, but many had gone belly up. In a standard business deal, the creditors have to wait in line to get their pennies on a dollar. Ivan's investors were likely his pals in the KGB. What if he had leveraged money from his pals into his investments?

Hey, Boris, do I have a deal for you!

Ivan could be in hock for debts owed to some very tough guys.

Hey, Boris. About that money I owe you.

It takes a lot of rubles to maintain a big yacht and a helicopter. Maybe that's why Ivan had cut corners and hired a couple of low-budget hoods rather than ex-KGB bone-crushers who'd be more professional, but more aware of his failing fortunes. In that context, the change Ivan could pick up from the drug trade might come in handy. A million here, a million there, and pretty soon you're talking real money. He could tread water until a piece of wreckage drifted by for him to cling to.

That possibly explained Ivan's dealings. What about Ramsey? His MO was similar to Ivan's. Borrow money and leverage the risk. If his fortunes were tied closely to the Russian's business flops, Ramsey too could be in big trouble. I couldn't see Ramsey pushing drugs, but he and Ivan were definitely up to something that could save their asses. And it had to do with MAC.

I drained my beer mug. "Okay, Alex. *Now* you may talk."

He smiled with relief. "What's going on, Soc? You rip my newspaper to shreds and ream me out. Then you put your arm around me and buy me a beer. What gives?"

"I'll spell it out for you, dear cousin. This is no longer a simple drug case. We, you and I, have stepped into a big pile of horse manure. The situation is far more dangerous and complex than either one of us could have imagined. Those two guys Chili was talking to are bad, in a very big way. The last guy to annoy their boss, they tied to a tree, poured gasoline on his head and made a one-man bonfire out of him."

Alex put his mug down on the table. I was pleased to see a healthy look of fear in his eyes. "You've got my attention," he croaked.

I laid my hand on his shoulder. "*Good.* Now here's the deal. I'm like a one-armed juggler. It's only a matter of time before I drop a ball. I can't help you if you get into trouble. But you can help *me* by doing what I ask."

174

"Okay. I understand. I think. What do you want me to do?"

"You want to play detective? This is how you do it. Go back to your office and start researching someone named Michael Ramsey. He's a venture capitalist. Dig out every nugget of information you can. Mostly, I want to know if he is as rich as he wants people to think he is."

Alex took a pad from his pocket and jotted down some notes. "I know people in the financial business I can talk to."

"Just be careful what you say to them. I don't want this getting back to Ramsey. Next, I want you to research a scientist named Sean Malloy. He owns a company named Marine Autonomous Corporation. MAC for short. It's near Woods Hole. When you dig out the information on these gentlemen, call me. If I'm not there, leave a message."

He made some more notes. "Is that it?"

I reached in my pocket and pulled out the ferry schedules. "That's it. The Steamship Authority boat leaves in twenty minutes. Go."

He gave me a handshake and a hug, then made a fast exit from the bar. I sipped my mug. My beer had gone flat, but I drank it anyhow. A few minutes later, I was in the MG heading toward Siasconset. Maybe it was time to check in on my client again.

The front door of the Daggett house was unlocked. I went in and heard shouting from the second floor. I climbed the stairs and followed the voices to Daggett's living quarters.

I pressed my ear to the thick wooden door. Rosen was speaking in a loud voice. I caught the word Starbuck uttered a few times, then something about a mutiny. I couldn't hear everything because a voice that was clearly Daggett's was shouting over Rosen's. The voices were getting louder. The temperature of the argument was definitely rising. I heard Rosen shout again. Nearer the door this time.

I edged down the hallway and hid in a linen closet. Daggett's door opened and shut. I heard Rosen laughing as he walked by my hiding place. I waited a couple of minutes, then emerged from my cubbyhole and knocked softly on Daggett's door.

He didn't answer right away. When he did, his voice was hoarse. "*Aye*," was all that he said.

"It's *Starbuck*, Captain Ahab."

Another pause. "Starbuck the *traitor*?"

Something had changed since my last visit. "No," I said. "Starbuck your first mate and friend, sir."

"What doest thou want?" He sounded almost fearful.

"Would the captain have time for a gam, sir?"

No sailor could miss out on a chance to exchange gossip. "A gam, yes. But come alone. And *unarmed*."

"As you wish, Captain."

I slowly turned the knob and pushed the door open. The captain stood facing me on the upraised floor in front of the big windows. He was holding his brass spyglass in two hands as if he were about to take a swing at a fast ball. His face was contorted in anger.

I stopped. "Permission to approach the quarterdeck, Captain Ahab."

"Granted, but do it slowly and stay where I can keep an eye on thee."

I advanced to within a couple of yards of the raised platform floor.

"Halt!" Daggett said. "Show thy hands. I'll have no weapons on my deck." He gripped the spyglass.

I spread my palms wide apart. "Why would I have a weapon?"

"*Mutiny*! Treachery. Murder most foul. 'Tis not the first time I've had to stove in the skull of a forecastle pirate who thinks he can take my ship from under my one good leg. It's a flogging and bread and water for any man who follows the lead of a mutineer."

"And I will stand by your side as your first officer. No one will take the *Pequod* from thee without a fight."

Doubt flickered in the angry eyes. "He said you were a traitor. That thou hast taken the side of the white whale that lopped my leg off and made me a poor limping cripple."

"Who said that, Captain?" I already knew the answer to the question.

"That scurvy forecastle hand who brings me my midday meal."

"Who would thou believe, Captain? A scurvy hand or your first mate?"

"Thou doubted me before, Starbuck. Thou couldst doubt me again."

"*Never*, Captain. My harpoon awaits to strike the white whale. Hast thou found him?"

The fire went out of his eyes. "*Aye*, Starbuck. Soon his carcass will be food for the sharks and we will be on our way back to Nantucket with the oil of the accursed creature cramming our holds."

He stepped off the raised floor and beckoned me to his chart table. Setting the spyglass down, he pointed to a chart of the Pacific. The ship's course was about to intersect with the path of Moby Dick. I tried to leverage Daggett's fantasy.

"There will be plenty of teeth for the crew to carve, Captain. Coffin will tell our story in ivory for those who await us in Nantucket."

Daggett looked nonplussed. "Who is this Coffin ye speak of?"

"The finest scrimshander on the ship, Captain."

He rubbed his forehead. "Of *course*. None finer. But what of the mutiny?"

"There *is* no mutiny, Captain. The men are ready to follow you to the jaws of hell."

The manic grin returned to his lips.

"Then get thee to thy duties, Starbuck. Tell the men that Ahab has ordered an extra round of grog." With new energy in his voice, he said. "And tell them that two days hence Moby Dick will pull us on a Nantucket sleigh-ride like no other." He was shouting now. "*Tell* them, Starbuck! And give the lads extra rations too, so they have the strength that will allow them to hurl their harpoons like lightning bolts and drive the lances into the heart of the beast!"

The door to the captain's quarters suddenly flew open. Dr. Rosen stepped in. "What are you doing here?" he said.

"Captain Ahab and I were chatting about the metaphorical aspects of Herman Melville's writing. See you later, Captain."

Rosen stared at Daggett's beaming face, then he followed me out into the hallway and slammed the door behind him.

"This man is under *my* care, Socarides. You are to stay away from him."

"Sorry, Dr. Rosen. You're only a deck hand. As first mate of the *Pequod*, I take my marching orders from Captain Ahab."

He stuck his jaw inches from mine. Dr. Rosen was younger than me, and his body hadn't been dissipated by my attempts to keep the breweries working a twenty-four-hour shift. He could have broken me apart. I'm a great believer in the adage that a kick in the crotch makes all men the same size. I tensed my knee for an upward swing. My calm smile must have warned Rosen that I had something in mind, because he backed off.

"You're a dead man," he said.

He spun on his heel and stalked off down the hallway. I let out the breath I'd been holding, and left the house. Rosen was nowhere to be seen. I hoped he was running off his anger, but I didn't really care. What's one more enemy, more or less?

Lisa wasn't happy after I ratted out Rosen for getting Daggett upset.

"I'm going to fire that man. He's nothing but a quack and he hasn't done a thing to help my grandfather. Now he's poisoning his mind. What in god's name was he up to?"

We were sitting on the deck of a harbor side restaurant where we'd gone for dinner.

"We haven't been pals since I questioned his treatment methods over breakfast. But it's obvious that he's trying to keep your grandfather in his confused state."

"Which is all the more reason to fire him."

I put my hand on hers. "Not yet. I want to keep him around until I figure out his connection to Ramsey."

"But in the meantime, he is damaging my grandfather and preventing his chances for a recovery."

"Then tell him that you know what has been going on. He'll say that I'm lying about it, but if he knows you're onto him, he'll back off. He'll go to Ramsey for marching orders."

"That's something else that has me puzzled. Why would Michael want to harm my grandfather? It makes no sense."

"It will in time, Lisa. We learn something new every day. Speaking of Ramsey, Lillian filled me in on the shell game the Navy played with her family land."

"It was absolutely heart-breaking. Lillian knew every square inch of the property. She took me there a number of times to show me where she played as a girl."

"Wondered if I could borrow a map of Mayhew Point."

"Why do you ask?"

"The Navy angle intrigues me. I'd like to take a closer look around, but I don't see any more cocktail party invitations in my future."

"I can show you how to get onto the property without anyone knowing. The point is flanked by extensive marshland and creeks. There used to be a bridge across one of the marshes. It's rotted away, but it can still be used to get to the property."

"Will you show me how to get there later tonight?"

She pinned me with her gaze. "How will roaming around

Ramsey's estate in the dark help my grandfather?"

"I can't answer that question, Lisa. I've never been wrong when I've followed my gut. And I have a gut feeling that practically everything I've learned about this case is connected to everything else. Ramsey seems to have a strong interest in your grandfather. Maybe it's time for *us* to have an equally strong interest in Ramsey."

"That's good enough for me," she said in a determined tone. "Where do we start?"

CHAPTER 21

Zero hour was set for nine o'clock.

The plan was simple. Lisa would go home and check on her grandfather. She'd make a point of telling Rosen that she had to attend a conservation trust meeting. We'd rendezvous around eight-thirty. She gave me the key to her office. I asked her to grab my duffel bag from the apartment.

From the restaurant, I walked a few blocks to the hotel Alex had staked out. I thought about sitting on the bench, but it was washed by headlights every time a car came around the corner. I hid instead in the shadows of a shop doorway where I had a clear view into the alley behind the hotel kitchen.

The dinner hour was in full swing. Delicious food smells flowed from the kitchen vent. The clatter of dishes echoed through the screen door that led from the kitchen into the alley. Before branching out into frozen pizza, my family had run a restaurant. I knew the drill. After dinner, the clean-up crew would scrub down the kitchen and get it ready for the prep crew's arrival in the early hours of the morning. The trash truck would arrive to empty the dumpster. The delivery trucks would roll off the first ferry with loads of produce, meat and baked goods. The kitchen crew would turn the raw materials into luncheon specials to be cooked up by the next shift.

More surveillance would be needed to figure out which truck carried the drugs back to the mainland. It was a pretty good system, although the taxpayers who paid for Chili's chef training in prison might not think much of their investment. The kitchen and alley were the distribution point for goods brought onto the island. For express deliveries, the truck could make an airport run and little packages of pills could wing their way anywhere in the country.

As head prep cook, Chili could hire his staff from a roster of names he'd picked up in jail. No one would ever suspect such nefarious doings at a posh hotel in the heart of old Nantucket.

That was my theory, anyhow. The big question was what to do about it. I could make an anonymous call to the police and let them clean up the operation. But that might get messy. The cops could find Alex's name and number in Chili's possession. The Socarides family name would be dragged through the mud. I decided not to try to sink the drug operation until I figured out the link to Ivan. Chili would have to wait.

I had some time before I met Lisa, so I walked over to Petticoat Row. Lights glowed in the windows of Sutcliffe's house. I went up the front steps and rang the bell. Sutcliffe opened the door and greeted me with a big grin.

"Wonderful to see you again," he said, ushering me into his living room. "Glad you dropped by. Can I get you a drink? I've got some Jameson."

"Maybe a glass of water." The clear head thing again.

He made a sour face. "You know what fish do in water, don't you?"

"Afraid so. I'll try not to think about it."

He disappeared into the kitchen and returned with two tinkling glasses. I eyed the amber liquid in his glass with more than a little longing, then glanced around the room, which had been cleaned up.

"Any leads on the break-in?"

He frowned. "Cops are up to their eyeballs with the summer craziness," he said. "An investigation into petty vandalism immediately goes onto the back burner. How about you? Making any progress on the *Moshup* caper?"

"Hard to say. It's tough digging into the past because all the witnesses are dead. Thought I'd start with the present and follow the trail back. There's an obvious link between the late Mr. Coffin and his ancestor."

"The legendary scrimshaw collection?"

"Not so *legendary*. This morning I talked to a New Bedford antique dealer named Mandel."

"Irving Mandel? He's a heavy-hitter. Ab used to talk about him. What did he have to say?"

"He said he learned about the collection from a dealer named Warner who's got a rep for selling antiques with vague ownership. When Warner told him about the Coffin collection, Mandel blew him off without taking a look. Later, he mentioned it to Ab at a scrimshaw weekend and Coffin apparently *did* see the collection. He was very excited about it because the pieces all had to do with whaling, unlike the commercial carvings old Coffin was best known for."

"That jives with what I know. Ab practically went off the rails after he'd seen the collection."

"Mandel said Coffin wasn't worried about the scrimshaw's provenance. Warner had told him there was a good reason no one had heard about the collection before. Coffin had kept it secret. When Coffin died, it was auctioned off as part of his estate to pay bills."

"Old Coffin was in dire financial straits. I'm surprised he didn't sell off the collection when he was still alive."

"I sent Warner a message saying I was a rich collector. Maybe he'll take the bait."

"I hope he can shed light on this mystery."

"Speaking of island mysteries," I said. "I heard about an old Navy base where there was some hush-hush stuff going on."

"No mystery there," he said with a smile. "You're talking about the naval installation at the end of Tom Nevers Road. The land is near the airport. It used to be a bombing range back in World War II. Then in 1955 the navy set up a submarine listening post to keep track of Soviet subs. Things got *really* interesting in the Cold War."

"In what way?"

"They built a bomb shelter for President Kennedy there. If he happened to be at Hyannisport during a nuclear attack, they would airlift him over here and he'd go underground. They had a sister shelter in Florida for when he vacationed in Palm Beach. The navy gave up Tom Nevers in 1976. The Nantucket Hunting Association uses the old shelter for storage."

"I talked with Lillian Mayhew. She told me about the navy taking her family property."

"More Cold War stuff. Heard the Navy built something out there, but I don't know much about it."

"Lillian is still upset about the land transfer to Ramsey."

"I don't blame her. That was a crappy thing. One more mystery that needs clearing up. You could be a busy guy. Sure you don't want a Jameson?"

"I'll take a rain check." I glanced at my watch. "Sorry to run. I've got a date."

Sutcliffe smiled. "If it's with Lisa Hendricks, I don't blame you for dashing off. She's a lovely and smart lady."

"I *agree*. Unfortunately, for now anyhow, she's the boss and I'm the hired gumshoe."

"Well good luck, anyhow," he said. "Come back again when you can stay longer."

We shook hands. I said I would keep him in the loop. From Sutcliffe's house, I made my way to Lisa's office. I found the Mayhew

Point map in the drawer where Lisa said it would be and spread it out on the desktop. The map was labeled: Proposed Land Trust Acquisition.

The point was shaped like a broad arrowhead, more or less equal on both sides. Extensive marshes and salt water creeks flanked the point. An unpaved road was the only access before Ramsey built his mega-mansion, but there was another access way, Lisa said, a bridge over one of the marshes, that was not shown on the map.

I was still poring over the map when Lisa showed up. She was wearing the fashionable pant suit I had seen her in earlier. She dropped my duffel, which landed with a loud thud on the floor.

"That's heavy! What do you have in there?"

"A few toys I borrowed from the Boston Police Department's storeroom."

She hiked an eyebrow and said she had better change. When she emerged from the bathroom she was wearing a dark red jump suit with white trim. Ninja chic, I guess. I went into the bathroom with my satchel to change into a black uniform that I'd liberated from the SWAT wardrobe at the Boston PD. I pulled my baseball cap down over my eyes.

She smiled in approval when she saw me. "At least *one* of us looks official."

"Since you'll be serving as lookout, one Ninja is all we need."

I must have been intent on the task at hand because I didn't read anything into the quick smirk that came to her lips. We left the office and headed west out of town in the Jeep. I asked how her grandfather was doing. She said Daggett seemed to have calmed down and was quietly happy. She suspected it had something to do with his expectation that Moby Dick would soon be in his sights. When she talked with Rosen, he was sugar sweet and never mentioned the encounter with me.

She was describing the conversation, but broke it off as we passed the metal gate to the Ramsey estate.

"Keep going for around a half mile," she said. "There's a sand road on the right."

I slowed the Jeep to a crawl when the odometer had ticked off another half mile. Bushes encroached on both sides of an entrance and almost hid the weathered Private Property sign tacked to a tree trunk. I turned the Jeep off the main road and stopped where a chain had been stretched across the road between two crumbling concrete pillars. Another Private Property sign hung from the chain.

"This chain is new since the last time I was here. Guess we'll have to walk."

"Not necessary." I got out of the Jeep and used the loppers from my bag to snap the chain. I got back behind the steering wheel.

We drove over the chain and followed the road for about a quarter of a mile to a sandy clearing.

"This is as far as the road goes," Lisa said.

We got out of the Jeep. I gave Lisa a halogen flashlight and told her to keep the beam shielded with her hand. She led the way along a path through the woods.

The rank smell of salt marsh mud became stronger. Soon, we stood on the high, grassy bank overlooking a meandering creek. The distance between one bank and another was only about fifteen feet, but it would have been almost impossible to cross the stream without bogging down in the thick mud. The bridge Lisa had mentioned was mostly rotted away. Twin rows of pilings were left and they looked pretty shaky in the light of the flashlight beam.

"This isn't exactly the Verrazano-Narrows Bridge," I said.

She pinched her chin. "It *has* deteriorated a little since the last time I was here."

"A *little?* And when may *that* have been?"

"About three years ago."

I shook my head. "How do you propose I get across?"

"Like *this.*"

She took the flashlight from my hand. Before I could make a

move, she put her foot on the first piling, then stepped to the next. She seemed to float across the ruins of the bridge to the other side.

"I knew those ballet lessons would come in handy some day," she said. "You won't have any problem. The pilings seem pretty stable. Just move slowly and deliberately."

I stood there with a dumb look on my face, then slid the satchel off my shoulder. "Head's up," I said, and lobbed the heavy bag to the other side where it thumped on the ground at her feet.

Lisa kept the flashlight pointed at the pilings. I stepped on the first one, which wobbled slightly with my weight, then placed my other foot on the next. No turning back now. I repeated the maneuver, pin-wheeling my arms a couple of times to keep my balance, before I stepped onto the banking next to Lisa who grabbed my hand to steady me.

I was amazed at the strength in her grip. Lisa seemed full of surprises, especially the next one.

She said, "Let's go!"

Dragging me along like a stubborn child, she strode off onto the darkness.

CHAPTER 22

Minutes later, we stood in front of a rusty fence post. Hanging at an angle was a metal sign warning trespassers away, under penalties to be inflicted by the might of the U.S government. Passing hunters of an anti-government inclination had peppered the sign with bullet holes. Rusty strands of barbed wire hung from the post.

After crossing the creek, we had trekked along a winding sand path through a stretch of scrub forest for a few minutes before encountering the sign. We kept moving, and trudged along the beach that ran around the perimeter. The main house was mostly in darkness, but lights blazed in every level of the rotunda, reminding me of my first impression, when I thought it resembled a lighthouse.

We stopped after a few minutes and I put my hand on Lisa's arm.

"What's wrong?" she said with apprehension in her voice.

"*Nothing*. Hold on for a second."

I scanned the house through binoculars. Most of the windows were dark, and there was no movement in those where lights glowed. I handed the binoculars to Lisa.

Pointing toward the ocean, I said, "Tell me what you see."

After a second, she said, "Lights of what looks like a large boat. It seems to be anchored."

"You're looking at the *Volga*. Ramsey's out on the yacht with Ivan."

She lowered the binoculars.

"What are they doing?"

"I don't know. That's why we're here tonight, to see if we can learn what's going on."

We continued along the sandy bluff to the blunt point of the Ramsey property, then started inland, following a straight line back toward the house. The ground began to rise into the brush-covered hill, shaped like a meatloaf that I had noticed on my first incursion onto Ramsey's property. We climbed to the top of the hill, which was about twenty feet above the ground.

"This is a strange little mound," Lisa said. "I've been to the house a number of times and never knew it existed."

"Good natural camouflage. You can't see it from the house. It blends into the landscape."

We descended from the top and walked around the hill to where the greenery had been cleared away to reveal a vaulted metal plate around eight-by-eight feet built into one end of the mound. There was a steel door set into the surface of the plate.

"What *is* this place?" Lisa said.

"It's probably not a Hobbit hut."

I brought the flashlight closer. The door was secured with a combination lock. I dug a small black box out of my duffel and placed it below the numbered keys. Magnets held the box in place. I pushed a button and a small screen glowed. I pushed another button and a set of numbers appeared in the digital display. I pressed the corresponding keys on the combination lock. A light on the lock glowed green. I turned a handle and the door opened. It did so silently, indicating that it had been oiled recently.

When the door swung open, the stale smell of cooked food and cigarette smoke assailed my nostrils. I removed the box, put it back in the bag, and told Lisa to stay close behind me. Behind the door was a corrugated tube about six feet in diameter. A wooden walkway ran along the bottom of the tube and into the hill for around thirty feet to a set of sliding steel doors.

The doors had been moved aside on their runners. I stood in the doorway and swept the flashlight beam around the arched corrugated walls and ceiling. It was evidently a Quanset hut that had been buried in the hill. I stepped off the walkway, went over to a wall switch and gave it a flick. Light flooded the room from a row of ceiling lamps in the high arched ceiling. There was nothing in the space except for a box-shaped structure, built of wood, at the far end.

"Not exactly the Nantucket Hilton, is it?" I said.

Lisa glanced around the room. "I've been in the JFK bunker at Tom Nevers. It looked a lot like this. I don't understand. Why would there be another fall-out shelter like that on the island?"

"Got me. Let's take a look."

We walked to the wooden structure, which was about the size of a two-car garage. An entryway and a couple of windows had been cut into the side. I pointed the light inside and saw that the box held twelve over-and-under bunks, a refrigerator, and a Primus camp stove. Shelves held breakfast cereals and cans of food. There was a portable electric heater, and a couple of folding chairs. There was a closet-sized bathroom and shower. Only one of the bunks had a mattress, and it was made up with blankets and a pillow.

A swivel chair was drawn up to a computer that sat on a folding metal table. Next to the computer were stacks of books. I picked up one volume. The title was: "Division of Labor in the Common Honey Bee and other Social Insects." I thought back to the photos of bees and other creatures that I had seen in the MAC lab. Another book had to do with "Autonomous Self-Organizations." It was mostly equations and technical text. More interesting was the author's name: "Sean Malloy."

"I can't believe someone's been living in this awful place," Lisa said. She had come up behind me and was talking in a hushed tone.

I put the book down. "From the looks of it, that someone has been forced to work."

"How do you know that? Oh, of course. Why would anyone live in here if they didn't *have* to be here?"

I checked the refrigerator and saw that it contained a few bottles of beer and some prescription containers. The prisoner was being allowed some creature comforts.

"We've seen all there is to see," I said. "We don't want to be around when the landlords return."

Lisa crossed her arms and shivered. "You don't have to ask me twice."

We hurried back to the tube and scuttled through it like a couple of crabs escaping a trap. The fresh sea air was as sweet as perfume after the claustrophobic underground interior. As I locked the door, I pictured JFK living in a hole in the ground while the world was going up in radioactive fire. I gave thanks that the human race is not always as stupid as it could be. I turned away from the bunker entrance, and that's when I saw that we had company.

Two Dobermans as big as ponies stared at us with their mouths hanging open, showing off their sharp teeth.

My thoughts jumped back to the shadows I had seen the night I stole Ramsey's Bentley. I moved protectively closer to Lisa, provoking a scary show of doggy gums and a growled warning. The dogs coiled their rear legs under their bodies, waiting for an excuse to spring. I tightened the grip on my flashlight, realizing as I did so, that it would be practically useless if they attacked. Lisa had been silent. I thought she was scared stiff. That's when she surprised me when she crooned:

"*Good* boy, Brutus! *Good* boy, Cassius!"

The dogs stopped growling and wagged their tails like a couple of puppies.

Keeping my eye on the Dobermans and my voice low, I said,

"You've met these guys before, I presume?"

"Michael introduced us the first time I visited his house. They're really a couple of big babies."

Each one of the babies must have weighed a hundred-and-fifty pounds.

"Could you tell the little tykes that we'd like to be on our way?"

She said, "*Sit*, Brutus. *Sit*, Cassius." When they obeyed immediately, she went over and patted their heads as a reward. They began to lick her face. Still speaking in her motherly voice, she said, "That's my good boys." Then in the same tone, she said to me, "Start moving away, Soc. I'll keep them preoccupied. Isn't that right, boys?"

I edged off to the side, keeping my eye on Ramsey's pets. Lisa said, "*Stay!*" and caught up with me. "Just walk slowly. I'm not sure how long before they figure things out."

I imagined us running for the piling bridge with the Dobermans nipping at our heels. It wasn't a pretty picture. Fortunately, about then, the dogs were distracted by the engine noise of a helicopter moving across the water toward the point. They began to bark and run around in circles as the chopper hovered near the artificial hill that contained the bomb shelter.

We sprinted away toward the beach and followed the dunes until we came to the woodland path we had used earlier. Minutes later, we were at the piling bridge. Lisa went across first, dancing lightly over the pilings. I threw my bag to the opposite banking, then followed her, far less gracefully.

We stopped to catch our breath, then we climbed into the Jeep, drove back onto the road and headed for Siasconset. Lisa began to laugh, softly at first, then louder until the tears rolled down her cheeks.

"What's so funny?" I said, miffed to be left out of the joke.

"Your reaction when you saw Michael's dogs. It was the first time since we've met when you haven't had a wry observation."

I had to admit it must have sounded funny from her angle. I forced a smile and said, "*Bow-wow.*"

We both laughed at the shared joke, but then Lisa stopped suddenly.

"Soc, we've got to get that prisoner out of there. No one should live like that. I can't imagine who it could be."

I murmured in agreement, but unlike Lisa, I had seen the name on the prescription bottles and knew *exactly* who was being held underground.

Sean Malloy, the owner of the MAC lab I had explored on the mainland.

I just didn't know *why.*

CHAPTER 23

The warm charm of the Daggett house kitchen was light-years removed from the world of snarling guard dogs, swooping helicopters and a prisoner held in an underground shelter built to house the country's government after a nuclear holocaust.

Lisa stood at the stove, grilling ham and cheese sandwiches on thick slices of homemade oatmeal bread. I sat at the long trestle table, letting a cup of herbal tea grow cold in front of me. The lovely smell of heated butter filled the air. We could have been any couple settling in for a late-night snack. Lisa served the sandwiches and sat down. I took a dainty bite, pronounced it the finest ham and grilled cheese sandwich I had ever tasted, and gazed across the table.

"DNA is a wonderful thing," I said.

She stopped with her sandwich poised in mid-air. "What in the world does DNA have to do with grilled ham and cheese?"

"I wasn't talking about the sandwiches. I was making a scientific observation. On top of the stress of having your grandfather accused of murder, tipping him into a temporary insanity, you have been shot at and growled at. But here you are, keeping it all together. Your harpooner ancestor, who hunted seventy-foot-long sperm whales with a spear, obviously passed on the steely calm and determination that he would have needed to do his job."

"Determination, *yes.* Not so sure about the calm." She puffed her cheeks out. "I'm *roiling* inside."

"That's a natural reaction. We had a run for our money tonight."

"It's not just our experience out there. I'm upset at the thought of someone being kept in that horrible bomb shelter. Do you think we should call the police?"

I slowly savored another bite while I pondered her question. "That's an option," I said. "Say we drive to the police station and tell the cops someone is being held a prisoner in an underground shelter on the property of one of the island's most prominent and richest taxpayers. What do you think they'll do?"

"They would have to investigate, no matter how rich Michael is."

"*Correct.* But they would tread carefully and respectfully, which would warn Michael of their intentions and allow him time to remove the prisoner and clean up the bunker. We would look like crazy fools."

"You make a good point. But what *can* we do?"

"*We* can't do anything. We're going to need help."

"Your scary friend?"

I nodded. "We'll have to wait until Flagg can lend a hand. I'll give him a call tonight. In the meantime, I suggest we finish our meal, turn in and get a good night's sleep. We'll tackle the problem with fresh minds in the morning."

"You're probably right," she said with a shrug of resignation. "Just keep that invisible bed board ready in case I wake up in the middle of the night with the shivers."

"I'll be sure to do that," I said. "Thanks for the snack."

I got up from the table and gave her a quick hug. She clung to me few seconds, then the Hendricks toughness reasserted itself. "I'll check on Gramps and crawl into bed. See you at breakfast?"

I said I'd be there at eight. I walked back to my garage apartment. Rosen's car was in the driveway and his cottage lights were out. I imagined him recording the household comings and goings from behind the shades. Well, *screw* him.

The light on my telephone answering machine was blinking. There were two messages. One was from Warner, the antiques dealer, saying he would love to meet with me to talk about the scrimshaw collection. He left a number to call. The other call was from Cousin Alex who said he had some information.

I called Warner first, apologizing for the lateness of the hour. He didn't seem perturbed and got right to the subject at hand. The lure of money is a wonderful motivator.

"I'm free tomorrow, Mr. Socarides. I'll be on the island in the morning, if that's convenient for you."

Since all I had to do the next day was to figure out how to rescue a prisoner and torpedo a drug ring, of course I said *yes*, and agreed to meet him at the ferry dock. I called Alex next. He was still up and working.

"I talked to some financial guys in Boston. They had friends on Wall Street. The word is that Ramsey has put all his eggs in one basket. Made some risky foreign investments and they've fallen through."

"Foreign, as in Russia?"

There was a pause, then Alex said, "Yeah. Russia. How'd you know?"

"I may have met one of his business partners. What's the skinny with your pal Chili?"

"I called him like you suggested and said I was ready to deal. That I'd come to Nantucket and see him. I could almost hear the bastard licking his chops."

"Thanks, Alex. You've done a great job. We'll talk soon."

"I could have done better with Sean Malloy. I made a bunch of calls to Woods Hole. Said I wanted to invest in his company, but I was told that his lab was closed. I found someone who talked to him a few months ago. Malloy said he had new financial backing that would allow him to devote more time to pure research rather than business."

"They tell you what kind of research he was doing at the lab?"

"Only that he's a robotics genius. Cutting edge stuff."

"That's very helpful, Alex. Give me a call when you have more. Thanks."

"Heck, no cousin. Thank you! And please be careful, Soc."

I told him I would. I went out onto the deck and blended the information Alex had uncovered in with what I already learned. What I came up with was an image of me drowning in a mind stew filled with all sorts of objects and people. It was my brain telling me that I was in over my head, I guess. As I promised Lisa, I went back inside and called the number Flagg had given me.

Flagg must have been busy saving the world. His recorded voice said, "Go ahead," so I did.

"Hi, Flagg. I'm calling to apologize and to ask for your help. You were right as usual. I'm out of my league with this thing. Ivan the Terrible is only the tip of a very big and nasty iceberg. Give me a call when you can."

I was too keyed up to sleep. As I hung up the phone, my eye fell on the copy of Swain's journal that I had borrowed from Sutcliffe. What better to lull me to sleep than a tale of murder and cannibalism on the high seas? I picked it up and settled into a wing chair.

Swain had entitled his journal: *A Sailor's True Tale of Suffering, Sacrifice, and Survival; the Sinking of the Ship* Moshup *After Being Stove By a Whale and How with Grit and Courage I Prevailed Against the Unforgiving Sea and Got Redemption.*

It didn't take a detective to see that Swain was a master of the run-on sentence and that he had an ego bigger than the whale that sank his ship. I turned to the first page.

I have always been a humble man, with faith in the Almighty and the goodness of Mankind, especially those hardy souls who toil in the ships of the Nantucket whale fishery. I write this short history of my travails not to profit from the misfortune of my loyal shipmates, but only as a way to feed my family.

Sutcliffe had annotated the journal.

"This is a huge whopper! The men who served with Swain all said he was a profane braggart who was despised by everyone aboard the *Moshup*. He was practically thrown overboard as a gambling cheat. He is lying about his reason for publishing the journal. He was well-off from his businesses and far from starving to death."

I kept reading. The *Moshup* incident was uncannily similar to the plight of the *Essex*. A battle-scarred bull sperm whale fights off its attackers, upending the whaleboats and battering their ship until it sinks.

Swain wrote of the encounter: *The harpoon bounced off the side of the whale as if the skin were of cast iron.*

Sutcliffe dashed cold water on this claim with a note: "Swain conveniently omits the fact that *he* threw the first harpoon at the whale, but it was a bad toss, the barb fell out and only infuriated the whale."

With the *Moshup* foundering, the crewmen salvaged supplies from the sinking ship, then set forth on an attempt to reach the nearest landfall a thousand miles away. The boats are scattered in a storm. Swain's boat is separated from the flotilla and the navigational instruments. The first men to die are thrown overboard. Then comes the agonizing pact to eat the dead. Eventually, the only ones left in the boat are Swain, Coffin and Daggett.

Swain describes how Coffin admits that he has developed a fondness for human flesh. Coffin is quoted as describing the texture and taste of various parts of the body, starting with the heart and liver. But the description was so finely detailed that I began to get the creepy feeling that Swain was talking about his *own* developing appetite rather than that of someone else.

As their situation grew even more hopeless, it became evident that the crewmen are not dying fast enough to supply the others with meals. Swain says that Daggett suggested that one man make the ultimate sacrifice to save the others. He says that he opposed the idea, but Daggett and Coffin out-voted him. They draw straws and Daggett loses. Daggett can't bring himself to commit suicide and asks for someone else to kill him. Coffin and Swain draw straws to choose the executioner. Swain picks the short straw, and is handed the knife to do the job. But he hesitates:

I could not bring myself, under the eye of all-seeing God, with respect for human life and for my good friend Daggett, to do the deed. I would rather die of starvation, as horrible as the prospect seemed. Coffin had no hesitation.

"If you'll not do your job, I'll do it for you," he said, and with that he snatched the knife from my trembling hand and plunged it into Daggett's chest. Then we both ate him, and his bones and marrow sustained us until we were rescued, poor wretches that we were.

I put the journal aside and stared off into space. A murder had been committed long ago on that drifting boat with its skeletal occupants. Swain said that Coffin was the killer. But Coffin was no longer around to defend himself. So Swain's account was the story that passed as the truth for decades. The descendants of Obed Coffin were forever stained by the supposed actions of their ancestor.

Sutcliffe had said Swain went on to exploit his misadventure, using his celebrity status for financial gain, but Coffin never got over the horror of the awful voyage. I imagined him sitting in the back of his narrow shop, lonely and despised, hiding from the world, ridden with guilt, carving beauty into ivory that had been pulled from the jaws of a whale like the one that had destroyed his ship and his life.

I put the journal aside and crawled into bed. I couldn't sleep and lay in the dark with my eyes wide open, thinking back over the horror of the events in the open boat. All the men involved were dead, their lips sealed by the grave. But the more I thought about it, the more I became convinced that if I listened, the ghost of Obediah Coffin would tell me the truth.

CHAPTER 24

Lisa left a note of apology taped to the refrigerator at the Daggett house. She said she had forgotten about a breakfast meeting at the airport restaurant with a potential donor who had deep pockets. He was flying back to New York and she wanted to put the squeeze on him while he was basking in the island afterglow.

I scrambled some eggs, slathered my oatmeal toast with butter and read *The Boston Globe* sports pages with a heavy heart. The Sox had lost the latest game.

After breakfast, I ripped a flap off a cardboard carton I found in the pantry. Then I used a black Sharpie to print the name WARNER on the cardboard square. I carried it out to the MG. Rosen's car was in front of his cottage, but there was no sign of its owner. Which was why it was surprising to glance in the rearview mirror minutes later and see the Miata behind me on Polpis Road.

At the outskirts of town, he turned off onto a side street. I parked at my usual spot and was waiting when the high-speed ferry made the turn at Brant Point lighthouse and tied up at the dock. As passengers streamed down the gangway, I lifted the cardboard square above my head like a hotel valet welcoming guests. A slim, well-dressed passenger separated from the crowd and came over to where I was standing.

"That's me," he said, pointing to the sign.

I lowered the cardboard. "Nice to meet you, Mr. Warner."

I introduced myself and we shook hands. I suggested we grab a cup of coffee at the dockside restaurant.

Mandel's description had led me to picture his rival dealer as an unshaven, shifty-eyed thief. Warner actually looked quite respectable. He wore neatly-pressed beige slacks, and a navy linen sports jacket. His steel-gray hair and mustache were trimmed short. His thin face was tanned. He carried an attaché case, which he set on the table.

I said, "Thanks for agreeing to meet me on such short notice, Mr. Warner."

"It was no problem, Mr. Socarides. I've been asked to come to the island to do an estate appraisal and tweaked my schedule slightly." He spoke in a crisp, boarding school accent. Warner slipped the aviator sunglasses off his face, revealing shrewd gray eyes under frosty brows. "I'm curious about how you got my name."

"From Mr. Mandel in New Bedford. He mentioned that you had been talking to Ab Coffin about a unique scrimshaw collection."

"Ah, yes," he said. "*Mandel.* And what scurrilous things did the dean of Johnnycake Hill have to say about me?"

"Sure you want to hear them?"

He let out a long sigh. "I'm sure it's no worse than anything he's said previous to this."

"You'll have to be the judge of that, Mr. Warner. He said you were thoroughly dishonest and conniving, and if you weren't so clever you'd have been arrested long ago."

His mouth turned up on one side and his mustache twitched. "I suppose I should take the *clever* part as a compliment. Apparently, you didn't believe what he said, Mr. Socarides, because you're not afraid to do business with me."

"I like to make up my own mind about people. I'm curious,

though. Why doesn't Mandel like you?"

He sipped his coffee, then set the cup down in exactly the same place and leaned across the table.

"Mandel spreads those stories because he's *jealous*. I've snatched a few choice collections out from under his big fat nose. He should know better than to get his knickers in a knot. This is a competitive business."

"What's the secret of your success?"

"In part, I use an extensive network of paid informants and I have a list of high-paying clients."

"And Mandel doesn't?"

"Yes, of *course*. We use the same informants in some cases, but Mandel is at an immediate disadvantage. He regards scrimshaw with a romantic eye. He falls in love with his acquisitions."

I remembered the almost sensuous manner with which Mandel had caressed a piece of scrimshaw.

"How is that a problem?"

"When you're emotionally attached to an object, you're slow to part with it. I'm known for fast turnover. I look at the pieces I handle as commercial art. Things to be bought and sold. Ingenious contrivances, curiously carved, as Melville described them. Carved in some instances by untrained artists of immense talent, but still things."

"How does the Coffin collection stack up?"

"Coffin was a master of his art. The workmanship is exquisite. The themes he carved into the ivory came from his heart as well as his hand. The collection is one of a kind."

"I think I'm missing something. If it's such a great collection, why haven't you done your usual quick sales turnover?"

"Because of slandering idiots like Mandel." Anger blazed in the cool gray eyes. "I'll admit to a sharp deal now and then, but everything I do is within the boundaries of the law. Unfortunately, aggressive business practices can provide fodder for malicious gossips like Mandel to build on. The reputation for shady deals scares away institutional buyers for the bigger and more expensive collections. They don't like making acquisitions that later turn out to be stolen goods."

I drummed my fingers on the table and gazed off across the harbor. My wandering eye lit on Rosen, who was standing on the other side of the marina, looking in my direction. He sensed that I had seen him and disappeared around the corner of a shop. I turned back to Warner.

"You've been honest with me, Mr. Warner, so I'll come clean before we get deeper into our discussion. I don't have the money to buy the collection. And I'm not a collector."

His silvery eyebrows dipped into a V. "I don't—"

"I lured you here on a pretense. I'm a private investigator and I'm helping the legal team defending Henry Daggett, the man charged with killing Coffin."

"Well, well," Warner said. "I appreciate your honesty, but if you're not interested in the Coffin collection, what *do* you want?"

"Information. And your expertise. In return for your help I might be able to help you move the collection to a *real* buyer."

There was a glint of interest in the flinty eyes. "And how would you do that?"

"By clearing up the Daggett case. I have serious doubts that Daggett was the murderer."

"I have no reason to help Daggett."

"Actually, you *do* have a reason. If the police suspect that the collection was the motive for the killing, they might want to confiscate the scrimshaw until the case is resolved. There will be appeals and challenges. The collection could be out of your hands for months, maybe years."

"Wouldn't Mandel just love to see that happen," Warner said, his voice dropping an octave. "Okay, then. What do you want to know?"

"It's no secret that Coffin wanted the scrimshaw. And that

Daggett said the provenance was a sticking point, which is why he didn't want the museum to buy it. Coffin called the meeting at the museum, saying he had information that might change Daggett's mind. Any idea what he was talking about?"

"Not a clue. But Daggett had a point. There *was* a slight shade of doubt as to the collection's provenance."

"*Tell* me about it."

"The history of a scrimshaw collection can usually be well documented because the pieces were passed down to the whaler-artist's family. Even with no paper documentation, there is frequently family memory to rely on. The Coffin collection was different."

"In what way?"

"The major portion of Coffin's known work wasn't created on shipboard. It was done in his Nantucket workshop. He had a brother, the sibling whom Ab Coffin is directly descended from, but he predeceased him. Coffin died intestate. No will. The collection was auctioned off after Coffin's death to pay off debts. The successful buyer was a Boston businessman. Upon the buyer's death, the collection went to his wife. It traveled an interesting path after that."

"How so?"

"The widow was a former showgirl who had been shunned by Boston society. When she died, the collection was passed on to her child, a playboy, who sold it to buy wine, women and song."

"That's not a bad trade-off."

"I don't disagree. The next owner of record owned a saloon. When he died in a bar brawl, the collection was stored in the bar's basement. It sat there for years, still in the same family. In time, the building was being refurbished for apartments. The owner found the ivory and assumed that the collection might be valuable. He came to me for an appraisal."

"All these ownerships are verifiable?"

"Every step of the way. Bills of sale. Affidavits. I have diagrammed the travels of the scrimshaw to the present day."

"Coffin was mainly interested in one item from the collection. What can you tell me about that?"

"He wanted a panorama bone plaque made from a sperm whale's jaw bone. I told him that the owner would only sell the collection as a whole. Coffin said he would try to get the Nantucket museum to buy it. The museum's trustees said they had more than enough scrimshaw, but it was only an excuse. The main reason for the rejection, thanks to Mandel, was my sordid reputation."

"Why didn't the owner find another dealer to represent the sale? Mandel, for example?"

"He was thinking about it, but I offered to buy the collection and take it off their hands. The owner had no sentimental family attachment to the work. I got the price down, but it was still a considerable amount of change."

"Did your ownership change the terms of sale you'd discussed with Coffin?"

"Would I sell it piece-meal? I'd sell it whatever way that would bring the most money. My ownership allowed me the opportunity to make a deal with Coffin. I'd let him borrow the piece to show to the museum along with verification of its rightful ownership showing that it was not stolen property."

"I understand you demanded a substantial insurance fee."

Warner shrugged. "The arrangement suited him, but I was the loser. The piece is missing."

"Can you describe it to me?"

"I can do *better* than that." He unsnapped his attaché case and removed an envelope. Inside was a stack of eight-by-ten color photos. He shuffled through the packet and set one photo in front of me. It showed a long, somewhat rectangular, flat piece of ivory. Several separate whaling scenes were carved into the surface. Warner took a magnifying glass from the case and handed it over.

The scenes were laid out like a comic strip, showing the progression of a whale hunt and its aftermath. He passed over photo enlargements of each scene. The series included the standard image of whaleboats closing in on their prey. In the panels that followed, the whale upends the boats, smashes head-on into the ship, sinking it, and the boats set out in a flotilla. They are separated in a storm and the action concentrates on a single boat. The images were vividly photographic in their detail and the lines flowed with action.

"This is pretty incredible stuff," I said.

"Oh, it gets *better*. Here's the reverse side of the piece."

He handed me a second set of glossy photos showing the backside of the bone carved with multiple panels, then individual scenes. They looked like something out of a graphic horror novel. The first image showed the men cutting up a dead body and handing the parts around. Then only three men were left in the boat. The names of the men were carved under the scene. They seemed to be gambling. In the next panel, one has a knife and he is stabbing another crewman. The last panel shows two men gnawing on bones like the animals they resemble. There is a ship on the horizon.

I said, "This is the story of the *Moshup*, isn't it?"

Warner nodded. "*Lovely*, isn't it? As you can see, it's not the type of art someone with a weak stomach would appreciate. I almost forgot to tell you the most interesting thing about it. The person who bought the collection, when Coffin's estate was being settled, was *Swain*, the man depicted in the boat with Coffin, gnawing the marrow out his shipmate's bones."

"That *is* odd. You'd think Swain would have avoided anything that reminded him of that experience."

"Yes," Warner said. "You would think so."

I peered through the magnifying glass again and noticed that the harpooner and the man with the knife were the same person. I stared in amazement at the panels.

"Could I borrow these photos?"

"I have copies." He handed me the envelope. "This has been fascinating, Mr. Socarides. I have to be going. Let me know if anything turns up."

"I'll *do* that." I took the business card from his fingers and put it in my shirt pocket. "This is a fascinating story."

The pan bone carving was a piece of history, and in its macabre way, a thing of beauty. But it was much more. What Coffin had painstakingly carved into the polished ivory was a homicide indictment of his fellow crewman. The harpooner in the initial attack on the whale and the man who'd stabbed, dismembered and eaten his crewmate were the same person.

Swain.

CHAPTER 25

Nantucket was turning out to be a big fat time warp. I came to the island to look into a murder case, but increasingly, I was jumping from one time zone to another. *Flick.* I was Starbuck chatting with Captain Ahab about the whereabouts of Moby Dick. *Double flick.* I was dodging bullets in a fake slice of Africa with a beautiful descendant of a harpooner. Then I was making nice outside a Cold War bunker with a couple of Dobermans who wanted to have me for dinner. Now I was being drawn into a homicide investigation that involved three starving men in a whaleboat casting lots to see who would be the early bird special.

I had to admire Swain's skill at shifting blame from himself, but the scrimshaw told a different story. He kills Daggett's ancestor, and conspires with Coffin to cover the whole thing up. After Coffin dies, Swain writes a journal accusing his late shipmate of murdering Daggett for food. He learns that Coffin carved the true sequence of events into a sperm whale's jawbone, which Swain buys at auction. Before he can dispose of the incriminating evidence, he's killed in a bar brawl and the bloody account of his crime goes into cold storage for a hundred or so years.

As I walked back into town, a familiar voice jerked my rambling thoughts out of the 19th century and back to the present.

"Hello, Mr. Socarides. Nice surprise."

Ramsey had popped out of an alley so suddenly that I had almost barreled into him. Maybe I'm a suspicious old gumshoe, but I guessed that Rosen had reported my travels to Ramsey so he could set up the convenient ambush.

"Hello, Ramsey," I said. "Small world."

"Nantucket is a *very* small world," he said.

"No argument there. Dr. Rosen was on the road behind me on the way into town and I saw him later near the marina."

"Then you see what I mean. Speaking of Rosen, how is Henry coming along under the doctor's treatment?"

I played along with the conversational side-step.

"Daggett still thinks he's Ahab. He's closing in on Moby Dick. So I guess you could say that Dr. Rosen's treatment isn't working very well."

Ramsey ignored my attempt to inject Rosen back into our friendly chat. He gave a wag of his head and furrowed his brow in a pretty good imitation of real concern. "That's a damned shame. What's the latest on the trial?"

I told him half of what I knew. "The assistant district attorney handling the case informs me that they are pushing for an early trial date. His boss is running for re-election and wants a quick conviction in a high-profile case."

"My *God!* What's the defense strategy going to be?"

"They don't have much to work with. My guess is that they'll accept a plea bargain. The D.A. drops the murder charge on insanity grounds if the defense agrees to place Daggett in a hospital rather than a prison. Even if he comes out of his Ahab phase, he'd be regarded as a threat to society. Whatever the outcome, he'll be out of circulation a very long time."

"It's hard to believe Daggett could have killed Coffin," he said.

I quoted Aeschylus about the sins of the fathers being visited upon the sons. A thoughtful look came to Ramsey's face.

"It seems that way, with Coffin and Daggett suffering because of what happened in that whaleboat. Hard to imagine how it must have been with these three men throwing dice to see who would sacrifice himself for the others. How's Lisa taking all this?"

"She's having a hard time with it, but she is a very tough lady."

"Yes, she is, but she's still going to need the support of her friends. I was on my way to her office. Maybe I can cheer her up."

From what I had seen, the best way for Ramsey to cheer Lisa would be to keep his hands and eyes off her body.

"She won't be there. She's at the airport trying to pry conservation money out of a potential donor."

He gave a back of the throat laugh. "Lisa is like a pit bull terrier when it comes to pursuing funds for land acquisition. She's pried a few dollars out of me."

"I'm sure there's plenty more where that came from," I said.

We got into a grinning contest that ended when my jaw muscles began to hurt. I know when I'm out-grinned.

"I don't blame you for thinking that I'm just a greedy Wall Street type who worships at the altar of the money god," Ramsey said. "But there are things about me that you don't know."

"I think that it's very possible there's a *lot* I don't know about you," I said.

I was thinking about the bomb shelter prison on his property and the question of why a respectable businessman had ties to a shady Russian thug called Ivan the Terrible.

Ramsey put his hand on my shoulder. "Come down to the marina and I'll show you that I have a much different side."

Ramsey was up to something. But I'd been scraping the bottom of my idea bin for ways to hook up with him again and here was my chance. I asked him to wait while I dropped some papers off at Lisa's office, which was a few steps away. I went up the stairs to the office and used the key she had loaned me to get in. I wrote on the outside of the photo envelope with a felt pen:

"Have new stuff on the *Moshup* incident. Went to marina with Ramsey." I added the time and signed it with a big S.

Ramsey was waiting patiently on the sidewalk outside the office. We made small talk about the traffic and tourists on the short walk to the Old North Wharf. When we got to the marina, Ramsey stopped and pointed to a pretty little sailboat nestled in a slip. It had a navy blue hull and white cockpit and sleek lines. The bright work looked as if it had been buffed with a toothbrush.

"That's my boat," Ramsey said. "What do you think of her?"

"Very sweet."

"She's an Arleron. Self-tacking jib. She'll turn on a dime. Twenty feet long."

"I would have expected something more along the length of the *Volga*."

Ramsey made a sour face. "I call Chernko's yacht the *Vulger*. That kind of thing is not my style."

"Could have fooled me, Ramsey. Don't forget, I've seen your house. You like *big*."

"My place *is* on the grand side. In the old days, a conspicuous display of wealth would be unseemly. Today, if you don't advertise what's in your bank account, it's seen as a sign of weakness. In my business, the strong devour the weak."

"That doesn't explain why you have a big house and a small boat."

"It's a Nantucket thing. Buy a million dollar boat on this island and there's always a guy who'll spend ten million. Besides, going against the flow shows that you've got enough dough to not give a crap what people say."

"Like wearing jeans to a fancy cocktail party."

"That's right. Do you have a few minutes to spare? We can take her out for a spin around the harbor. We'd be back in less than an hour."

"Fine with me," I said.

We walked out onto the dock and got into the boat. Ramsey cranked up a small battery-operated outboard motor while I cast off the dock lines. Then he backed out of the slip and motored away from the marina toward the harbor. When we got into open water, we unfurled the mainsail and the jib. I hauled in the sails until they stopped luffing and caught the wind. He shut down the motor.

"You handle the sails and I'll take the tiller," he said.

He pointed the boat so that the wind was off our stern. I slacked the main sheet and let the sail out on the starboard side until it was at right angles to the hull. I did the same with the jib on the port side of the boat so the sails were in the extended position called wing-to-wing.

Ramsey kept the boat headed across the harbor and then we turned and came across the wind. I trimmed the jib and mainsail, and the boat picked up speed and heeled.

"Good job, Socarides. You've sailed before, I see."

I had sailed on big boats owned by guys who needed crew for the Figawi race between the mainland and Nantucket, but I didn't want to give Ramsey any more than I had to.

"A little, back in Camp Hiawatha."

Ramsey grinned, this time for real, and for a moment we bonded like a couple of old sailors dancing on the wind.

That moment passed quickly when Ramsey said, "Lisa tells me that you've been using her grandfather's boat. The *Pequod II*."

"She offered it up, but I haven't had much time with all the detecting work."

"Reason I asked, we passed Daggett's slip on the way out and I saw it was empty. I wondered where the boat is."

I tried to deflect the lining of questioning. "Boat's out of the water for repairs."

"Really? Lisa didn't mention that. Who's doing the work?"

"Don't remember the guy's name. He seemed okay. Besides, I'm not paying the repair bill."

"You have to watch the locals. Some of the local mechanics are real land pirates. I had to pay a small fortune for some front end damage to my Bentley."

Uh-oh.

"Too bad. My last chauffeur was a lousy driver, too. Had to fire him."

"I don't *have* a driver. My car was stolen from my garage and used as a battering ram."

I let out a low whistle. "I read in the *Inquirer* that drugs are a big deal on the island, too. Maybe someone stole the car to buy drugs."

"I don't think so. The car was found in town."

Ramsey was playing games. Someone in the helicopter had seen the registration number when Daggett's boat sank under me. It would have been easy to trace its ownership. Ramsey would have casually asked Lisa about her grandfather's boat, and she, innocently, would have replied that she had been offered to let me use it. I detected a growing edge in Ramsey's voice. With his concentration diverted, he had let the boat drift off course.

I said, "Wind's shifting. Get ready to jibe."

A quick frown came to Ramsey's handsome face, but he gradually pushed the tiller to prep for the maneuver. I hauled in the main sheet for a controlled jibe, so that the arc of the swinging boom didn't snap the mast off. I hauled in the jib and we set off on a new course with the mainsail extended at right angles in a broad reach.

"Nicely done," Ramsey said. "Want to take the helm?"

"Thanks." We traded places and I pointed to the ferry dock where the big yacht was tied up. "How does Chernko like you calling his yacht the *Vulger*?"

"I've never told him."

"Don't blame you. Some guys don't have a sense of humor. How long have you known him?"

Ramsey hesitated. "A few years. We've put together some business deals."

"How's that working out?"

"Fine. We're into developing markets. I can give you some tips if you have some extra cash to invest."

"Thanks. I may take you up on that. Lisa said you're a venture capitalist."

"Some people call us *vulture* capitalists, or even worse, because we swoop down on weak companies, acquire them, do our magic and sell them at large profits."

"Any company I might know?"

"Probably not. Most are pretty obscure. How is your investigation for Lisa going?"

"Slowly. I'm following up on some unexpected leads."

"Such as?"

"Ready about?" I said, giving Ramsey the warning that it was time to swing the bow around for a tack.

He gave that quick little frown again. Then the bow swung across the wind and the mainsail filled out on the other side of the boat. He hauled in the sail and the boat heeled, again picking up speed.

"Nicely done again," Ramsey said.

We switched places again.

"Boat handles like a dream. Thanks for the sail."

"My pleasure. I'm glad to have this chance to talk to you. Take some advice from a fellow sailor. After we tie up, get on the ferry, and leave the island. Tell Lisa you've learned all you can, collect your paycheck and get lost."

I glanced at him. "I don't get your drift, Ramsey."

"Ivan told me all about you. He said you and he have a history."

"I suppose you could call it that. I talked to a newspaper reporter who asked for my theory on a murder. I was quoted in the newspaper. Ivan thought I was talking about him, which I wasn't, and sent a couple of his goons to threaten me. A day later someone torched my boat."

"You think Chernko had something to do with the loss of your boat?"

"It had crossed my mind."

"So you came to the island to exact your revenge."

"I came to the island to work on the Daggett case."

"Have it your way, but it would have been far better if you had simply let the insurance company pick up the tab for your boat. My advice? *Forget* about it."

"You're Chernko's pal. Why are you so concerned about my welfare?"

"I'm not," he said in a flat voice. "You've unwittingly blundered into something bigger than you could ever understand. That's your mistake, but Lisa's right in the line of fire and she could get hurt."

That really caught my attention. Maybe the cold-blooded plutocrat had a streak of humanity when it came to Lisa.

"Who would hurt Lisa?"

"That's not important."

"Here's how I figure it, Ramsey. Say I took your advice. I'd go back to the mainland, reconstitute my charter business with a shiny new boat. One day I'd get a charter from four buddies. We'd be miles at sea, which is when they'd tell me they were friends of Ivan the Terrible. They'd slice me up and feed the pieces to the fishes. Chernko strikes me as a guy who likes to tie up loose ends. He might figure Lisa had been too close to me and she'd have to go, too."

"I would do my best to see that didn't happen," he said in a dead voice.

"Then you admit it's a possibility."

"I told you that this is *big*. It's even bigger than me. Ivan is a force of nature. He usually gets what he wants."

"And in this case you want the same thing."

Instead of answering, he turned to start the little outboard.

I furled the sails as we moved toward the slip. He spun the boat around and guided it into the slip stern-first. I climbed out of the boat and said, "Thanks for the sail. See you later, Ramsey."

He gave a sad shake of his head. "I don't think so. Sorry, but events seem to have moved more quickly than I anticipated."

I turned to make a snappy retort which is when I noticed the name *Moshup* on the boat's transom. *Flick.* The Nantucket time warp.

I walked from the slip to the parking lot. Some thoughtless jerk had left his vehicle directly in the way. I went to go around the black Chevy Tahoe. Four doors simultaneously flew open. Chernko's goons emerged from the front seat and two dark-skinned guys popped out from the back.

They hemmed me in, two in a side, and the Tall Guy said, "Get in!"

He gestured with a hand that held a switchblade like the one that had been used to decorate my old boat. In fact, they all had switchblades dangling at their sides. I knew that if I got in the car the chances of living a long and healthy life would be slimmer than slim. They closed in, herding me like a stray sheep. Then they began to shove. I dug my feet in to prevent from being pushed into the back seat, which was fortunate because at that instant there was a loud thump and the SUV jerked several feet to my right.

The cause of its sudden lurch was a black Ford sedan that had crashed into the rear bumper like a pool cue hitting a ball. The door on the driver's side opened and John Flagg stepped out. He checked the front of his car and the back of the SUV, then came over to where we were standing. The switchblades had miraculously disappeared from sight.

"Sorry about that. Hit the gas instead of the brakes. Everyone okay?" He glanced around. "Good. Who's the owner? No big damage. Guess we should exchange licenses and registration."

Guess he was wrong. Tall Guy snarled something in Russian

and he and his friends piled into the Tahoe. A second later, the SUV took off so fast that it fishtailed, then headed out of the parking lot and was lost in the traffic.

Flagg watched them go and slowly removed his sunglasses. Flagg tends to be stone-faced, but his thin lips widened in a beatific smile and his heavy-lidded eyes half closed.

"Don't you love it?" he said.

"Love *what*, Flagg?"

"Don't you just love it when the Indians come to the rescue of the palefaces?"

CHAPTER 26

I'd never admit it to Flagg, but I'd been humbled by the ease with which Ramsey delivered a savvy, smart guy like me into the hands of Chernko's Russian gangsters and their pals.

"What was *that* all about?" Flagg said as he watched the departing Tahoe merge into the slow-moving traffic.

"We need to talk," I said.

"Thought you'd never ask. Got a better place than this?"

I thought about it, and then asked him to drive me to the MG and tail me out of town. Flagg never goes anywhere without his personal arsenal. If the Russians tried a second pass, he'd be in a good position to discourage them. Still, as I drove onto Polpis Road, I glanced frequently in the rearview mirror. The only car I saw was Flagg's rental.

About a mile from Siasconset, we turned off onto a side road that ascended to the Sankety Head lighthouse. The light tower is perched atop a hundred-foot-high bluff that offers a sweeping view of the elements that define Nantucket: rolling heath and dunes. The deep blue sea. And the greens and fairways of a golf course that caters to the corporate royalty who can afford the stratospheric membership dues. As we strolled from the parking lot to the light,

I asked how he had found me at the harbor.

"I got your phone message. Sorry for the delay. I was on the other side of the world, up to my eyeballs in water buffalo dung. I'm supposed to be in Langley now for a debriefing. I told my boss I had to make a stop on the Vineyard. Made a slight detour to Nantucket."

When he couldn't reach me by the phone, he had rented a car at the airport. He drove to the Daggett house and talked with the housekeepers, who said they had seen me go out earlier in the day. Flagg still had the business card with Lisa's office address. She was meeting with her client, but she showed Flagg my note and gave him directions to the marina.

Flagg had noticed the Tahoe parked near the boat dock and didn't think anything about it until he eyeballed the four tough-looking guys lounging near the SUV. They were looking out at the harbor at an approaching sailboat. He had a pair of pocket binoculars and used them to see that I was on the boat. When the men got back into the SUV, he assumed they were waiting for me. And that they were up to no good. Flagg has always said to use the nearest weapon at hand. In his case, it was his car, which he employed as a battering ram.

We walked around the lighthouse, keeping away from the camera-toting tourists snapping pictures of the red-and-white brick tower. Flagg looked wearier than the last time I had seen him only a few days before. Wrinkles had deepened around the mouth. His nut-brown complexion had darkened to a chestnut tone and the skin was shredded on his eagle nose. I noticed pouches as big as suitcases under his eyes when he stopped and removed the mirrored aviator sunglasses to let the sunlight bake his face. His eyes were closed and he was taking deep breaths of the air which smelled of seaweed and salt-spray rose.

"You okay, John?" I said.

His eyelids opened to a half-squint. The rare use of his first name seemed to catch him by surprise. "Yeah, thanks. I'm all right. Must look like crap. Saving the world takes a lot more out of me than it used to. Getting older."

"Judging from the blisters on your nose, you were saving the world in a warm climate."

"It was *warm* all right. Not Miami Beach by a long shot, though."

He looked out at the sea with the gaze that soldiers call the fifty-yard stare. Flagg had pretty much seen it all, so his assignment must have been a tough one this time around. There was nothing I could say that would help. I kept my silence to allow Flagg to work it out as he always had.

He finally said, "I apologize for the black-out, Soc. Some of the stuff I see is getting to me. Especially the kids." He filled his lungs and exhaled. "Smells good after twelve hours in a plane." He took a few more breaths and looked up at the cast-iron lens housing at the top of the lighthouse. "Damned pretty sight. Seventy-feet high. Built in 1850 to keep ships off Nantucket Shoals."

"Didn't know you were a tour guide, Flagg."

"Just digging into my Native American roots. Sankety's a Wampanoag word that means *highland*. Guy from Aquinnah named Vanderhoop was one of the principal keepers. I remember him talking about it. Old keeper's house is gone, but it must have been some gig working out here. Imagine seeing this view every day." He slipped the sunglasses back on. I could feel his eyes boring into me through the silver lenses that reflected my face. "Okay. Tour's over. What the hell was going on with you and those hoods at the harbor?"

"Two of them were Chernko's goons. The same guys who tried to rough me up back on the mainland, and probably torched my boat. I don't know the others. They wanted me to go for a little ride. I don't think they had a sightseeing tour of the island in mind."

"Do *tell*. I never knew Nantucketers were so friendly."

Flagg had a dim view of the snooty island to the east of Martha's Vineyard.

"*Friendly* isn't the word for it. It's a good thing you came along when you did."

He pasted a phony sad smile on his lips. "Last time I was in these parts, you were dodging bullets. Hell, Soc, you riling folks up again with your wise-ass jokes?"

"I wish it were that easy." I let out a big sigh.

"I advised you to cool it with Chernko. Guess you ignored my sage advice."

"You were right. I'm in *way* over my head."

"I figured that things were hitting the fan after I heard your panicked phone message. You never learn, Soc. Now you're looking for help because you've got a big bad Russian on your ass."

"This is a lot bigger than the little feud over my boat, Flagg. I'll tell you about it when you're through with the sermon."

"Okay. I'm done. Now tell me what's going on."

"I'm not sure. Maybe you can figure it out."

I told Flagg about the talk with Tanya and her mention of the *Volga*'s midnight cruises. Flagg had known me a long time, and wasn't surprised when I said I'd shadowed the yacht, and spied on the *Volga* when it anchored off shore where Ramsey had his house.

"Refresh my memory. Ramsey was the big businessman you mentioned. Friends with Chernko."

"That's right. *More* than friends. They're business partners."

"Okay, so the yacht goes out to do some night-fishing. What's the big deal?"

"If they were fishing, they were using some funny-looking gear. I saw them lower something into the water using an A-frame crane. The object looked like a big box, but I couldn't be sure because of the darkness and the distance. Then the yacht just sat there. I got bored and after a while, started for home. I'd only been on the move a few minutes when I got hit."

"Hit by *what*, Soc?"

"Don't know." I described the weird multiple rapping that

preceded the boat's sinking, the blue lights in the water and the ragged hole in the hull. Flagg responded with a grunt that could have meant anything or nothing.

"Go on," he said.

"Next thing, the helicopter from the yacht was hovering overhead. I hid under the boat and eventually the chopper went back to the yacht. Then my boat sank. I swam to the beach. Ramsey's mansion made a good landmark."

"My guess is that you didn't knock on the door and ask for a shot of Johnny Walker."

"I thought it might be rude to just drop in. Besides, Ramsey was out on the yacht. I started inland, which was when I came across the old Cold War bunker."

"Now you've *really* got my attention, Soc."

"Ramsey's property used to belong to the navy. Rumor has it that he acquired the land through some sort of sweetheart deal. Kennedy used to vacation across the Sound at Hyannisport. The feds built a shelter for JFK near the Nantucket airport so they could protect him in case of nuclear attack."

"I knew about the airport shelter. Never heard they built a second one."

"The second one had sleeping quarters for twelve. I figured it was staff."

Flagg shook his head. "Leadership of the Free World would have been a bunch of folks scared out of their minds, hiding in a hole in the ground. How'd you get home from Ramsey's place?"

"I broke into the garage and stole one of Ramsey's cars. A Bentley. I busted through the front gate and left the car in town."

"*Bentley.* You've got good taste. Sounds like you had a lucky night. Ride in a nice car and you got clean away."

"Not exactly. I bumped into Ramsey in town today. I thought that it was a little too convenient, but I went along when he invited me to go out for a sail in his boat. I was hoping he might tell me something I didn't know."

"And *did* he?"

"Unfortunately, *yes*. He had tracked me down through the boat's hull registration. He knew I was spying on the yacht that night. He even knew that I had boosted his car. He said that I'd blundered into business that could get me killed and warned me to get off the island."

"From what I saw, he gave you good advice."

"A tad late. When he saw the welcome party on the dock, he said something about events moving faster than he expected. It was almost an apology. Strange."

"You saying he *didn't* set you up?"

"I think he was *in* on the set-up, but was looking for an out. Unlike Chernko, who wants me dead because he thinks I know more than I do about the big project."

"First thing you've said about a project. But you haven't told me what it is."

"That's because I don't *know* what it is! Tanya mentioned that she'd overheard Ramsey and Chernko talking about something called Max, over on the mainland at Woods Hole. I poked around and learned MAC was the name of a high-tech company. Marine Autonomous Corporation. The owner was a guy named Sean Malloy. I found the lab, but it was deserted."

"Which meant there was no one to stop you from snooping around."

"True. They had surveillance cameras, but I neutralized them. I think."

"You *think*?"

I explained how I'd covered my body and head with a trash bag.

"Smart," he said, deadpan. "They're gonna be looking for a walking trash bag. You get inside the lab?"

I nodded. "There was a deep pool that looked like it might have been used for testing underwater gear. There were some empty computer cubicles and photos on the walls. Pictures of ants and bees."

Flagg frowned. "Run that by me again."

I did, including details on the diagrams I'd seen on the blackboard. "Stuff didn't make sense."

"They may make more sense than you think, Soc."

"You know something?"

"Maybe. What about this guy, Malloy?"

"He's a robotics scientist. And he's among the missing. My cousin Alex has been trying to track him down."

"*Alex?* That little druggie puke we had to straighten out back in the day?"

"That's the one. He's a family man now with two kids and a law practice."

"He grew up to be a lawyer? Huh. That figures."

"He says Malloy has disappeared off the face of the earth. And we've since learned that Chernko is heavily involved in the international drug trade."

Flagg let out a low whistle. "Gets better and better."

"There's lots more," I said. "I'll tell you about it when you explain what you've been hearing around Washington."

The lips parted in a quick smile. "Here's the thing. I've been picking up rumors. Top secret, so it's nothing official. Just give me a little time and I'll tell you where I'm heading."

"Fair enough. Back to your question, I think Malloy is right under our noses. He's being kept prisoner."

I gave him a shortened version of the uninvited visit Lisa and I made to the bunker.

"You've been a busy boy, Soc. Bringing that pretty lady into this mess wasn't smart."

"All she knows is that someone has been living in the old bunker. I didn't mention the Malloy connection. I don't want to place her in danger."

"Might be too late for that, Soc."

"I know. That's why I want to get back into that bunker tonight. Will you help me?"

Flagg didn't hesitate. "Okay. I've got to get down to D.C. for a debriefing and a hot shower. I'll fly back to Nantucket later tonight and we can make our move. Watch your ass in the meantime, in case the Ruskies come looking for you again."

"I'll lay low until you get back." We shook hands and walked to the parking lot.

Flagg leaned against his car. He surveyed the scenery and let out a loud sigh.

"I was hoping for a little R and R. Shoulda known better." He slapped me on the back, got into the car, and started the motor.

I watched his car for a moment, then strolled around the lighthouse. I let the sea air blow through one ear and out the other. My thoughts went back to the sail with Ramsey. He had said that it was hard to believe Daggett could have killed Coffin. When I quoted the Greek thing about the sins of the fathers being visited upon the sons, Ramsey had agreed with that assessment, saying it seemed that way, Coffin and Daggett suffering because of what their ancestors did in that whaleboat.

Hard to imagine how it must have been with these three men throwing dice to see who would sacrifice himself for the others.

Back up, Soc. I asked myself how Ramsey knew they threw *dice*. The story I had heard from Sutcliffe was that they drew *straws*. How had Ramsey known about the dice unless he had seen Coffin's scrimshaw record and the panel labeled: The Fatal Toss?

I turned my back on the lighthouse and got behind the wheel of the MG.

Maybe I'd find the answer to my questions in the Nantucket time warp.

CHAPTER 27

The household shrink must have been exhausted from the rigors of stalking me all over Nantucket. As I drove up to the Daggett place, I noticed that the Miata wasn't in front of his cottage. With Rosen away, this would be a good time to see Daggett. The second I set foot in the house, my nostrils quivered at the delicious scents flowing from the kitchen. Mrs. Gomes was stirring a big pot on the stove.

"Kale soup?" I said.

She flashed her lovely smile. "I know it's a little heavy for the hot weather, but the captain loves it. I used my summer recipe. Local turnips instead of potatoes, so it's lighter than winter soup. Want to try some and see if it's okay? I usually test it on my husband, but he's in town."

"Testing kale soup is one of my specialties," I said.

She grabbed a bowl from the cupboard and filled it with the steaming concoction. I slurped down a spoonful without blowing on it and burned my mouth. I didn't care. The earthy taste of kale combined with the spice of linguica sausage was a marriage made in heaven. I quickly emptied the bowl.

"I guess it was good," she said.

"Better than good. *Fantastic.*"

She held the ladle over the pot. "Want some more?"

"Maybe after I see Mr. Daggett. How is he today?"

She tasted a spoonful of soup and added more salt to the pot. She frowned, but it had nothing to do with the soup. "Phil said that he's changed in the last day or so."

"In what way, Mrs. Gomes?"

"He says the old man paces back and forth a lot. Keeps looking out that big window with his spyglass. Crazy-eyed. Doesn't say much. He's letting himself go, too. Phil says his beard looks like a bird's nest. He only eats breakfast and lunch. Doesn't touch his dinner."

"Maybe your soup will cheer him up. I'd be happy to take some into him."

She filled another bowl, and set it on a tray with a spoon and napkin. I carried the tray up the main stairs to the captain's quarters and knocked on the door with the side of my foot.

"Who *goes* there?" Daggett called out.

I switched to Melville-speak and growled, " 'Tis Starbuck, Captain Ahab."

"Don't *stand* there, Starbuck. Approach the quarterdeck, lad."

I juggled the tray with one hand, opened the door with the other and stepped inside. The captain was standing on the raised floor with his back to the window.

"Cook asked me to bring you some grub, Captain."

I set the tray on the table after noticing that the top had been cleared of charts. Daggett stepped down from the window and removed his slouch hat. His unkempt hair hadn't seen a comb recently. The mouth-watering smell of the soup was too much for him to resist. He limped over to the table, sat down and scooped a big spoonful into his mouth. That was the end of his fast. He dug in until the bowl was empty. Drops of soup got into his matted beard, but he didn't seem to care. He sat back and motioned for me to take a chair.

"Tell Cook that I'll soon reward him with enough fresh whale meat to slice up for a hundred steaks from the carcass of the white whale. The evil creature's end is near."

"How soon, Captain?"

"Not soon enough! The *morrow*."

"Is that what the charts tell you, sir?"

"The charts have served their purpose. We are entering the devil's den. Today I gammed with the captains of the *Rachel* and the *Delight*, two Nantucket ships that only days before had lost good men to the unholy wrath of the white whale. I will avenge them as well with this very hand, Starbuck. Will ye stand fast with me in the boat?"

"Aye, Captain. I'll be there."

"Good!"

He stood, pushed the chair back and raised his arm in the air, his fingers balled as if clutching something.

"The lance that will end his days has been tempered by blood and lightning. I will place the point in that hot place behind the fin where the white whale most feels his accursed life."

His words rang like hammer blows on steel.

"And once that is done, Captain, what then?" I said.

A manic grin came to his lips.

"Art thou mad, Starbuck? The white whale will be dead."

"And once Moby Dick is dead, will *that* be the end of it, Captain Ahab?"

"Aye, Starbuck. The white whale is gone to the hell that spawned it. I am done."

Daggett was starting to annoy me. Since arriving on Nantucket I had been shot at, pushed around, lied to, growled at by attack dogs and stalked. Daggett on the other hand, gets himself into hot water, then retreats into the protective bubble of his fictional personality. I wasn't sure at this point whether he was truly crazy or whether he had simply found a clever way to escape life's slings and arrows.

Either way, I resented it.

I wished I had the *Moby Dick* paperback so I could shove the book in his face and say that I was onto him and to stop using Melville and Ishmael and Stubbs, and yes, good old Starbuck as shields while the rest of us poor slobs had to deal with everything life threw at us. But I didn't. Because there was always the possibility that he was temporarily insane, and if I tried to drag him back to reality, it would send him over the abyss.

Instead, I spoke softly and said, "But what of the *Pequod* and the crew? What of me? Are we doomed to become rotting corpses sailing a ship of the damned for all time?"

"If need be. It will be out of my hands."

I had the feeling that I was losing Daggett. That he would drift off into the safety of his madness and wither away until he was beyond reach of anyone. Daggett was at the center of a whirling vortex. I wasn't about to let him drag me and others down with him. His mania seemed to be peaking. I had no idea what might happen when he at last confronted the white whale in his fevered brain. Would the shock suddenly snap him back to the present, or would he be drawn further into his madness, never to emerge?

Speaking firmly, I said, "It's not for you alone to say, Captain."

He glowered at me. "You think me mad, Starbuck, but it's *your* brains that are addled. This ship is my *kingdom*, the crew my loyal knights and serfs. I care *not* for the mindless prattling from the fo'c'sle."

"But there others who *do* care, Captain. Your granddaughter, Lisa. Your sweetheart, Lillian. They'll be at the water's edge waiting for the first sight of the *Pequod*'s sails."

"I know not—"

"They want your voyage to end. They want you to walk the cobblestones of Nantucket again. To sit and gam with other whaling captains. To end your days at sea forever. They *miss* you, Captain."

The heat went out of his eyes. "I miss them, too. Dear God, I miss them, too."

"Then come home now, sir. They're waiting."

His face contorted, as if he were going through a fierce internal struggle, then his features hardened and his voice grew icy.

"My time will come, but first there must be *blood*."

It's not easy playing at being Sigmund Freud, especially when your skills of psychoanalysis are non-existent. What I did have was something no professional shrink, even a legitimate one, would ever have. Daggett thought I was Starbuck. As his first mate, I could reach him in a primal level. He had responded when I mentioned the names of his granddaughter and sweetheart. It wasn't much, but it was a crack in his Ahab façade.

I said, "Excuse me, Captain, but I must tend to my duties."

"Aye, Starbuck. Tend away. And I must prepare for the glorious hour."

"You do that, Captain."

He rose slowly from the table, placed the hat on his head and walked back to the window. He stared through the glass without speaking. I picked up the tray and bowl and edged out of the room.

Lisa had come home and was in the kitchen alone. She was scooping the bottom out of a soup bowl. I sat across from her.

"I see you've been recruited as a soup tester, too."

"You've already had some? It's heavenly, isn't it? I could finish off the whole pot."

"Better not. Mrs. Gomes made it for your grandfather. I took him some and he practically ate the bowl, too."

"Thank you for doing that."

"How did your airport meeting go?"

"Good. I got a substantial contribution. It was hard keeping my mind on the conversation. I kept thinking about the prisoner out on Mayhew Point."

"You can relax a little. I got in touch with Flagg. He's offered to help."

"That's a relief. It's difficult enough dealing with Gramps and his problems. How is he doing?"

"Hard to tell, Lisa. Tomorrow may be a turning point."

"Why tomorrow?"

I told her about my conversation with her grandfather. "I was going to use tough love on the old guy, Lisa. I thought if I accused him of scamming everybody, it would snap him out of whatever spell he's under and bring him back to life."

Her brow furrowed. "You think he's been pretending all this time?"

"It crossed my mind. Maybe because Rosen is a jerk and I didn't trust his conclusion that Gramps is out of his mind. I told you when you hired me that I wouldn't bend the facts to suit the needs of my client. It's whatever it is."

"And what is it?"

"We won't know the truth until your grandfather comes out of his Ahab spell."

She gave me a bleak smile. "Then that's it. Gramps goes to court, they find him crazy and put him away forever."

"Not necessarily. Dr. Socarides may be rough around the edges, but he gets results."

I told her about Daggett's reaction when I mentioned her name and Lillian's. She reached across the table and grabbed my hand in hers.

"Sorry for doubting you. That gives me so much hope. Maybe he *can* come out of it."

"It will raise new problems if he becomes lucid before his trial. He won't be able to use the insanity defense, which means there may be a prison cell in his future."

She squeezed my hand until it hurt. "He would *die* in prison, Soc."

"Then let's keep him out of prison. Dr. Rosen is convinced that Henry will never recover. Maybe you can use his questionable diagnosis to help Gramps. Tell Rosen that your grandfather seems to be reaching a crisis. That he's starting to remember things. And that it wouldn't help if Henry had a meltdown in the courtroom. Ask him to back you up when you tell the D.A. that you want a trial postponement."

"You think it will work?"

"Maybe." I paused, then said, "There's one other thing. I think it's time you visited your grandfather and talked to him as a person, not as a specter."

"Dr. Rosen says if I did it will drive him over the cliff."

"Do you trust Rosen?"

"No. I don't. Okay, I'll go see my grandfather, but I'm not sure how he'll react."

"What do you have to lose?"

"Not much, unfortunately." I was a little sad when she released her warm grip. "Thanks for everything, Soc. Will you be here when I'm done seeing him?"

"Probably not. I've got to check my telephone messages, then get back into town to do an errand. How about dinner later on?"

Lisa said that would be fine and we arranged to meet at a restaurant she suggested. As I walked back to the apartment, I worried that I had given Lisa bad advice. Working as a detective in Boston and later on my own, sometimes I acted like an amateur shrink. A practical knowledge of human behavior can help when you're trying to get information out of someone. But I had never met anyone as crazy as Daggett.

The red light was blinking on the telephone. I retrieved the messages. My mother had called to ask how things were working out with Alex. And there was a call from my cousin saying that Malloy had called his daughter a few weeks ago, said he was going hiking in Nepal, and might be out of telephone range for a while. How convenient.

I had a few hours before Flagg's return so I called Sutcliffe and said I had something I wanted to show him. He said he'd be at the whaling museum, but would meet me at a nearby bar. On the drive into town, I pictured the surprise on his face when I showed him the scrimshaw photos that implicated Swain as a murderer. Silly me. I'd forgotten that the Little Grey Lady of the Sea is never predictable. As I would soon find out, she had more than one secret hidden in the thick folds of her foggy skirt.

CHAPTER 28

Sutcliffe was waiting for me at the Brotherhood of Thieves. It was the quiet time in between lunch and dinner, so we were the only people at the bar. We shook hands and I set the envelope in front of him without saying what was in it. We ordered a couple of beers and made small talk. Between sips, Sutcliffe kept glancing at the envelope. Finally, his curiosity got the best of him.

He tapped the envelope with his forefinger. "Is this for *me?*"

"Depends on whether or not you buy me another beer."

"No-brainer," he said.

He signaled the bartender, then undid the clasp and slid the photos out. He was familiar with Coffin scrimshaw and knew right away what he was looking at. He examined each image, his eyes widening.

"Holy *crap*, Soc! This is a scrimshaw record of the sinking of the *Moshup* and the aftermath."

"That's not *all* it is. Take a very close look at the panels."

He studied the carved scenes that showed the hunt for the whale, the overturned whaleboats and the whale's attack on the ship. He brought the photos close to his face when he came to the panels that depicted what happened after the ship went under and the crew set off in the whaleboats. I heard a sharp intake of breath.

"*Find* something?" I said in an off-handed voice.

"Oh *yeah*. And don't you know it." He placed his forefinger on the panel detailing the dice throw, then slid it over to the scenes of the killing and the grisly aftermath. His finger stopped on the image of the two survivors gnawing on the bones of their fellow crewman. "This shows what *really* happened in that whaleboat. That lying sonofabitch Swain was the killer."

"If you can believe Coffin."

"I believe him. The sly old bastard Obed must have known Swain would try to frame him for the murder. So he told the story the best way that he could, with his art."

"Which would explain why Swain scoffed up the entire scrimshaw collection when Coffin died. He had covered up his crime the first time, when he persuaded Coffin to go along with the phony story about Daggett killing himself. Again, when he wrote the journal implicating Coffin. And a third time when he acquired the incriminating evidence."

"A cover-up of the cover-up of the cover-up. Where did you *get* this stuff?"

I took him along the trail that I had followed to New Bedford, my talk with Mandel and how that discussion led to the meeting with Warner.

"Forget all those jokes I made about Sherlock and Nick Charles. You're better than either one of them."

"Thanks. It was something any red-blooded, Greek-American detective could have done with a little perseverance and lots of luck."

"*Luck*? Like hell. I've been digging around in this stuff like a pregnant pig, but I never found any truffles."

"Not sure I like the pregnant pig analogy, but I agree that this is a rare find."

"And it's going to make an even bigger book, thanks to you."

"In good time," I said, shoving the photos back into the envelope.

Sutcliffe looked like a kid who'd been told to hand over his lollipop. "All the actors in this play have been dead for a hundred and fifty years," he pleaded. "Nobody's going to get hurt. Not even Swain."

"Someone's *already* been hurt," I said. "Remember Ab Coffin?"

"Oh yeah. That's right. Damn!" His face crumpled in a mask of disappointment. "Okay then," he said with a deep sigh. "Where do we go from here?"

"Let's start with the premise that the evidence of Swain's guilt was what got Coffin excited. He sees an opportunity to set the record straight about his ancestor. He tries to acquire the evidence, but Warner says no-go. Collection has to be sold as a whole, although he'd entertain an expensive compromise. Coffin finds the money to essentially *rent* the piece. He plans to show it to Daggett as a way to persuade him to buy it for the museum. Something goes wrong. Coffin ends up dead. Daggett's in *Moby Dick* land. The piece is missing."

"That's a pretty good summary. But what went wrong. And why would Daggett kill Coffin?"

I shrugged. "Maybe Daggett was still being stubborn about the acquisition. Coffin won't take no for an answer. He gets physical. In self defense, Daggett grabs the boarding knife off the wall and skewers Coffin."

"Do you really believe in that scenario?"

"Hell, no. It's ridiculous. But it's a story the prosecution will tell the jury."

Sutcliffe slurped his beer. "Doesn't make sense. Daggett's a Nantucket history buff, too. He would have seen the value of the piece to set the record straight. It would have made great publicity for the museum and a hell of a tourist draw. What a story, man!"

"So why didn't that happen? Why didn't they join forces to persuade the board of directors that this was a major find?"

"I don't know. *Why?*"

"Because someone didn't *want* the record set straight," I said. "Let's assume there was a *third* person at the meeting."

"Interesting theory. Do you have anyone in mind?"

"Put that question aside for now. Picture this. Coffin and Daggett *both* believe the scrimshaw should be made public. They set up a meeting. Coffin gets there first. The third person is waiting, and kills him. When Daggett shows up, Number Three whacks Daggett with the pommel of the knife. He wipes down the knife, puts it in Daggett's hands and exits the scene of the crime."

"How does Number Three get into the museum?"

"Good question. I don't know, so let's stay with what we *do* know for now."

"Okay. The cops got a phone tip about the murder. Number Three again?"

I nodded. "Unfortunately, Daggett regains consciousness before the police show up. He sees Coffin's body, and the knife in his hands. Figures maybe he killed his friend. He makes it to his car and tries to drive home, but instead stops at the Serengeti, a place that is near and dear. The blow on the head, the shock of finding his pal dead, the possibility that he is responsible, send him over the edge. He takes refuge in his Ahab persona."

"Not bad," Sutcliffe said.

"There's another possibility. The bad guy knocks Daggett out and transports him to the Serengeti."

"More complicated, but possible. Can you prove any of these theories?"

"Nope. But I'm open to suggestions."

Sutcliffe drifted off thought, but only for a moment. "Maybe we should get it straight from the horse's mouth. Let's take a walk."

Sutcliffe paid for the beers and we emerged from the dim bar into the summer sunlight. I thought Sutcliffe was taking me back to his house. Instead, we walked along a narrow lane lined with antique houses and followed Sparks Avenue to an old cemetery at the edge of town.

Sutcliffe climbed over a split-rail fence and I followed him into the burying ground.

"They used to call this the Old South Cemetery," he said. "Nothing but pasture land back in the 1700s, but as you can see, the town has expanded this way. Fifteen or so sea captains are planted here."

We walked by a row of headstones. "There's a Mayhew. Lillian's family," I said.

"Check out the date. Mayhews go back to the 1700s. There's Susan Veeder, who went on a five-year whaling voyage on her husband's ship, and gave birth to a little girl in Chile. The child died in Tahiti. They didn't want to leave her body so they brought it back in a sealed coffin and buried her here in the family plot."

I read the inscription on the headstone. "Sad story," I said.

"But not untypical. Nantucketers sailed around the globe to places most Americans never dreamed existed. But they wanted their remains back on the island. One guy ended up in Salt Lake and before he died, he directed that his heart be taken from his dead body and buried here." We tromped down another row of stones. Sutcliffe stopped and said, "*This* is what I wanted to show you."

His finger pointed to a headstone of red marble that was at least twice as big as the markers around it. The top of the stone was arched, rather than horizontal, which allowed space for a carving of whaleboats attacking a whale. There was no date on the face of the stone, only a single word. *Swain.* The stone was enclosed within a granite brick border a couple of inches high.

"Any connection to our friend from the *Moshup*?" I asked.

"Yup. You wouldn't know it from the inscription, but that block of granite marks the burial spot of Nantucket's most famous cannibal."

I read aloud the name on the smaller, left-hand stone. Trixie Swain.

"That's his wife. The ex-prostitute. Stone on the other side is for Charles Swain, his only son."

I pointed to the reddish monument. "Is this the horse's mouth you were talking about?"

He nodded.

"You forget to mention that the horse was dead."

"The *dead* tell tales, too, my friend," he said in a hollow voice.

There were a dozen or so rectangular white stones behind the three monuments in front. By moving from slab to slab, we traced the Swain progeny from the 19th century into the 20th. Charles had eight children, which meant that the family had grown exponentially. New names were added into the mix as women married into the family and had children of their own.

Sutcliffe, who was a step or two ahead of me, knelt before the last stone in the chronology and read the names on it.

He brushed some yellow lichen off the granite. "Now *that's* interesting."

I squatted beside him and read the name of the deceased. "And *that's* an understatement if I ever heard one." I reached out and traced the letters with my forefinger. "You didn't know about this?"

"God, no! I would have followed up in a minute. This is great stuff."

I stood and looked around at the mute stones in the old burial ground. "Island fog."

It was a clear sunny afternoon. When Sutcliffe gave me a funny look, I told him the theory that I had come up with to explain the curtain of mystery that seemed to hang over the old island.

"That's a good way of putting it. But thanks to the miracles of modern science, I can cut through the fog. The historical society has a database on the stones in all the cemeteries. I'll check it out and see what I can dig up."

"Let me know when you do."

"Could be a coincidence."

"You really think so?"

He stared at the headstone. "I've written thousands of words about the history of Nantucket, but with something like this, I don't know *what* to think. Want to talk about it over another round of beers?"

"Another time. Got a dinner appointment with Lisa," I said.

We walked back into town. Before we went off on our separate ways, Sutcliffe promised to get back to me after he'd visited the historical society. We shook hands and he said, "Guess we jumped the gun thinking that the dirt you dug up on Swain was the end of the *Moshup* story."

I couldn't deny that I'd been hit with a case of hubris, the Greek term for the exaggerated self-confidence that can incite the wrath of the gods. After all, this was Nantucket, a Chinese puzzle box mated to a Rubik's cube. Just when I thought I was out of the maze, I came up against a blank wall.

"No, it isn't the end," I said. "Not by a long shot."

CHAPTER 29

Flagg had only been gone a short time, but I already missed him. On the drive back to Siasconset, I kept a nervous eye on the rearview mirror. The attempt to stuff me into an SUV had me on edge. If the Russians and their friends tried once, they would try again. At any second, a carload of thugs could come roaring up from behind and drive the little MG off the road.

All I saw in the mirror were the golden rays of the setting sun filtering through rows of striated purple clouds. It's called a mackerel sky because the cloud formation looks like the scale pattern on the fish of the same name. It's usually a sign the weather is about to change. The yellowish tinge to the waning light meant wind and rain were in the cards. Bad things coming, any way you looked at it.

Lisa's Jeep was in the Daggett house driveway. Behind it was the Gomes's pick-up truck. Rosen's car wasn't in its usual place in front of his cottage. I parked next to the garage and climbed the stairs to my apartment. I dug out my Ninja outfit and stacked the dark clothes on my bed in readiness for the night's work. Lisa arrived with dinner a few minutes later. She was casually dressed in tan shorts and an aqua tank top. She was holding a tray and on it were some covered dishes and a bottle of *Prosecco*.

"I decided to have dinner at home, if that's okay." She breezed by me and set the tray on the kitchen table. "Wine glasses, please?"

"At your service, mademoiselle. May I suggest that we dine on the deck?"

"That would be perfect," she said as she rounded up dishes and placemats.

I got two glasses out of the cupboard and set them on the deck table. The air was calm, allowing for a couple of candles. Lisa dished out chicken *piccata* and sauteed spinach with rosemary-flavored potatoes. In between bites and sips, we talked about inconsequential things like the weather, and the traffic in town. We topped off our meal with Italian-style salad and a fruit cup. I pushed back from the table and patted my stomach.

"Does that mean dinner was okay?" she said.

"Let me put it this way. If you serve another meal like that, you may never get rid of me."

She gave me her appraising look. "Thank you. Consider it a reward for suggesting that I see Gramps."

"You're smiling, so I guess it went well."

"Better than well. I knocked on the door, and when he asked in his gruff Ahab voice who it was, I simply said, 'It's your granddaughter.' There was a pause of a few seconds, as if he was thinking it over, and he told me to wait. After a minute, he said it was all right to come in. That's when I got my first surprise."

"A good or bad surprise?

"*Good.* He had combed his hair and beard." She wrinkled her nose. "He smells a bit ripe and could use a hot shower. Anyhow, I got my second surprise when he said, '*Lisa.*'" She wiped a tear from her eye. When she spoke again, there was a slight catch in her voice. "Sorry for the waterworks, Soc, but it's the first time he's recognized me since he went into his delusional state."

"That's enough to make anyone cry for joy, Lisa. Does your

grandfather still think that you're only a dream?"

"It's hard to tell. He stared at me for the longest time, then he stepped closer and reached out to touch my cheek. He drew back after a second. I think he was afraid that if he touched me I'd disappear like a soap bubble."

"Did he say anything else?"

She smiled. "He said, 'art thou real, granddaughter?' "

"How did you answer him?"

"I said, '*Yes*, grandfather. I'm real. It's time to come home to Nantucket.' He seemed to recoil at the suggestion. He said he couldn't come home, that he was fated to hunt down the white whale."

"He's confused. He knows Melville's book ends with Ahab tangled up in the harpoon lines, Moby dragging him down into the sea."

"If he goes along with that scenario, in his mind he'd be dead. So I cut away at the foundation of his delusion. I said, 'It's only a story, Gramps. *I'm* real, but Moby Dick isn't. Don't you remember all your books? He came out of Herman Melville's imagination. The *Pequod*. Ahab. Ishmael. They're all fiction."

"You were taking a chance."

"Yes, I know. But I was so frustrated. And I think it worked."

"In what way, Lisa?"

"He's aware that the story doesn't *have* to end for him the way it does in the book. He's fighting that. He's lost that sour Ahab scowl. His features were more relaxed and he looked like my old Gramps again. He said he had to rest, that there was much to do. Here's the good part. He told me to come back in a little while."

I leaned back in my chair and tented my fingers. "Congratulations, Ms. Freud. I think you've made a breakthrough."

"I'm *sure* of it. As I was saying goodbye, he called out, 'I miss Lillian, too.' "

"You're definitely on the right track, Lisa. When do you plan to see him again?"

She frowned. "I don't know. Soon. Dr. Rosen saw me coming from the captain's quarters and quizzed me on what I was doing there. I told him what happened. He got angry and advised me, that as the court-approved shrink, he must forbid me from seeing Gramps. I told him he was fired and had half an hour to vacate the cottage."

I let out a whooping laugh and raised my glass in toast. "To the swift return of the *Pequod*'s captain to the real world."

"I left a message with the D.A. outlining my reasons for a delay in the trial. Hoping to hear by tomorrow."

"That's good. We need time to develop some leads."

I told her what I had learned about the scrimshaw collection and showed her the photos of the Coffin pieces. She studied the pictures and said, "These are fascinating in a gruesome sort of way, but I'm not sure how they relate to my grandfather's case."

I arranged the photos in a row.

"What we have here is eyewitness evidence in another murder case. Swain murdered Daggett and he and Coffin covered up the crime. Later, Swain acquired the scrimshaw so he could extend the cover-up. Flash forward to the present. The incriminating scrimshaw surfaces again. Ab Coffin realizes the significance and tries to bring the collection into the open. Someone stops him. Conclusion, counselor?"

"Swain wasn't the only one who wanted to suppress the truth," Lisa ventured. "Someone more recently may have wanted the story behind the *Moshup* squashed."

"*Bingo*. That person was at the museum the night Coffin was killed."

Her jaw sagged. "Which would make the third person the murderer. Do you have any idea who that is?"

"Not yet." I glanced at my watch. Flagg was due in soon.

"*Sorry*, Lisa. We'll have to pick this up later. I have an

appointment."

I began to clear the table. As we carried dishes into the kitchen she said, "This is an odd time to be meeting someone. Is this anything to do with my case?"

"Not exactly. I'm going to the airport. Flagg is flying in."

"Thank goodness," she said. "Does that mean you'll be going back to Mayhew Point?"

"It's a possibility."

As we passed the bedroom on the way to the kitchen, Lisa glanced through the open door. The black clothes were clearly visible on the bed.

"It looks like *more* than a possibility," she said.

I shrugged.

Without hesitation, she said, "I want to go with you."

"That's not an option, Lisa. It's too dangerous."

"Don't patronize me, Soc. It doesn't become you." She set the dishes down on the counter so hard that they rattled and turned to me. "I'm not anxious to go back there, but I'm thinking of *your* safety. As I recall, *I* was the one who prevented you from being chewed up by Michael's guard dogs."

I did a verbal tap-dance step. "Tell you what," I said. "Let's let Flagg decide."

"You've got a deal."

She threw her arms around me in a quick hug, and said she had to go get her own Ninja outfit. I was off the hook. If I knew Flagg, he would never agree to Lisa's request. As I would soon discover, I didn't know Flagg well at all.

The airport lobby was almost deserted. I asked the woman at the rental car counter if she had seen anyone come off a plane. She pointed. Flagg stood behind me holding a leather satchel. For a big man, he has the amazing ability to materialize like a ghost.

"You're ten minutes early," I said.

"Old habit. I never arrive when I'm expected," he said. "Hello, Ms. Hendricks."

"Lisa."

"Hello, Lisa," Flagg said. He shot a questioning glance in my direction.

I shrugged. "Why don't we discuss it in the car," I suggested.

We went out to the parking lot and headed for the Jeep.

"Lisa knows about tonight," I said. "She wants to go along. There are two big dogs on the property, and the last time we visited she had them wagging their tails."

Flagg said, "You know the property well, Lisa?"

"I've been there a number of times. Michael Ramsey is an acquaintance."

"That's good, Lisa, but here's the thing. It's always riskier to visit a target the second time around. Security cameras might have picked you up on the first visit. So they could be on the lookout for intruders. We may look over-the-hill, but Soc and I have experience in this kind of thing."

"Speak for yourself, Flagg."

"See. Soc's getting touchy in his old age. What I'm saying, Lisa, is that we go back a long way. We've got to get to the bunker and rescue whoever is being held prisoner. Having you along could make it dangerous for us, too."

"I realize that I could be a liability. That's why I propose I only go as far as the bridge that crosses the creek to Michael's property. I can keep an eye on the Jeep and be available if you need any help from the outside."

Flag nodded. "Sounds okay. That okay with you, Soc?"

I gave Flagg a hard look and Lisa one that was only slightly softer. I was outnumbered and outgunned. Arguing would be a waste of time.

"Just as long as we stick to the plan. Lisa hangs back while the over-the-hill gang does its thing."

Lisa squeezed my arm, melting away my last shred of resistance. "I promise, Soc. But what are you going to do about the dogs?"

Flagg hefted his bag. "Got some stuff here that'll give the pups a little nap."

"Guess that's it," I said. "We've got one thing going for us on this trip."

"I'd like to hear what that is, Soc."

"The element of surprise. They won't be expecting us to do anything so stupid."

CHAPTER 30

Mayhew's Point was less than a half hour's drive from the airport. I wheeled the Jeep off the blacktop onto the rutted track that led to the clearing Lisa and I had used as a jump-off for our first incursion onto the Ramsey estate. The moon was veiled by a thickening overcast. Inky darkness enveloped us the second I killed the headlights.

Flagg climbed from the back seat with his satchel and pulled a halogen flashlight from the bag. He turned it on, and without a word starting walking at a brisk pace toward the path that led to the old bridge.

Lisa and I followed the bobbing bull's-eye to the banking that overlooked the creek.

"How'd you know the way to the bridge?" I asked.

"Us Indians carry a natural compass," he said.

"Sure you do. Now how did you *really* know the way?"

"Sometimes we use the white man's *mojo*. Satellite images in this case. I memorized the terrain on the flight from DC. Got a pretty good idea of the lay of the land." He pointed his flashlight at the bridge. "*Whoee!* You walked across on top those poles, Soc?"

"What's wrong, old-timer. Twinkle-toes not twinkly as they

249

used to be?"

"I'm fine, but your twinkly mouth is going to give us away."

"Pretty lame, Flagg."

"Best I could do for now. Sorry for the trash talk, Lisa. Soc and I haven't worked with each other in a while. We've got lots of bad jokes saved up. Must seem crazy to you."

"No apology needed, John. I've only known Soc a few days, but it's long enough to discover that he's, uh, unconventional. It stands to reason his friends would be, too."

Flagg laughed, louder than he should have on a clandestine mission. "*Unconventional.* I like that."

He was still chuckling as he strode off in a loping walk and we followed the dancing light back to the Jeep. Flagg took a satellite photo from his jacket pocket. He flattened the photo on the hood of the Jeep and asked me to point out the bunker. I tapped the photo with my fingertip.

"It's this elongated dark area between the edge of the lawn and the dunes. Sort of shaped like a meatloaf. From the ground it looks like a low hill covered with grass and brush, so it blends into the trees."

"What do you figure is the best way to get there without being seen?"

"I suggest we make our way to the point, then head in toward the house, using the hill to shield our movements."

Flagg grunted an okay, excused himself to Lisa, then stripped to his underwear and slipped into a black cover-all from his satchel. I got into my Ninja uniform. He dug out two sets of night-vision goggles, handed me one and passed around hand radios set on vibrating mode.

"Will you be okay out here alone?" I asked Lisa.

"Being look-out is the easy job. Careful, both of you. Don't take any chances."

Flagg put on the goggles and pulled a black skull-cap down over his forehead. "Don't worry, Lisa. Soc and I are better at running than we are at fighting."

I pulled on my goggles and hit the power switch. The darkness vanished, and in its place was a grainy amber and black image of trees and bushes. We headed toward the creek. When we got to the old bridge pilings, Flagg hardly slowed his pace. He stepped off the banking, then moved from pole-to-pole with an ease no one would expect from someone with a physique so big and top-heavy.

He stepped onto the opposite banking and watched me cross the bridge with only slightly more grace than the first time across.

Flagg extended his hand. "You looked a little shaky."

"Still getting used to these goggles," I said, which was only partly true.

"*Now* who's being lame?"

"Best I could do. This way."

I took the lead and we followed the creek to where it emptied out into the cove, then walked through the dunes to the beach. We trudged along in the sand, skirting the edge of the peninsula, until we came to the point. Lights glowed off shore.

"That's Chernko's yacht," I said. "He and Ramsey are on one of their nocturnal cruises."

"That doesn't mean we should be any less careful," Flagg said. "Keep a sharp eye out. We might not be the *only* ones with night vision." He looked to the right and the left. "What about those dogs you mentioned?"

"Probably watching a re-run of *Lassie*," I said. "They'll find us. Hope you brought along some dog treats."

"Nope. I've got something better."

Flagg reached into his backpack and pulled out what looked like three pipes of varying lengths lashed together in parallel fashion. The apparatus had a strap, which he slung over his left shoulder.

"What's that thing?" I said.

"Glorified blow-gun. Ready?"

We climbed a ridge of dunes and struck off inland, using the rotunda as a beacon. The ground rose gradually and the landscape changed from dunes to low brush, then we were in the strip of scrub forest that bordered the vast lawn. Once we were among the scraggly oak woods, I navigated by dead reckoning. After a couple of minutes, we came to the bunker. I was eager to show Flagg my find, and quickened my pace. He reached out and grabbed the back of my shirt.

"*Down*," he said. My Marine training returned. We dropped belly first onto the ground. "There," he whispered.

I followed his pointing finger. Someone was walking along the base of the hill that concealed the bunker.

"Crap," I whispered. "Place is under guard."

We watched the figure until it disappeared around the end of the mound. I was thinking we might be able to time an approach with the guard's rounds, but the first guard was only out of sight for a couple of seconds before another one appeared at the opposite end of the bunker. There were two of them, moving counter-clockwise around the hill.

Flagg brought his arm close so we could see the second hand moving around the glowing dial of his watch. He timed a patrol cycle.

"We've got twelve seconds before the first guy disappears and the second one pops out at the other end. Plenty of time to cover ground. You do the count."

I watched until both guards were out of sight and said, "Up!"

We were on our feet and running. I counted ten to myself and said, "Down!"

We hit the ground simultaneously around a dozen yards closer to the bunker. The guard popped out a second later.

"Cutting it a little close, Soc."

"I'll do an eight count this time. *Up!*"

We got our legs under us again and did the sprint and drop with plenty of time to spare. We repeated the exercise two more times. On the last drop, we were both panting.

"Outta shape," Flagg said between breaths.

"Can't be age," I panted.

"Hell no! One more and we're there."

Up again and down again. This time we landed so close we could have thrown a stone and hit the passing sentry. Flagg slipped the pipe arrangement off his shoulder, snapped open a folding stock to its full extension and braced it against his shoulder. He squinted through the cylinder on top of the other pipe.

"That thing works on humans?" I whispered.

"It was *designed* for humans." He snickered. "Your tax dollars at work. Now zip your mouth."

Flagg led the slow-walking guard by a hair, and pulled the trigger. There was a soft *thut* sound, not much louder than someone blowing out a cake full of birthday candles. The guard grabbed his shoulder, spun around and crumpled to the ground. Then the second guard appeared and Flagg popped him nicely, too.

The fast-acting drugs in the dart had put the guards to sleep almost instantly. They lay crumpled on the ground within yards of each other. Both men wore black jumpsuits and if we hadn't been using goggles, we would not have seen them guarding the bunker. The machine pistols they had been carrying lay on the ground. Each weapon had a night vision spotting scope.

Both men were in their thirties. Their eyes were glazed and drool came from their mouths. Flagg knelt down and removed the darts. He made sure the guards were on their sides, so they wouldn't suffocate on their own saliva. Then we bound their hands and feet with duct tape from a roll Flagg carried in his sack. I led the way to the door at the end of the bunker. I had my black box with me and used it to neutralize the lock.

When the green light flashed, Flagg produced a Sig Sauer pistol and pushed the door open. I haven't packed a weapon since I left the Boston Police Department, but Flagg always carries a personal arsenal, so I let him take the lead.

When the door opened, there was the stale smell of cooked food and cigarette smoke that I had noticed on my first visit. We passed through the radiation lock, then into the main space. I found the wall switch and the big room flooded with light. Flagg looked around, wonder in his eyes.

"What a dump."

"Your taxpayer dollars at work," I said.

We walked to the box-shaped structure and stepped inside. There was a man lying on the only cot with bedding. He was covered with an army blanket. I went over and put my fingers against his neck. His skin was warm and I could feel blood pulsing through his carotid artery. I shook his shoulder, but he didn't respond.

"He's alive."

Flagg lifted the man's chin. "This your friend Malloy?"

"Never saw the guy, so I don't know what he looks like. I'll take a ball park guess and say yes." I called Malloy by name, but he didn't respond. "Out cold. We've got to get him away from this place."

Flagg peeled back the blanket. Malloy was dressed in a rumpled navy blue running suit and sneakers. One wrist was chained to the bunk frame. Flagg produced a pair of metal cutters from his miracle bag. He made short work of the chain and we lifted the man up onto rubbery legs. We draped his limp arms around our shoulders, put him between us and dragged him back through the bunker and out the air lock.

We decided to head straight back to the bridge rather than take the long route out to the point and along the beach to the creek. We would be in the open, but our exposure would only be a few minutes. We were almost at the low brush bordering the lawn when I glanced back. Two blobs of fuzzy light were headed in our direction across the wide expanse of lawn. As the blobs neared, they sprouted legs.

"Uh-oh," I said. "Brutus and Cassius."

Flagg must have been puzzled at the mention of a couple of old Romans. He said, "What the hell are you talking about?"

"Ramsey's guard dogs."

"Why didn't you *say* so?" Flagg said. "No problem."

Unlike Flagg, I thought there *was* a problem, actually *two* problems. Without Lisa around to pacify the Dobermans, within seconds they'd be sinking their fangs into our ankles. Flagg told me to hold Malloy up and slipped the blow-gun off his shoulder. There was that soft puff sound again. I thought Flagg had missed because the lead dog kept on coming, and was almost on us, but after a few seconds, his gallop slowed and he crashed to the ground.

The second dog slowed to avoid his fallen pal. There was another *thut*. The dog leaped into the air, came down in a clump and lay there. Flagg went over to the limp forms and removed a dart from the chest of one dog and the flank of the other.

"They'll be fine. They'll wake up in an hour or so after their nap."

He tossed the darts into his bag with the others, grabbed Malloy's arm and threw it over his shoulder. It was slow going because we had to stop from time to time for a rest. Flagg was right. Neither one of us was young again. But somehow, with a lot of grunts and surges of adrenaline, we made it to the creek. We stretched Malloy out on the ground face-up and caught our breath. Then I called Lisa on the hand radio and was happy to hear her voice.

"Everything okay?" I said.

"All quiet here. What about you?"

"Mission accomplished. We're about to cross the creek."

"Were there any problems?"

"A few. No big deal, though,"

"That's a relief. I've ranged from high anxiety to extreme boredom."

"The boredom part is about to end. We could use some help with a package."

I clicked off and went over to Flagg. "Figured it out yet?"

"*Yeah*. You grab his legs. I'll take his arms."

Flagg squatted and got a lock grip on the wrists, then stood again. I did the same, grabbed Malloy under the knees and lifted. Malloy sagged like a full hammock. We moved forward onto the pilings. First the right foot, then the left. Our human load rocked from side to side, threatening our balance. A couple of times we teetered. Slowly, laboriously, we got him to the other side and stood him upright again. My shoulder muscles were screaming.

Lisa emerged from the woods and saw us with Malloy. "Who *is* that?"

"We'll explain later. We've got to get him to the Jeep."

She ran ahead, showing us the way with her flashlight. I had about reached the end of my rope physically when we emerged into the clearing where the Jeep was parked. We lifted Malloy into the back seat. Lisa flashed the light onto the ravaged face.

"He looks terrible," she said. "We've got to get him to a hospital!"

"Can't risk it," Flagg said. "They'd ask too many questions."

He took Malloy's pulse, put his head against his chest, and looked into the man's gaping mouth. "I think I know the drug they used to knock him out. It won't kill him. He's going to need somewhere quiet to sweat it out of his system."

Lisa wasn't through yet. "A hospital would be quiet."

Flagg said, "The guys who did this to him won't let some nurses or doctors stop them. They'll kill anyone who gets in their way. Then they'll kill him."

"Flagg's right," I said. "Whoever had him locked up is going to come looking for him. He needs to be somewhere he can't be found."

Our warnings must have sunk in. Lisa stopped protesting. And after a moment of thought, she said, "I know just the place."

CHAPTER 31

The outline of Henry Daggett's dune shack loomed from the fog shrouding the beach. Lisa unlocked the door and Flagg and I trundled Malloy inside. We rolled him into the bunk. The cottage was damp and musty, but it quickly dried out and was almost cozy after we fired up a load of kindling in the stove and lit a couple of kerosene lanterns.

Flagg said he would keep watch on Malloy. He sat in the rocking chair and closed his eyes in a deceptive pose. Flagg had a cat-like ability to maintain a steel-spring alertness even while he slumbered. Sometimes I wondered if he ever really slept.

On the walk back to the main house, Lisa asked if Flagg would be okay on his own.

"He'll be fine. Flagg by himself is the equivalent of a Marine platoon."

"Will that poor man be all right?"

"He's in good hands. Flagg is a trained paramedic."

I advised her to get a good night's sleep. She gave me a quick hug and headed for the main house. I went up to my apartment and popped a beer to settle me down. I drank it out on the deck and stared into the fog, letting the events of the night tumble over in my mind. I finished the beer and was headed for the bedroom to turn in when I heard a knock at the door. It was Lisa, in her nightgown and pink terry cloth bathrobe. She apologized, said she was unnerved by the rescue mission, and asked if she could bundle.

Once again, like a Colonial lad of yore, I slept in my clothes, within inches of a warm and beautiful woman, separated by an imaginary wooden board.

My eyes blinked open at first light. Mr. and Mrs. Cardinal serenaded me while I brewed a pot of coffee. The toasty fragrance woke Lisa and drew her into the kitchen like one of those cartoon characters floating off the floor on a heavenly aroma. The pinched, worried expression of the night before had faded.

I filled a couple of coffee mugs and sat across the table from her. "Sleep well?" I said.

She took a sip of coffee and said, "Yes, thank you. *Considering*."

"Considering the fact that you helped a CIA spook and his pal rescue a kidnap victim being held prisoner in a secret nuclear war bunker?"

She compressed her lips in a quick, tight smile. "Something like that. I was worried about the man you rescued."

"With any luck the drugs have worn off by now. I'll check on him in a few minutes."

"Thank you." She bit her lower lip. "Maybe I shouldn't have gone with you and John. I'm a country lawyer. I'm not cut out to be a Green Beret."

"For a country lawyer on your first special ops mission, you were a pretty cool customer, Lisa."

It was good to hear her laugh. "I was *beyond* cool. I was practically frozen stiff with worry. You said last night that there were a few problems."

"Brutus and Cassius were there to greet us."

"You didn't hurt them, did you?"

"Flagg likes dogs. Maybe better than people. He used a

tranquilizer gun to give them a nap. They're awake and probably chasing rabbits by now. If it's any consolation, he used the same technique on the guys guarding the bunker."

"There were *guards*?"

"*Two* of them. Surveillance cameras probably picked us up on our first visit. The mission didn't exactly go with 007 precision, but Flagg and I have worked together before and we muddled through." I got up and said, "I'll take some coffee and breakfast down to the dune shack. You can come if you want to."

She shook her head vigorously. "This is way out of my league. I'll go back to the house and get dressed. Then I'll spend some time with Gramps. Maybe I can bring him a step closer to reality."

"With Rosen out of the picture I see that as a distinct possibility."

"I hope so, Soc. This whole thing is so . . . ."

"Insane?"

"Yes. *Insane*. It's hard to believe Michael is so deeply involved in this mess. He must have known someone was being kept a prisoner on his property. Why would he allow that?"

"I can't answer that question, Lisa. Maybe we'll know more after we talk to the guy from the bunker."

Lisa headed back to the main house. I showered and changed into shorts, a T-shirt and sandals. I put some food and a thermos of coffee into a wicker picnic basket I found in a closet and made my way along the sandy path to the beach shack. Flagg was sitting in a rocking chair on the front porch, his shoulders wrapped in a blanket, a short-barrel shotgun resting on his knees. He looked like a landowner defying the bulldozers in an eminent domain taking.

His hair was lank from dew and there were dark half-moons under his blood-shot eyes, suggesting that he had little or no sleep. I poured him a mug of coffee from the thermos and he exchanged the shotgun for hot buttered toast wrapped in aluminum foil. I pulled up a chair, resting the shotgun on my knees, and stared off at the sea. The fog had retreated and thick clouds blocked the sunlight, giving the water a leaden look.

"Thanks for the hot chow," Flagg said. "Gets chilly near the ocean. Damp, too."

"How's the patient doing?"

"Just checked on him. He was awake. Took one look at me and passed out again. Guess I scared him. Don't know why."

Malloy's reaction wasn't exactly a surprise. Flagg's physical presence can be intimidating, and after a sleepless night on the beach he looked like the ghost of Geronimo.

At Flagg's suggestion, we walked around the cabin for a surveillance check while he stretched his legs. The only signs of life on the beach were a few gulls wheeling above the ribbon of sand that stretched out in both directions. Malloy was awake when we went into the cottage. He lay on his right side and he had pushed himself up on his elbow. I tried to reassure him with a grin and cheery good morning.

"You okay to sit?"

Malloy nodded, but he kept a fearful eye on Flagg. I helped him sit on the edge of the bed. Malloy had a wide face framed by ginger-colored hair and beard. In normal circumstances, he probably resembled a tall leprechaun. Even in the dim light of the cottage, I saw that Malloy had dark pouches under his sea-blue eyes and his lips were dry and crusted.

Flagg pumped a glass of water and handed it over.

"You don't take in liquid your kidneys will shut down," he said. "Your body's been dehydrated, but you'll be okay, Malloy."

He nodded dumbly, then a look of sheer terror came to his eyes.

"*Malloy*? Dear God! I don't know who I am!"

He tried to stand, but his legs buckled like wet noodles. I grabbed him before he fell on his face, lowered him back onto the bed and propped a couple of pillows behind his head. I dragged a wooden chair up to the bunk and sat so that we'd be at eye level. I told him to take slow easy breaths. He followed my instructions.

After a minute or two, his panicked breathing had slowed to normal. He raised his hand to his heart.

Flagg poured him a mug of coffee. Holding the mug in both hands, Malloy slurped down half the contents. Then he demolished the slice of toast.

"Thanks. I'll be okay."

"Good. We'll get back to who you are in a minute, but let's start with us. My name is Socarides. I'm a private investigator. This is my friend John Flagg. He works for the U.S. government."

"All right. I've got that," he said in a doubtful voice.

"Tell us what you remember."

He furrowed his brow. "I'm getting bits and pieces. I remember being chained to the cot in that crummy room." He stared at the handcuffs dangling from one wrist.

"We'll get those off as soon as we can," I said.

"That would be nice." He blinked a couple of times. "What the hell *was* that place?"

"It was a Cold War bunker built on Nantucket, probably for the president's staff."

He glanced around the cottage and sniffed the sea air coming in the window. "Where am I now?"

"You're in a beach cottage on Nantucket."

"How'd you find me?"

"I discovered the bunker during an investigation. Do you have any idea how you got there?"

"Everything is fuzzy. It's like my brain is surrounded by a white curtain."

"That's because it *is*," Flagg said. "The curtain's made up of chemicals that induce amnesia. It's the same stuff they use in surgery, so you won't remember the tough part. You'll get your memory back slowly."

I said, "Maybe we can speed it up if you're willing to try."

He asked for more water, then signaled with a wave of his hand that he was ready.

"Okay. I'll do my best. I just hope my brain cells haven't been destroyed."

"Brain cells are overrated," I said. "I've washed thousands of them away with booze. Close your eyes and picture a resume form in front of you. Imagine that you are filling out the blank spaces. Start with your first name."

He scrunched his eyelids. "It's Sean. My name is Sean Malloy."

"Good. Date and place of birth?"

He struggled with that one, but after a moment gave me an answer I assumed was correct. I asked him where had been raised and had gone to school. He answered, slowly, and each successful reply helped link him with another. He'd been born in Englewood, New Jersey, attended the University of Pennsylvania, and did graduate work at MIT. He recited his academic record with wonder, as if he couldn't believe his own accomplishments.

"I wrote some books, too, but I don't remember the titles."

"That will come. Tell me about your daughter," I said.

A broad smile lit his face. "She's a smart kid. Studying statistics at Stanford."

The mention of his daughter cracked the dam blocking his memory, because when I asked him where he lived and worked, he replied with no hesitation. "Cataumet, Massachusetts. I've got a lab there called MAC." His eyes flicked open. "That is I *had* a lab there. *Bastards!*"

Flagg said, "Good job, Soc. I think Mr. Malloy here has returned to planet Earth."

"Stuff is coming back." Malloy looked as if he had a sudden headache. "Oh *no!*"

"What's wrong, Sean?"

"I just remembered. We've got to stop it."

"*What* do we have to stop?" I said.

Malloy looked like the unhappiest man on earth. When he

spoke it was in a harsh whisper.

"The *swarm*. The deadly swarm."

CHAPTER 32

Malloy was on the verge of a full-blown panic attack. His face was ashen and he was taking big gulps of air into his lungs. I was afraid he'd pass out before he explained what had triggered his anxiety.

I put my face close to his, and in a calm voice, said, "Tell us about your books, Sean."

The diversion seemed to work. In order to answer, he had to slow his rapid breathing. His eyes, which had been darting around the cabin, refocused. "You know about my writing?"

"I saw the books in the place you were held prisoner. Didn't have time to browse."

"They're pretty dry stuff to most people." He rattled off some highly technical sounding titles. "They dealt mostly with the concepts governing chain-based path formation in swarmbots."

"Flagg and I can be a little dense, Sean. You'll have to speak English."

"Sorry." He must have realized it was like a teacher explaining quantum physics to a golden retriever. "Swarmbots is short-hand for *swarming robots*. Groups of autonomous machines that have the ability to self-organize and perform a task you set out for them. It's a concept you find in nature. Think of the way some insects work as a unit."

I had a flashback to the MAC lab. "There were photos of ants and bees on the walls of your lab."

"You've been to my lab?" he said.

"A couple of days ago. Tell us more about what you did there."

He nodded. "It was an attempt to replicate nature. Ants and bees, for example. Another parallel might be wolves hunting as a pack. These seemingly unorganized groups organize themselves to do a job without benefit of outside control."

A snort came from Flagg. "Sounds like the way you and I work, Soc."

Flagg's antipathy to authority sometimes got him in trouble, and his preference for improvising had gotten us *both* in trouble.

"Probably a lot more efficient than the way we work."

Malloy laughed. A good sign. "You guys teamed up to get me out of a nasty situation, so from my point of view, your working arrangement is a raging success. On the other hand, you'd be hard-put to top the efficiency to be found in an ant hill."

"You obviously gave it a try," I said.

"Pardon me if I sound smug, but we gave it *more* than a try. We actually mimicked the way it is done in nature. Picture an anthill. Hundreds of insects scurrying around in seemingly random patterns. One ant discovers a dead cricket. The ant tries to haul it back to the nest, but it's too big. So the ant goes for help. It lays down a trail of *pheromone,* a chemical that attracts other ants, so they can follow it back to the cricket."

"Smart ant," Flagg said.

"It would seem that way. You can find intelligence in organisms in the lowliest of creatures, and it's the same with man-made brainpower. You only need enough computer capacity for a few relatively uncomplicated jobs. The beauty of the swarmbot is that each unit in the group only has to be smart enough to perform simple tasks."

"Kinda like the government bureaucracy," Flagg suggested.

"That's not a bad analogy, except an anthill is more productive. The collectivity of the group allows it to perform complex tasks that can't be done individually. The ants need only the capacity to dismember the cricket and find their way back to the nest. *Bang.* Mission accomplished."

Flagg uses the latest in technical gear in his day job. While I was trying to wrap my mind around the ant and the cricket, he homed in on the nuts and bolts.

"How do you get a machine to lay down a chemical trail? You'd have to use mechanical odor detectors. Could get cumbersome."

"I agree. In fact it would be next to impossible, and would get away from the simple approach we wanted. In my concept, the bots form *chains* with other bots that serve as trail markers. You don't have to give each unit its control mechanism. You achieve complex behavior at the *colony* level."

"Like the ant nest," I said, trying to get my oar in the water.

"Exactly. Let's imagine that you want to form a path between the nest and the prey. The bots have no clue of the target's location. They're scattered about, moving in a random search pattern. One encounters another bot and forms a chain. If no prey is detected right away, they break apart and keep searching. When one finds the prey, it scurries around until it finds others to join it in a chain between the nest and the prey. Maybe several chains are formed. Together they work to accomplish the task."

"You got that far in your experiments?" Flagg said.

Malloy nodded. "The key was self-acquisition. Using ants for my inspiration, I developed an algorithm that induces a division of labor at the group level."

"And it worked?" Flagg said.

"Beyond my dreams."

I listened with glazed eyes to the talk of algorithms, but I was thinking of another component of Malloy's work. "What's your definition of *prey*?" I said.

"Practically anything you want. Swarm concept is readily adapted to military use. Ancient horsemen roamed vast plains, singly or in small groups. When they detected the enemy, they closed in, destroyed it, then vanished into the sunset. U-Boat wolf packs used the same technique in World War II with deadly efficiency. The Office of Naval Research has been looking into swarms as a way to protect ships in shallow water or to use to attack if necessary. They're worried about China, which has been building up its navy. I had no trouble getting a navy contract. "

"What did the navy want from your lab?"

"My contract was to develop swarming robots for mine detection and neutralization. I built the lab, hired staff, and development was moving along. About a year ago, the navy got hit by budget cuts. ONR chopped funding for experimental high-concept research. We switched to non-military applications like toxic waste clean-up, search and rescue, collecting specimens in hostile environments. There was interest, but no one wanted to spend on R and D. Not long after I shuttered the lab, I got a call from Nantucket Capital Investment Partnership."

"Michael Ramsey's outfit," I said.

"That's right. You know Ramsey?"

"We've met. What did he want?"

"Ramsey said he owned NCIP and explained that it was a company that bought out sick businesses, pumped a little life into them, and sold them at a profit."

"How did Ramsey know about MAC?" I said.

"I asked Ramsey the same question. Navy contacts," he said. "Seemed to make sense. I was low-hanging fruit. I said I'd talk to him. He came by the lab for a demo. It impressed him, I guess, because he made me an offer I couldn't refuse."

"What did you do?"

"I *refused* it. I'd done some research, learned that folks in Wall

Street called the Nantucket bunch, 'The Young Cannibals.' I asked Ramsey about that. He laughed and said don't worry about it. Didn't like the smell of things. Ramsey kept calling. My bills kept going up, so eventually I caved in."

"What was your deal?" Flagg asked.

"Ramsey's company would become stockholders, but I would retain majority holdings. In return, he promised a cash infusion from a foreign investor. I said that was a deal-breaker. My research still had military potential, and foreign involvement could kill any future navy work. Ramsey backed off and we did the deal one-on-one."

"What happened next?"

"The money arrived as promised. I hired lab staff, started doing field tests. Ramsey got very excited when he saw us do a robot launch and target retrieval. I was higher than a kite. Then Ramsey pulled the rug out from under me. He said the money used for the investment had come from loans made against the company. Since I was the major stockholder I owed big bucks."

"Or you could bring in the foreign investor," I said.

"*Bingo*," Malloy said.

"Sounds like a set-up," Flagg said.

"That's *exactly* what it was. This time I said okay. That's when I met Ivan Chernko, my new partner. He came by for a demo. Had a couple of hard-assed bodyguards with him. He pulled me aside and suggested that I go back to military applications. I refused. He told me to think about it."

"What made you change your mind?"

"The photos of my daughter that arrived in the mail a couple of days later. Someone with a camera had followed her around. There were pictures of her apartment, her car, and she and her friends. No note, but I knew it was Chernko sending me a message."

"Where was Ramsey in all this?" Flagg said.

"I called him after I got the photos and said I wanted out. He said that it was no longer in his hands. That I should do what Chernko wanted. I figured that even if I played along, there was no guarantee that my daughter or I would be safe."

"You were probably right about that," I said. "It would only have been a matter of time before you both had outlived your usefulness."

"That's why I decided to take a gamble. I figured I had one card to play. The algorithm. I told Ramsey that the whole system was inoperable without it." Malloy shook his head. "I was in deeper than I thought. A few hours later, Chernko's thugs showed up at my door. They took me to see Chernko, who said that if I didn't cooperate I would watch my daughter die. Then they knocked me out with an injection and I woke up where you found me. Only time I was allowed let out was for sea trials on Chernko's boat."

"Tell us about the trials," Flagg said.

"The chopper would pick me up at night and fly me to the yacht. The first time they did this, Chernko was already aboard. He told me that he wanted me to reprise my military research."

"Specifics?" Flagg said.

"He wanted autonomous swarming robots that would attack a ship."

Flagg's chair creaked as he leaned forward. "Tell me about the hardware."

"Each bot is around eight inches long. I relied on nature again, so the bots have a chubby fish shape, like a miniature nuclear sub. The design allows for a battery, the computer circuit and motor. The nose contains a small but powerful explosive with a triggering device."

"How would the bot deliver the explosive without destroying itself?" Flagg asked.

"It's designed to self-destruct. The computer isn't much more complex than what you'd find in a toy, so each unit can be built at low cost."

"Kamikaze robots, in other words."

"You've got it. That way there is no evidence to leave behind."

"How are they launched?" Flagg asked.

"The nest is a plastic platform, towed behind the boat that floats just below the surface. If the bots don't find their target within the range of their battery power, they are programmed to return to the nest. It is circular in shape, with docking ports to accommodate each pod of twenty fish. There is an electrical contact on top of each bot, like the conning tower on a sub that plugs into a low-level power source that recharges the battery. It deactivates the explosives, too. When the bots are ready to launch, the same connection sends a signal over the power line that arms the bot for action."

"What prevents the swarm from attacking the launch ship?" I said.

"Good question. That was one of the first things we looked at. Before each launch, waterproof transmitters are dropped off the bow, both sides and stern of the ship. They broadcast a signal that activates a turn switch in the bot. If a fish encounters this perimeter while it is searching for the prey, it automatically turns away and looks elsewhere for its target."

"How does it identify the target when it does find it?"

"It uses a combined sound and laser system for detection and communication."

"Lasers," I said. "That would explain the blue lights in the water!"

Malloy furrowed his brow and stared at me. "Damn! That was you out there a few nights ago, wasn't it?"

"Guilty as charged. Tell me what happened."

"It was a launch and retrieval test. The unarmed swarm was supposed to scour the programmed search area and come back to the nest. Only this time they found an unexpected target—your boat—and went into attack mode. They formed chains and threw themselves against the hull of your boat as if they were trying to blow it up."

Flagg said, "You lucked out that night, Soc. You'd be dead if the bots had been armed with explosives."

"Yeah, lucky me." I turned to Malloy. "The swarm kept whacking away at the hull until they punched a hole in it."

"I saw the helicopter go out to investigate," Malloy said. "When the crew returned to the yacht they were talking in Russian, but I heard Chernko tell Ramsey that the bots had taken out a boat. Chernko was pretty happy that the swarm did its job even without explosives. Unfortunately, your experience set things up for the real world test on a real moving ship."

"What ship is that?"

"I don't know. Our discussion never got that far. I pointed out that people would certainly die during this demonstration. He said that was irrelevant. I refused to do the test. Chernko said his men could carry out the test without me."

"Can they do that?" Flagg said.

"The system is set up so it can be operated without a lot of technical expertise. Once he said that, I thought I was dead, but they just knocked me out and tucked me away, probably in case anything went wrong that I would have to fix." He stared into space. "Good God. What have I done?"

"It's not your fault, man. We can straighten this out, with your help."

"I'm still worried about my daughter."

"We can make sure she's safe," Flagg said.

"I'll hold you to that. Okay, where do I start?"

"Chernko say where or when this test is happening?" Flagg said.

"They knocked me out again, but I must have built up a resistance to the drug because I didn't go under right away. I heard Chernko and Ramsey talking." His thoughts seemed to drift off. Flagg grabbed the back of Malloy's neck like a faith healer treating a patient.

Flagg said, "Stay with us, Sean. Think about what they were

saying."

Malloy took a deep breath to steady himself. "They were arguing. Ramsey said he didn't want blood on his hands. Chernko laughed and said he *already* had blood on his hands. He said Ramsey owed him for a big favor. Then Ramsey seemed to back down and he asked when and where. Chernko said it was better for Ramsey not to know, given his sensitivity. But if he wanted to lay low, that it would take three days for the observers to arrive."

"Did he say who they were or where they were coming from?"

"Not specifically. Like I said, the U.S. Navy thinks the Chinese have been showing the strongest interest in swarmbots."

"My boat sank two nights ago. The third day after that would be tomorrow."

"Chernko say anything about location?" Flagg said.

"I'm sorry. Everything went black after that."

"You did just fine," Flagg said.

He handed him a cell phone and told him to call his daughter. Malloy punched out the number and broke out in an ear-to-ear grin when his daughter answered. Flagg let the happy reunion go on for a minute, then signaled Malloy to cut the conversation short.

"Tell her some folks will be picking her up in a little while. They'll say they are friends of mine and will mention my name. If anyone else comes by before they get there, tell her to dial 911. My friends will take her to a safe place. You'll meet her there."

Malloy conveyed the message to his daughter, hung up and turned to us. "Thank you for that. What now?"

"It's best to get you off the island until Soc and I sort things out." Flagg asked Malloy where his daughter lived, and then he called a number on his cell phone, had a brief conversation and hung up. "Plane's waiting for us. Team is on its way to your daughter's place. You okay to walk?" he said to Malloy.

After talking to his daughter, Malloy said he was ready to *dance.* Not quite. He was still shaky and we had to support him on each side on the walk from the beach house to Flagg's car. Lisa's Jeep was in the driveway. She was probably still with her grandfather.

We tucked Malloy in the back seat. I drove while Flagg rode shotgun. We got to the airport without incident and escorted Malloy to a Cessna Citation in the section of tarmac reserved for private planes. The pilot Flagg had called from the beach shack helped Malloy into the plane and made sure he was belted in. Minutes later, we watched the plane taxi down the runway and leap into the darkening sky.

On the walk back to the car Flagg said, "If what Malloy told us is the truth, we've got to move fast or some people could be hurt real bad. You come up with any ideas, Soc?"

"Doesn't seem we have a lot of choice, does it? If we want more info on the test, what better place than the horse's mouth?"

"Chernko?"

I nodded. "He knows what we want to find out."

"You going to bribe ol' Mr. Ed with a sugar cube?"

"Wish it were that easy. You got any better schemes, I'd love to hear them."

"What about Ramsey? Bet we could get some answers if we rough him up."

"First we'd have to find him. Chernko advised him to lay low."

"No guarantee Chernko is around. He could be on the high seas."

"Let's assume that Malloy is right and the observers are coming from China. Any way we can check up on that? See if there's any connection to Ramsey or Nantucket Capital Investment Partnership?"

Flagg said he'd make a few calls, which he did. After he hung up with the last one, he said it would take time. "I originally thought I should call in the Marines and raid the yacht with guns blazing, but if the Chinese are involved, this might complicate things."

"It's *already* complicated. Chernko is a pretty important guy back in Russia and Ramsey is a big-deal businessman with lots of contacts. We might look real silly if we shot up the yacht and didn't find anything except a few cases of vodka and caviar."

"You've got a point. Okay. You do recon. I'll cover your ass. Just like the old days back in Nam."

"Wish you had used a better example, Flagg. As I recall from my days in Vietnam, we won the battle, but lost the war. And don't give me any of that 'we, white man' stuff."

Flagg had faced discrimination as an Indian kid growing up on Martha's Vineyard, and when I first knew him he maintained that Vietnam was a case of the white guys against the darker-skinned guys, no different than General Custer and the Sioux. But he has mellowed through the years, so I was happy to see his grin and hear his reply:

"In that case, *we'll* just have to do better this time around, Soc."

CHAPTER 33

Despite my manly-chest thumping, I knew that walking into the den of a murderous mobster nicknamed Ivan the Terrible wasn't conducive to good health. I needed an *edge*. And I knew just where to find one. Chernko had been out on his yacht last night. That meant Tanya would have been kicked off the *Volga* for a shore-side shopping spree.

I asked Flagg to drop me off at the Jared Coffin House, suggested he scout out the yacht and said I'd meet him at the ferry dock. I only got as far as Tanya's first name before the young woman at the inn's reception desk gave me a broad grin. "Oh yes, I know who you mean. She comes in with all those shopping bags."

"That would be Tanya," I said. "I wonder if I could get a message to her. She stayed here last night."

The receptionist checked her computer. "Sorry. That reservation was canceled."

Alarm bells went off in my head. Tanya always stayed on shore the nights Chernko was running tests. I thanked the receptionist and headed for the ferry dock. The summer carnival was in full swing. There were the usual couples and families with kids, oldsters and youngsters, one group tanned, the other pale-faced, like two different tribes.

I stood near a T-shirt shop and scanned the happy crowd until I saw the top of Flagg's head moving above the milling throng. He homed in on my waving arm.

He had an ice cream cone clutched in his big hand. He went to take a lick, then paused to offer the cone. "Want a bite?" he said. "It's peanut butter cup."

I eyed the dripping blob. "Maybe I'll reward myself with a treat after my talk with Chernko."

"Don't blame you, Soc. Guy makes me want to puke my guts out and I don't even know him." He gnawed off half the cone like a hungry T-rex. "Tell you what, pal. I'll buy you a double scoop."

"You've got a deal. Ready to go?"

Flagg hefted the bag of tricks slung around his shoulder so that the contents clanked, then he finished off the ice cream, and wiped down his sticky hand with a paper napkin. "I'm ready," he said.

We headed for the yacht dock. The *Volga* was a major tourist attraction. Knots of camera-toting tourists stood around snapping photos, unaware that the pretty yacht that filled their viewfinders was the lair of a monster.

From the sleek white-hulled vessel, Chernko's slimy tentacles snaked out to Viktor Karpov, burned alive; to my cousin Alex, dragged once again into the drug world he had left far behind; to Malloy, held prisoner and squeezed to make him give up the dangerous technology he had worked so hard to create. Then there was me. My new boat was destroyed, and I'd almost lost my old pal Kojak. Just because Chernko was annoyed.

Now *I* was annoyed. If my mother saw the angry fire smoldering in my eyes, she would know that was no small thing. Some personal history is in order here. After I beat up a bully in defense of my younger brother, Ma began to worry that I had inherited the genes from her Cretan grandfather, a mild-mannered farmer who had waged a one-man war against Turkish occupiers. He had become a *pallikari,* an embodiment of all that is good and manly, but in his campaign to defend the weak against the strong, he became a cold-blooded killer.

My mother had urged me to study the classics in college, hoping that philosophy would soften the harder aspects of my personality. It came as a disappointment, but no surprise to my mother, when I quit school and ended up in a far-off land fighting a war that blurred the line between the good guys and the bad guys. Blood will tell, she said.

As I stood on the dock next to Flagg, my simmering blood wanted revenge. Not just because of the trouble Chernko had caused me, but for the woes he bestowed on others and his plans to inflict even more pain in the future.

Flagg and I had talked strategy on the ride in from the airport. Since we didn't have a lot going for us, it was a short talk. We would keep it simple. Get on board. Take a look around. Get off in one piece. I didn't try to kid myself. I was pushing middle age and my body suffered from the rewards of a lifestyle that was far from wholesome and pure. Maybe this wasn't a bad thing, because it made me realize that I'd need more than muscle to deal with a professional criminal like Chernko and his small army.

I told Flagg about my stop at the Jared Coffin House and my suspicion that Tanya was being held on board the yacht. He grunted and told me what I already knew, that Tanya complicated a complex situation and that I would have to be extra-special careful. We slapped palms for good luck. Flagg began to shoot photos of the yacht, and I strolled up to the gangway.

Access to the yacht was barred by a crewman who could have gotten a job as a car lift in a garage. His chest strained against the seams of his sky blue T-shirt. His close-cropped head sat directly on his broad shoulders. He wore baggy gray workout pants that could have concealed an entire gun show. He was about six feet tall and half as wide. He untucked one of the arms folded across his chest and shoved a palm in my face.

"Go away," he snarled. "Private property."

I snarled back. "Tell Chernko I want to see him."

I must have out-snarled him, because he slowly pulled his arm back and removed his mirrored sunglasses. Chernko's minions came in different shapes and sizes, but they all had the same apathetic expressions that you see in the bad guy posters tacked up on post office bulletin boards.

"*Name*," he said.

I told him who I was. He studied me for a moment, then, with a studied deliberation, slid the shades back onto his eyes and removed a radio from his belt. He carried on a conversation in Russian, keeping watch to make sure I didn't try to dash past him and up the gangway. His lips turned down to form a reverse image of the dark mono-brow that connected his eyes. He switched off the radio, stood aside and jerked his thumb at the yacht.

I deliberately brushed him with my shoulder and climbed the gangway to the deck where I was greeted by two clones of the dock guard. They were both wearing sidearms. When I stepped on board, they crowded in from both sides in a deliberate effort to intimidate me. They weren't doing a bad job of it.

One man said, "That way," and pointed to a door at the deck level of the yacht's superstructure. Allowing myself to be dragged into the bowels of the *Volga* didn't seem prudent.

"*Nyet.*" I shook my head. "I want to see Mr. Chernko out here. On the deck."

So much for the direct approach. They grabbed my arms in a steely grip and tried to muscle me toward the door. I planted my feet and swung my elbows back and into their guts. They both made a sound that was surprisingly high-pitched for a pair of tough guys, then doubled over and released my arms.

Things started to happen fast. Flagg had been watching from the dock. He started toward the gangway in a brisk, deliberate pace, his hand reaching into his satchel. The deck crewmen were recovering from my sucker punch. They were holding their stomachs with one hand, reaching with the other for their belt holsters. There was murder in their tear-filled eyes. The dock guard had been watching the encounter, and now he was sprinting up the gangway to join our jolly threesome. The whole idea of a civilized visit with Chernko was about to swirl down the drain.

That's when the door in the superstructure swung wide open and Chernko popped out.

He shouted in Russian. The two men backed off, shot me a see-you-later glance, and headed for the door they had wanted to drag me through into the superstructure. Chernko came over and waved away the approaching gangway guard who turned around and went back to his post. Flagg had frozen in place when he'd seen Chernko, waiting for a signal from me. His hand was in the open satchel.

Chernko saw Flagg staring at him. "Is that large gentleman a friend of yours, Mr. Socarides?"

"A very *good* friend. If I disappear from his sight, he will summon more friends who are waiting nearby. At the same time, he will reach in that bag for the portable rocket launcher that he will fire at the waterline of your pretty boat. Then he will take out an automatic weapon and hand grenades, and he will storm the sinking yacht. Your men may eventually stop him, but not before he takes out the primary target."

"Which is?"

"Ivan Chernko," I said.

I was bluffing about the back-up and I wasn't sure whether Flagg had a rocket launcher, but I wouldn't have been surprised if he carried a nuclear warhead in that bag of his. Chernko gazed at Flagg for a moment, a slight smile on his lips, then turned to me.

"That will hardly be necessary, Mr. Socarides," he said with the friendly Uncle Ivan voice I had noticed on our first encounter. He dragged a couple of deck chairs close to the rail. He sat in one and gestured toward the other.

I plunked myself down, making sure my head and shoulders were visible from the dock, and gave Flagg a wave. He removed his hand from inside the satchel and waved back.

If the moment had unnerved Chernko, he didn't show it. He was dressed casually in white slacks, loafers and shirt and he lounged in his chair like the rich yachtsman that he was. He regarded me in silence; his chiseled marble face showed no hint of emotion. He obviously was waiting for me to say something. I obliged him with a smile and a quick glance around the deck.

"The *Volga* is even more impressive up close," I said.

"Thank you. I added a few touches to the original design."

Chernko may have been talking about the cushion colors of the deck chairs around the swimming pool for all I knew. What I saw was that the *Volga* was a hybrid. With the A-frame, the stern-facing bridge, the powerful winches and the helicopter pad, the yacht was as well-fitted as any salvage vessel I had ever seen.

"It's a large ship and crew for only one passenger," I said.

"Perhaps, but I often have guests."

"Like the young lady who was with you the night of Ramsey's party?"

"She was transient, and has since left the ship to return to Bulgaria."

The little voice inside my head was reminding me that Tanya said she would rather die than go back to Bulgaria. Tanya's shore leave had been canceled for some reason. What I was less sure of was her fate. Chernko would think nothing of having her killed, stuffed into a weighted-down body bag and tossed into the sea. I pushed the image out of my mind.

"That's too bad. She was quite attractive, as I recall."

He replied with a slight shrug. "Pleasure plays a secondary role on board this ship. The *Volga* serves as both my home and my place of business. Now, if you don't mind, what business brings a private investigator to see me?"

"I've talked to Malloy," I said.

"*Sean* Malloy?"

"You admit you know him?"

"Why would I deny it, Mr. Socarides? Malloy owned a research company in which my organization bought a controlling interest."

"You forgot to mention Ramsey's involvement in the deal."

"That's hardly a secret. You could read about our joint ventures in *The Wall Street Journal*."

"Would I also read about Malloy being held a prisoner on Ramsey's property?"

"*Absurd*. Malloy owned a company that I acquired working with Ramsey's company, Nantucket Capital Investment Partnership. We invested heavily, but his lab was a money loser. Eventually we had to close it."

"That's not how Malloy sees it. He says you grabbed his company, threatened his daughter and made him work for you."

"Malloy was very upset over losing control of his company. He has obviously become unhinged."

"He seemed quite rational when I talked to him a little while ago."

"And what did Malloy have to say?"

Chernko would know by now that Malloy was missing from the bunker, but he found it hard to believe that I had anything to do with it. I tried to change his mind.

"He told me all about the swarmbots you've been testing."

There was a slight change in the smooth facade. A miniscule narrowing of the eyes. A tiny down turn at the corner of the hard mouth. I had finally gotten through to him.

"What *else* did he tell you?" His voice was quieter, more menacing.

"*Every*thing," I said.

It was an answer that was vague and specific at the same time.

It had the desired effect.

"What do you want, Socarides?" A growl.

"This is more about what *you* want. *Malloy.* I'll turn him over to you for a consideration."

Chernko could swat me down like a fly, but I suspected that he feared the wrath of his KGB debtors. He had to make the demonstration work so he could get the money from the Chinese to pay off his pals. And having Malloy on the loose could spoil his plans.

"You're quite straightforward, Mr. Socarides."

"I try to be."

"What sort of consideration did you have in mind?"

"A replacement for my boat, to start with."

"Is that what this is all about?" he chortled. "Your *boat?*"

"That's a big part of it."

He tented his fingertips and stared through me. "We have only known each other a few days, Mr. Socarides. In that time you have managed to insinuate yourself into the most private corners of my business, so I find it hard to believe this is about something so trivial."

"You wrecked my boat. That's not trivial. You got sloppy. I'm an opportunist. Besides the boat, I wanted *revenge.*"

He raised a brow. "*Bravo*, Mr. Socarides. Revenge is something I can understand. Obviously, the possibility of extracting payment from me has mitigated your desire for vengeance."

I shrugged. "Obviously."

"You could have picked up the information on Malloy's research from a number of other sources. Why should I believe you actually talked to him?"

"Because he told me about the live test you're planning."

That tidbit convinced him because he said, "What's this going to cost me?"

I tossed out a figure that seemed like a fortune to me, but he didn't blink. It was either small change to him, or he had no plans to pay it because he said, "That would be no problem. How do you propose to close the deal?"

"I'll give you the number of a bank account into which you'll deposit the money. It will take time to arrange. Say forty-eight hours from now."

He gave me a bull-dog frown. "I can't wait that long. I need Malloy tonight."

"Then I'll require payment in cash, upon delivery."

"That's better. I'll be sailing at ten o'clock. I want him on board the *Volga* before that."

"Malloy won't come willingly." I looked around. "We couldn't cause a scene in a public place."

"That won't be necessary. I'll order the *Volga* moved to an anchorage in the harbor and send a boat ashore to pick up the package."

"And deliver payment, too."

"Yes, payment will be delivered at that time."

"It will be tough to find a place private enough for the exchange," I pointed to the harbor island. "Let's do the deal there. Boat to boat."

"*Agreed*. Do you need help handling Malloy?"

"My large friend on the dock is very capable."

"Nine o'clock then." He rose from his chair. "I believe our business is done for now."

I stood to leave, but I knew our business was only beginning. Chernko would renege on the deal as soon as he had Malloy. The art of the double-cross was part of his DNA. He'd get rid of Tanya because it was the smart thing to do and kill me in revenge for making him look bad. I thought of offering Malloy in exchange for Tanya, but discarded the idea. Chernko would see my connection to Tanya as a weakness to be exploited. I wondered if Lisa might be swept up in my feud with Ivan. Possibly, I thought, but Ramsey liked Lisa and might run interference. Ultimately, the one certain way to stop worrying about the threat Chernko posed was to eliminate him as a threat.

"One more question," I said.

"Yes," he said impatiently.

"You seem like a careful man. Why did you have someone take a shot at me in the fog the other day?"

He stared at me with wariness in his eyes, then said, "I don't have a clue what you're talking about, Socarides."

With that, he spun on his heel and headed off at a brisk pace along the deck.

No one tried to block my way when I left the yacht. I took Flagg up on his offer for an ice cream cone and he bought a second one for himself. As Flagg and I walked back toward the center of town, I filled him in on my tete-a-tete with Chernko.

"What do you want to do next?" he said.

"I want to get on the yacht."

"You were just *on* board."

"Yes, but this time I want to visit the *Volga* without being seen. I'm worried about Tanya."

He thought about it for a moment. "You can slip into the water where no one will see you and sneak aboard."

"Chernko told me he's moving the yacht out into the harbor. That's a long swim."

"No problem. We use a boat to get in close to the yacht. We get on board and find Tanya."

"A distraction would help."

"That's easy. We time it for when we're supposed to give up Malloy. I'll drop a dime, call the cops and Coast Guard, and say there's a drug deal going on at the island. By the time the Ruskies explain what they're doing, we get us on and Tanya off."

"That may work," I said. "Take me back to the house and we can start things rolling."

We finished our ice cream and walked to the rental car. Flagg dropped me off at the Daggett house and went to line up a boat. There was an antique Ford beach wagon in the driveway, the same car I had seen on my visit to Lillian Mayhew's house. The Ford's owner was standing on the porch, talking to Lisa, who smiled and waved when I got out of the car. I saw Lillian watching Flagg as he drove off. She must have been curious about who he was, but her Yankee reserve wouldn't allow her to ask questions.

We shook hands. "Nice to see you again, Ms. Mayhew."

"You too, Mr. Socarides. Lisa has told me how helpful you've been in bringing Henry back to the present."

"He *wants* to come back," I said. "I gave him a compass heading to show him the way."

"How appropriate," she said with a smile. "Starbuck was intensely loyal to Ahab even though he thought the captain was dangerously obsessed." She turned to Lisa and said, "Well. Let's see if Henry remembers me."

She went into the house. Lisa lingered for a minute and said, "Did everything go well with Mr. Malloy this morning?"

"He's fine. He left the island on his way for a reunion with his daughter."

"Have you and John found out what this is all about?"

"We'll have it wrapped up within twenty-four hours."

"That's wonderful."

She gave me a hug and we were still embracing when Lillian stuck her head out the doorway. She smiled approvingly.

"Come, Lisa. It's a long voyage to the 19th century."

Lisa hurried into the house and I headed to my apartment, ticking off a mental list of preparations for Operation Tanya. The phone was ringing when I stepped through the door. I picked it up, said hello and heard the hushed voice of my cousin say, "Soc. I've got a problem!"

Another voice came on the phone. It was low and gravelly, and it had been years since I last heard it, but I recognized Chili, the cocaine dealer who had crawled out from under a rock to drag Alex back into drug world.

"Your little cousin has got it wrong, Socarides," he growled, "*You're* the one with the problem."

CHAPTER 34

The first time I met Chili, he was running a cocaine operation out of a rented beach house on Cape Cod. He was aiming for the big time in the hard drug trade, but what he got was *hard* time in the Big House. He took up residency at Cedar Junction, the one-star hotel for unlucky felons south of Boston, after being nailed in a drug bust. Alex had been sucked into Chili's drug business, but I snatched my cousin from the clutches of the law seconds before the narcs moved in.

"Guess what, Socarides," he said, slowly pronouncing each syllable so it sounded like *Sock-Ah-Ree-Dees*. His voice was deeper and more gravelly than I remembered and it had a slyness that had replaced the coke-addled mumblings of his youth. "I've got your pretty-boy cousin sitting here in front of me. He's looking down the barrel of an AK-47. I'm trying to decide what to do with him. You got any suggestions, Socko?"

"*Yeah*," I said. "I suggest you put Alex back on the phone. *Pronto.*"

Chili laughed. It was a nasty laugh. There were mirthful echoes in the background which told me that Chili wasn't the only one with Alex. "Still playing the hard-ass private cop, old man. What are you going to do if I refuse? You going to drop a load in your Depends?"

Old man? First Flagg with his geezer wisecracks. Now Chili had me wearing adult diapers for incontinence.

"Nope," I said. "I am going to hang up at the count of three."

I wasn't indifferent to my cousin's predicament. Chili was stupid and violent, and after schooling by his fellow inmates, he would have graduated from Cedar Junction with a degree in criminal methodology and a resolve not to go back to jail. He'd be a lot more dangerous than on our first encounter. At the same time, I knew that *any* sign of weakness on my part would doom Alex. I kept counting and got as far as two. Alex's voice came on the phone.

"Soc, I'm sorry about this." He sounded more contrite than scared.

"Skip the apologies for now, cousin. Tell me what happened."

"Chili said he wanted to make a deal. I couldn't reach you, so I came to Nantucket."

Alex acting out his private eye yearnings again. Chili and his pals were waiting to escort Alex when he got off the boat. I felt a triple-hitter of guilt. For being the bad role model Alex aspired to emulate. For not being around when he tried to reach me. And for failing the promise to my mother to protect my cousin.

"Are you okay, Alex?" I asked.

"Yeah. For *now*."

There was a pause and Alex's voice was replaced by Chili's guttural one.

"Alex is a smart boy. He knows that he's a dead man unless his cousin Aristotle comes through." He pronounced my given name in that annoying, slow way. *Ah-Ree-Sto-Tol.*

"I don't have time to play games, Chili. What do you want?"

"I spent ten years in the can because of you."

"I didn't have anything to do with your arrest. You got sloppy and thought you were smarter than the cops. You were wrong."

"Don't give me that. You were there, watching the whole thing!

You knew the cops were onto us. You made sure you got your cousin out. You could have tipped me off about the bust. You didn't, which makes you just as guilty."

"Like they say, Chili, if you can't do the time, don't do the crime. If you'd been dealing in grass instead of coke you'd have gotten a slap on the wrist instead of ten years."

"You should be glad I didn't do *twenty*, Socarides. I want a hundred thousand from you for every year I served, and a pain and suffering bonus for the guy who tried to cut my throat."

That explained the guttural voice. "Too bad he botched the job."

"He botched more than that. The pain and suffering was his when I had him clipped."

"You're really scaring me with that tough talk, Chili, but I wouldn't give you that kind of money even if I had it."

"Tell you what, Socarides. You're not dealing with a kid snorting the profits up his nose. I know all about your family's business. A million would be chump change to them."

Chili had done his homework. Parthenon Frozen Pizza made lots of money. They might even part with it to save the life of a family member, although I wasn't sure about that. I knew this wasn't all about the money. Even if I paid the ransom, Chili would kill us as soon as he had the cash clutched in his grubby fingers. I dug into my fertile imagination, trying to come up with something that would work. But my thoughts got tangled up with the threads of Chernko's scheme. I did the only thing I could do. I stalled.

"I'll have to talk to the family," I said. "In person. They're not going to do it over the phone. I'll have to leave the island. I can have the money in forty-eight hours."

"Make that twenty-four hours or the lawyer boy is dead."

I swallowed hard. "Okay. Twenty-four hours. How do I get in touch with you?"

"You *don't*. Make sure you're by the phone tomorrow at this time waiting for the call." He hung up.

I slammed the phone back into the cradle. I didn't like putting Alex at risk, but there wasn't much choice. Chernko was testing the swarmbots tonight, endangering an unknown number of people. Alex was one person, and I still had some breathing room to bail him out. I had one thing going for me. Chili didn't know I had followed him to his cottage and that I knew where he lived.

I borrowed the bird-spotting scope from my apartment and carried it down to the MG. The Ford beach wagon and the Jeep were still in the driveway. Lisa and Lillian were off sailing aboard the *Pequod* with Captain Ahab. I wondered how the voyage was going, but I'd find out later. There was a family matter to take care of.

I drove to the Madaket end of the island and turned onto a sand road not far from the driveway to Chili's cottage. I parked off to the side of the road and hiked through a scrub pine forest. After about five minutes, I emerged from the trees onto a grass-covered expanse between the woods and the cottage a few hundred yards in the distance.

The offshore islands were crawling with wood ticks and some carry Lyme disease, but I took a deep breath, got down on my hands and knees and went about fifty yards, skirting patches of poison ivy. When I came to a ridge behind the cottage I parted the grass and squinted into the eye-piece of the birding scope.

Four vehicles were parked next to the cottage. A black Tahoe SUV had a license plate with the words CHILI on it. There were also two other SUVs and a pick-up, all new. I lowered the scope and pulled the baseball cap visor down to keep the hot sun out of my eyes. I moved the lens from window to window. The shades were down so I couldn't see inside the cottage.

Half an hour passed with no activity. I would have to leave soon to hook up with Flagg. I decided to give it fifteen minutes. Only ten had gone by before the front door opened and five men emerged. Two were Chernko's goons, Sergie and Pitir, which explained why I hadn't seen them on the boat. Two were the big Jamaicans I'd seen behind the restaurant kitchen in town. And the fifth was Chili. He had been stocky when I met him, and probably lost weight in prison, but he'd developed a beer belly living the good life.

The guys hugged each other, high-fived and fist-bumped in a druggie love-fest. The Jamaicans left and the others went back inside the cottage. I watched for another quarter of an hour. There was no further activity. I made my way back to the car, checked myself for ticks and was happy to see that I was clean.

When I arrived back at the Daggett estate, I found a note from Lisa tacked to the door of my apartment. She said she was going out to dinner with Lillian. She added: "Good session with Gramps. See you soon."

I went into the apartment and took a shower to wash away any hidden ticks and maybe as a ritual cleansing, warrior style. I'd take any edge I could get. I got back into shorts, T-shirt and sandals, packed my Ninja outfit in a bag and followed the winding sand path that led to Daggett's beach cottage. The breeze had freshened and it carried the smell of food cooking. The scent was coming from the barbecue on the porch. I opened the barbecue lid and saw sweet potatoes cooking on the grill. As I lowered the lid, I felt hard pressure at the back of my head.

"*Bang*, you're dead!" a quiet voice said in my ear.

The wind was churning up the surf, but Flagg could have ambushed me in the quiet of a church. I turned to see a boyish grin on his wide face. He was holding the spatula whose handle he had pressed to my skull.

"Hello, Flagg. You're starting to remind me of the valet who jumps out at Inspector Clouseau in the Pink Panther movies."

"Kato was an amateur. We Indians have got sneaking-around genes that allow us to creep up on the bad guys." He hefted the pan in his other hand. "Picked up a couple of steaks on the way in. Grab some plates and implements of destruction while I warm up the rib-eyes. I like them burnt and bloody. That okay?"

I nodded and went inside the beach shack. I found some mismatched plates and a couple of steak knives. After a while, Flagg came in with a platter of rare steaks which we attacked and quickly demolished. In between bites, I told him about Alex and the deadline with Chili.

He kept eating without comment until he had finished the last morsel, which is when he said, "You did right putting him off. We'll have plenty of time to deal with Mr. Chili after we wrap things up tonight."

"Speaking of tonight, it occurred to me while we were devouring a whole steer that we hadn't pinned down our plans."

"Hell, Soc, you know I hate too many details. You over-plan, something's bound to go wrong, so I like to build in a lot of improvisation. You know that."

"Indeed I do, pal, and I have the scars to show it. But for the sake of argument, if we *did* have a plan, what would it be?"

"Plan the prep and prep the plan," he said, which in Flagg-talk, could mean almost anything.

In my experience, Flagg liked to build a plan around the available firepower. He got up and went over to his bag of tricks on the cot and began to pull out enough weaponry to outfit the overthrow of a small country. He laid out a couple of handguns, a short-barreled shotgun and a compact machine pistol with a sound suppressor on the barrel. Then he extracted a short black tube around a foot-and-a-half long and three inches in diameter.

"Real cute," he said. "Just developed. It's a personal rocket launcher."

I laughed and said, "I told Chernko you might have something like this, but I was making stuff up." I took the weapon, unfolded the pistol grip and squinted through the sight. "Didn't know they made Patriot missiles this small."

Flagg chuckled, and pulled a narrow, pointed projectile around a foot long from the bag. "This little baby's got more punch than the Patriot. We can sink a whole ship with one shot."

I thought about the *Volga*. "You talking about Chernko's yacht?"

"If we have to. Matter of life or death."

I nodded. "I think you've brought along sufficient hardware. Now let's go over the operational details."

Despite Flagg's preference for improv, we needed an action timeline if we wanted to accomplish a mission as delicate as the job we had in mind. Flagg said he had hired a sixteen-foot inflatable Zodiac with a hundred-fifty-horsepower, four-stroke motor. We studied the harbor chart that Flagg had picked up at the boat lease shop. Before starting for the *Volga*, we'd call the Coast Guard with an anonymous tip that a boatload of armed men could be found doing a drug deal off the harbor island. Taking advantage of the distraction, we'd sidle up to the yacht and climb aboard using a grapnel and rope ladder. We'd look for Tanya, and when we found her, would leave the same way we came.

We went over the plan several times until we were sure we could carry out the mission with our eyes closed. Flagg has a built-in mental clock so I didn't even bother to look at my watch when he folded up the chart, zipped his satchel shut and said: "Time to go, Soc."

CHAPTER 35

Flagg's bag of tricks would have sunk the inflatable, so he left some hardware in the trunk of his car. The inflatable still sagged with our weight and that of the remaining weaponry. I sat in the stern, started the motor, and steered out of the marina into the harbor. Flagg perched in the bow and scanned the harbor through his night vision binoculars.

The *Volga* was anchored off by itself around a half mile from shore, away from the flotilla of moored boats that bounced at anchor in the chop kicked up by the freshening breeze. I tried to keep the inflatable at an even keel. The rounded bow was made for skimming the sea rather than cutting through it, so the boat bounced in the wavelets like a rubber duck in a tub. Flagg was having trouble focusing the binocs. He let out a string of curses, followed by a yell of triumph.

He turned and shouted over the buzz of the outboard, "They're on their way! Boat just left the yacht and is heading for the island."

Timing was crucial. Flagg had called the Coast Guard station using his untraceable cell phone when we were halfway between Siasconset and Nantucket town. He had said that there was a boat with armed men in it heading to the harbor island to make a drug deal.

He had clicked off his cell phone and grinned. "That should start things rolling." From his position in the prow of the Zodiac, he did a play-by-play narrative. "Coast Guard boat's left its dock. Lights moving out into the harbor. Real slow. There's another boat with it. They're not taking any chances. Okay, Soc, make your move."

My move consisted of a push on the tiller, swinging the inflatable toward the yacht. I put the motor on low idle and let the rising wind push the boat back toward the yacht. We wouldn't need a grappling hook. The boarding ladder was down in anticipation of the yacht's launch return with Malloy.

Quick short bursts of the throttle kept us on track to the ladder. When the Zodiac thumped against the hull, Flagg uncoiled like a Jack-in-the-box, grabbed the lowest rung, and hooked the line onto it. The inflatable came to a jerking stop at the end of the line and we both almost tumbled into the drink.

Flagg grabbed a backpack, slung it onto his shoulders, and started up the ladder, with me right behind him. He halted at the top, looked around, then waved me on. We hit the deck belly-down, then slithered like salamanders toward the shadow of a large, looming silhouette under the A-frame, which was upright in operational position. It must have been stowed in the hold, because the object wasn't there when I visited the yacht earlier.

The object was covered with dark plastic. Flagg lifted the edge of the covering and crawled through the opening. I followed, but couldn't see him in the darkness. When I whispered his name, he said, "Over here."

He flicked on an electric torch that had a red light beam. The shaft moved back and forth, illuminating a honeycombed framework of metal and plastic. Dozens of oblong objects were stacked in rows. Flagg whispered again. "It's the nest for Malloy's little fishes."

The light went out and we crawled out from under the nest.

We stood, and in a hunched-over position, began to make our way forward from the stern. We stepped over a thick cable that ran from the superstructure to the edge of the deck and skirted the pale waters of the swimming pool. A dim light glowed through the tinted windows of the salon. The door was unlocked. We stepped inside and made our way around the sofas and chairs, and past a bar to an exit, marked by a light, at the back of the salon.

I placed my ear against a door. There was only the hum of the yacht's power plant. We slowly cracked the door and stepped through into a passageway that bisected the living quarters.

We moved from cabin to cabin. We'd listen for a second, knock softly, then try a door. None of the cabins were locked, which probably wasn't thought to be necessary, given the number of armed men on board. It was a risky maneuver; if anyone answered, we'd have to come up with a quick excuse, but none of the luxury cabins were occupied.

I jerked my thumb down.

"We're wasting our time here. They wouldn't put Tanya in a first class cabin. She'd be down in the crew quarters."

Flagg was a step ahead of me. We descended to the lower deck. Flagg slipped a Glock 9 mm pistol with a sound suppressor out of his pack and let it dangle loosely at his side. We knocked, listened and opened doors again. The cabins were a quarter of the size of those in the deck above, and each had bunks for two people. All were empty.

"Maybe I was wrong about Tanya being aboard."

"Or maybe they killed her," he said.

"She could have left the yacht on her own."

"You really think—"

He stopped in mid-sentence, brought the pistol up and pointed it at a door that was labeled *Laundry.* He raised his free forefinger to his lips and took a couple of slow steps forward. Flagg's hearing is on the subsonic level, but this time I heard the noise, too. A soft moaning sound that came from the storage area. A tight smile creased his jaw. Then he stood back, keeping the gun leveled at the door, and gestured for me to open it.

I turned the knob and swung the door open. The room was in darkness. I reached around to the inside wall and hit the light switch. Along one wall of the room were a heavy-duty washer and dryer, and across from the appliances were shelves stacked with towels, sheets, soaps, laundry detergents and cases of bottled water. Tanya lay on the floor, her right wrist handcuffed to one of the steel uprights that supported the shelves.

Tanya had been demoted to the equivalent of baggage. She was dressed only in her bathing suit bottom and a T-shirt and lay on a couple of blankets. She probably didn't notice the hardness of the floor because she looked unconscious or dead. She was neither, as it turned out. When I knelt by her side and lifted her head, she slowly opened her eyes and blinked as if coming out of a deep sleep. Her eyes widened for a second, then closed and she let out the same kind of moan we had heard outside the door.

"Drugged, like Malloy," Flagg said. He tucked his gun into his belt and pulled a pair of metal cutters from his pack, using them to cut the chain between the handcuffs.

I took a bottle from a shelf, and tried to get some water into her mouth. Most ran down her cheek. I poured water onto a washcloth and pressed it against her forehead. Her eyes opened again. This time there seemed to be recognition in them.

We lifted Tanya to her feet. Her wobbly legs were incapable of bearing weight. We had to drag her out of the corridor, up the stairway and into the salon. We headed across the room to the door that would take us out onto the deck. We heard voices, and a second later, saw figures moving along the deck on the other side of the wrap-around windows. We ducked behind the bar, dragging Tanya's limp body with us.

As we huddled behind the bar, we could hear the voices inside the salon, talking in what sounded like Chinese. Then Chernko's unmistakable steel-edged voice cut in.

"Well, gentlemen, we seem to have a bit of excitement," he said, speaking in English.

"What is happening, Chernko?" someone said.

"The Coast Guard checked one of the yacht's boats and became quite excited when they learned that my crewmen carried arms."

Tanya started to move and her eyes and lips opened. Flagg clamped his hand over her mouth. He was trying to be gentle, but she resisted. I put my lips close to her ear and whispered, "Sleep, Tanya. Sleep." Her eyes drooped and she stopped jerking her head. Flagg removed his hand.

"I don't like this, Chernko," said another accented voice. "This was supposed to be a risk-free operation."

"And that's what it will be. The Coast Guard has been assured that my men are all licensed for their weapons as security personnel aboard the *Volga*. They will soon release them. Once they are on board, we will get underway. Would anyone like a drink in the meantime?"

Flagg brought his pistol around and pointed it upward. The first person to lean over the top of the bar would have his head blown off. There was a negative murmur of voices.

"No takers?" Chernko said. "Well later, maybe when we have something to celebrate. Let us go to the bridge where we'll have the best view of the demonstration. I'll have our stewards bring up some refreshments for you to have while you enjoy the show."

This time the response was more positive, and a second later the salon went dark and quiet again.

CHAPTER 36

Funny how the mind works in times of stress. I was crammed between an oversized Native American and a stoned-out Bulgarian woman, thinking how strange it was to be on the floor *behind* a bar instead of in front of one. Fortunately, Flagg wasn't given to humorous flights of fancy. As soon as the voices faded from the salon, he uttered a half-grunt of a command.

"*Up!*"

We untangled our arms and legs, peered over the top of the bar like a couple of characters in a Mel Brooks movie, then lifted Tanya to her feet and dragged her to the door leading onto the deck. Tanya was as slim as a fashion model, but in her drugged state, her limp body seemed to have gained a hundred pounds.

We muscled her across the floor. Tanya was too out of it to care. We had to get back to the Zodiac before the boat crew detained by the Coast Guard returned to the yacht. They would find the inflatable, and with no way to get off the yacht as it moved out to sea, we would be hunted down like rats.

We had one thing working for us. The center of action on the *Volga* had gravitated to the bridge. The decks were deserted. Once we saw that the coast was clear, we hustled back to the boarding ladder. I was on Tanya's left, with my arm around her waist, and Flagg was holding her on the other side, his free hand clutching the Glock.

As we moved along the deck, I glanced off as the cluster of boat lights split in two near the island where the Coast Guard had detained Chernko's boat crew. The Coast Guard boat was headed back to the station and Chernko's thugs were on their way to the yacht. Seconds later, we were at the boarding ladder. If we got back into the Zodiac soon, we could make a run for safety. Getting Tanya down the ladder into the inflatable bouncing at the end of the grapnel line was going to be a challenge.

Flagg told me to go first. He picked Tanya up, threw her over his broad shoulders and backed down the ladder like a fireman making a rescue from a burning building. I stood on the bottom rung and helped ease Tanya into the Zodiac. The inflatable was sloshing around in the waves beating against the hull.

Flagg was right about getting older and out of shape. I was panting like a leaky organ bellows. My arms and legs had turned to putty.

Flagg was huffing like the big bad wolf, so I gaped with amazement when he stood on the lowest rung of the ladder and said, "Wait here, Soc. Got something to do."

By then, Chernko's boat had cut the distance to the yacht by half.

"Are you *crazy*, Flagg? The bad guys are almost here."

"If I'm not back in two minutes, get your ass out of here. Get that girl some medical help. Don't give me any crap, Soc. This is important!"

He handed me his Glock, then scrambled up the ladder and disappeared through the opening in the ship's railing. I turned away at a cry from Tanya, who was stretched out on her side in the boat. The water rolling over the rounded sides of the inflatable had splashed into her face and revived her. She was trying to push herself up, and was having a hard time doing it on the squishy wet boat bottom. I tucked the pistol in my belt and put an arm around her shoulders, trying to calm her. In her disorientation, she tried to push me away.

Tanya's panic gave her an unusual strength, and her shove was strong enough to knock me off balance. My arms wind-milled. The Glock fell out of my belt and splashed into the water. It was a comedy of errors, but I wasn't laughing.

The sound of Chernko's boat motor was getting louder. A spotlight probed the water in its path. I had maybe thirty seconds to make my escape.

My hand went to the ignition switch and the motor caught on the first try. I reached up to loosen the line to the boarding ladder. I could hear voices from the approaching boat. To make things even more interesting, Tanya was trying to stand. She was swaying on her knees and if she got to her feet, she'd topple over the side. I took my hand off the throttle, gave her a quick apology, pushed her back down into the boat and sat on her.

If not for the delay, I would have been off and running and Flagg would have missed the boat. Literally. As I went back to the throttle, I heard someone yell. Flagg stood on the deck at the top of the ladder. He tossed the knife in his hands out into the water, then half-climbed, half-fell down the ladder. Without the line to hold it, the inflatable was drifting away from the hull. I gave the throttle a quick twist and steered close to the boat so that the rubber pontoon brushed the hull.

Flagg did a swan dive off the ladder into the inflatable. The impact rocked the boat, and for a second, I thought it would capsize and throw us all into the drink, but his weight actually stabilized us. I cranked up the throttle and steered away from the yacht. Our troubles weren't over.

Chernko's boat had been angling toward the yacht, and was around fifty feet away when the Zodiac started moving off. The spotlight from the boat caught us in its beam. There were shouts from Chernko's crew and the boat changed course, going into a quick turn to follow our wake.

Flagg rolled over and scrambled to a kneeling position in the stern.

He stuck his hand in the air. "Where's my Glock?"

I pointed down. "I lost it. In the water. Got an extra?"

Flagg's curse was audible against the noise of the motor and wave slap. Tanya was lying on his backpack and he had to shove her out of the way to get to it. He unzipped the bag, stuck his hand in and came out with a pistol so small it was barely visible in his big hand.

"Is that pea-shooter the best you can do?" I yelled.

"It is unless you want to dive for my Glock. Stinking little .22 Beretta. About as useful as a cap pistol in this situation."

With three people aboard the Zodiac, the outboard pushing the blunt-nosed inflatable through the water was inadequate to the challenge of outrunning the bigger, more powerful boat. Soon, they'd come up beside us and blast away with what I guessed would be bigger guns than the Beretta.

It was a miracle they hadn't tried. We were in easy range. My guess was that they didn't want to attract any more attention to the yacht than was necessary and would make their move once we cleared the *Volga,* which was about to happen.

I aimed the Zodiac toward a thicket of moored boats anchored between us and the shore, then did a slow slalom turn around a big cabin cruiser. I heard the staccato popping of gunfire and shattering glass as the bullets slammed into the cruiser's pilothouse.

I mumbled a silent apology to the boat owner, then gave the marine insurance companies more claims to pay. I did another S-turn, this time around a pretty sailboat that I commandeered as a bullet buffer. I tried to avoid boats that had cabin lights, which would indicate that there were people aboard. The tricky maneuver may have saved innocent lives, but put ours in jeopardy. The pursuers figured out my strategy, and swung their boat around in a big turn that would cut us off once we emerged into the open again.

I could delay the inevitable by weaving in and out of the boat fleet, but they were getting closer with each turn. Even if I didn't run out of gas, they'd catch up. It was only a matter of time and physics. Then I heard a shout from Flagg.

"We're losing them!"

Flagg wasn't entirely accurate. They were losing *us*. Chernko's boat had turned around and was now on its way back to the *Volga*. Maybe Chernko had been feeling the pressure from the guests who had come all the way from China to witness his murderous demonstration. I cut the motor to an idle and we drifted. I was exhausted, frustrated and enraged by overwhelming helplessness. It was Flagg who brought me down to earth.

"Got to get this girl to a doctor pretty quick," he said.

He was cradling Tanya's head in his lap and brushing her damp hair back away from her pale face. It was an uncharacteristically tender gesture. There are times I forget Flagg is a human being. I glanced around the harbor to get my bearings and saw the flashing beacon of the little Brant Point lighthouse. I goosed the throttle and pointed the boat toward the Coast Guard station near the light. They'd have the emergency medical techs who could tend to Tanya.

I reasoned that once she was taken care of, we could again turn our attention to Chernko. I could only hope that we wouldn't be too late.

CHAPTER 37

The U.S. Coast Guard may be the best government deal going for the American taxpayer. For a mere fraction of the annual budget, the men and women who work out of the stations along the country's coasts monitor pollution, combat drug smuggling, and rescue mariners in distress under the most terrifying sea conditions imaginable. They've pulled me out of a jam more than once. So it pained me immensely to be upbraiding the commander of the Nantucket station for not doing his job.

Not that I blamed him. It's doubtful the Coast Guard has a protocol that tells a station commander what to do when a lunatic walks in the door and demands that a cutter be dispatched to chase down a private yacht. The captain was handling me a lot better than *I* would have handled me. I paced back and forth in front of his desk, ranting about bureaucracy, red tape and foot-dragging.

Captain Tom Gwinn simply nodded in agreement and made an occasional note on the pad in front of him as if he dealt with crazies every day. From time to time, he glanced over at Flagg, but I doubt if he read anything in my friend's bland expression.

Captain Gwinn finally jumped in when I paused to take a breath. "Why don't you and Mr. Flagg sit down and start from the beginning."

I wanted to tell him that there *was* no time. That there was a boat out there in the dark carrying armed underwater robots that could attack another ship and send it to the bottom. But even in my agitated state, I was aware that I walked a fine line between appearing upset and just plain bonkers.

I plunked into a chair. Flagg took a seat beside me. I looked at him, then at the captain and let out a deep sigh. Nantucket is a genteel place. It's not every day two scruffy characters in black Ninja outfits show up at your door with a drugged Bulgarian.

I said, "Sorry to come down on you, Captain Gwinn. It's a long story."

"We only know the part where you arrived at the station with the young lady who is now in sick bay. Could you tell us what happened?"

Flagg was ready for the question. "My friend and I were taking a cruise around the harbor when we saw this young lady swimming. We pulled her out of the water. She said she had been on a yacht and had a fight with her boyfriend. He wouldn't bring her back to shore, so she jumped overboard. She was drunk at the time she said, but her English is hard to understand."

Not a bad cover story, even if it was untrue. Tanya had been fully awake by the time we arrived at the station, and she was babbling as if she had too much to drink. Gwinn stared at Flagg for a few seconds and then looked at me. I nodded in agreement. I had replaced my raging lunatic face with a calm, innocent expression, but I don't think the captain was buying.

"Did she say *what* boat?" he said.

Flagg and I shook our heads.

Gwinn shrugged. "I'd better call the police in."

"Maybe not," Flagg said.

Gwinn narrowed his eyes and drummed his fingers on the desktop, a signal that he was getting annoyed. Flagg reached under his shirt for a waterproof pouch that hung around his neck. He unzipped the pouch, extracted a laminated ID, and placed it on the captain's desk. Gwinn picked the card up, glanced at the photo, then at Flagg's stolid face.

"Looks like we work for the same employer, the federal government," he said.

"Looks that way." Flagg retrieved the card and slipped it back into the pouch. "I could make a few calls, but that will take time. I'm wondering if you can help us out."

"Okay. What do you need?"

"I'd like you to find a yacht called the *Volga* that left the harbor a little while ago."

Gwinn's face lit up. "That's some dreamboat. We can see it from the station. What's going on?"

Flagg said, "We have reason to believe that the *Volga* has armaments aboard and that if not stopped, it will use them in an attack against another vessel."

Gwinn's smile vanished. He leaned forward onto his desk and stared at Flagg.

"You're serious, aren't you? But *what* vessel and *where*?"

"We don't know that yet. Only that the attack will be made soon."

Gwinn shook his head. "You need the U.S. Navy. We're not equipped for naval battles."

Flagg said, "I agree. If I can borrow your phone I can start the wheels moving, but we have to find the *Volga* in the meantime."

"Shouldn't be hard to do. The yacht is a commercial vessel, so its transponder will be broadcasting its position."

"Don't bet on it," I said. "The yacht's owner doesn't want to be located."

"That could pose a problem. I can call the Otis air base and get a helicopter in the air for a rescue op, but I'm going to need you to make those telephone calls you mentioned."

Flagg asked him to get started. While Gwinn began the process to ask for the dispatch of the helicopter, Flagg used his cell phone to round up government backing for an interception. I paced the floor.

Gwinn hung up the phone. "They can have a chopper in the air in thirty minutes," he said. "I said I would call with more position info. Any idea where the yacht could be?"

I pointed to a wall chart that showed Nantucket Sound. "It's been about an hour since the yacht left. It moves fast, but there's a lot of area to cover."

Gwinn rose from his desk and went to the chart. "There's usually a lot of traffic out there, ferries and so on. But the *Volga* is a big vessel and should be easy to find."

"There's a time issue," I said. "The attack could come any minute."

We gazed at the chart as if the squiggles and lines could tell us a story. A young female Coastguardsman entered the office. She had been the one to wrap Tanya in a blanket and take her into the medical room.

"Your friend is doing better," she said. "She says she wants to talk to Feeshermenz."

"That would be me," I said.

While Flagg and Gwinn studied the charts and made more phone calls, I followed the Coastguardsman into a small room that held some medical cabinets and an examining table. Tanya sat on the table with the blanket wrapped around her shoulders. Her hair had been pulled back and tied in a braid and her face was pale. Her beautiful eyes were no longer blurry and unfocused as they had been.

"Hi, Tanya," I said. "How are you feeling?"

Her mouth widened in her usual careless smile. "Lak ded feesh," she said.

A puzzled look came to the Coast Guard woman's face.

"Tanya says she feels like a dead fish."

Tanya nodded vigorously. "This naz womens very good dekter."

I went to translate, but the young woman said, "I get it. Thanks, Tanya, but I'm not a doctor."

I asked if Tanya and I could have a few minutes alone. The woman must have assumed that we were boy and girl friend.

She smiled and said, "Let me know if you need any help. I'll be in the next room."

Tanya waved goodbye, then unwrapped the blanket and slid off the table. She was wearing borrowed jeans and a Coast Guard sweatshirt. She extended her arms wide in invitation to a hug. I obliged. For a slender woman, she had a lot of strength in her arms. I helped her into a chair and pulled up another to face her.

"What happened with you on board the *Volga?*"

Tanya's linguistical locutions were a challenge even for someone who was used to them, but I got the gist of what she was saying. Chernko had told her the yacht was going out for the night again. She had arranged for her usual room at the Jared Coffin House. She had packed her overnight bag, but forgot her credit card and went back to look for it. She couldn't find her wallet and decided to borrow money from Chernko.

He kept a wad of cash in his office desk, which was off their living suite. Chernko was in his office talking to someone. She recognized Ramsey's voice. They were arguing. She wasn't sure about what they were saying, only that Ramsey felt strongly about something. He stormed out of the office with Chernko close behind him, so quickly that she didn't have a chance to leave. Chernko told Ramsey he would see him after the event, grabbed her by the arm and asked how much she had overheard.

She used her excuse, "My Angleesh steenks," but he didn't believe her. He called in two of his thugs, who punched something sharp in her arm. She didn't know what happened next. I told her she'd been drugged, and that Flagg and I had found her in the laundry room. She reached over and gave me another hug and a big wet kiss on the lips.

"Do you remember *anything* about the argument?"

She scrunched up her face in intense thought. "Remzee wants Ivan to wet."

"Wait for what?"

Tanya shrugged. "Ivan sez Chineez here for tez. No goink bek."

Interesting. Ramsey wanted to postpone the test, but Chernko overruled him. I asked her to close her eyes and try to remember if she heard anything else.

"Ok. I rimimber." She paused, searching for the right adjective. "Lots talk about *eeyanoh*." She smiled, proud of her recall.

"You don't know *what*?"

She shook her head. "Not, 'I don't know.' *Eeyanooh*."

I tried another tack. "Say the word slowly."

"Okay, feeshermenz." She pursed her lips, then parted them. "Eeyanooh." I told her to go even slower. She laughed and said, "Ee. Yan. Oh."

The alarm bells started clanging inside my thick skull.

"Iyanough?"

She nodded vigorously, and her arms went wide for another hug, only to find empty air. I was already out of my chair and making a dash for the door.

CHAPTER 38

Captain Gwinn was hanging up the phone when I barged back into his office. He said, "Good news. In addition to the helicopter out of Otis, Woods Hole station is sending a cutter to look for the *Volga*, and an unknown target."

"No longer unknown, Captain. It's the steamship authority ferry, *Iyanough*," I said.

Gwinn's jaw dropped. "The car ferry is the target? Are you sure?"

"*Very* sure. I just talked to the woman we brought into your station. She was on the *Volga* and heard the attack plan being discussed."

Gwinn went to his computer and called up the ferry schedule. "The *Iyanough* is about mid-point in the crossing."

"Can you call the ferry and have it turn back?" I said.

"Follow me," he said.

A moment later we were in the communications room and he was instructing a radio operator to contact the ferry. The ferry captain's voice crackled over the speaker and identified himself and the boat.

"This is Nantucket Coast Guard station," Gwinn said. "I'd like you to turn your boat around and head back to Hyannis."

There was a pause, then the ferry captain said, "Say again?"

"This is Captain Gwinn on Nantucket. Please reverse your course. Your boat may be in danger."

"Danger from *what?*"

Captain Gwinn glanced at Flagg, who put his forefinger to his lips.

Gwinn nodded. "I can't tell you specifically, Captain. My source hasn't told me the details. Only that the ferry is in danger. What's your approximate position?"

"We're more than three-quarters of the way to Nantucket," the ferry captain said.

Gwinn told the ferry captain to stand by.

I drew a map of the Cape and Islands in my head. The Coast Guard was used to emergencies and would have a boat underway with minutes, but the distance the cutter would have to cover to the intercept spot was too great for help to arrive on time.

"How long before the cutter gets to the ferry?" I said.

"Within an hour. Seas are kicking up, so it's hard to say."

"That's too long. What about the chopper?" I asked.

"They're about to lift off. When they get there, they may use up a few minutes searching before they find something."

They may not *have* a few minutes, I thought. The *Volga* could be already at midpoint, ready to ambush the ferry and send it and its passengers to the bottom. I turned to Flagg.

"You're the guy with clout," I said. "Anything you can do?"

"Lots I could do if I had the time," he said.

"You *had* the time," I said. "This thing has been brewing for weeks, *months* maybe. While you were shooting off in your private jet saving the world, I practically stumbled over a big deal right in your backyard. What do you and your spook friends *do* down there?"

He shrugged. "We do our best, Soc."

Flagg and I were friends, but I needed someone to blame for

my frustration. Flagg was a convenient target. Mostly, I was in full fury at my own ineptness.

"Okay. When and how are you going to prevent a lot of innocent people from getting killed?" I swept my hand toward the wall chart.

He gave me an enigmatic smile. "Maybe I already *have*, Soc."

Gwinn cut in. He was on the phone talking to the air base again. "Chopper's in the air," he said. "Any ideas on what it should do if it finds the *Volga*?"

"See if you can make contact with the yacht," Flagg said. "Tell them that a Coast Guard chopper is on its way to locate them. They may not try anything if the chopper is keeping an eye on them."

At Gwinn's order, the radioman made several attempts to reach the *Volga*, each with a warning about the imminent arrival of the chopper, but there was no answer.

I felt bad about scolding Flagg, so said, "Good move. We may have given the bad guys something to think about."

"Thanks, Soc. You know this guy. Think we've scared him off?"

"Probably not. That might have worked with anyone other than Chernko."

He asked Gwinn to contact the ferry captain.

"Ask him if there are any other vessels in his vicinity."

Gwinn complied with the request.

The captain's voice back with an answer. "Yes and no. We can see someone on radar, about a half mile away. Just sitting there. But we can't see their running lights. Visibility is bad with the rain coming in."

While Gwinn was dealing with the ferry captain, Flagg said, "What did Malloy say was the range of his little fishies?"

"Half a mile."

Flagg turned to the captain. "Tell them to try to avoid the other boat. Tell them to keep at least a mile in between if they can."

Gwinn relayed the suggestion to the ferry captain. He asked for the ferry's position and gave the coordinates to the chopper. After

312

a few minutes of waiting, the helicopter called back.

"Come in, Nantucket. Repeat coordinates please."

Gwinn gave them the ferry's last position.

We waited anxiously for a few minutes before the helicopter called back again. "Doing a circular search pattern."

Another tense wait. Then the voice from the helicopter again.

"Seeing debris in the water."

Too late. The big slow-moving car ferry would have been an easy target. My heart felt as if it had been filled with molten lead.

I had to go somewhere. *Anywhere.* I walked back to the sick bay. Tanya was lying on the gurney, her eyes closed. Sleeping. My shoulders sagged. I cursed myself for not figuring this thing out sooner, or moving faster. I knew there was nothing that I could have done, but it felt good to whip myself. I felt a hand on my shoulder. Flagg had come up behind me in that uncanny quiet way of his.

"She going to be okay?"

"Yes," I said. "Just sleeping it off. Well, Flagg, at least we saved *one* person."

"Maybe *more* than one," he said. "You ran off before we got the call." He took my arm and guided me to the window which overlooked the harbor. A boat was rounding the Brant Point light. It was the *Iyanough.*

"I must be hallucinating," I murmured.

"No such luck," Flagg said. "That's the real thing."

I stared at his grinning face. "You *knew*?"

"Like I said, we do our best. Remember Malloy answering your question about how the *Volga* put up a protective field to protect itself from those crazy little robots swarming around in search of the target?"

"Sure. He said there were four hydro transponders hanging off the bow, stern, port and starboard. They were connected by cables."

"Like the cable we stepped over when we first got on board."

I remembered how Flagg had left me as we were trying to get

Tanya off the yacht, his last-minute return, the knife arcing into the sea.

"You *cut* the cables?"

"Only had time to slice the one on the starboard hull. I figured that twenty-five percent was enough of an opening to find if those fish were as smart as Malloy claimed. I guess I was right."

The dark cloud I'd imagined hanging over my head vanished in a puff of smoke. I laughed so loudly that Tanya stirred in her sleep.

"*Finestkind*, Cap," I said. "Finestkind."

CHAPTER 39

The ambulance showed up a few minutes later to give Tanya a ride to the hospital. She was fully conscious and talking non-stop in Bulgarian as she was loaded onto the stretcher. Captain Gwinn had called in the rescue squad as a precaution. My guess was that it had more to do with the distraction Tanya was causing at the station among his male subordinates.

Flagg and I watched through the station window as the EMTs rolled Tanya into the ambulance and closed the doors.

"Nice lady," Flagg said. "Don't understand a word she's saying, though."

"Doesn't matter. She saved the passengers on the ferry boat."

He made the rumbling sound in his throat that passes for a laugh. "We're getting too old for this kind of stuff, Soc."

"I'm glad you made that a plural pronoun. I'm going to sooth my aching joints with some alcoholic painkillers. Want to join me?" Knowing Flagg doesn't drink, I tried to entice him with an offer to buy him a Shirley Temple.

"I'd like that, but some of my people are flying in and I've got to stick around here so I can update them on Chernko."

"Don't forget I'm going to need your help getting my cousin

315

Alex out of trouble."

"I've been thinking about that. Deadline's tomorrow afternoon, you said. I got a plan that could roll things up real quick. You going to be at your place? I'll see you after I deal with the folks from Spook Central."

We shook hands and I said I'd walk back into town. I wanted to clear my head. I stepped out of the station. The wind had come up, making the rain come in horizontally. The raindrops felt good splashing against my face.

A few minutes later, I pushed through the door of the Rose and Crown into a noisy and well-oiled crowd that was dealing with the inclement weather by staying dry on the outside and wet on the inside. I bellied up to the bar and ordered a Jack Daniel's neat. It went down too fast and I liked it so much I ordered a second. I slowly sipped the second glass as I tried to order my jumbled thoughts.

My feud with Chernko was at an end. I'd had my revenge, but I still wondered why Chernko had denied being behind the shooting in the Serengeti. He'd almost been insulted. Chernko liked to set people on fire, so maybe it just wasn't his style.

What *was* clear was that someone still out there had a grudge against me. I suspected that it was linked to Henry Daggett. Finding Coffin's killer would unravel the unholy mess. I was convinced of it. I was tempted to order another drink, and let myself slip into a blissful sea of forgetfulness, but I knew that before long, my guilt would conjure up Lisa's face in the bottom of the glass.

Leaving the bar, I struck out into the rain again and walked to Lisa's office. The light was on in the second floor window. I climbed up the stairs with water sloshing in my sneakers. I didn't want to startle her so I knocked softly on the door. "Hi, Lisa. It's Soc."

She said to come in. I opened the door and stepped into her office. She looked up from her paperwork.

"Dear God! What happened to you? Are you all right?"

"I'm a little damp, but fine otherwise."

She went into the bathroom and came out with a towel which I used to dry off my face.

"Where have you been?" she asked.

I sat in a chair, took a deep breath and let it out. "I'll tell you later about my adventure on the high seas. I wondered how you were coming with the trial continuance."

She got behind her desk, smiled and put her hand palm down on the stack of papers in front of her.

"I just finished the request for a delay in the trial. I've incorporated the findings of the new psychologist I'm bringing into the case, along with my own observations and those of Lillian."

"And what were those conclusions?"

"He's coming out of it, Soc. I'm sure seeing Lillian did it. He recognized her right away, called her by name. He's remembering things he should know as Henry Daggett."

"What about Captain Ahab? Is he still chasing the white whale?"

"Ahab is quite persistent. He doesn't want to let go. Gramps has lapses, falls back into the Moby thing, but then he'll smile as if he knows he's being silly. It's as if one personality is fighting to be in charge. Gramps is winning, I'm sure of it."

"Does he remember the night of Coffin's murder?"

"In fragments. Right now he is neither fully himself nor Ahab, but some personality in between."

"Once we get the trial delay, Henry's doctor will have time to draw out the real self and banish Ahab."

"That's right. As I told Michael—"

"You saw Ramsey?"

"He wanted to have dinner at Wauwinet. I said I was busy. I couldn't see him, knowing something of what he's involved in, but we chatted about Gramps's improving condition."

Ramsey hadn't left Nantucket as Chernko had advised. Something was keeping him here.

"I'd better let you finish up your paperwork," I said, rising from the chair. "Would it be all right to talk to Henry to see if he still thinks of me as Starbuck?"

"Could you? You were the one who got him started on the road to normality."

"Maybe we can go in together. I'll stop by my place first and clean up."

"That would be just fine. I've got to make copies of this stuff and I'll be a few minutes behind you."

"See you at the house," I said, pulling on my rain slicker.

Polpis Road was practically deserted. Gusts of wind coming across the moors slammed against the little sports car. The miniature windshield wipers were practically useless against the driving rain, and I barely made it through puddles as deep as lakes. I was glad when I pulled into the driveway, but that feeling quickly vanished. Ramsey's Bentley was in the driveway in front of the main house.

I parked behind the car and went up onto the porch. The front door was unlocked. No one was in the kitchen. I went upstairs and knocked on the door of Daggett's quarters. There was no answer.

"Captain Ahab!" I called as I stepped inside. "Henry Daggett. *Gramps.*"

None of the old man's revolving personalities replied.

I went back to the first floor and encountered Mr. Gomes coming in the front door.

He removed his baseball cap and shook the water off. "Nasty night out there."

I was in no mood for a weather report. "Where's Mr. Daggett?" I said.

"He's in his quarters. I was just going to check on him for the night."

"I've already done that. He's not there."

318

"You're *sure?*"

"I went inside and called for him. Lisa told me that Daggett never left his rooms."

"That's right. He was afraid to leave. Thought the house was surrounded by the ocean. Maybe he went off with Mr. Ramsey?"

"I saw the car, but there's no sign of Ramsey. How long has he been here?"

"He arrived about an hour ago. He said he wanted to chat with Mr. Daggett. I left to have dinner with my wife and was on my way to settle the old man in for the night." Gomes looked as if he'd lost a winning lottery ticket. "I feel responsible for him wandering off. He's not going to get into trouble, is he?"

I was more worried about Ramsey than the police. I didn't know what Michael was up to, but I was certain nothing good could come of it.

"It isn't your fault and maybe the police won't mind if we get him back soon. Lisa will be home in a few minutes. I'd appreciate it if you could stay here and tell her what happened."

"Should she call the police?"

"Yes. The police can track him through his ankle bracelet. Tell Lisa that I've gone off to look for him around the property."

I stepped out of the house onto the porch and squinted as if that could help penetrate the curtain of raindrops. Use your brain, Socarides. Daggett didn't simply wander off on his own. He was with Ramsey, who obviously wanted to take him somewhere. Ramsey's car was still in the driveway, which meant he was still around. As I stood there, I became aware of a sound that was a backdrop to the pelting drumbeat of rain on the roof. The low roar of pounding surf. And it was telling me exactly where I should look.

CHAPTER 40

Nothing is more humbling than a nighttime romp on a rain-swept beach in the teeth of a gale. You quickly discover that you might as well have left all six senses at home. You can't see, and even if you know where to go, the mushy wet sand will grab at your feet or spiky clumps of beach grass will try to break your ankles. You can't hear, because your auditory nerves are overwhelmed. The relentless army of waves thundering against the beach sounded like a fleet of locomotives at full throttle. Raindrops pelted my skull as if someone were using it for a timpani.

The flashlight Mr. Gomes had loaned me was practically useless. The beam was shredded by thousands of glittering raindrops. I pointed the light down, a few inches ahead of my slogging feet, which worked out better, because my head was bent to avoid the bullets of rain. I made my way slowly toward the crashing surf. Eventually I'd stumble onto the beach. If I fell in the ocean, I'd have gone too far.

I lost my balance a few times and fell to my knees like a supplicant to King Neptune. Finally, after what seemed like hours of walking, my feet crossed from dune grass to sloping sand. The spray cast up by the waves breaking against the beach flew through the air like foamy birds. I guessed that the beach shack was off to the right. I wiped the water from my eyes with the back of my hand and saw a glint of yellowish light that quickly vanished. I struck out toward the direction I had last seen the light, trudging blindly through the rain like one of the surf men who used to patrol the beach on the lookout for ships in trouble.

There was nothing but darkness ahead. I thought I had made the wrong choice. Then, I saw a pinpoint of light blink on and off again. I staggered on, buffeted by the wind, and glimpsed the blink again, brighter now. The light gained contours and I saw that it came from a window. The stroboscopic effect was caused by the intermittent sheets of rain.

I made it to the shack and peered through the side window. The glow that had attracted me like a soggy moth came from an oil lantern sitting on a table. Next to the table was the rocking chair Flagg had used when he was guarding Malloy. And slumped in the chair was Henry Daggett.

I stepped onto the porch, unlatched the door and pushed it wide enough to stick my head through the opening. With the lantern throwing the only light, half the cottage was in shadow.

And it was from this darkness to my right that the muzzle of a rifle emerged and a voice said, "Don't be shy. Come in out of the rain."

I did as I was told. I couldn't see the person in the shadows, but I knew the voice.

"Thanks for the invite. Any port in a storm."

Ramsey stepped out of the shadows. He held a stubby-looking rifle, chest-high, with his finger wrapped around the trigger. In his other hand was an unlit lamp similar to the one on the table.

"Sit down and keep your hands folded on the table where I can see them," he said.

I lowered my dripping wet body into a chair.

Ramsey placed the lamp on the floor and sat in a chair opposite

321

me, resting the rifle on the tabletop, the muzzle pointing toward my heart. He saw me staring at the rifle. "If you're thinking that you'd like to snatch the rifle out of my hands, I'd advise against it."

"I was admiring the telescopic sight. That's a Walther sniper's rifle, isn't it?"

"Good call, Socarides. It's shorter than most rifles used for that purpose."

"Is that why you missed when you were using the gun in the Serengeti?"

"How did you know that it was me?"

"Three reasons. Lisa hired me to keep the Daggett case open. Someone didn't want that to happen. And that someone is holding a sniper's rifle."

"Have you figured out why *someone* would not want the case to remain open?"

"Still working on it, but Rosen was the staff shrink for one of your companies, so maybe you can tell me why he was trying to keep the old man crazy and confused."

"What would have happened if Rosen hadn't botched the job?" Ramsey said.

"Daggett would have been sent off to a mental hospital for the rest of his life."

"Which would have been the kindest course of action, don't you agree?"

"That wasn't the way it was going down, though, was it? Daggett was coming out of his Ahab delusion despite Rosen's attempt to keep him in la-la land. When Lisa hired me, that messed up your plans."

"You have a high opinion of yourself, Socarides. You crash around like a bull and break a few pieces of china, but you can't put the pieces back together."

"My detective skills weren't an issue. I connected on a personal level with the old man, and in time, he could have told me things you didn't want to hear. You tried to cut me out of the picture. I can't figure how you'd miss an easy shot with the high tech piece of hardware you're holding."

"Killing you would have brought even more attention to the case. I was trying to avoid that.

It was only a matter of days to the trial. If I scared Lisa off until then, Daggett could be tried and committed. Case closed. But that didn't happen."

"With Rosen gone, Daggett started to improve. Lisa told you tonight that he was getting back to normal, and you couldn't let that happen."

"Would *you* have allowed that if you were in my place?"

"I wouldn't *be* in your place." I nodded toward the old man. "Is he dead?"

"Oh, *no*. He's under the influence of a drug I acquired from Dr. Rosen. I administered it with a high pressure hypodermic after we came to the cottage."

Malloy and Tanya had both been put under using the same technique.

"Why did you bring him here?"

"After Lisa told me he was coming out of his Ahab hallucination, I wanted to see how far he had progressed. She wasn't exaggerating. He was still slipping in and out, but his mental state was definitely improving."

"Improved enough to remember that you were at the whaling museum the night Coffin was murdered?"

A tight smile came to Ramsey's lips. "Nice try. You want me to say that he never saw me at the museum and was unconscious on the ride to the Serengeti."

"Sorry. It always works in the movies."

"It works in real life, too. Daggett never saw me."

"Then why worry about the old guy?"

"Because the police would find out that I was supposed to be at the museum that night to meet with Coffin and Daggett."

"To talk about the Coffin scrimshaw collection?"

"That's right. Do you know what was so unusual about the collection?"

I tap-danced around the question. "I talked to a couple of dealers. They said it was some of the best work done by possibly the best scrimshaw artist in the country."

"Very good. I told Chernko he shouldn't underestimate you," Ramsey said. "I did some research and saw where you'd broken some complicated cases."

"Is that why you set me up after our sailboat ride?"

"I tried to warn you off the island. Chernko's operation moved faster than I anticipated."

"Glad you brought up Ivan. That's another thing I don't get, Ramsey. Why kill old Coffin? He had nothing to do with your big score with Chernko."

"That's where you're wrong. Coffin had *every*thing to do with the deal. Coffin had information that could have hurt a major acquisition my firm was involved in. The money from that deal was the foundation for an even bigger venture with Chernko."

"How could Coffin—?" I stopped short, remembering what Malloy had said about Nantucket Capital Investment Partnership. "Why do they call your company the Young Cannibals? Why not say you're vulture capitalists like other outfits?"

"Because vultures are scavengers who prey on the dead. Nantucket Capital Investment Partnership gobbles up companies that are weak but still alive."

"Just like your ancestor, William Swain, who gobbled up his weak shipmates?"

Ramsey reacted as if I'd thrown a switch. A dark cloud passed over the smirking expression on his face and his features contorted into something brutish. I was no longer looking at the handsome business executive with the charming manner and expensive dental work. Maybe it was the shadows, but the broad sloping forehead, the wolfish expression in the eyes, the hungry, open mouth were those of the murderous cannibal that Coffin had etched into his scrimshaw.

"How did you know that?"

Even his voice had changed into a low hiss that was more reptilian than human. A shiver ran down my spine. This was how Coffin and Daggett must have felt when they realized that they were trapped on a boat with a monster who wanted to devour them.

"The scrimshaw trail led me to a headstone in the cemetery. Interesting family lineage you have."

The Michael Ramsey persona reasserted itself. He gave the flashing car salesman smile.

"My group was acquiring a fast-food company, and my family background would have made great fodder for the headline writers in the *Wall Street Journal*: **Cannibal's Descendant Wants Quick Meal**."

"Not very catchy, but it isn't the kind of thing that would get you invited to a celebrity roast."

"Very funny, Socarides. It would have killed the deal and made my company a laughing stock."

"So you killed Coffin instead."

"He should have left the past undisturbed. He showed me the photos, trying to get my support for the acquisition. "

"That was you who broke into this beach shack and Sutcliffe's house, wasn't it?"

"Coffin didn't have it with him at the museum. I was desperate to find the scrimshaw piece."

"And *have* you?"

He shook his head. "That old fool says he doesn't know where it is."

"You'd better think it through, Ramsey. I'm not the only one who knows you met with Daggett tonight. They'll figure things out."

"I'm way ahead of them. I'll say that Daggett wasn't in his room.

I went to look for him and found the beach shack on fire." He placed the flickering kerosene lantern on the floor and picked up an unlit lamp, placing it on the table. "This one is filled with gasoline rather than lamp oil. I'll toss it into the shack on my way out. Crazy old man escapes confines, knocks over that lamp and this one, and set himself on fire. I didn't expect a visit from you, but that's even better. Your body is found in the burned wreckage, apparently killed with the harpoon hanging on the wall. Kinda like Coffin. They'll assume Ahab finally caught his white whale."

He rose from his seat, still holding the rifle on me, reached onto the cot, and picked up something that looked like a pistol of the future. I guessed it was the pressurized hypodermic because he moved closer and pointed it at my chest.

"I'll be humane about it. You'll be unconscious and won't feel a thing."

My mouth got very dry, but I managed to get out a simple declarative sentence.

"Chernko's plan is dead in the water."

The pistol hand froze, but the muzzle was still aimed my way. "What are you talking about?"

"The *Volga* sank. The swarmbots malfunctioned and attacked the yacht instead of the ferryboat. The Coast Guard picked up Chernko and his Chinese pals. The CIA has been brought in, so it won't be long before the FBI is knocking on your door."

"You're bluffing," he said.

I *was*, but I said, "Do you want to take that chance?"

Michael Ramsey, the ruthless but rational businessman, would have said *no*. But Ramsey did a quick switch into his Dr. Jekyll and Mr. Hyde mode. I was dealing with the genetic and insane resurrection of William Swain. With the clarity that comes with impending death, I knew that Ramsey was Swain and Swain was Ramsey.

"*Yes*," he said in that peculiar hissing voice. Again, I felt a chill run along my spine, but this time it was caused by the door opening and letting in the wind and rain. I heard Lisa's voice.

"*Michael!*" she screamed. "What are you *doing?*"

I had been staring into Ramsey's, or Swain's, cold blue eyes, trying to anticipate his next move. He shifted his gaze for an instant as his brain processed the new development. I grabbed his wrist with both hands, but my palms were slippery with rainwater. I stood up and used my body's leverage to twist the hypodermic from his grasp. He let out a yelp of pain. Both hands were on the sniper rifle, bringing it around to shoot me.

Our eyes locked for an instant, and then I shot him in the face with the hypodermic. The jet hissed out of the muzzle at supersonic speed. He screamed in agony and dropped the rifle so he could bring both hands to his eyes. He staggered blindly around, and knocked over the lamp on the table. His flailing arms hit the gasoline lantern. It smashed to the floor, splashing its contents onto the kerosene lamp.

There was a *whump* sound and gasoline flared up around his knees. By then, the drugs kicked in and he crumpled to the floor.

I turned and saw Lisa standing there, transfixed.

I grabbed Daggett's arms and pulled him up. "Help me with your grandfather!" I yelled.

She snapped out of her trance and took Daggett by the ankles. We carried him out of the cottage and into the rain where we set him down on a dune around fifty feet away.

I ran to the cottage and tried to get through the front door, but the combination of old wood and the mix of kerosene and gas was too potent for the rain to extinguish. The blistering heat drove me back.

I returned to where Lisa was standing over her grandfather. She would have stared at the burning shack until it went to ashes, but I said. "We've got to get him out of the rain."

She nodded numbly, then we dragged the old man along the

dune path. The house was illuminated by the flashing lights of a police car.

A police officer came over and said, "We're investigating a call from someone named Gomes. What happened to the old guy?"

"There was a fire in an old beach cottage," I said. "He tried to rescue someone who was inside."

The officer quickly got on his hand radio. Two fire trucks and a couple of ambulances showed up fifteen minutes later. Firemen and EMTs raced toward the glow from the beach. A pair of EMTs stayed behind to check out Daggett inside one ambulance. They said he needed to go to the hospital. Lisa asked if she could ride in back. Before the doors closed, I saw her mouth the word, "Thanks."

The ambulance passed more incoming fire trucks and police cruisers. I looked around at the pandemonium, and was reminded of the fire that had destroyed my boat and launched me into this madness. Then I staggered to my apartment, locked the door, found a bottle of bourbon, and drank most of it before I crashed onto my bed in a drunken sleep.

CHAPTER 41

It was not the chirping of the cardinal family outside my window that woke me out of my brain-dead sleep, but a deep voice that said, "You dead, or dead drunk, Soc?"

I rolled over, slowly opened my right eye, then the other. I squinted against the hard morning sunlight streaming through the window. Flagg stood at the foot of the bed holding a steaming coffee mug.

I let out a groan. "I know I'm not dead because I can feel little men hammering on the inside of my skull, my tongue is made of cardboard and you're not an angel. How'd you get in? I thought I locked my door."

"You *did*." He lifted the mug. "There's coffee in the kitchen. Still some whiskey in the bottle in case you want a little hair of the dog that bit you."

I gave him a *look*. I was suffering from more than a simple dog bite. My stomach reacted with a silent protest when I rolled out of bed. I stood on wobbly legs waiting for the room to stop spinning. I made it to the bathroom, put my head under the faucet and drank a gallon of water to replenish what was lost to alcoholic dehydration. Then I stripped down, took a long hot shower, and after I had toweled my body dry, got into clean shorts and T-shirt. I padded out to the kitchen. Flagg prefers coffee the color of unrefined petroleum, which was fine with me.

I carried my mug out onto the deck where Flagg sat having his coffee. The rains had stopped, and the clouds had cleared out, leaving a bright azure canopy over an ocean of jade. I shaded my eyes to keep the strong sunlight out of my sensitive eyes. Flagg handed me his aviator glasses.

"You need these more than I do," he said.

I slipped the sunglasses on and inhaled a deep breath of fresh air. The smell of burned wood came to me on the breeze.

"Crap," I said.

"Bad hangover?"

"I've had worse. I just remembered last night."

"I heard there was quite the ruckus around here. Care to fill me in on what happened?"

"I'm not exactly sure I can tell you exactly *what* happened," I said. "But I'll give it a try."

I drank more coffee and began a reconstruction of the events of the night before, starting with my damp walk into town from the Coast Guard station, going on to the craziness with Ramsey at the beach shack and finally, my unwise decision to dive into a whiskey bottle.

"Close call, Soc. Good thing for you Lisa showed up at the beach shack."

"No argument there. Did you see any sign of her when you pulled in?"

He shook his head. "I saw the fire trucks and cruisers. Talked to Mrs. Gomes who said old man Daggett was taken to the hospital and his granddaughter was still with him. So I came looking for you. Glad you're okay."

I paused for a moment in thought, then said, "It could have gone badly for me even after Lisa distracted Ramsey. I had grabbed the injection gun and had it pointed at Ramsey, but I hesitated. I couldn't shoot him in the face. But then it was no longer Ramsey's face and it was Swain instead, looking as if he wanted to have me for dinner. Scared the crap out of me. I froze. But my body took control from my mind and sent an order to my trigger finger. Does that sound crazy to you?"

"This whole *thing* is crazy. First, Daggett thinking he was two people, then Ramsey trading places with his ancestor. Maybe this stuff is catching."

"*Maybe.* From what I know, Ramsey seemed ambivalent about the swarmbots. One minute he's backing Chernko's mad scheme to the hilt. The next he's backing out. Wonder if his two personalities were battling each other."

"The Jekyll and Hyde thing? You got me, Soc. Here's what I *do* know. The Coast Guard picked up a life raft with some people from the *Volga* on it."

"Chernko one of them?"

"No word yet. I'll let you know."

Flagg said his colleagues from Washington had been delayed coming in because of the weather, and when they finally arrived, the de-briefing had gone into the wee hours. He caught a power nap at the station, and when he woke up, drove out to my place.

"Main reason I came by was to see what you wanted to do about your cousin."

Alex. "Hell, Flagg, I forgot all about him in the excitement. We've got to do something. Chili gave me twenty-four hours to bring in a million dollars."

Flagg glanced at his watch. "We've got time for breakfast. You can fill me in over scrambled eggs. I've got one important question now, though."

"You want to know where I'm going to get a million dollars?"

"Hell, no, Soc. Okay if I use the *chirizo* you've got in the fridge?"

Forty-five minutes after we'd wolfed down eggs scrambled with Portuguese sausage, Flagg and I were crawling through the thicket of tall grass near Chili's house. Flagg was moving slower than I was because he was dragging his heavy satchel with him.

At one point, he stopped and belched. "You know something, Soc, we never should have had that *chirizo.*"

"Hey Flagg, that was *your* idea."

"I know, man, but that was before I knew we were going to be crawling around on our belly like a couple of lizards."

Whining is unbecoming from a man built like a bulldozer. I told him I'd buy him a bottle of Maalox, then squirmed through the grass a few more yards and raised my hand in a stop signal. Flagg moved up beside me and parted the grass enough to peer through it.

"Pretty quiet," he whispered. "You sure this is the place?"

"*Positive.* I saw Chili and his pals the last time I was here." I pointed to the Tahoe which was pulled off the shell driveway onto the grass.

"Nice wheels."

"Check out the name on the license plate."

"CHILI. Guess that nails it," he said.

"You see the problem," I said. "This is as close as we can get without being seen. Anyone approaching the house is walking through a kill zone."

"That's why we're not going to do anything that dumb. We're going to make them come to us."

He dragged the satchel closer, rolled onto his side and opened the bag. He reached inside and extracted the portable rocket launcher he had showed me earlier. Next, he pulled a missile from the bag and slid it into the breach.

"You can't use that thing on the house, Flagg. They've got Alex inside."

He gave me his sad-eyed look. "How long have you known

me, Soc?"

"Sorry. Okay, I trust you. Just be careful! What do you want me to do?"

"Cover your ears," he said.

He got up on one knee, squinted through the launcher's tubular sight and squeezed the trigger. There was a loud *whoosh* and a white streak leapt from the front of the tube toward the Tahoe, magically transforming two tons of steel into a fiery red and white sunburst of flames.

It took only seconds for the front door of the house to fly open. Chili burst out, followed by his Jamaican pals and Chernko's Mutt and Jeff thugs. All of them were armed with AK-47s. The weapon dangled at Chili's side as he stared at the smoky blaze where his SUV used to be. He began to dance around as if he'd stepped on a hornet's nest. He tried to get closer to the vehicle, but a secondary explosion drove him back toward the house.

The Russians were babbling with excitement at each other, but the Jamaicans behaved with a deliberate calmness that suggested they'd had some military training. They held their AKs at waist level, pivoting their bodies, scouring the woods and grass around the house. Flagg waited until they were looking away from us and then he went hunting again.

There was another *whoosh*. The pick-up truck on the other side of the driveway exploded in flames. Flagg set the launcher aside and had his Sig Sauer in hand, prepared to lay down a line of preventive fire in case they started back to the house. Watching the second vehicle transformed into molten steel convinced Chili and his friends that they were over-matched. Rather than go back into the house, they ran up the driveway and disappeared around a bend in road.

Flagg was laughing so hard tears streamed down his wide cheeks.

I took my heart out of my mouth where it had been while Flagg was destroying vehicles, and got to my feet. While Flagg kept watch, I trotted between the blazing vehicles to look for Cousin Alex. I found him in a bedroom, lying on a dirty mattress, tied hands and feet. I got a knife out of the kitchen where I saw stacks of small packages wrapped in white paper, cut him loose and asked if he was okay.

"I'm a little stiff," he said as he rubbed the circulation back into his wrists. "Boy, am I glad to see *you*."

I patted Alex on the back, then hustled him back to where I had left Flagg. He was watching the woods behind us in case Chili and his friends figured things out and tried to cut us off on our way back to the car.

I told him about the packages I'd seen and suggested Chili and his friends might venture back for their stash. We made double-time back through the woods to our car and didn't let our breaths out until we were in the clear.

The billowing black smoke must have been visible for miles because we passed a police cruiser and fire truck both going in direction we'd come from. For insurance, Flagg made a cell phone call to a friend at the DEA suggesting that the agency might like to talk to Chili after the police got through with him. Chili might still try to implicate Alex, as he'd threatened, but it was unlikely that his word would stand against a respected young lawyer. With any luck, Alex's old pal would have another ten years or more to put his cooking skills to use at a federal prison. Maybe Chernko's goons could teach him some Russian recipes.

Flagg hung up and turned to me. "That was fun. You got any plans for the rest of the day?"

"Not much has been planned with me lately, Flagg. Things just sorta happened. Why do you ask?"

"I was just thinking. I saw a couple of rods and reels back at your place. I still got the Zodiac under rental. What say we go fishing? You, me and Cousin Alex."

Alex had been silent up to then, probably still in shock, but he said, "Go *fishing*? After all this stuff we've gone through? He's got to be kidding, Soc."

"Not at all. It would be a good way to put some of that stuff behind us."

Alex laughed, a good sign. "I'll buy the beer."

I must have been feeling better because I said, "And I'll *drink* it."

CHAPTER 42

As it turned out, the fish lived to bite another day.

The operation had gone off with surgical precision. Flagg rounded up the boat. Alex got the beer. I bought the Italian sub sandwiches. We piled into the Zodiac with our supplies and fishing gear, and motored to a quiet part of the harbor. The lines went in the water. The beer cans popped, except for the Mountain Dew for Flagg, and we dug into the sandwiches.

Then Flagg's cell phone trilled. He stuck it in his ear, listened intently and muttered, "I'll be there as soon as I can."

He clicked off and shook his head, a look of chagrin on his face.

"Don't tell me," I said.

"Yup. I have to save the world again. Got to leave immediately. Sorry, guys."

"Serves me right for having the Man from U.N.C.L.E. as my fishing buddy."

"Haven't told you the *good* news. That *was* Chernko they picked up in the life raft. Some Chinese guys were with him."

"What about the crew from the yacht?"

"Some made it. Some didn't."

"What are they going to do with him?"

"Here's the problem, Soc. Yacht's on the bottom, blown to smithereens. Malloy is going back to work for the navy on super-secret stuff. The fact that Chernko had Chinese guys on board was no big deal. Anyone can go out for a ride with their pals. Thanks to you, Ramsey's history so we can't use him. Surviving crew from the yacht aren't going to talk, and my people don't want them blabbing about what they saw anyhow."

"If we can't prosecute Ivan, can we send him back home?"

"Might be hard. Chernko's still got friends at State who think he's got connections with the top brass in Moscow. They'd need a reason."

"Let's give them one. The DEA puts the squeeze on Chernko's thugs, the guys who were working with Chili, and they may get them to connect their boss to the drug deal and the murder of Viktor Karpov. Maybe they can use that to kick Chernko out of the country."

"What's that going to accomplish?"

"A *lot*. Chernko is heavily in debt to his KGB pals. He did the drug stuff to keep the gas tank full on his yacht. The swarmbot deal with Ramsey was going to bring in cash he could use to pay off his debts. He was trying to sell cutting edge military technology to the Chinese instead of the Russians. I wouldn't be surprised if someone made an example of Mr. Chernko."

"I'd be more surprised if they *didn't*," Flagg said.

"Then that settles that. There's a big lunker of a striper out there just waiting for Alex and me to haul him in."

"I don't know, Soc," Alex said. "I think maybe I better get home to my family. Talked to my wife a while ago. She says the kids really miss me."

I put my arm around Alex's shoulders. "No problem, cousin. Family comes first."

Flagg suggested that we finish the sandwiches, which we did in short order. Then I pulled in the lines and we putted back to the boat rental place to return the Zodiac. Flagg and I shook hands and promised to get together soon for some fishing.

"Hey, Soc," he said. "All that stuff about getting long in the tooth. Hope you didn't take it personally. Just kidding."

"Hell, Flagg, I know we ain't the hard-muscled hunks of our youth, but we can still whip our weight in bad guys. Think about it. Chernko's in trouble. Ramsey's with his ancestors. Chili will be going to the federal lock-up for a post-graduate degree in cooking."

Flagg gave a wide grin. "Damn straight, Soc. We are some bad-ass dudes."

I watched him disappear into the stream of pedestrian traffic on his way back to his rental car. Then I walked Alex to the ferry dock. When it was time for the ferry to leave, I gave him a hug and told him to stay out of trouble.

With Flagg and Alex gone, and villains no longer nipping at the heels of my sandals, I suddenly felt very much alone. I walked over to Lisa's office, but no one was there, so I drove the MG back to the Daggett house. Mrs. Gomes was puttering around in the kitchen. I asked if she had seen Lisa and she handed me an envelope with my name on it. Inside was a note from Lisa:

"Dear Soc:

"I've been trying to get in touch to let you know that I've flown to Boston with Gramps. I persuaded the D.A. to allow his ankle bracelet to be removed. You may be called in as a witness. We will meet with his lawyers to discuss how we can clear his record of charges, and he'll be undergoing further psychiatric treatment at Mass. General. We'll be away several days. I'll be in touch so we can deal with unfinished business. Thank you so, so much for all that you have done, and what you will do. Love, Lisa."

I folded the paper and put it in my pocket. Then I wrote a note to Lisa saying that I was leaving the island to deal with personal matters on the mainland, and that I hoped we would talk soon. I would leave the MG in its parking space and the key in her office.

I asked Mrs. Gomes to give her the note and went to my apartment to pack my bag. Before long, I was tooling along the Polpis Road in the red sports car for one last time.

A couple of hours later, I picked up Kojak at my neighbor's house. She was happy to see me, because she was running out of Kojak food. She gave me the pitiful amount she had left and I drove Kojak back to the boathouse. I opened the windows to let out the dampness, but it didn't help much because fog was blowing back in. The fog reminded me of Nantucket. Which reminded me of Lisa. Which reminded me that I missed her. I distracted myself with a few beers at a local pub known as the 'Hole, and got a good night's sleep.

Kojak nosed me awake for breakfast, and I realized that I missed Mr. and Mrs. Cardinal, too. But Kojak wasn't the only one with a full plate. Over the next few days I spent hours dealing with the insurance adjustors and paperwork. Officer Tucker called with some good news. One of Mr. Glick's associates had turned whistle-blower. His boss was being charged with charging the feds for non-existent rest home residents. Glick would be too busy defending himself to sue me.

I thought of Lisa from time to time. Let me correct that. I *yearned* for her. But I assumed she was wrapped up in her grandfather's case. Henry Daggett was still one can short of a six-pack and he was still the defendant in a murder case.

I got a call from the district attorney's office to appear at a deposition. I testified how Ramsey had kidnapped Daggett, confessed to murdering Coffin and would have killed me if Lisa hadn't distracted him. Since I was the last one to see Ramsey alive, I left out the part about shooting him in the face with the high-pressure hypodermic. I simply said he caught fire when the gas-filled lantern got knocked off the table. I tried to ignore the glower on the D.A.'s face. District attorneys, especially those running for re-election, never like to admit they are wrong.

When I was reasonably sure that I would soon have an insurance check to buy a replacement boat, then, and *only* then, did I find the courage to tell my family about the loss of their investment. Brother George was quick to jump down my throat, and got into a spirited exchange with sister Chloe. But my mother was pleased at the way I got Alex out of trouble, and joined my little sister in my defense. I said I would be able to make up lost fishing income from my fees in the Henry Daggett case.

My mother had only one condition. That I would name the new boat the *Thalassa II*.

I found my new boat at the price I wanted at a boat yard north of Boston. The owner was getting out of the fishing business. I drove up to take a look and liked what I saw. I had it trucked to a Cape boatyard near my house where I spent my time outfitting her with the latest in electronics and adding some luxury touches to the cabin.

I had talked to the dock master in Hyannis. All the slips had been taken by then, but he had one in reserve and said it was mine if I wanted it. I got in a supply of baseball hats and T-shirts to sell customers, bought some new fishing gear, and pulled in an IOU from my reporter friend Sheila Crumley. She did a nice feature story on me with a photo of my new boat. The piece stirred up a dozen or so calls from potential charter customers.

I was making the arrangements to have the boat delivered to the marina when I got a call from Lisa.

"Hello, Soc," she said. "How are you? Sorry to be so long getting back to you."

It had been nearly two weeks since we talked, and my Nantucket adventure seemed like a dream, but hearing Lisa's voice again made my heart do a little jump for joy. I apologized and said I had been away from home a lot anyway.

"I was advised not to talk to you pending the depositions," she said. "They took testimony from me as well."

"How's the case looking?"

"Our stories must have matched or I would have heard by now. The D.A. still wants to prosecute Gramps, but we're pounding away at his case. Can you hop over to the island? We have some unfinished business to take care of."

I'd been anxious to get a cash flow going to my family, but hadn't wanted to call Lisa looking for money. I asked when she wanted to get together. She suggested that afternoon, proposed that we have dinner, and that I stay the night in my apartment. I had a couple of days before my first charter. I checked the ferry schedule and we agreed on a meeting time. I gave Kojak enough food to last him overnight, and drove to Hyannis.

Late in the afternoon I stepped onto the ferry dock and saw Lisa waiting for me. She was wearing a cranberry and white Nantucket Conservation Trust T-shirt with a stylized logo of a bird flying over the wave-tops, and pale green shorts. We walked toward each other like one of those movie encounters where the man and the woman embrace in slow motion. All that was missing was the up swell of violin music.

She had the Jeep instead of the MG, and said she needed room for another passenger. I tossed my bag in the back and we drove out of town onto Milestone Road. I thought we were going to the Daggett compound, but near the cutouts of African animals, she pulled off the road and parked at the edge of the Serengeti.

We got out and I followed her along the path we had taken the night Ramsey had used us for target practice. Unlike that time, there was no fog blow. I was able to see the figure walking in the field we had crawled through when there were bullets whizzing overhead. The man was wearing tan chinos, a blue long-sleeve shirt and a floppy white cotton hat. He was carrying a bird-watching scope.

He had his back to me, but turned when Lisa called out, "Gramps. There's someone here to see you."

My jaw dropped in amazement. Henry Daggett was clean-shaven and his face had none of the torment of his Ahab persona. In its place were the features of a handsome older man blessed with a broad smile. Laugh crinkles framed eyes that had lost the blazing hellfires of their former owner.

"This is Mr. Socarides, Gramps. Soc, this is my grandfather."

We shook hands and he held on with a firm grip as he studied my face as if it were one of Ahab's charts.

"You look familiar, Mr. Socarides. Have we met before?"

"Maybe," I said. "But it would have been a long time ago."

"Mr. Socarides is the private investigator we hired. He's been a great help."

He pumped my hand again before he let go. "Lisa has told me about you. Thank you so much for all your hard work."

"My pleasure, Mr. Daggett. I'm pleased to see that you've recovered."

He chuckled softly. "I understand I've been on quite the journey. Luckily, I only remember part of it, or I'd *really* be stark raving mad."

"Anyone would be confused after your experience, especially after a blow to the head."

"That wasn't what prolonged Gramps's condition," Lisa said. "Dr. Rosen was putting a hallucinatory drug in his food. It was discovered when Gramps went for routine blood tests in Boston."

"Nice to see that my suspicions were justified when it came to the good doctor."

"He won't be a doctor much longer. His license to practice is being revoked and he's got a criminal investigation breathing down his neck."

"Do you feel well enough for me to ask you some questions, Mr. Daggett?"

"I'm not sure I can be much help. I'm told my memory of events will come back in bits and pieces. I only remember what happened before I went to the museum, and finding myself on the beach watching my shack burn down. Nothing in between."

"Okay, then. Let's start with the events leading up to the meeting with Coffin."

"As you know, Ab Coffin and I argued over the acquisition of the scrimshaw collection. Lisa has showed me the photos of the plaque, so I know now why he was so insistent."

"He wanted to exonerate his ancestor."

"I didn't know that at the time. He felt that if I saw the plaque I'd change my mind."

"And when you saw it?"

"Oh, I never saw it."

"I was under the assumption that Coffin brought the plaque to the museum."

"Oh, *no*. We were only supposed to *meet* there. He was very secretive. Said he didn't want to carry it around."

"The missing plaque has been a sticking point with the district attorney," Lisa said. "He says Ramsey had no motive without the actual scrimshaw to prove it."

"What about the photos Warner took?"

"They want the real thing. I think they're just using it to delay a ruling."

"Did Coffin give you any hint of where he was taking you that night?"

"No. When I asked him why all the mystery, he smiled and recited a quote from *Moby Dick*."

I'd had it up to my ears with Moby, but I said, "What was the quote, Mr. Daggett?"

"It has to do with the 'sweet mystery about this sea, whose gently awful stirrings seem to speak of some hidden soul beneath.' "

It took a moment for the words to sink in, but when they did, I was transported from the Serengeti to Coffin's antique shop. I was chatting with the manager about the Red Sox and she was pointing to the pennant over her head. But this time my eye lingered on the words etched in brass on the painting of the ship sailing in a puddle of moonlight.

"Can you give me a ride back into town?" I said, trying to keep the excitement out of my voice.

Gramps got into the Jeep with us and I directed Lisa where to go. When we entered the shop, I walked directly to the far end. The shop manager was at her computer. She looked up and recognized me.

"Nice to see you again," she said with a smile.

"Good to see you, too. If it's not too much trouble, I wonder if I could take a look at that painting over your head."

"No problem."

She unhooked the painting and handed it over. I read the title of the painting aloud. "Sweet Mystery of This Sea." Then I turned the painting over. Taped to the back side was the missing scrimshaw plaque.

Lisa and I celebrated this latest development at Topper's. I was able to pick up dinner with the substantial check she gave me for my investigative services. She asked me to file for any expenses. I gritted my teeth and told her about the loss of her grandfather's boat. Which in turn led to a condensed version of the great swarmbot saga.

She said the boat was insured, and that she was grateful that I was still alive. "I had no idea when I asked you to join this case that I was hiring James Bond." She gazed off at the lights across the harbor. "It's hard to believe that Michael could be so evil. Greedy and full of himself, but not a vile person like Chernko."

I thought of William Swain's genes being passed through generations, and said, "People can surprise us. Are we caught up on unfinished business?"

"*Almost,*" she said. "We can discuss it later."

We drove along Polpis Road with the top down in the MG. The bad weather had cleared out the clouds and the stars seemed to pop out of the velvet sky. I dropped her off at the house and said I'd see her in the morning, which was why I was surprised a while later when I was sitting on the deck and heard a soft knock at the door. When I let Lisa in, she was wearing a lavender colored silk bathrobe instead of the pink terry cloth one she had worn before.

"Hello," she said. "Hope it's not too much trouble, but I wondered if I could sleep with you tonight."

"No trouble at all," I said. "I'll get the bundling board."

Sometimes I can be a little thick. I didn't get what was going on until Lisa smiled and said, "I don't think we need a board tonight."

The next morning Lisa rose before I did. I heard the shower running and called her name. She told me to join her, which I did. Later, over coffee, she said she had to go to Boston for a conservation meeting.

"Lillian will tell you about it when she gives you a ride into town. Unless you can stay another night?"

With great reluctance, I told her I had to get back to my cat. She gave me a big hug and a long lingering kiss. "I'll call you when I get back," she said.

Lillian Mayhew arrived about an hour later. I had come back from the beach after checking out the beach shack ruins. The building had been completely cleared away. I thought back to what had happened on that night, and decided I was glad to see it gone. I got into the station wagon and we exchanged pleasantries until we were out of Siasconset, when Lillian asked if Lisa had told me about the conservation deal. Not in detail, I replied.

"Then you'll be pleased to know that negotiations are underway to acquire Mayhew Point and turn it into a nature preserve. The house will be used for international conferences on how best we can save the planet."

I said that I couldn't think of a more fitting use for the property. When we neared town, I asked Lillian to drop me off on Petticoat Lane. As I was thanking her for the ride, she affixed me with a twinkle in her blue eyes and said, "Lisa is quite entranced with you. I hope you'll honor us with a return visit to the island, Mr. Starbuck."

"I'll be back as soon as I can, but not as Starbuck."

"I'll look forward to your next visit." She smiled and said, "You'll always be Starbuck to me, Mr. Socarides."

A minute later, I was knocking on the door of Sutcliffe's house. He asked me in, but I said I had to catch a boat. I gave him back the copy of Swain's journal that he had loaned me. I said that I had been on Nantucket to see Lisa, and was on my way back to the mainland.

"That's too bad," he said. "Awful about Ramsey dying in Daggett's beach shack. I checked the record, you know. He was a direct descendant of William Swain. This whole thing is crazy. There's a book in it, but I don't know where to begin."

"I suggest that you go back to where it all started. There's an interesting piece of scrimshaw you might want to see at the museum. I wouldn't wait too long, though, because the district attorney may be marking it as an exhibit in the murder case."

He bubbled over with questions, but I said I had to run. I made the ferry with minutes to spare. As I stood on the stern deck watching the church spires recede in the distance, I pulled out the dog-eared copy of *Moby Dick* that I had borrowed from Daggett's shack and read the rest of the Melville quote about the sea.

"For here, millions of mixed shades and shadows, drowned dreams, somnabulisms, reveries; all that we call lives and souls, lie dreaming, dreaming, still; tossing like slumberers in their beds; the ever rolling waves but made so by their restlessness."

I read the passage several times, and when I looked up again, Nantucket Island, the Little Grey Lady of the Sea, was hidden by her misty shrouds. I put the book aside, and then I walked around to the bow, so that I could catch an early glimpse of the shores that lay ahead.

The End

ABOUT THE AUTHOR

My fiction-writing career owes it start to the bad navigation of an 18th century pirate. For it was in 1717 that a ship, the *Whydah* went aground, reportedly carrying a fabulous treasure. In the 1980s, three salvage groups went head-to-head, competing to find the wreck. The controversy over the salvage got hot at times and I thought there might be a book in their story. I was working for a newspaper at the time.

I developed my own detective, an ex-cop, diver, fisherman, and PI named Aristotle "Soc" Socarides. He was more philosophical than hard-boiled. Making his first appearance in "Cool Blue Tomb," the book won the Shamus award for Best Paperback novel. After many years in the newspaper business, I turned to writing fiction and churned out five more books in the series.

Clive Cussler blurbed: "There can be no better mystery writer in America than Paul Kemprecos."

Despite the accolades, the Soc series lingered in mid-list hell. By the time I finished my last book, I was thinking about another career that might make me more money, like working in a 7-11.

Several months after the release of "Bluefin Blues," Clive called and said a spin-off from the Dirk Pitt series was in the works. It would be called the NUMA Files and he wondered if I would be interested in tackling the job.

I took on the writing of "Serpent" which brought into being Kurt Austin and the NUMA Special Assignments Team. Austin had some carry-over from Soc, and another team member, Paul Trout, had been born on Cape Cod. The book made *The New York Times* bestseller list, as did every one of seven NUMA Files that followed, including "Polar Shift," which bumped "The DaVinci Code" for first place.

After eight NUMA Files I went back to writing solo. I wrote an adventure book entitled, *The Emerald Scepter*, which introduced a new hero, Matinicus "Matt" Hawkins. I have been working on the re-release of my Soc series in digital and print, and in 2013, responding to numerous requests, I brought Soc back again in a seventh Socarides book entitled, *Grey Lady*. My wife Christi and I live on Cape Cod where she works as a financial advisor. We live in a circa 1865 farmhouse with two cats. We have three children and seven granddaughters.

To learn more about Paul Kemprecos, check out his website at http://www.paulkemprecos.com.